Mean Spirits

Mean Spirits

Roger Chiocchi

Writers Club Press
San Jose New York Lincoln Shanghai

Mean Spirits

Writers Club Press
an imprint of iUniverse, Inc.

For information address:
iUniverse, Inc.
5220 S. 16th St., Suite 200
Lincoln, NE 68512
www.iuniverse.com

ISBN: 0-595-22840-2

Printed in the United States of America

To all good spirits, past, present and future.

Especially you, Joe.

Contents

Part I: Psychic Dust: Stirring Up the Past

Part II: A Murder in Newport, 1928

Part III: Pollock Rip

Prologue

The New England Coast
November 9, 1620

Captain Christopher Jones gazed out from the mid-deck remarkably composed, an island of calm, while his crewmembers, more nervous than frightened, silently wondered what he was planning. His ship was in a box, a tight box.

"Four fathoms, sir!" The leadsman called out.

Only twelve feet between his keel and the sandy bottom and Jones just stood there, as cool and calm as if he were in the mid-Atlantic running before a twelve knot breeze. His men all swore ice water flowed through his veins.

"Three and a half fathoms, sir!"

All day the leadsman had punctuated this cruise down the Cape Cod coast with his frequent soundings, scraping the ocean's floor with his hand lead and reading out the depth of the sea from the marks on his line. For hours, his readings wavered around ten fathoms. But Jones knew not to relax. In earlier voyages to this strange elbow of land, Gosnold, Champlain and Smith had found its coast a treacherous puzzle of abrupt shoals and shifting currents. So it was no surprise when ten fathoms turned to nine, and nine to eight, and then seven and six…

It had been a long day for Jones, a remarkable day. At six-thirty, after sixty-four days on the North Atlantic, he had first heard the lookout sing out those two long-awaited words—LAND HO! LAND HO! LAND HO! Robert Coppin, his second mate, assured Jones that the thin strip of wooded beach lining the horizon was

1

indeed Cape Cod, the same strip of land Coppin had sighted on a voyage several years earlier. Jones did not doubt it. For the last two months he had drawn a beeline across the Atlantic on the forty-second parallel. If he were any Captain worth his rank, that strip of land *had to be* Cape Cod.

Word of landfall spread quickly throughout the ship. Little Ellen More, up unusually early, overheard the crew's excited chatter and ran below to break the news to her parents. Within minutes, drowsy-eyed adults sprouted up from the hatch below. By seven o' clock, only half an hour after the lookout had first sighted land, every one of the one hundred passengers stood pressed to the rails, straining for a glimpse of their new home. They were happy, jubilant. Jones could not remember the last time such jubilation chimed the timbers of his vessel so early in the morning.

For the past nine hours—throughout the morning and well into the afternoon—Jones had followed a southwest course in pursuit of their intended destination: Northern Virginia Colony at the mouth of the Hudson. A fair wind—first from the west then clocking to the north before weakening from the east—pushed them down the back side of Cape Cod. Jones stood quietly on deck throughout, gauging the wind with his brow and the currents by watching flotsam drift in the sea. Then, late in the afternoon—

"Shoal water ahead, sir! Shoal water ahead!" The lookout shouted from the maintop, sighting breakers and lighter water before them in the distance.

Crewmembers ran about in a fury while Jones stood silent on the half-deck, determining his options. The most prudent course of action would be to turn back to deep water. In fact, the more Jones thought about it, it was his *only* possible course of action. After everything they've been through, he couldn't risk having the voyage end with his ship run aground in shoal water, roaring breakers thrashing at her sides, only miles from the shores of their new continent. But, inside, he wavered: *they barely had several day's worth of provisions left, would they ever make it to the Hudson if he turned around now?*

"Three fathoms, sir!"

Jones pondered it one more time, then called out to his chief mate. "Tack her about, Master Clarke. To the Northeast."

Clarke snapped the crew into action. Jones walked up to the forecastle deck and silently watched, his eyes fixed on the telltales hanging off the main shrouds. They hung limp, only occasionally stirring. The east wind that had helped push them along their southwest course was dying. He could only hope, before expiring, it would give him one or two last puffs, freeing them from the shoals.

Slowly, the ship swung around on its keel, the passengers lining the rails, watching their new world spin away from them. The sea drenched its timbers and sprayed the starboard deck. Jones looked back towards the shrouds, watching the telltales. Still, they hung limp.

"Hold 'er steady." Master Clarke sang out to the steersman, his eye fixed on the compass. They were on their new course, headed to the northeast.

"Three and a half fathoms, sir."

Jones realized the next half-hour would be critical. The tide was on the ebb, working in his favor. But without the cooperation of the wind, it might all be for naught; his ship still might shiver her timbers on the shoals. Jones stood calm, his defiant confidence, itself, propelling them onward.

Then, suddenly, from across the deck:

"Man overboard! Man overboard! Man overboard!"

Jones looked up, startled.

A frenzied crewman rushed towards him. *"I seen 'er do it. I seen 'er do it, Captain! She jumped over the taffrail when we tacked about! The Ashford's servant-girl, sir. I know it was 'er. I seen 'er. I seen 'er do it."* The young crewman shook as he addressed his Captain.

"Four fathoms, sir." The leadsman yelled out from abaft.

Long ago, Jones had learned to deal with the perils of the sea. Above all, he had to remain composed, assuring himself that by dealing with one tragedy, he would not be causing another. It had been a rough voyage. Just several days ago, he had lost the young

Butten boy, thrown overboard in heavy seas. And in mid-Atlantic, one of his crewmen had succumbed to some strange attack.

"Four and a half fathoms, sir."

"*Sir?*" The nervous Clarke almost shouted, breaking Jones' concentration. "What shall we do?"

Before the Captain had a chance to respond, a passenger thrust himself in front of him: Charles Pennfield. "You're certainly not going to turn back, Captain. You wouldn't risk us crashing on the shoals, would you?"

"I'm not sure if that decision is entirely in my hands." He answered and then looked away.

"But certainly, you wouldn't turn back, Captain. Would you?"

Jones turned back towards Pennfield, paused for a moment, then looked him in the eyes. "You speak like a man who's running away from something."

Pennfield froze. "No, not at all, Captain. It's just that I'm concerned with the welfare of our passengers. I just—"

Before Pennfield could finish, Jones turned abruptly away and looked up towards the maintop. In the brief instant his eyes roamed around the sky and his ship's rigging, he noticed the telltales streaming straight ahead towards the bow. *Somehow, almost magically, the wind had shifted to the south, pushing them away from the shoals.*

"Five fathoms, sir."

Jones bit his lip, quickly assaying his options. The tide was on the ebb, running with him to the northeast. The south wind was now blowing strong. He was piloting a ninety-six foot merchantman around a strange coast. Nightfall was approaching. Deep water lay ahead. If he turned around now, the wind and breakers would be in his face with nothing but shallow water and darkness before him. It boiled down to a simple equation: it was the slim possibility of saving one servant girl's life balanced against jeopardizing the lives of all his passengers and crew. There was only one decision he could make.

"Hold course," he ordered. "To the northeast."

As the ship ploughed farther and farther from the shoals, the poor servant girl, wallowing in the breakers, could barely make out the words painted in large letters on the tall ship's stern. She jumped up and down, pushing herself off the sea's sandy bottom, flapping her arms in desperation. The letters melted in the dusk: *Mayflower of London.*

PART

I

Psychic Dust: Stirring Up the Past

1

Nantucket Island
September, 1994

When Jonathan Pennfield arrived at Nantucket on that tranquil September Friday, he had no idea that before he left the island's historic waters he would connect with his family's past.

"Supposed to be a great one tomorrow, Mr. Pennfield. Clear all day with a six to ten knot breeze." The young freckled-face pilot of the Nantucket Harbor launch extended his hand and helped Pennfield onto the small skiff, the afternoon sun casting a golden path across the quiet harbor.

"About time, wouldn't you say, Red?" Pennfield smiled. He was happy, *extremely happy*. The anticipation of the next day's sailing gave him a rush that was nothing short of narcotic. Him and The Speedwell, alone, against the forces of nature. Escape. Therapy for the inner spirit.

Red revved the engine, pushed off from the dock, and headed out to a patchwork of vessels moored across the harbor. Sailboats of all sizes and shapes. Sloops. Yawls. Ketches. Twin-engine diesels with twenty foot bridges. Single-engine cabin cruisers.

"Number twelve, Mr. Pennfield?" The young pilot asked.

"Yep, twelve."

Jonathan Pennfield, Executive Vice President of GlobalAir, Inc., had an office far above Park Avenue with a view of the East River, a six bedroom home in Greenwich, Connecticut, a quarter share in his family's Newport cottage, a condo in Florida and a multi-million dollar trust fund, but *The Speedwell*, his thirty-five foot Tartan fiberglass sloop with polished teak, a state-of-the-art nav center, a furling genoa, self-tending winches, and room for six below was his most valued possession, his place of peace and solitude.

Silence. Red cut the engine. As the launch floated up to *The Speedwell's* mooring, Pennfield glanced quickly at the headline on a newspaper left on one of the skiff's benches: "HAITIAN REFUGEES LAND AT KEY WEST." Non-plussed, he shrugged his shoulders, slowly lifted himself from his seat and picked up his duffel bag. He threw it onto the deck of his boat, and jumped on as Red steadied the launch. Then, reaching into the pocket of his blue jeans, he pulled out four singles and handed them down to Red.

"Thanks a lot, Mr. Pennfield. And have a good sail tomorrow."

As the launch pulled away, Pennfield quickly unlocked the hatch, threw his duffle bag below, took the cushions out of their locker and laid them down on the long bench seats in the cockpit. Then he stretched himself out and relaxed, waiting for the sun to dip below the horizon. *Don't worry, Red. I'll have a good sail tomorrow. I'll have a great sail tomorrow.*

Months later, Pennfield would realize the signs began that night as he slept out on the cockpit, directly under the stars. The cool, salt air soothed him into such a peaceful trance that the nighttime clanks and rattles of the harbor were silent to him. Predictably, he dreamt of the sea—clear blue frothy water, bright yellow rays of sun, and pungent salty air filled his nighttime thoughts. *Nirvana!* On his imaginary horizon he remembered seeing an old boat, a deep-bellied tall ship ploughing through the peaceful waters. Its giant canvas sails luffed in the tranquil afternoon breezes. Then, unexpectedly, a disturbance in this sea of tranquility: *a figure, a human figure, dressed in white, wallowing in the breakers off the tall ship's stern.* Strange how the ship just sailed off with no apparent concern, the lone white figure gasping for help to no avail…

The next day started out as every bit the paradise Pennfield had hoped for. A stiff southerly breeze, a glassy-smooth Atlantic, and *The Speedwell* skimming across the surface. Pennfield took a deep breath. He ran his fingers across his taut, brisk cheeks, surveyed the Indian Summer New England coastline and breathed out. Picture perfect. Crisp, clear, clean, colorful and quaint.

He thought about all he had left behind. Stacks of files, notes from countless dysfunctional meetings, about thirty-seven phone calls to return. All still there to welcome him back on Monday. Trading the island of Nantucket for the island of Manhattan would be no fair deal, not at all, he grimaced.

He leaned over from the cockpit and loosened the jib sheet. The wind caressed his shoulder and gently filled the bellowing sail. He loved it out here. Sixteen and a half miles from Nantucket Harbor. Monomoy Point lay low on his beam, the shoals of Pollock Rip and the "backside" of Cape Cod running off his bow out to the horizon.

He had been out a good three and a half hours when he first saw the ripples on the water, about a hundred yards off the port bow. The wind was picking up, a mass of cold Canadian air pushing a frontal system down along the Coast. *Funny, but the morning's weather report said the storm wouldn't come until well into the night, the cool air's leading edge of low pressure sucking up a delightful ten knot breeze across the Sound all day long. Oh well, this wouldn't be the first time a weather report was incorrect.*

It was time to head back. He loosened the port jib sheet and slowly worked the helm toward starboard. As the boom swung overhead and the jib back winded, he threw the port sheet off its winch and pulled rapidly with his right hand on the starboard sheet, steadying the wheel with his opposite hand. He quickly tightened the wheel lock, grabbed the winch handle, threw the line around the self-tender, and rapidly winched until the jib filled sufficiently.

Close-hauled. A heeled-over helm slicing through the sea. Exultation. Two and a half hours back to Nantucket Harbor. He would beat the storm. The wind whistled through the slot between the jib and the mainsail, whizzing past Pennfield's face. Sea water sprayed his leeward deck. *Damn, it felt great!*

As *The Speedwell* rolled to the rhythms of the Atlantic, Jonathan wondered if Charles Pennfield, the Pilgrim, his twelve times great-grandfather, had felt sheer ecstasy like this standing on the deck of the Mayflower. Or was it pure hell, all of them stuffed into a small, stinky boat with little provisions and even less chance of surviving?

Curiously, he then thought of that headline he saw last night on the newspaper in the launch: "HAITIAN REFUGEES LAND AT KEY WEST." He smiled, almost laughing. Funny, but as he thought about it, his revered ancestor—the Great Charles Pennfield—was no different from any of them, those Haitians on their make-shift boats. A refugee, an outcast, running away from a home where he was no longer wanted. Ironic, wasn't it, that over three-hundred years later most of the descendents of those original Pilgrims would be among the very first to keep today's refugees out? It was exactly the attitude of his brother Christopher. Snobbery personified. *Mayflower Societies. Mayflower Balls. Social Registers.* Pennfield shook his head. Thank God, unlike his brother, he had never bought any of that crap.

Swisssh! A giant spray of salt water tickled Pennfield's face, stunning him back to the here and now.

During the twenty-odd minutes Pennfield stood there daydreaming, the approaching front had plowed a slow, languid swell through the once smooth sea. The long, lazy swells were becoming choppy rollers. The Speedwell's bow rode up their undersides, slammed into their frothy crests and crashed down in a series of thuds.

He looked back. The gray line of clouds that had appeared so innocent creeping over the horizon forty-five minutes ago had leap-frogged onto his stern, defying all known laws of meteorology. The wind rushed against his cheek, flapping his sails and spraying the deck. He looked down at his instrument panel. Twenty-seven knots. *Holy Shit!* A real storm brewing, maybe even a gale.

The Speedwell heeled over more than fifteen degrees. The wind whipping at its sails. The storm approaching with sprinter's speed. *The sails had to be dropped. Now!* He jerked the wheel to port, pointing his bow into the eye of the wind. Quickly, he threw the jib sheet off the winch and pulled rapidly on the furling line, fighting with it, *struggling with it,* until the jib was back on its furler. He tightened the wheel-lock, ran up to the mast, undid the main halyard, dropped the mainsail, and secured the bunched-up canvas to the boom, hanging on for dear life.

BOOOOOOOOOOOM!!!

A thunderous explosion of wind, water, light and noise. The rancor of the sea-gods punished The Speedwell, rocking it, bouncing it. He bear hugged the mast, swinging around furiously as the wind knocked it back and forth. He forced himself to concentrate, think: *Calm down. Go with it. Don't fight it. Wait for your chance, dash below, slam the hatch and wait the storm out.*

He looked over the stern. *A black line. A straight vertical black line. A buzzsaw of wind!!*

He spun around like a top, flipping and flapping as the boom batted him back and forth. The Speedwell's deck plunged in and out of the sea as the furious waters funneled into a tight, swift whirlpool. A giant wall of water spanked the hull, crashing into frothy white foam right over his head. *He had to get below! He had to go for it! NOW!!!*

He dove headfirst for the hatch. But, just as he remembered reaching for it—*Smack!*—the boom jerked down upon his head and slammed him squarely on the temple. He toppled into the cockpit, unconscious.

*   *   *

The bright sun glared into his eyes, sending brittle lines of pain across his forehead and a deep, throbbing sensation to his temples. It was later, he was sure. Slowly, he lifted his hand to his head and fingered soft, puffy flesh over his right eyebrow. He looked up, surprised to find the sky clear and the sea peaceful, just as in the morning. But he felt strange, dried-out, hungover.

It seemed to take hours, but eventually he managed to prop himself up. He sat behind the Speedwell's wheel and rested his hand lightly on top, allowing it to rock gently with the rhythm of the sea. As the boat swayed with the calm waters, the boom swung freely back and forth, the mainsail bunched up awkwardly around it from his efforts during the storm. He stood up, hoping to walk over to the mast and raise his sail, but he was far too weak. He sat back down in the cockpit; took a breath of fresh air, switched on the engine, and set his course for Nantucket Harbor.

"Jesus, where'd you get that shiner, Mr. Pennfield?" Red asked him that evening as the harbor launch floated past the Speedwell's mooring.

"Afraid my boat got the best of me during the storm, Red," Pennfield answered.

"The storm?"

"What's the matter? Why are you looking at me like that?"

"Well, it's just sorta funny, I guess."

"What do you mean?"

"Talked to almost everyone who went out today and no one told me anything about a storm. According to everything I heard, conditions were practically perfect. Where'd it happen to you?"

"Off Monomoy, near the shoals."

"Hmmph. I could swear Mr. Walsh told me he was out there all afternoon. Said he had clear skies and a six knot breeze."

"Are you sure?"

"Couldn't be more sure, Mr. Pennfield."

All day, Red's comments gnawed at Pennfield, until they became an obsession: a major disturbance. *Of course there was a storm, he had seen it with his own two eyes, he had lived through it, bumped his head because of it!* Pennfield was so distraught over it he paid a visit to the Nantucket Coast Guard Station the next morning. Unfortunately, the officer on duty seemed more intent on processing paperwork than helping Pennfield explain his enigma at sea.

"No Sir, no storms at all out near Monomoy and the shoals yesterday afternoon," the officer told him.

"Are you absolutely *sure* about that?" Pennfield asked.

"As sure as I possibly could be. Weather maps were all clear and our logs don't show any reports from anyone. Except you, of course."

"Yes, but look at this bandage on my head," he pointed. "Something had to have caused it."

"I don't doubt that something caused it. It's just that, according to our official report, it's highly unlikely it was a storm at sea, Mr. Pennfield."

"*How the hell can you be so sure!*" He pushed himself into the officer's face. "I was there. I saw it."

"Look, Mr. Pennfield. I'll say it again. There's no record of any weather in that area until around eight o' clock last night, not three in the afternoon. It could've been a random local squall or something like that, but I tend to doubt it. Now, if you're through asking your questions, I have some reports to file."

Dazed, Pennfield lumbered out of the station, his thumb rubbing the bandage over his right temple. Silently, he wondered: *what the fuck was happening?*

2

As much as Jonathan Pennfield loved his time alone on The Speed-well, his older brother Christopher reveled in late peaceful eve-nings on the front porch of the family's Newport, Rhode Island cottage. Built just east of Bailey's Beach in the 1880's by Alfred Pen-nfield, Jonathan and Christopher's great-grandfather, the "cottage" stood atop a lush green hill on a point surrounded by craggly rocks, overlooking the Atlantic's frothy waters. Not nearly as large or ostentatious as the mansions of nearby Bellevue Avenue, the cot-tage had, nonetheless, served first as a comfortable home and later as a summer retreat for three generations of Pennfields. Over the hundred odd years it had stood so proudly at the top of the point, the cottage became as much a part of the landscape as the sea and the foliage.

Christopher Pennfield sat out on the porch that night completely relaxed, unaware of the strange forces about to collide before him. The hard, wooden runners of his favorite Boston rocker rolled slowly back and forth over the squeaky gray floorboards: a large glass of scotch in his hand, ice cubes clinking to his motions, and an occasional drag on a cigarette. Of course, he *should* be relaxed tonight he thought. After all, part of the reason for this entire weekend was relaxation. When "the news" broke on Tuesday, Winnie had phoned him immediately and suggested it.

"It's not every day that a dirty old man gets to be a keynote speaker, Unk!" She exclaimed from her New York office.

"Winnie? How did you find out so quickly?"

"I have my sources. So tell me, what's going to be the theme of the keynote address at Pennfield College's one hundredth anniversary ceremony?"

"The minute I figure that out, you'll be the first to know. I need to relax and contemplate over that one for awhile."

"What better way to relax and contemplate than a weekend at the cottage with your favorite niece?"

"My sentiments indeed. But what would I tell Elizabeth?"

"Must I do *all* your thinking for you?" she answered. "Tell her that I'll be up from New York to meet with you and the architect about the renovations. Tell her I have a social event to attend in Newport that evening. A short trip, a quick in and out."

"Yes, indeed. Perhaps several."

A lush, Irish sweater insulated Christopher from the brisk air and the occasional puffs of wind off the water. He was at peace. It was late, past ten thirty. After a more-than-stimulating evening, Winnie had just retired to the third floor master bedroom and he was free to sit here and contemplate as long as he wished. He took a quick sip from his half-full glass and wondered.

Was he fooling himself, did he really make a difference? Or was Professor Christopher Pennfield just a good showman, standing up in front of his daily audiences of malleable minds, putting on repeat performances of his same well-rehearsed material semester after semester? That very question had plagued him for years. Surely he filled the role well. Standing tall and silver-haired, blessed with a golden tongue, stately, perfectly-mannered and extremely erudite. Everything so professorial. But what had he done to advance the state of his art, to take his discipline to a higher plane? Oh well—he melted into his rocker—he was happy, wasn't he? He had more money than he knew how to spend, all the attendant material possessions, a dedicated wife, two sons, his occasional flings and the respect of his colleagues. And, indeed, wasn't *he* the one just chosen to be keynote speaker? For a brief moment, he swelled his chest. But, then—his chest sagged—that constant question: was all of that enough? He walked into the kitchen and poured himself some more scotch.

He figured he *deserved* his scotch tonight. He should be proud about being chosen as keynote speaker. *Very proud.* After all, it was *he* who had dedicated his career to the College. It was *he* who was Chairman of the Philosophy Department and Tenure Committee. And it was *he*—certainly not his younger brother Jonathan—who upheld the Pennfield family tradition.

Ahh...yes, the Pennfield family tradition. A smile ran across his face. A whole line of Pennfields, back to the Mayflower, paving the way for the betterment of the American system. He pressed his lips against the cold rim of his glass, tipping it towards his mouth. The scotch tasted good tonight, swishing around his mouth, coating his throat, and warming his chest.

Unlike Jonathan, he was proud of his family's heritage. *Damn proud!* He gulped more Scotch. *Fuck moderation for once!* Tonight he would drink past his limit. He was proud of who he was and where he came from and he would drink in honor of all that! He thought of them all. Alfred Pennfield, his great-grandfather, founder of the Pennfield Foundation, a philanthropic organization which funneled family money into hospitals, libraries, and worthy social causes throughout New England. His grandfather, Benjamin Pennfield: his cunning and guile and poker-faced approach to the game of business built railroads, factories, public utilities and even a small airline. And his father, Richard Pennfield: most of the time cold and unapproachable, *but a fucking good lawyer, damnit!* Isn't the name of today's most prestigious Wall St. law firm, McGrath, Moore *and Pennfield?*

All in all, an impressive breed. No matter what direction the fortunes of the Pennfield clan may take from hereon in, no one of objective mind would disagree that the Pennfields had achieved greatness. Then, like a spark, a thought: *what a great opportunity to tell the whole world at the College's One Hundredth Anniversary ceremony!* Yes, indeed—he sat up straight in his chair and smiled—*that would be the theme of his speech next June!* He would relay the story of the Pennfield legacy—all the way from the Mayflower through thirteen generations—and how it resulted in the founding of Pennfield College. Of course, it would take time for him to research it all, but such a glowing tribute to his family would be well worth it. He could envision it already.

A bright June day. Hundreds of friends, alumni, celebrated academics, public figures—and, of course, the press—seated reverently on temporary stands set up across the college's sprawling green lawns. The college's belltower chiming throughout the small, quaint campus to signal the beginning of the ceremony. Someone important—perhaps college President Collins or maybe Governor Winters; well, whatever, he'd have nine months to decide—would introduce him. He would walk respectfully up to the podium, place his speech down before him, raise his eyes to the sky, and then begin:

> *Governor Winters, President Collins, Senator Hessler, Provost Murray, Reverend Clergy, Distinguished Guests. We are here today to celebrate the legacy of a great American family. A family of which I feel both humbled and privileged to be counted as a member…*

Yes, yes! He smiled and rocked. What a great idea! But he mustn't let the time fritter away. He must begin soon. For sure, he would need a research assistant to help. That wouldn't be a problem, though: there were plenty of eager young students around. Better yet, if the student was female and attractive, he smiled.

Looking back, he would realize it was at that precise moment in time when his life had reached its apex. The events about to ensue would cause everything to come unraveled.

As he placed his glass down on the floorboards, he thought he heard something. A rustling sound, perhaps. But, of course, it could always be the shifting winds or the frothy breakers washing up on the cottage's craggly shoreline. Slowly, his eyes surveyed the lawn. A light fog misted the air, making it difficult for him to see out to the water. Gray wisps of mist floated before him, forming odd shapes. Again, he thought he heard something far off near the sea wall.

"Walter! Walter!"

A stiff breeze blew in from the water, sending a shiver through his bones. He heard the sound again, this time closer. He squinted, again looking out on the lawn.

He saw her distinctly: a young woman. Slowly, she walked toward him from out of the fog. There was something different about her, ethereal, he thought. Young and blonde in a formal white dress, she appeared oblivious to his presence, as if he didn't matter.

Staring at her, he stood up from his rocker. For an instant, he felt queasy. But, quickly, it subsided. He looked at her again, squinting into the fog. Most likely, a refugee from some charity ball at one of the mansions nearby and undoubtedly stewed to the gills. Wasn't there something going on at the Breakers tonight? Probably, she and a group had skipped off to Cliff Walk for a little party of their own as they found the more formal one too stodgy for their liking. *But, Jesus, did they have to wander up to the cottage, couldn't they stay down on the walk?*

"There's no Walter here," he called back to her.

She glanced at him, and then looked back toward the walk, as if at the very same instant realizing that she had both strayed from her friends and wandered onto someone else's property. She stood in place for several seconds and then ran back towards the walk, blending into the fog. He shook his head and lifted the scotch to his lips.

"Unk?" Winnie yawned and twisted in the sheets as Christopher joined her in bed several minutes later.

Shit! He prayed she wasn't completely awake. "Yes, dearest," he answered.

"How about an encore performance from the maestro?"

"But, Winnie, I'm dead tired. I couldn't possibly…"

"Perhaps then it's true."

"What's that?" He snapped, hoping she wasn't referring to the disparity in their ages. *That was a sensitive subject and she knew it!*

"Why, of course—that all great artists require motivation." In one lithe movement, she sat up in bed, flicked on the light behind her, and slowly unwrapped the sheets from her naked body. She hovered over him, two young, ripe breasts dangling before his face.

"Jesus Christ, Winnie! You're going to wear me out."

He slept peacefully at first. He remembered floating, floating comfortably on his mattress, every muscle in his body supple and relaxed. A light, euphoric feeling titillated his skin, his cells effervescing. Then, after several hours of restful sleep, abruptly: a deep black chasm. Falling, tumbling, *nosediving* down the endless spiral. Then, *Thud!*, bottom. A sack of potatoes slammed onto concrete. He woke up with a gasp.

He remembered forcing himself to open his eyes, or at least he thought—or dreamt—he did. Lazily, his eyes wandered around the textured white ceiling, now a muddy shade of gray, lit only by the moonlight from the windows at the foot of the bed. He figured he had slept at least two hours. Instinctively, his eyes shifted over towards the clock on the dresser. He strained, both pupils as far to the edge as his eye muscles would allow. He couldn't quite see the clock. He forced himself to turn his neck. *Nothing.* Again, he tried. *Again, nothing.* He squirmed and sweat and struggled, but he could not move. *Damnit, it was happening again!* His neck, along with the rest of his body, was frozen in place, nailed to the bed! *Nailed to the fucking bed!*

It was the most baffling experience he had ever encountered. Paralysis? Or *suggestion* of paralysis? It was so fucking frightening, so nerve-tingling. A prickly, paralyzing non-sensation of a feeling needling away at his chest and upper arms. The flesh stretched so taut against his cheekbones so as to render his mouth incapable of slurring out even the least intelligible grunt. As much as he wanted to, as sure as that cold, fearful drop of sweat slid across his forehead, he simply *could not* lift himself off the mattress. A large invisible lead weight hung over him, pinning him, crushing him against the bed.

His brain sent a massive shot of current to the fingers of his left hand, signaling them, *pleading with them*, to move, even slightly. But they wouldn't. His lungs furiously pumped air to his throat, hoping that his larynx would have the good sense to form a sound. But, he heard only a soft gurgle as the gasps ricocheted off the roof of his mouth. He desperately, *violently*, tried to do anything to prove to himself he had control of his faculties. But, nothing. He lay there, helpless, like a lifeless mass of jelly.

Winnie! Winnie! He silently screamed. She was two feet—*two fucking feet*—to his right and nothing, absolutely nothing, he could do. He was convinced, yes convinced. No matter how many times this had happened before, he was convinced. Every ounce of cholesterol he had ever ingested, every gram of sodium that had ever entered his bloodstream, every drop of that God-damned scotch that had ever bathed the tissues of his liver, was coming back to extract payment.

This was it! He was dying, dying! He thought he could feel a lone tear trickling down his cheek.

He drifted into a state of semi-consciousness, unsure whether it was a body's natural demand for rest, some conundrum of a dream within a dream, or the last juices of life being sapped from his veins that cast this drowsy shadow. Gradually, though, the needles left his arms. He ran each of his thumbs across his fingers, sensing that crude feeling somewhere between touching a detached, inanimate object and an actual part of one's self.

He wiggled his fingers. Slowly, he was regaining the faculties of a relatively healthy fifty-two year old man. His strength was back. He could lift himself now, he was sure. He placed both hands against the mattress and tried to push his torso off the bed.

Damnit! He should have known better.

It was still there. Something pushed so hard against his mouth, jaws and cheeks so as to render them useless. He tried, but he could barely let out a muffled groan. He struggled desperately to lift his forearms off the mattress, but someone or something wrapped around his wrists, pushing his arms back against the bed. With all his might, he pushed back. Whatever strength he could summon ran through his biceps, pumping his forearms against the invisible force. He grit his teeth, focusing whatever he had left in one final climax of strength. *More. More. Mooooore.* His arms collapsed against his chest, the force crushing him, stronger than ever, stuffing his wrists back into his face. He was scared, very scared.

Our Father who art in heaven...

It flapped, it kicked, it punched.

Hallowed be thy name...

A small tornado hovered over him, whipping at him, wrestling with him. Drilling his chest. Slapping his face.

Thy kingdom come, thy will be done...

It was responding. The fucking thing was responding! It could read his mind, siphoning more and more energy from his silent thoughts. Some fucking anti-Christ was beating the shit out of him because he was invoking the name of God. So forceful, so malevolent, so—

He opened his eyes.

Time had passed, he was sure. Cold beads of sweat drenched his cool, clammy face. The room was calm now. Quiet, devoid of any sensation but the quick heaves of his chest and the rapid palpitations of his heart. He could move again.

Savoring the simple joy of rotating his neck, he looked to his right. Grey shades of darkness. Winnie, sound asleep, unaware of the massive struggle between good and evil in which he had just battled. It was almost amusing, now that it was over. A nightmare, that's all it was. Something must be bothering him. There has to be some explanation. Some rational, scientific explanation. He would discuss it with his colleagues, that's what he would do. One Friday afternoon at the faculty club, between his second and third scotches, he would bring it up. Clinically, of course.

He pushed off the mattress, repositioning himself to finish the night's sleep face down. No need to take any unnecessary chances.

Against his better instincts, though, he forced himself to glance at the window.

Why he did, he did not know. He would never understand. A strange compulsion, but he did it. By day, the two large windows, draped in plunging maroon, framed an ever-changing landscape of the sea. But at night, the picture was far more menacing.

He was not alone.

They were there again, looking at him. Two people near the window. Shrouded in a veil of cloudy grayness, but they were there. They talked among themselves, pointing at him, looking at him like he was a specimen in some museum. It bothered him, bothered him immensely. Whomever they were, they were invading his own personal space standing there so quietly at the foot of his bed. He wished he could jump up and strangle them! But he was too scared. He started to turn over, daring himself to take one final look.

They moved. *They fucking moved!* They were moving towards him. He could see their faces. Two men. Two big men. They walked towards him, almost in a trance, as if directed by some outer force. They looked at him, one of them drawing back his arm. He was holding a knife. Pennfield curled into a corner of the bed and whimpered, *"Jesus Christ, please, please don't."*

As the man was about to thrust the knife, Pennfield flipped over, dove face-first into the pillow, and pulled the covers up to the nape of his neck. He breathed rapidly, his eyes shut tight. He braced himself, awaiting a sharp blade plunging through his spine. But—he winced—nothing. He gasped. Still nothing. *He had to be dreaming, had to be!* That was the only explanation. Some nightmarish dream within a dream within a dream. That's what it was, definitely.

When he closed his eyes that final time, he had prepared himself for the worst. So he was both relieved and surprised when several hours later a warm beam of morning sun shone upon his face. He looked around. First to Winnie: still asleep, her soft white face buried in the pillow as if nothing ever happened. Then, over towards the windows: a shot of adrenalin burst through his veins when he looked at the very spot where, several short hours ago, two anonymous intruders brandished a sharp knife at a whimpering, pathetic man. He told himself that he must be sure to do something about these strange episodes, see a doctor perhaps. But, now that he had survived yet another, he knew he never would. *It's a dream, that's all it is,* he would convince himself.

All of that seemed the right and proper way to dispense of the pestery little episode until later that afternoon when he bumped into Rupert Hobbes, the owner by inheritance of the cottage directly to the west—between the Pennfield's and Bailey's Beach. Christopher had never liked Hobbes and, in fact, felt chagrined that the common rules of decency forced him to be civil to this self-important knave merely by virtue of contiguous real estate. Back in prep school they had a word for spoiled brats like Hobbes: *wussy.* Christopher could easily imagine Hobbes as a chubby little ten year old in tight navy blue Bermuda shorts and knee socks, crying to *mummy* whenever he didn't get his way.

"Christopher, Christopher!" Hobbes, winded and sweaty from a slow jog along the point, flapped his arms wildly and called out to Pennfield as he drove by in his Jaguar.

Pennfield stopped and lowered his window, "Mr. Hobbes, getting a little exercise are we?" He snickered. He could swear Hobbes looked like a puffed-up doughboy in that awful red polyester running suit. And that yellow iridescent sweatband, *Jesus Christ!*

"Have you heard about the Phillips estate?" Hobbes caught his breath.

"No, I'm afraid I haven't, Rupert."

"I just heard yesterday. Some real estate man from New York bought it and there's rumors he's toying with the "c" word."

"The "c" word?"

"Condominiums, Christopher. Right along the beach. Lord knows what kind of people that'll attract."

"My. My." Christopher shook his head.

"Perhaps we should band together and hire an attorney."

Christopher almost laughed: to think Hobbes thought he was *one of them!* The Hobbes' family fortune was a product of turn-of-the-century manufacturing, making them practically *nouveau riche* by Pennfield standards. "Indeed we should."

"It's just terrible what this area's coming to, isn't it, Christopher? Why, they might as well let the Haitian boat people drop anchor right off Bailey's Beach. It's not like it used to be, that's for sure."

"Indeed," Christopher said. "I'm sure you were as upset as I about the intruders last night."

"Intruders?"

"Yes, on the walk. They must've drifted over from that gala at The Breakers. What was it, the The Greater Rhode Island United Way Ball or something like that?"

"No, that was *last* Saturday night, Chris."

"Oh really?"

"What time did you see them?"

"I'm sure it was between eleven and eleven-thirty. A girl strayed up from the walk right onto our lawn. I saw her myself. I was out on the porch at the time."

"You sure?"

Pennfield raised his eyebrows. "You don't think I'd make it up, do you Rupert?"

"No, didn't mean anything of the sort. It's just that I went for a stroll on the walk about that time myself and didn't see a thing."

Sometimes Christopher wondered why prestigious Wall St. investment houses felt it their obligation to provide sniveling little twerps like Hobbes with lifetime six-figure employment; a rationalization, perhaps, for their paltry existences. But, he couldn't say it didn't bother him that Hobbes seemed so intent on refuting his story about the young woman on the lawn. Pennfield wondered if Hobbes' motivation was some kind of perverted one-upsmanship or if it was genuine sincerity.

It tugged at his mind as he drove Winnie to the train station in Kingston later that afternoon. He began to wonder if *he ever really did see* that woman on the lawn.

"Why are you so quiet, Unk?"

"Quiet," he answered. "I wouldn't say I'm quiet. Just enjoying the foliage of a wonderful fall day."

"C'mon, I know you better than that. You haven't said a word since we crossed the bridge. What's up?"

"Nothing really. Except perhaps…"

"Perhaps what?"

"It's just this strange recurrent nightmare I've been having."

"Really?" Her ears piqued. "Do tell."

"Well, I wouldn't overblow it, but I wake up in the middle of the night thinking that I'm paralyzed, stiff as a stone, can't move a limb. And then, just when I regain my faculties, I see these two men hovering over me with a knife."

"And what kind of repressed guilt do *we* have floating around in our mind?" She grinned at him.

"Don't start, dearest." He looked over at her and then back to the road. "There was one other thing that seemed a bit strange, though. When I was out on the porch last night, I could swear I saw a young lady calling for someone named Walter, at least that's what I thought I heard. I just figured she was a straggler from some party who had too much to drink. But, then I saw that imbecile Hobbes this morning and he said he was walking along the beach at that time and saw no sign of anyone."

"So, the plot thickens, huh?"

"Perhaps.

"So what are you gonna do?"

"I don't know, what would you do, Winnie?"

"Simple." She grinned. "My standard solution for any problem of this sort. Go see a shrink."

He scowled. "Edwina, you know very well how I feel about that. I've lasted fifty-two years, thank you, with no help at all from those pseudo-scientific charlatans and I don't intend to start now."

"Jesus, it's no big deal, you know. I'm up to three times a week myself."

Perhaps it *was* guilt, he thought. Perhaps his mind had allowed him to deny what was going on between himself and Winnie for all these years. Perhaps now everything was catching up with him, exacerbating its effect, causing him to awaken scared stiff, hallucinating about large men in his room and a mysterious young woman on his front lawn.

It had begun between the two of them innocently enough, and he certainly wasn't the aggressor. Actually, an unsuspecting victim if the truth be told. It was six years ago. After fourteen years of European boarding schools and living under the supervision of a legal guardian—as strictly prescribed in her parents will—Winnie had arrived in the States. Both Jonathan and Christopher thought it an excellent opportunity to use their annual family Labor Day weekend at the cottage as an occasion to become reacquainted with their niece. Neither had seen her for over nine years.

Her personality was a magnet. Christopher's two teenage sons, Richard and Robert, developed immediate crushes on her. Jonathan's little Alex adopted her as a big sister. Jonathan secretly lusted for her and Elizabeth and Susan admired her refreshing combination of spunk and refinement. But, it was between Winnie and Uncle Chris where the chemistry really meshed.

That first Saturday night Winnie and her uncle stayed out on the old wraparound porch until 2AM—he, comfortably settled in his sturdy wooden rocker, a bottomless glass of scotch in his hand, puffing out cherry-scented smoke from his pipe; she, sipping on an occasional beer, in blue jeans and an oversized pullover, sitting on the cold wooden slats. Their discussion ran the gamut. Politics. Philosophy. History. Ethics. What being a Pennfield meant. The lasting impact of the Beatles on the future of music. The ten historical figures whom each admired most. Is there such a thing as perfection? Was MTV creating a generation of zombified illiterates? Springsteen, Madonna, Reagan. That night when Christopher finally went upstairs to bed, he thought he had adopted a daughter. The next afternoon he realized the flaw in his thinking.

The aroma of sizzling burgers scented the air. Jonathan was tossing a football to the boys in the backyard and Elizabeth and Susan sipped gin and tonics as they watched over the barbecue. When

Christopher ran upstairs to the bathroom, Winnie called him into her room. She was stark naked on the bed.

He was shocked. He considered a brief admonition or maybe just walking out, but he couldn't deny himself the outright thrill of what he was seeing. It was both beautiful and serendipitous—*and, Jesus, did his juices flow!* He tried to force himself out the door, but he couldn't take his eyes off her. He stood silent, gazing at the center-fold on the bed. Finally, after what seemed an eternity, she walked over, kissed him, undid his fly, and, giggling, buried her hand in his crotch.

The guilt that would plague him for months afterward didn't begin until the drive home that night. He clenched the steering wheel and thought it all out. She had lost her parents at an early age. She was vulnerable. Elizabeth and the boys were right in the backyard and, worst of all, *she was his dead brother Robin's daughter for goodness sakes!*

Despite it all, their dalliances continued. Not frequently, but two or three times a year. It became a perfunctory thing, like going to the dentist or getting a haircut. Certainly there was romance, and there was lust, plenty of it. But these little trysts didn't lead anywhere, they just happened. Surely, they weren't hurting Winnie: she was a big girl acting of her own free will. And given Elizabeth's almost non-existent sexual appetite, why would she care if her husband was forced to find another outlet? After all, she wasn't going to pack up and leave over these trivial little things.

"I want you to make me a promise," Winnie shook him as he pulled up to the train station.

"What's that?"

"If you wake up in the middle of the night again and feel like you're watching re-runs of the Twilight Zone, you won't hesitate to get some help." She blew him a kiss.

"Don't hold your breath," he answered. "It's non-negotiable."

3

Jonathan Pennfield squeezed his way out the train, lunged onto the platform, and along with hundreds of other commuters slowly made his way toward the main terminal of Grand Central Station. As he reached the main floor, he stopped for a moment and fingered the small bandage over the corner of his right eye. Although the previous weekend's adventure on *The Speedwell* may have been less than ideal, it was still a welcome escape from *this*. He looked around, drinking in the massive marble-plated terminal, as if it was the first time he had ever seen it. People scuffled by him, rubbing shoulders, bumping elbows. *Jesus, what were we all coming to?*

He remembered how it was when he first started working in Manhattan. Instead of the New Haven Line it was the Lexington Avenue Subway that had deposited him daily in this Palace built in deference to the working commuter. A wet-behind-the-ears twenty-four year old, he was in awe of the place back then.

Grand Central was an unappreciated spectacle the way the young Pennfield saw it. Its magnificent ceiling one hundred and twenty feet above the floor. The stars of the Zodiac painted across it. Taurus the Bull watching down over the information booth. Cancer the Crab over the West balcony. Cassiopeia, Orion the Hunter, Leo the Lion, Pisces the Fish all in their correct places along the celestial path. And those great, magnanimous arching windows with their intricate metal grate work overlooking Vanderbilt Avenue. And then the delicate, understated ledge lining the terminal's arching ceiling, like an exquisite fringe lining an elegant tablecloth. He wondered how many of the preoccupied commuters below—busily scurrying off to wherever they had to be, day after day after day— ever even noticed it.

"Spare a quarter, gotta quarter, man?"

He bumped into the exact same guy every day—Capt. Jack, he called him, a black guy with a speckly-grey beard, wearing a beat up Army jacket—working the same crowd for their daily nickels, dimes, and quarters. As easy as it was to reach into his pocket and slap down a coin, Pennfield never had.

He could rationalize it, rationalize it very easily. *Theory number one:* Captain Jack was a con-artist. If in the course of a ten hour day, Capt. Jack could con a thousand quarters, that would be two hundred and fifty dollars a day or a thousand two fifty a week or sixty-five thousand a year, tax free. Not bad. *Theory number two:* Whatever money he gave him would just be squandered on drugs or alcohol which would only contribute to the poor fellow's already huge problem and indirectly perpetuate the underground empire controlled by organized crime and South American Drug Lords. *Theory number three:* So maybe the guy really did need the money. But there were legitimate social services he could turn to. No one who truly needed help would ever be turned away. And hadn't he given over two thousand dollars to the United Way last year?

Poom!

Some young turk, hellbound for Wall St. or some ad agency, sneakers on his feet, a Brooks Brother suit draped over his frame and briefcase in hand, grazed Pennfield's shoulder without even noticing. Not even an "excuse me." Which, of course, lead to *Theory number four:* Thousands of young turks like that fellow bustled through this building every day, so preoccupied with oiling the wheels of commerce that they didn't even notice Captain Jack. At least *he* took a few seconds to think about the Captain Jacks of this world.

He bit his lip. The more he thought about it, though, the more it bothered him, pissed him off. Everything that was wrong with this world—everything his instincts had told him years ago—was summarized every single morning right here in Grand Central Terminal. The utter preoccupation of the masses with just churning the engine, keeping the flywheel moving, struggling to get one step—or one half step—ahead of the next guy. All in fealty to that King of Capitalism, the almighty dollar, plowing right over and through whatever poor, unfortunate souls stood in their way.

At that moment he thought of the unusual dream he had during his night on The Speedwell the previous weekend. That poor young girl drowning: although silent, it was clear from the images that she was begging for help, the tall-masted wooden ship sailing off as if she didn't matter, had no worth. There was a message in it, he was sure. Just like what was happening here: the engines of progress running roughshod over the less fortunate of the world.

Then it struck him as he walked through the revolving doors into the Met Life building: *how dare he be the one to criticize!* He was thinking as if he were an observer, some detached social-scientist taking notes on the human condition when truth was, somehow, someway, over the years he had rationalized everything away. He didn't do anything—didn't even make a feeble attempt—to help solve the problem anymore. He *ignored* the problem—or worse, *escaped* the problem—running off to his hundred thousand dollar yacht whenever he couldn't take the heat. *Jesus, he was one of them!*

The sheer shock of the thought caused him to stop dead in his tracks. *If he really believed all this, then why did he allow himself to continue on?* He didn't need the job, didn't need the money. If he allowed everything to continue, it would only get worse, he would only become more immune to the whispers of his conscience. Perhaps it was time to do something about it?

He stepped out onto Forty-Fifth Street. Cars sped by, taking advantage of the street's two block "freeway" separating the Met Life and Helmsley Buildings. At times, he wondered how he had survived all these years of crossing Forty-Fifth street unscathed, except, perhaps, for that gradual, well-documented gain in systolic pressure. Today was no exception. He waited for an opening. Unaided by anything resembling a traffic light, he had to do it on instinct. He saw what he considered to be a pretty wide gap. Briskly, he strode across the street. Then, *Shit!*, he stutter-stepped, a black Saab dusting the cuffs of his pants. *Bastard!*, Jonathan grimaced. That fucker actually sped up. *Actually, sped up.* These urban barbarians weren't satisfied in attaining whatever it was *they* wanted. They had to fuck up someone else in the process as well!

It was definitely time to do something about it! he told himself as he rushed through The Helmsley Walkway. He couldn't be part of it, couldn't support the existence of this all-consuming, dehumanizing machine anymore. He stepped out the walkway, a bright morning sun lighting up Park Ave's grassy median. He looked up the Avenue. Banks, hotels, law firms, giant publishing houses, shining towers of industry. People, busy people, important people, rushing about their business. He winced. Yes, it was time to get back to his roots, drop out from all this bullshit. Take some time off, step back, and then figure out how he could best contribute.

By the time he passed the Waldorf-Astoria, the issue was no longer *if*, but *how*. Of course, Don would take his resignation hard, consider it practically abandonment given all the troubles at the airline these days. But, as much as he loved and respected Don Piersall, this wasn't about abandonment. It was about liberation, getting back to one's true roots. There was a real person deep down inside his Brooks Brothers suit—a person who hadn't seen the light of day since 1973—and it was about time to let him out again, damnit!

He had gone through this thought process many times before, but today he would not talk himself out of it as he approached the GlobalAir Building on Fifty-Third Street. There was a reason to stick to his resolve this time, *a damn good reason!* The pressure was beginning to get to him, fuck his brain. It had to be some sort of neuroses that caused him to imagine that storm during the weekend, had to be! And that neuroses had to be a product of his high-pressured life. He was losing it, losing control and he was embarrassed about it. He picked up his pace, swelling his chest in ridicule of the life he was about to discard.

"Good morning, Mr. Pennfield."

He looked up at the security guard. "Oh, hi, Charlie."

He had been so deep in thought, he didn't realize he had reached the GlobalAir Building. He turned inside the revolving doors to the building's marble lobby. He took a deep breath: now the hard part. It wasn't the act of resigning that was so daunting, it was the necessity of facing *him*. He pushed the button to the elevator and then, while he waited, forced himself to look down towards the end of the long, arched hallway where a painting of his grandfather, Benjamin Pennfield, kept watch over the building's lobby.

Those eyes, those two beady eyes, locked right onto him. The defiant grimace across his lips, his strong pronounced jaw, the determined crossing of his arms, his caliper-like grip on his cigar: all told Jonathan that Benjamin Pennfield knew whatever treasonous thoughts violated his grandson's mind.

That painting had not changed one bit in the twenty years Jonathan had worked there, but each day those same expressions— his dark eyes, his jutting jawbone, his suffocatingly-crossed arms, his cigar tipped up just above the lower edge of the frame—sent a different message. Benjamin Pennfield may have been dead for over thirty years, but he still minded his business, protected his interests.

Jonathan quickly looked away. *No, grandfather, not today. It's time to get this fucking Pennfield albatross off my back. This time, I'm going to do what's right for me.* The instant the elevator door opened before him, Pennfield stepped in. There was no turning back.

When he stepped off onto the twenty-first floor, the office was surprisingly quiet. Usually he was barraged the minute he showed his face. But, today, no one ran up to him as he strode down the hall. Everyone moved out of the way, allowing a clear path to his office. He could sense whispers all around. He stopped at his secretary's desk.

"Good morning, Linda."

"You're wanted right away up in the boardroom," she answered.

Jesus, what now? He knew something was wrong. The staff reserved the silent treatment for only the *really big* problems. Shit, what was it going to be? He could only imagine. Then he smiled: whatever it was, it wouldn't affect him. He was about to resign, wasn't he?

"Fine, I'm on my way."

The entire board of directors stood silent around the long mahogany table when he entered the boardroom. *Jesus, is this a wake or something?* Slowly, he scanned the faces of the board members. Leonard Samansky, financier. Al Mayfield, corporate attorney. Bob Shapiro, CFO. Maxwell Curtis, General Counsel. Don Piersall—his mentor and friend—President and COO. And then, finally, Arthur Mapletree, the Chairman of the Board.

"Yes, gentlemen." Jonathan broke the silence.

Mapletree cleared his throat. "Jonathan, after much thought, we've decided that a change is called for. Don has done a commendable job under the most trying of circumstances, but it's time to move the airline in another direction."

Silence. Pennfield looked over at Piersall who nodded at him.

Mapletree smiled. "And we think you're the man to set the course. We've just elected you President and Chief Operating Officer of GlobalAir."

*   *   *

Susan Pennfield pulled on the parking brake to her family's Volvo wagon, rested for a moment in the driveway, and eyed the half-open window in the second floor guest bedroom of their ten room colonial. "How odd," she thought. She was sure she had shut the window earlier in the day. As her eye slowly wandered around the window frame, her thirteen year old son, Alex shot out the passenger side door and ran up the house's front stoop.

"Hey, ma, what you waiting for, Christmas or something?"

"Just one minute, Alex. I think I see something. Let me check the security system."

She was puzzled. Was it a burglar who raised the window, or was it just her memory playing tricks? Slowly she opened the car door, walked up to the front stoop, and within eyesight of the keypad to her home security system, noticed the small light was a bright, steady red. No one had tripped the system since she had left the house forty-five minutes earlier.

"C'mon, c'mon," Alex fidgeted on the stoop, "I've got things to do."

"Okay already." She grasped for the key in her pocketbook.

As Alex bounded up the stairs to his bedroom and computer, she stopped for a moment, glanced into the mirror in the entrance hallway and doffed her short brown bangs. Then she hung her pocketbook over the banister and breezed through the living room, straightening the picture over the formal white mantle as she passed. When she swung through the archway into the kitchen, she immediately noticed something wasn't right. It was the microwave door, slightly ajar. Just as she was about to correct it, she stopped short: *wasn't she absolutely sure she had closed it after she heated her soup at lunchtime?*

Without ever answering herself, she tipped it closed and walked through the french doors at the far end of the kitchen and out onto the deck. The soft rays of a late September sun felt so good she settled back onto the chaise. When she closed her eyes for a moment, she thought again of the guest room window and the microwave door. Normally, small things like those wouldn't have bothered her, but it was just yesterday that she found the living room candlesticks unexplainedly awry. And then last week, she came home from the store one day only to find the books on the mantle tumbled over like a row of dominoes.

Come on, get real! she told herself. *Didn't she have bigger things to worry about?* She stretched back on the chaise. Perhaps the years had made her so paranoid that she focused more upon creaks in windows and open microwave doors than the *really important* things in her life. These little imperfections were nothing compared with what was going on with Alex. Growing pains, the therapist had told her this afternoon. Alex was a little smaller, and brainier, and, yes, *nerdier* than his classmates. It's no wonder he didn't fit in socially right now, no wonder that he withdrew sometimes, no wonder that he played sick sometimes. It would all even out some-day, the therapist assured her: twelve years from now when Alex was graduating Harvard Law or receiving his PhD from MIT, where would the others be?

As her lids grew heavy, Susan reminded herself not to get too comfortable. Against her better instincts, she pushed herself off the chaise, yawned and stretched her arms, allowing several more sec-onds of afternoon sun to seep into her skin. She opened the french doors and stepped back into the kitchen. She stopped.

There was something wrong.

She shook her head and fixed her eyes on the table. *That canister wasn't there when she walked out onto the porch just five minutes ago, she was sure of it.* She stood there silent for several moments until the telephone rang, interrupting her train of thought. Slowly, she picked it up.

"Hello?"

"Suz?

"John?"

"Fasten your seatbelt. You'll never guess what happened today."

"You know what really pisses me off. No one was more dedi-cated than Don. No one knew the airline better than Don, and still they did it to him," Jonathan told Susan that evening as he sat at the edge of his easy chair, scotch in hand.

"You're doing a great job of laying one mega guilt trip on your-self," Susan said. "So if you think they screwed Don so bad, why'd you accept?"

"I had to. I had no choice. If they let an outsider in, he'd run Glo-balAir into the ground."

"So why do you care?"

"I guess I care because…well, I know this sounds funny, but I guess I care because I'm a Pennfield."

"Jesus, that's a change of tune. Wouldn't your brother like to hear that."

"I know. I know." He swirled the glass in his hand, clinking the cubes. "But, still, it's my grandfather's airline they'd be destroying. It's just that Don's the right man to turn GlobalAir around, not me."

"I think you're being much too hard on yourself," she answered. "Who's been at Don's side for the last seven years."

"I'm not *denying* I was an asset to Don. But he set the direction, I just executed." He paused for a moment and then looked up at Susan. "You know, maybe this thing is just one big set up."

"What do you mean?

"Well, we all know the Board's scared shitless. If things don't turn around soon, the stock price'll plummet and then the corporate raiders'll be all over our backs. So they needed to extract their pound of flesh, they needed an available body to blame last year's poor performance on. And Don just happened to be the available body."

"Okay. But, that happens all the time. No one's immune to that."

"Yeah, but now the Board's in the unenviable position of having to name a successor. Now, whomever they name, if things don't turn around—whether or not it's that person's fault—the Board's in jeopardy of being ousted or getting itself caught in the middle of a hostile takeover. So the convenient candidate—a candidate they can name without being subject to the `I told you so' syndrome—would logically be a Pennfield. Better yet, if he's already in-house. And I was the available Pennfield."

"C'mon, Jonathan, give yourself a break, you're much too—*Jesus, look!*" She turned white.

"*What?*" He heard rattling, strange rattling.

Shivering, she pointed to a far corner of the room.

"Holy shit!" His jaw dropped.

It was the ashtray, the ashtray on the end table at the side of the sofa. Rattling, shaking uncontrollably. Together, they watched it rattle off the smooth cherry surface, suspend itself in mid-air for several seconds, then drop to the floor.

For the next several days, Susan attempted to blot the incident from her memory, write it off as some sort of optical illusion or freak occurrence. But after trying in earnest, she could not. Forgetting where you placed a book or canister or candlestick was one thing, but watching an ashtray float magically off a table and hang in mid-air was quite another. Although Jonathan put up a good cover, she suspected, deep down, he thought of it as well. The Great Unmentioned Floating Ashtray Incident, she dubbed it.

It gnawed at her, though, every day until one night the following week she decided to break the silence. She placed an open dictionary in Jonathan's lap and pointed to an entry:

> pol-ter-geist n. [G.: polter, uproar+geist, a spirit] a ghost supposed to be responsible for table rappings and other mysterious noisy disturbances.

"This doesn't mean anything, Suz." He closed the book and placed it on the living room floor. "Just because someone invented a word to describe it, doesn't mean it exists. Anyway, it reads, and I quote, a ghost *supposed* to be responsible.'"

"But, we've been in denial over this thing for a week, John. After all, it *did* happen. We *did* see it."

"Yes, we saw something last Wednesday night. But there were so many other things going on. It could've just fallen for Chrissakes. With all the excitement and stress over me being named President, we could've *imagined* we saw it."

"Fine if only one of us saw it. But we *both* saw it."

"I know. I know. I know. Problem is, I'm trying to forget it and you won't let me."

"And that's not all. What about your storm at sea?"

He turned his head. "What about it?" He stretched out in his chair.

"The storm that only you saw and no one else."

"What are you saying, one's related to the other? You've gotta be out of your gourd, Suz."

"Why not? Why couldn't they be?"

"Because things just don't happen that way, that's why."

"That's not true. Not true at all." She paused for a long moment. "I spent some time in the library the other day. It seems as if there are many, many reports of these types of things, these poltergeists, every year. And the people it happens to aren't Satan-worshippers or anything weird like that. They're normal, everyday people. And the researchers, the parapsychologists, seem to have a theory that…"

"Susan Winters Pennfield, I thought you gave up smoking dope in 1978."

"Give me a break, John. Something's happening around here and I just want to know why. That's why I followed up on it."

"Don't tell me you…"

"In one of the books I read, there was the name of this man, an investigator. He's from New Jersey. Who knows, maybe he could help."

"Jesus Christ, Suz, the last thing we need is to bring in some kook from New Jersey to confuse us."

"I don't think he's a kook. Sounds like he's very highly regarded. Here, I followed up and got his number." She handed him a piece of paper:

EDWIN SWANN

732-524-9237

Investigator of the Paranormal

4

It was on his sun porch where Christopher Pennfield did his best work. Jutting from the south side of his Victorian home on a pleasant, tree-lined street in downtown Percer, Vermont, the porch provided him with the perfect setting for thought and contemplation. He had drafted some of his most noteworthy articles there, articles that had helped create a not unenviable reputation for the Chairman of Pennfield College's Philosophy Department. And it was there where he would begin the most important missive of his impressive twenty-five year academic career: the keynote address for Pennfield College's one-hundredth anniversary ceremony.

Anxiously, he forced a piece of white bond into the carriage of his old Smith Corona and then, before typing, looked out onto the street. The bright sun beaming in through a maze of branches and leaves created a perfect source of inspiration. He sniffed a dose of fragrant air, scented by the many flowers and plants tastefully placed around his work area. Slowly, he pecked one finger at a time. The first paragraph would come easily. After all, he had practically committed it to memory that evening out at the Newport cottage— the scotch helping the words flow effortlessly through his mind— and then had embellished it during the ensuing three weeks as he would occasionally daydream through a lecture or walk across campus deep in thought. Now he had it perfect. It was only a matter of putting it down on paper:

> *Governor Winters, President Collins, Senator Hessler, Provost Murray, Reverend Clergy, Distinguished Guests. We are here today to celebrate the legacy of a great American family. A family of which I feel both humbled and privileged to be counted as a member. A family whose legacy is intertwined with the history of our great nation ...*

He sat back in his chair and studied the words. He smiled. Yes, the perfect opening, the perfect set of words to set the tone for the entire piece. Now, the not so unformidable challenge would be to pay it off on the next fifteen or twenty pages. He looked out onto the street as he searched for ideas. He was so deep in thought that when the phone rang he ignored it, allowing Elizabeth to pick up in the kitchen.

"Chris!"

He shook his head abruptly. "Yes, what?"

She opened the porch door and slipped halfway in. "Your brother's on the phone."

Christopher grimaced. *Didn't Jonathan know he mustn't be disturbed!* He grabbed for the phone and thrust it to his ear. In only several short moments, the two brothers were at odds.

"But the woman makes *no sense*, Jonathan! I mean, she's practically ready for the looney farm and you, in one of your self-righteous pangs of guilt, are ready to give in to her every whim!"

"No, Chris, I'm not doing that at all." Jonathan answered. "I'm not saying that cousin Xenobia's right, but I *am* saying it's about time we seriously think about the real value we're getting out of the cottage."

"But the cottage is as much a part of us as our very flesh and bones, Jonathan!"

"Look, I'm just saying the house is...well, it's getting to be a white elephant."

"A white elephant! Bite your tongue, Jonathan!"

"Don't get me wrong, Chris. I don't mean that in a pejorative way. All I mean is that it's getting very, very expensive to maintain and how many weekends a year do we really use it?"

"Yes, and just because attendance may be off at Carnegie Hall, doesn't mean you tear it down to build a parking garage!"

"Oh come on…don't get haughty on me, Chris."

"I beg your pardon! I was *not* being haughty, I was merely serving up a very valid analogy."

"Come on, Chris…you know you don't have to play your professor games with me. Look at it from Xenobia's viewpoint. She really never uses the place and you're asking her to put up thirty-five grand for her share of the improvements. How would you feel?"

"I'll tell you exactly how I'd feel. I would feel honored to have inherited a share in such a family treasure. And, as a Pennfield, I would feel it my obligation to do whatever I can to help properly maintain it."

"But think of all the good we can do with the money, Chris. It's choice real estate. Think of the price it would bring. We can use that money to help house the homeless, feed the poor. We could start a whole new Pennfield legacy."

"Yes, and right now I would brand you a bleeding heart liberal if it wasn't for the fact that I know, without one iota of doubt, you could do all that on your own without *ever touching* the cottage."

"But, you're missing my point, Chris."

"And I think you're missing *my* point, Jonathan. What that cottage represents goes way beyond its mere monetary value. Think about all the family history inhabiting those walls."

"Granted, the cottage is rich in family history. But, this isn't about the past. It's about where we go in the future."

"Oh, hogwash, Jonathan! Our great grandfather, Alfred Pennfield, built that cottage himself. He probably came up with the very idea for the Pennfield Foundation right there. Think of all the good that's done."

"Yes, but…"

"But, nothing! And what about our grandfather? God only knows what deals he put together there—how many companies he started, how many jobs he created—in that very house! That cottage was probably the birthplace of GlobalAir, for goodness sakes! And isn't that where we spent the best days of our childhood? And how about Robin? Why, he stood up to father right in that parlor."

Silence.

"John? Jonathan?"

Jonathan smiled. *His brother Robin.* He swore he would always remember that night. Was it sixty-two or sixty-three? Robin had been quiet at dinner, clicking his lighter—a nervous habit of his—through the main course. Then, just as the help was about to clear the table, he stridently announced that he was going off to Europe to marry Gabrielle. Father stared at him with a vengeance, then barked across the table that he would *certainly not* go off to Europe and that he *certainly would* go off to Yale to pursue his law degree. Robin just sat there quietly through dessert, clicking his lighter with abandon. Then, thirty minutes later, fully tuxedoed for a night on the town, he ran down the stairs, threw his champagne glass against the parlor wall, and valiantly proclaimed that he was his *own* person, that he *would* go off to Europe and marry Gabrielle.

"Jonathan? Jonathan? Have we a bad connection?"

"No, no," Jonathan answered. "I was just thinking of Robin. I hate to admit it, but I haven't had a spare second to think about him in months."

"Well, I'm sure if he were with us today, he would shudder at the thought of us surrendering the cottage."

Jonathan laughed. "How can you say that? Have you been conversing with his ghost or something?"

"There you go again, John, trying to make folly of a serious family matter. At my expense, to boot. I just don't—

"Listen, Chris, I have an idea. We're getting nowhere. Let's call a truce for now, for Robin's sake. And why don't you and I get together in a few weeks to discuss this face to face. We haven't seen each other in how long? Maybe we should even meet at the cottage, a little stroll through the halls of our childhood may do us both some good. Who knows, maybe if I spend a few hours at the place, I'll begin to see things your way. Fair?"

"I suppose I should applaud your apparent act of generosity. But why do I find myself wondering if you have an ulterior motive?"

"Now that's the brother I know so dearly. Not only are you strong willed, you're neurotic as well," Jonathan answered. "By the way, I understand congratulations are in order. That's great about the keynote address."

"Thank you. Likewise, I was pleased to hear of your good fortune."

When he hung up, Christopher again looked out onto the street, searching for his next set of words, as if the conversation between his brother and himself had never taken place. He set his fingers on the keys, waiting for inspiration. Yes, he would meet with Jonathan at the cottage, it couldn't hurt. But, now, back to the address. That was of most importance, his chance to shine—*the Pennfields' chance to shine*. He paused for a moment and then pecked out a draft of his second paragraph:

> *Just like our nation, the Pennfield legacy had the most humble of beginnings. One wonders what it must have been like for our ancestor, Charles Pennfield, as he sailed with his Pilgrim brethren down the English Channel in the vessel Speedwell from Leyden, Holland to join the Mayflower in Southhampton. Did he realize he was about to embark upon a voyage of historic proportions? Did he realize that this small group of religious outcasts, looking only for a home safe from persecution, would plant one of the first and most fertile seeds in what would blossom into the greatest nation on the face of this earth? An heroic voyage it was, indeed, but a voyage that was not without its share of setbacks. Think about the despair our forefathers must have suffered when that very Speedwell, which was to accompany the Mayflower to the new world, sprung a beam just a few short days out of Mother England. Think of the havoc it wreaked with their well-made plans, forcing the two vessels to turn back to Plymouth, England where the most able pilgrims from both were crammed into the Mayflower for a treacherous sixty day voyage across the North Atlantic...*

*   *   *

The Mayflower, At Sea
September, 1620

"Yah Separatist swine! Heavin' up and down the rail like yer beggin' to yer Lord. Pray to 'em now, yah snivellin' scabs! Yah shoulda prayed to yer Mighty Saviour before He led yah tuh slaughter on this decrepit heap uh driftwood and pitch!"

The robust young man with the jagged front tooth skirted up and down the Mayflower's deck dodging the never-ending pulses of sea-spray. With a crooked walking stick he poked at the passengers, taunting them as they clutched over at the rail. He laughed, glaring into their faces and watching their vomit spew into the dark green sea.

"Yah think you're sufferin' now, do yahs? Wait'll a *real* storm rattles this heap uh timber and scum. You'll be *beggin'* for mercy then, yahs will!"

At least twenty of the hundred voyagers stood hunched-over at the rail, their stomachs so unsettled they had no choice but to subject themselves to the young crewman's ire. The Mayflower rocked on its keel, batted back and forth by angry waves. The sea boiled, spouting and foaming, its deep green-gray swells mixing up a bubbling witches' brew.

"Hah!" The crewman laughed, pointing at the sea with his stick. "Heave again, why don't yahs, maybe your suppers'll make it to the New World. Lord knows, your carcasses n'er will!" He laughed again, limping along the rail until, beneath the crashing of the timbers and the rolling of the swells, he heard something.

"One prays that a righteous Lord forgives you for your wretched words."

The crewman stopped, pushed his strangled hair off his face, and searched for his accuser. "And which uh yah pukin' scum dares be so bold?" He looked up and down the rail until one of the passengers pushed himself slowly away and turned towards him.

"I do," said Charles Pennfield.

"And what in the name of Beelzebub flames the spirit of a coward?"

"Perhaps the coward is the one who blasphemes." Pennfield, his face white, looked the crewman in his eyes.

"No," the crewman glared at Pennfield, "the coward is the one who deceives his brethren."

If Pennfield's face could have turned more pale, it did at the instant the young crewman spoke his words. Pennfield turned back at him to respond, but could think of nothing to say. Then, quickly, his stomach weakened again. He turned back to the rail and vomited.

"Hah, heave again, you lyin' coward!" The crewman skipped away, bounding off his stick.

Pennfield could not even begin to rest that evening. The words of the young crewman haunted him throughout the night. *The coward is the one who deceives his brethren.* What did this vile young man know? Was it something to do about what happened at Plymouth? But even if it was, Pennfield wondered what wrong he had done. Wasn't he only doing what was best for himself and Patience? As much as he tried to calm himself, to convince himself he had done no wrong, Pennfield could not fall asleep.

Two days later, what the vile young man knew became quite clear. It was a calm day, the Mayflower steady, the sun streaming across its decks. Crew and passengers alike strolled on the main deck drinking in the glowing rays and calming breezes. But the day quickly turned turbulent for Charles Pennfield when he went below to retrieve some items from his provisions. As he climbed down the hatch, he thought he heard strange sounds from a dark, lonely corner of the 'tween deck. He took several steps in their direction and stopped. He heard them again—breathing, he thought, and the squeaking of timbers. He took another step and, through a curtain of gray shadow, thought he saw something.

"Keep to yourself yah rotten scum!" A figure leaped off the floor and bounded in his direction.

Startled, Pennfield stepped back, rubbed his eyes, and then studied the scene carefully. The young man—the same vile young man who had taunted him during the storm—had been coiled up in that dark, lonely corner with a jug of wine and the Ashford's servant girl.

"And is this what you do when you're not blaspheming the Mayflower's God-faring passengers?" Pennfield looked down upon them. The servant girl turned her head away.

"God faring?" The young man cackled and then took a slurp of wine. "Do you call what you did at Plymouth God-faring, Mr. Pennfield?"

Pennfield collected himself and said, "Your accusation deserves no answer. But I did nothing wrong at Plymouth."

"Hah," he took another slurp. "Nothing wrong? You lied about that child, made it up, to assure room for the mighty God-faring Pennfields on this decrepit vessel. And what happened to the Perrins? Led like lambs to slaughter back to Mother England!" He slurped again, glared at Pennfield, and spit wine at him. "Yah pukin' coward."

Pennfield wiped the wine from his face and glared back at the crewman, his lips quivering. "If I ever again hear those lies pass through your lips, I will report this incident to both Captain Jones and the Ashfords."

The crewman scowled at him. "The words of a cowardly scum put no fear in my bones, Mr. Pennfield."

Pennfield looked at him again—*wouldn't this world be better off without such despicable vermin?*—started to say something, then decided not to. As he turned to leave, the crewman dropped to his knees and entwined himself around the servant girl.

Each day thereafter, the words of that vile young man clamored more profoundly in Pennfield's mind. Somehow, someway, that wretched young man knew about Plymouth, as if he had read his mind. *But how?* How did this young man know so much?

What bothered Pennfield most, though, was the power that young man now had over him. All that young man need do is open his lips to the Elders of the congregation and he would be shamed. Of course, Pennfield was absolutely certain he had acted in his best interests at Plymouth. There was hardly any room left on the Mayflower once the Speedwell sprung its beam, and there was no assurance that he and his wife, Patience, would be among those chosen as passengers. If not, they would be forced to fend for themselves in England, where the religious climate was not at all forgiving to sympathizers of the Separatist cause. As each day passed—and the Elders took their time deciding upon the final list of passengers—Pennfield worried that he and Patience would be left behind.

The idea came to him only two days before the Mayflower was to finally sail. When Pennfield stood in line for food, he noticed something about the young Perrin boy: didn't that rash on his arms and legs look familiar? He had heard it was a burn, the result of an accident with a kettle of boiling water. But, couldn't it, perhaps, be something else?

"Did you see that strange rash on the young Perrin boy?" he had mentioned to several members of the congregation the next day.

"Yes, what of it, Charles?" One of them answered.

"Doesn't it cause you to worry at all?" said Pennfield.

"Why should it? It's a burn. His brother dropped a pot of boiling water on him."

"I'm certainly not one to cause undue panic," Pennfield answered, "but couldn't that rash be a sign of the smallpox?"

As Pennfield's suggestion passed from member to member of the congregation, it grew into a serious concern. Could the Perrins have fabricated the story of the boiling water? Wouldn't a smallpox epidemic sabotage the entire voyage before they ever reached the New World? The news left the Elders with little choice. There was no way they could subject the congregation to such risk. The Perrins and their three children had to be stricken from the passenger list, assuring room for Pennfield and his wife.

As the Mayflower slowly traversed the North Atlantic, Pennfield convinced himself he had done the right thing. The New World would mean bountiful new opportunities for Patience and himself; he had acted in their best interests. Indeed, only two questions remained: how did that vile young man know about it all, could he read his mind? And what would the Elders do if that young man twisted the truth and convinced them that Charles Pennfield had deceived them?

The more he thought of it, the more Pennfield could not stand the possibility of being shamed. He envisioned himself as one day being a leader of the congregation: an Elder, himself, of this ambitious new colony planted in the New World. But should that young man tarnish his reputation with the Elders, everything he and Patience had worked so hard for would be ruined before they ever reached their new home. They would be nothing but outcasts, never able to assume their rightful positions within the Congregation. Pennfield realized he could *never* allow that to happen, he would do *anything* to prevent it.

"And what corrupts your conscience this fine morning, yah snivellin' liar!"

Pennfield grimaced and then turned around. Standing behind him was that vile young man. Even on a calm, tranquil morning—the oblique, golden rays of the sun just skimming the eastern horizon—Pennfield could feel no peace. Now that the crewman knew he had disturbed him, he would taunt him again and again. Every hour of every day that crewman would stalk him and, whenever he found him alone, would remind Pennfield of the Perrins.

"I would strongly advise you cease your campaign of lies lest I report your crude behavior to Captain Jones," Pennfield answered him.

"Now that's a fine trick fer yah, being called a liar by a liar!" The crewman grinned at him and then skipped off, sipping from his cask of wine.

As Pennfield watched him limp across the deck, he wondered if he would ever escape the young man's taunts. How much longer would it be before this vile young man would spew his twisted story to the Elders? Could he bear it much longer? If he did nothing to stop him, the young man would surely strike. As Pennfield thought more about it, considering every possible course of action, it became clear there was only one solution that was certain to quiet the young man. *But could he do it?*

"Heave again, yah pathetic drops of bilge!" The young man skipped along the Mayflower's rail on a blustery, gray afternoon, poking at the passengers with his stick and sipping from his jug of wine. "'Tis nuthin' but a strong breeze and yah swill-suckin' land-lubbers can't stomach it!"

The five passengers wondered what sickened them more, the rolling swells of a heavy sea or the foul words of this terrible young man. Stooped over at the rail, they silently wondered how many more days they would have to tolerate his ugly words. Gleefully, he danced around them as if taking pleasure in their suffering.

"Wait'll later, yah heaps uh rubbage, then you'll really heave!" He bounced up and down on his stick, sipping his wine, and howling at the passengers. "Yep, the Lords uh the sea'll curse yah snivellin' sacks uh—

He stopped short, reached for the rail, and gasped out a strong belch. His neck bulged under his collar. He reached for his stick, hobbled around the deck, and made a strange, deep grunting sound. As he gasped for breath, his face turned pale, then blue. Slowly, he poked at one of the passengers with his stick and mumbled, "Yep, the Lords uh the sea uh'll..." He stopped, clutched his belly, and fell to the deck. A puddle of urine drenched his crotch.

A commotion stirred around him. From all over the Mayflower, passengers and crew rushed over. Even one of the seasick passengers slowly pushed himself from the rail to help. But Charles Pennfield made no effort to come to the young man's aid. Instead, he stood across the deck and watched in silence as the vile young man inhaled his last gasps of breath.

By late that evening, the skies had cleared. Pennfield stood by himself at the Mayflower's stern and looked out upon the darkened sea. His problem was gone, done with. The vile young man's remains had been tossed overboard at sunset, now miles behind them. He had done it quickly and cleanly, secretly sprinkling the young man's jug of wine with drops of a poison stolen from the ship's carpenter. As he listened to the Atlantic's waters stream gently past the Mayflower's hull, he weighed the consequences of what he had done: was it worth breaking a commandment of the Lord to assure a better life for himself and Patience? It had to be, he thought, Divine Providence had left him with no other choice. Now his secret was safe; he and Patience were free to proceed on with their lives.

"Master Pennfield?"

Stunned, he froze—*wasn't he alone?*—and then slowly turned around. He squinted. In the night's darkness, he saw a luminous fuzzy figure, the light of the moon projecting a silver halo around it.

"It was you."

"What?" He squinted again. It was a woman, dressed in white, blonde hair flowing to her shoulders. He cupped his hand over his eyes and looked at her. The Ashford's servant girl.

"It was you who did it," she said.

"Did what?"

"You killed him, poisoned him."

"Rubbish!" He scowled. "Where did you hear such lies?"

"I just know." She shivered as she spoke, yet glowed through the mist of the night.

Anger flamed from the eyes of his reddened face. "You know nothing! Now be gone with you!" He glared at her, sweat oozing from his collar. Then, without warning, he slapped her across her face.

As she fell, he began to walk away. Then he stopped abruptly, turned around, looked down upon her, and said, *"Should I ever hear any of this again, I'll tell the Ashfords you were his whore. I'll scorn you. I'll scorn you with everyone, whore!"*

He rushed away across the hard, wooden deck never realizing how profoundly this single incident with the Ashford's servant girl would affect the lives of Pennfields for generations to come.

5

"And now I will make answer to you, O my judges, and show that he who has lived as a true philosopher has reason to be of good cheer when he is about to die, and that after death he may hope to receive the greatest good in the other world..." Professor Christopher Pennfield paused, removed his glasses, and stared off to a distant corner of the lecture hall. Then, with a perfect sense of timing, he turned his head back towards his students and continued: "And so Socrates, the great educator, sets the tone and by so doing posits one of life's most mystifying questions in the Phaedo, the last in the series of Plato's great Socratic dialogues. Now, who'd like to set the scene for us here?" Pennfield looked down at his seating chart, "Ummm...Mr. Kravitz."

Michael Kravitz, a well-tanned young man with curly black hair from Hewlitt, New York, according to the seating chart, stood up, looked down at his notes and began. "The Phaedo is umm...the story of the last day in Socrates life...it's uh...told by Phaedo to Eh-Eh-Eh-hecrates a few months after Socrates was forced to kill himself."

Pennfield's eyes roamed around Alden 302: twelve rows of well-worn wooden benches—and their accompanying long wooden tables—cordoned off in three triangular sections working their way down to the pit, from where the don stood at the lectern and cultivated young minds. He focused on the center section. Rows of sneakers. Orange sweat socks. Faded blue jeans. Ski parkas. Denim jackets. Football jerseys. All the accoutrements belied the tradition of the college's Gothic architecture and clinging ivy. Pennfield could remember the times in the mid sixties when he was a newly-appointed Assistant Professor and all the students in the all male school were required to attend classes in jackets and ties. Thank God the college had gone co-ed in 1968.

"Yes, all true, Mr. Kravitz...but the focus, the central 'focus?" Mimicking his hero, Socrates, Pennfield posed a question to the young student.

"Well it was the story of how Socrates didn't fear death."

"More specifically..."

Pennfield could tell that Kravitz was nervous. If this were a senior level course, he would have badgered the young man until he came up with the correct response. But Pennfield was no ball-buster, a trait which contributed to his immense popularity among the students at this small, but highly respected, academic enclave in rural Vermont.

"Okay, let's see who can come to Mr. Kravitz's aid." Before Pennfield had a chance to look down at his seating chart, a hand shot up in the back of the room. Elyssa Shrimpton, working on a 4.0, wanted to make sure she would receive a star for today's session in Pennfield's grade book.

"Yes, Miss Shrimpton." Pennfield obliged her. If he would allow her, this librarianish-looking academic machine working on preserving her space in the entering class for Harvard Law School two years hence could probably recite the Phaedo, and an analysis thereof, verbatim. But, that would defeat the whole purpose of this pedagogical exercise. Nonetheless, the controlled use of the Elyssa Shrimptons was necessary to keep the flow of discussion going.

"The central focus of the Phaedo," Miss Shrimpton began confidently, "is the relationship of the soul and the body."

"Of course, of course. And what does Socrates say about this relationship?"

"Well I would say his central thesis is that the soul and the body are disparate entities with the soul being everlasting and the body being corporeal and transitory…"

God, Pennfield thought, is she laying it on thick and heavy today. *Thesis. Disparate. Corporeal. Transitory.* What does this woman do, sleep with a thesaurus? Her personality could well benefit from a few less hours with the books and a few more at the weekly Phi Mu Beer Blast. Only half-listening as Shrimpton further developed her argument, Pennfield surveyed the faces of his students, deciding who would be on the receiving end of his next pointed question. Jonathan Becker. No, he had a tendency to ramble. Mary Powers. Maybe, she was pretty bright and usually grasped the basic concept. Jennifer Winston. *Ahhhh, Jennifer…*

Pennfield cleared his throat, giving Miss Shrimpton a not-too-subtle clue to finish up, and then looked toward another section of the lecture hall. "Within the Phaedo there's another analogy, brought on by Simmias, I believe…Miss Powers?"

Without hesitation, Mary Powers responded. "That would be the analogy of the lyre and harmony"

"Yes, of course, Miss Powers. Go on…"

Each semester, there was a woman in one of Pennfield's classes whose eyes were riveted on him from the moment he walked into the lecture hall until the moment he walked out. One semester, it would be an intellectual nerd like Elyssa Shrimpton. Another semester, it would be a Plain Jane like Mary Powers. But, this semester…*thank goodness, this semester*…it was Jennifer. Jennifer Winston.

"There's a certain philosophical term we use for the argument that Simmias makes here?" Pennfield questioned his students.

"Epiphenomenalism," Elyssa Shrimpton blurted from the back row.

"Correct," Pennfield cleared his throat for emphasis. "As always, Miss Shrimpton."

Giggles filled the hall. He was on to her and they knew it.

"And how does Socrates counter this argument?" He looked down at his seating chart. "Mr. Clarke?"

Pennfield wondered if the first time a baby ever opened its eyes, it looked at the world with the same enthusiasm and exuberance as Jennifer Winston looked at him. *God was she beautiful!* Long, straight blonde hair down to her elbows. Never a touch of make-up on her perfectly sculpted face. A lithe, athletic figure rendered almost transparent by her tight fitting jeans. And those firm breasts that protruded from her loosely-fitting Pennfield College sweat shirt. He was nervous, though. She had been practically gawking at him for more than half a semester, and she hadn't tried to make personal contact yet. She hadn't come to his office to discuss a grade, she hadn't been among the entourage that followed him, listening to his pontification, as he walked from Alden 302 to his next class, she hadn't asked for one-on-one counseling.

There was a moment of silence in the room. Pennfield had day-dreamt right through Clarke's answer.

"Okay," Pennfield quickly filled the void. "Now there's another analogy, brought about by Cebes…Miss Hart?"

"The weaver and the coat analogy?"

"Yes. Indeed."

Pennfield had lectured on Cebes' weaver and coat analogy countless times. It was nothing compared to the Jennifer Winston Paradox. He couldn't bear to wait any longer. All he wanted was a sign that she was willing to take her infatuation one step further. He had to be careful, though. She had to come to him, not him to her.

Instinctively, Pennfield looked up at the old clock in the back of the lecture hall. There were nine minutes left. Just enough time to sum it all up.

"So what does this all mean?"

"Professor Pennfield?" Richard Creighton, a wise-ass frat boy, but relatively smart kid, held up his hand.

"Yes, Mr. Creighton?"

"You know," Creighton started, "I've been reading in the papers about this old farm house near Rutland. You know, the one they said where the family moved out 'cause they claimed it was haunted. Isn't what Socrates is saying in the Phaedo…doesn't

that...well,   uh,   couldn't   that   support   the   existence
of...um...ghosts?"

Pennfield stiffened behind the lectern. Without warning, Richard
Creighton's innocent question had struck a tender nerve. Suddenly,
he was in that bedroom at the cottage. His neck would not turn, his
fingers would not wiggle, his body would not move. Pinned to the
bed, his body pummeled by some unseen adversary. Ghastly, forbidding figures staring at him from the windows, thrusting a knife
in his direction.

"Yes," Shrimpton cut in, "if it's true that the mind is the seat of
true wisdom and the master of the body, why need it cease to exist
when the body dies?"

Pennfield stood there, expressionless. Those thoughts, those terrible memories of the incidents in the bedroom distracted him so
much he paid little attention to Shrimpton's question. But he forced
himself to snap out of it. After all, this Professor of Philosophy was
not about to give up his corporeal existence. Not yet. Not as long as
Jennifer Winston was around.

"Well...ummmm," Pennfield mumbled, realizing that he was in
deeper than he would like on this subject, "...uh...Socrates obvi-
ously was making a very significant point, but I don't think he was
referring to ghostly apparitions. No, I don't think he was being that
literal."

"But...but...," Creighton spoke up again, "you read about people seeing ghosts all the time."

"Well...um...you may...in some of the more yellow tabloids...but I don't think it's ever been *scientifically* proven," Pennfield responded.

"Yeah," Leonard Persky chimed in, "but didn't Socrates say the
physical sciences couldn't explain spiritual matters?"

Pennfield paused for a second, both for dramatic effect as well as
inner reflection.

"Well," he began, "now that I think of it, I suppose Mr. Creighton
does raise a valid question, particularly if one is willing to accept
the principles espoused by those two great academic titans, Messrs.
Ackroyd and Murray."

A muffled giggle from the room.

"But last time I visited the library, I noticed that their landmark treatise on the subject of Ghostbusting was all mired in slime and ectoplasm."

The room was now full of laughter. The Old Master had done it again, deflecting a pointed, almost unanswerable question with a witty retort. It was the little things like this that fed his ego. As the laughter died down, Pennfield made one final pronouncement. "For our next session, be prepared to discuss the first three books of The Republic."

That was it. Another session of Plato 341 had come to a close. Students shuffled up the aisles and out the doors in the back. Although he had definitely left them laughing, Pennfield was a bit annoyed with himself. The out-of-left-field comment by Creighton had detracted from his well-rehearsed final summation of the Phaedo, where he drew several insightful comparisons and crystallized what he considered to be the true meaning of the piece.

Oh, well, he could use the beginning of the next session for a brief recapitulation. Borrowing several minutes from his opening thoughts on The Republic would be no difficult task. He looked down at the lectern and collected his papers for the five minute cross-campus trek to his next roomful of young minds.

When he looked up, he was surprised to see Jennifer Winston standing directly in front of him, poised to ask a question.

Thank God!

On Fridays, Pennfield's full afternoon of lectures would culminate with a rather healthy session of academic back-and-forth at the Pennfield College Faculty Club. Behind his back, younger members of the faculty referred to these sessions as Pennfield's Court. It was an unwritten rule that the oversized winged leather chair next to the tall arching window overlooking the College Commons was without question always reserved for the Senior Professor of Philosophy and Chairman of the College's Tenure Committee. To be seated in one of the other chairs or even on the couch around the large mahogany coffee table in that corner of the room was considered a privilege onto itself. Assistant and Associate Professors would patiently sit in other nooks and crannies of the dark, imposing Club for years before they would muster up the courage to venture over to the corner known as Pennfield's Court.

"Pervasive paranoia, that's what it is today, gentlemen. We run amuck in a world of pervasive paranoia." Phillip Wentworth, venerable professor of English Literature, lifted a glass of scotch off the tray offered to him by the white-gloved black waiter.

"Oh, Phillip, that's pure bosh." Kingsley Harris, Professor of History, countered. "Surely when historians look back upon these times they will certainly concede that the quality of human life enjoyed its finest hour. Wouldn't you agree Christopher?"

"An interesting proposition," Pennfield pondered the large antique grandfather's clock across the stately cherry-paneled room as he sipped scotch from his glass tumbler. "I tend to agree with the one major caveat, though. I have to say that it would be virtually impossible for one to truly appreciate the refinement of the ancient Romans and Greeks from mere literature and artifacts."

"I think Phillip makes a real point." Julian Weisman, the bearded and bespectacled Associate Professor of Physics, practically stepped on Christopher's statement, "Just watch any TV news program or read any newsmagazine."

"And what exactly do you mean by that, Jules?" Christopher challenged the young upstart.

"When we're not counting our cholesterol or watching our caloric or salt intakes, we're querying our potential sexual partners about the recent histories of their intimate relationships or, better yet, convincing ourselves that should we consume more than several sips of liquor a week, we are immediate candidates for admission to Betty Ford." Weisman, half way through his second scotch, rambled on. "I mean, in the sixties it was `If it feels good, do it' and today it's `If it feels good, it must be worth feeling guilty about.'"

"Surely, Jules," Pennfield chuckled, "you're not suggesting that the quality of life in the sixties was superior to what we enjoy today?" Christopher liked Weisman. He was feisty, always challenging, pushing the frontiers of inquiry. Now, if it wasn't for his unfortunate ethnicity…

"Why not?" Weisman answered, practically out of breath. He looked over towards his three younger colleagues for support.

Ira Hirschfeld from Psychology, Kevin Nordstrom from Biology and James Becker from Chemistry all nodded feebly. Their loyalties were split. Children of the Love Generation, yet they were all up for tenure this year. The discerning eye of Pennfield was always watching.

"I think the man makes a point, Christopher," Wentworth said. "The sixties were a time of experimentation, a questioning of life's basic values. Today, we just plod along looking over our shoulders and protecting our backsides."

"Oh, Phillip, you've been reading too much Ibsen." Harris cut in. "We can always tell exactly where you are on your syllabus. What was it this week? A Doll's House? An Enemy of the People? Or, perhaps, Ghosts?"

"Ghosts…" Pennfield laughed, almost with exaggeration.

"What is it, Christopher?" Harris asked. "I feel an Ibsenesque comment coming on."

"The mention of that particular work of Ibsen…," Pennfield's sweaty hand lifted the tumbler of scotch to his lips, "…reminds me of a rather amusing incident in my Junior Level Plato course this afternoon."

Pennfield paused, waiting for someone to encourage him. Wentworth obliged. "Well," he continued, "I was lecturing on the Phaedo and some young lad…of average intellect, at best…in the middle of one of my more insightful comments on Platonic Duality, questioned whether or not we can use Plato's reasoning as justification for ghostly apparitions like that nonsense up in Rutland that was covered in all the papers."

They all looked at him, expecting to hear more.

"And I suppose a comment like that is to be expected from a sophomoric mind. But the interesting thing was that the brightest students in the class immediately jumped to the young man's support."

That was it. A trial balloon. After contemplating it for weeks, the incident in today's lecture had finally given him the opportunity to toss it up for discussion. Now he would see if it would stick. One could say many things about his colleagues in the corner of the room, but, at very least, they all shared one trait in common: they were among the very brightest minds within miles of Percer. If there were any validity at all—scientific, historical, theological, psychological—to these phenomena he had experienced, they would know about it.

"I'm not too surprised by that," Hirschfeld commented. Not quite as bold or iconoclastic as his colleague Weisman, Hirschfeld was very careful when he spoke in the legendary Pennfield's Court.

"What?" Pennfield played the Devil's Advocate.

"I'm not surprised your brightest students would be intrigued with ghostly apparitions." Hirschfeld answered. "After all, parapsychology is one of the last great untapped areas of scientific inquiry."

"Rubbish." Harris countered. "Didn't you read what the National Research Council had to say about parapsychology? Why, they practically branded it a pseudo-science."

"I vaguely recollect skimming an article on that." Pennfield lit a cigarette, a common practice after his third scotch. "I remember something about experiments where they put ping pong balls over subjects eyes…"

"I believe the National Research Council report said something like the entire field suffered from poor scientific methodology." Harris added.

"True," Hirschfeld conceded. "Most of the current evidence of parapscyhological phenomena is anecdotal. But that's only because the whole field is so far on the edge of scientific inquiry that we still don't know how and under what conditions to replicate it consistently in a laboratory environment. But wasn't the law of gravity anecdotal at the point when Newton was hit with the apple? Wasn't the existence of electricity anecdotal when Franklin flew his kite? Just because a certain phenomena is anecdotal today doesn't mean it won't withstand the rigors of scientific methodology tomorrow."

Hirschfeld's line of argument impressed Pennfield. The young associate professor had been taken on by that old buzzard Harris and he didn't back off, actually coming back at Harris with a vengeance. But more than that, Pennfield was enlightened.

"So what do you all think?" Pennfield was more manipulative in his control of these intellectual forays at the Faculty Club than he ever was in an undergraduate lecture hall.

"I couldn't agree more," Weisman announced. "Think about it. On a clear night, when we look up at the sky, we see hundreds and thousands of stars. Yet, how many of them exploded into nothingness years ago? So then, what are we seeing, the star or a *ghost* of the star?"

"Yes," Harris responded quizzically, "but that's a completely different line of reasoning. It has no bearing whatsoever to…"

"Okay, here's another one for you," Weisman continued. "Suppose I asked Christopher to leave his seat. And then suppose I had a camera with heat sensitive infra-red film and I took a picture of his empty chair. When I developed the film…Surprise, Surprise…we'd all see a fuzzy but very recognizable image of Christopher sitting there, as plain as day. The camera, of course, would have picked up the elevated temperature in the area of the seat where he was sitting. So, is the image we see Christopher or Christopher's ghost?"

Harris distorted his face, squinted at Weisman through his scotch, and answered. "But your reasoning is completely circuitous. You're playing a game of semantics with us."

"No, I'm not. Not at all. My point is very simple, Kingsley. We all accept the existence of brainwaves. Don't we? So who's to say that during certain times in one's life these brainwaves become so intense, so energized, that they can exist as disturbances in the atmosphere for an indefinite amount of time, maybe forever. And who's to say that under the right atmospheric conditions and in the presence of a person who is particularly sensitive to them—a person in what parapsychologists would call a `high psi' state—that actual images from the past can't be recreated?"

"My dear fellow," Kingsley sat forward and looked Weisman straight in the eyes, "this is a college campus, a seat of higher learning. Your fabrications are nothing but pure and utter fantasy."

"Well, maybe they are to you, Kingsley." Weisman took another sip of scotch. "But, I say the existence of ghostly apparitions today is no more implausible than the existence of radio was a hundred and fifty years ago. The only difference is that the transmitter and receiver are the human brain, not pieces of electronic gadgetry. As a matter of fact, I would bet that within the next hundred years or so, it will all be proven beyond any reasonable scientific doubt. There's all sorts of theories. Some even say ghostly apparitions are the result of a discontinuity in the space-time continuum."

"And *what* do you mean by that?" Harris censured him.

"Two moments in time occupying the same physical space. Temporarily, of course."

"Jesus, that's a mouthful." Pennfield snickered.

"I even remember hearing a story, about a woman who had just bought an old restored farmhouse in Pennsylvania," Weisman continued. "She sits down for a quiet evening in front of the TV and, lo and behold, sees the apparition of a man in a bathtub right in the middle of her living room. Funny thing was, he appeared as scared of her as she was of him."

"Christopher, Phillip," Harris mumbled, looking at his older colleagues, "and what do you think of all this rubbish?"

Wentworth smiled. "Well, surely...at very least...our friend Weisman has proven to us that he potentially has a very lucrative second career as an author of science fiction."

Wentworth and Harris chuckled. Christopher also appeared to smile, but his mind was much too preoccupied contemplating the substance of what Weisman, a very gifted scholar in Physics, had said.

"Kevin? James? You both appear to be silent on this subject." Pennfield addressed the younger members of the group.

"Well," Becker, the chemist, began, hoping that he would have been able to avoid the subject, "I have to admit as an avid fan of science fiction and the tales of the supernatural, I am quite intrigued by what I read in some journals…"

"What journals?" Harris challenged. "The Star or The Enquirer?"

"No, not at all," Becker answered. "Real, legitimate academic journals. I'm sure you may even read some of them yourself, Kingsley. And, sure, all evidence of these type of phenomena are anecdotal, but they're too many commonalities…too many cases of over a period of years of several people, with no knowledge whatsoever of each other, seeing the same apparition at the same spot in the same house, and then finding out that these apparitions all bear an uncanny resemblance to someone who once lived there. Too many cases of poltergeist hauntings and out-of-body-experiences occurring under the exact same conditions. As a man of science, I think there's really something to what parapsychologists call the `psi' state…"

"Well, gentlemen," Christopher cut in, "I don't know about you, but the only state I plan to experience this evening is that of Vermont."

Pennfield's comment would have served as a final punctuation to the evening's session, had it not been for Nordstrom's desire to contribute at least one comment.

"Come to think of it," Nordstrom began, "I can't claim to be as well read on the subject as my colleagues here, but I think Jim makes a point with this commonality thesis of his. I remember reading several times about what I believe they call a `hypnogogic trance,' when one appears to be half asleep and half awake, sometimes even to the point of feeling paralysis or rigidity, and then seeing an apparition."

Startled, Pennfield grabbed the arms of his chair and slumped back.

"Yes, even Jung wrote about that," Hirschfeld added, "I remember it vividly. He was a guest in someone's home and at night experienced that same state of rigidity and paralysis during which he saw an apparition of a head of a woman."

"Yes," Wentworth quipped, "and I'm sure whomever she was, she had a mouthful to say."

They all shared one final laugh.

Except Pennfield. Suddenly, he felt an odd discomfort as he realized he had agreed to meet his brother Jonathan at the Newport cottage the next weekend.

6

From the moment he set foot on the cottage grounds, Christopher felt queasy. It was cloudy and dark, no stars filling the sky. Curtains of damp autumn wind breezed by him, chilling his bones. He proceeded with caution, standing on the edge of the property, carefully scanning the area before allowing himself to proceed further. Ahead of him the old cottage melded into the night, its swirling piazza grasping into the darkness. He turned slowly and watched the bushes sway to the rhythms of the wind, dancing with the rolling fog. His eyes halted on the spot where he had seen the young woman. He froze. The constant hiss of the sea seduced his imagination. *Was she here again? Was she watching him?*

His eyes roamed. Was what he thought to be a rising column of fog really the form of a young woman? Was she hiding behind the bushes, laughing at his cowardice? He stiffened. Or, perhaps, she was merely energy particles, brain waves etched into the atmosphere, forever calling out to some long-gone Walter, never to receive an answer. He shook.

Don't be foolish, he told himself. That wasn't a ghost or some meta-physical presence he had seen there last month, it was a sloshed young society girl who had drifted onto his property after having become thoroughly underwhelmed with some stuffy Newport party. Forget Weisman's and Hirschfeld's pseudo-science. Forget the sophomoric ramblings of his students. Hell, forget Platonic duality for that matter. His own logical judgment told him it could be nothing more.

Confidently, he stepped forward, his shoes scraping across the gravelly driveway. Half-way to the front steps, though, he felt the sudden urge for a cigarette. He stopped and lit up. As he puffed slowly—hoping to stretch out this short break as long as possible— his eyes drifted to the upstairs windows settling on the master bedroom's. Again, he froze. His mind obsessed: *Those creatures. Those two despicable creatures hovering over his bed. And that damn knife plunging towards his spine.* He sucked on his cigarette and wondered if this time their knife would hit its mark before he awakened.

He threw the cigarette on the ground and squashed it under his shoe. *Phooey!* Jonathan would be here shortly, and then, once occupied, his mind would cease playing these nonsensical games with him. He marched towards the front steps with confidence. As he placed his foot on the bottom step—*click!*—he shivered, bathed by a quick flash of bright light. He took a breath and wiped his brow. *Jesus!* The motion detector had clicked on like that thousands of times before and never had he reacted with such fear. *Get a grip, old boy!* He drew a beeline for the front door, twisted the key into its hole, and rushed toward the kitchen.

He plucked two cubes from the icebox and tossed them into a glass, drowning them in scotch. He stood at the sink and took a quick gulp. *Thank God! Thank God!* Nothing soothed him like a good swig of Johnny Walker Black. He stood at the sink and gulped again. He tipped back his head, closed his eyes, and breathed in through his nostrils, allowing the scotch to work its full magic. As he placed the glass on the counter, he opened his eyes and reached once more for the bottle, a refresher. He took another gulp, stopped short, and looked out the window. *No, it couldn't be.* He squinted. *Were there people in the back yard?*

He looked carefully. Two vague figures shimmered through the reflection of his taut face. Of course, this must be an optical illusion, he thought. There couldn't be anyone in the back yard. Not at seven o'clock on a dark November Saturday evening. He squinted again.

Through the reflection of his forehead, he was sure he saw movement. Then, an idea: he flicked the light off.

It was dark, but, indeed, he could not deny seeing two tall, husky figures in the back hovering over some large object: *a box perhaps?* They went on with their business clearly oblivious to Pennfield's presence. He flicked the light back on. One of them—what appeared to be a barrel-chested fellow with large brown eyes— looked right at him, directly into the window, yet registered no apparent awareness of the light or someone watching. How strange, Pennfield thought. He flicked the light off again. Once. Twice. Three times. Nothing. The men in the back yard worked on, talking amongst themselves and repositioning the object, undisturbed by the blinking kitchen light. At that moment, Pennfield's instincts took over. He rushed for the back door, burst outside, and flicked on the spotlight over the tool shed.

The branches of the weeping willow swept back and forth, chilled by the night time breeze. Cold bristles of November grass crunched as he walked. He stopped and focused on the spot where he was sure he had seen them. Nothing. Not even the slightest hint of a disturbance. If anyone had been there, they had escaped scot-free in the few short seconds it took him to run from the kitchen sink to the back yard. He rubbed his eyes, hoping to see something upon a second look. No luck. He tensed up and wiped his face. Surely, he must be losing it. Without doubt, he must do something about it, he must do something soon. *But, certainly, he must not mention a word of this to Jonathan.*

The clicking began at almost the precise moment of Jonathan's arrival. At first Christopher made nothing of it. Perhaps it was an animal outside—a loud cricket, or maybe a woodchuck. It could even be the cottage's antiquated plumbing or something in one of the radiators, he thought. But as he shared cocktails with his brother in the parlor, it began to pester him. In mid-sentence, he tilted his head to the side and listened, causing Jonathan to notice.

"Something wrong, Chris?"

"Not really," he snapped his head back to attention. "I just hear a bothersome noise. Do you?"

Jonathan put down his drink and listened for a moment. "No, can't say I hear a thing."

Christopher shrugged his shoulders. "Perhaps it's the pipes. Maybe I should have a plumber in."

They dined at the Inn at Castle Hill that evening. Even on a cold, foggy night they appreciated the Inn's panoramic view of Newport's historic waters as they enjoyed a fine meal and sipped chardonnay. The evening progressed precisely the way Christopher had orchestrated it. A nice non-confrontational brotherly chat to break the ice, an opportunity to tighten the loosened bond with Jonathan before the more serious discussions to come in the morning. By the time they arrived back at the cottage at half past eleven and shared some after-dinner sherry in the parlor, Christopher had all but forgotten about the clicking.

"My only point, dear brother, is that we have to accept cousin Xenobia for what she is."

"An eccentric?" Jonathan answered.

"Unfortunately, you're being far too charitable."

"Just because she doesn't happen to agree with you about the cottage, don't paint her a freak, Chris."

"But should we deny it? I've had Mr. Forsyth, the handyman, keep an eye on her for several years now and the picture he paints is not pretty, Jon, not at all."

"So my older brother, the esteemed professor of philosophy, dabbles in neighborhood espionage, does he?"

"Indeed I do. And if the purpose is the protection of a cherished family estate, I am damn proud of it, Jonathan. You should hear what I've learned about her. Her entire neighborhood is scared of her, to a person they are absolutely convinced she's some sort of witch." He stopped and cocked his head to the side.

"Aren't you going to continue?" Jonathan asked. "Why stop now, why not assassinate her character completely?"

"Shhhh!" Christopher placed his finger over his lips. "I hear something. I think it's that sound again. Listen."

Jonathan turned his ear toward the stairway, paused, and then smiled. "Well, it disappoints me terribly, Chris, but I regret to inform you that you're not losing your mind. I hear it too. For some reason, it sounds awfully familiar."

At that precise moment, the clicking became more pronounced. A short gust of wind swooshed down the stairway, luffing the draperies and jingling the blinds. The temperature in the parlor plummeted to a chill, the lights flickered.

Click. Click. Click. Click.

They both heard it clearly now, coming from the top of the staircase. Together, their eyes walked up the steps, one-by-one, until they settled on the top landing. Without doubt, there was someone there, an intruder.

"Shit. It can't be." Jonathan gasped.

"Oh, no! Oh, God, no!" Christopher's face whitened.

Standing in the darkness was their dead brother Robin. Wavy and transparent, he smirked at them, almost to the point of laughter, and puffed on a cigarette. He stood there, smirking and puffing, for a good thirty seconds before he nodded his head and flickered away into the darkness.

Christopher doubled over, then rushed for the bathroom, sick to his stomach.

*   *   *

It was not a night for sobriety. They sat in the parlor well into the morning: short bursts of bewildered conversation punctuated by long stretches of somber quiet; Christopher fogging the air with cigarette smoke, Jonathan staring aimlessly into the fireplace. They drank for hours, pondering.

"The gleam in his eyes. That smirk on his face. Even the way he lifted his cigarette. It didn't just look like him, that *was* him at the top of the landing tonight. And that clicking. His lighter. He was trying to tell us he was here. Don't you think?" Jonathan nuzzled a glass of scotch under his nose and took a strong gulp.

Christopher sat across the parlor in an old leather easy chair and gulped from a glass of scotch as well. "It's as if someone filmed him twenty-five, thirty years ago and projected it onto the landing wall. But, *Jesus*, all my instincts tell me it *couldn't* have been him."

"How can you say that? We both saw him, didn't we?"

"Well, let's not jump to any conclusions. Maybe we did, maybe we didn't."

"Jesus Christ, Chris, you lost half your dinner over it."

"Yes, but perhaps it was something in the food or maybe a bad bottle of sherry."

"Bullshit."

"Well, then it must've been a trick, a practical joke."

"By whom?"

"An optical illusion. Something that we both thought *looked* and *sounded* like Robin, but wasn't."

"Chris, get real."

Silence, then—

"Well, then, I don't know what's happening to me. Maybe I'm just sick! I'm just fucking sick and now I'm infecting you!" Christopher pounded his fist on the end table.

"What?"

"There's something terribly wrong with me and I don't know what it is, Jonathan. I see them all the time. Everywhere I look I see them. It's gotten to the point where I can't escape them."

"What do you mean by *them?*"

"Ghosts. They're all over the place. I can't stop seeing them, Jonathan." Christopher paused and wiped his eye. "There's at least four or five of them. Out in the bushes near the point, there's the ghost of a young woman. In the back, near the tool shed, I could swear I saw two men tinkering with a big wooden box. In the master bedroom, there's two more men hovering over the bed, brandishing a knife. Its gotten to the point where I fear sleeping here. I feel like a child, Jonathan."

"Chris, I can't believe I'm hearing this."

"I can't believe I'm saying it. Do you think I'm proud of the fact that our cherished family cottage is chock full of ghosts?"

7

Ed Swann leaned over, placed his palms on the wooden ledge and looked down the long narrow tabletop. He dipped his right hand in the gutter, rubbed his fingers in the sawdust, then held them up to his mouth and puffed softly. He grasped for the shiny red puck, held it up to eye level, and spun it between his finger tips. He placed it on the edge of the table and, with both eyes, focused on the two blue pucks sitting on the far end of the table—one perched cleanly in the three point zone, the other on the line between the two and the three. A total of five blue points sitting in the clear. If this shot didn't hit its mark, he would lose: twenty-one to seventeen. He spun the red puck on the smooth lacquered table, squinted, and with a fair degree of body english, let it fly. Whizzing down the table, it sliced into the near blue puck, caromed off, and hit the second blue head on, knocking it off the table. Then, as if attached to Swann's hand by an invisible string, the red puck stopped abruptly on the far ledge, a small sliver of it hanging over. Four points, a hanger. The small crowd of regulars at the bar hooted.

"Sonuvabitch." Old Jimmy Egan scowled from the opposite end of the shuffleboard table.

"Just a little luck, Jimmy. Just a little luck," Swann's rosy cheeks shined across the dark saloon.

"Luck? I think yah spooked it, Eddie. Had one uh yer ghosts er goblins guide it down the boards, I bet. Gonna let me get you back?"

Swann looked down at his watch and waved him off. "Can't Jimmy. Got a pot roast to stick in the oven."

"Hope it's tough as leather."

"No need to put a curse on my supper, James. Be back at my stool tomorrow afternoon. Ready, willing and able to take on all comers. Practice up a bit, will you. You're becoming an easy mark."

"Sonuvabitch." Egan mumbled.

Swann stepped back over to the bar, took a last swig from his beer, and picked his golf cap up from the stool he occupied most weekday afternoons. He adjusted the cap carefully, covering his bald pate, and wrapped himself in his old blue down jacket, stuffing his red plaid scarf into its collar. He slid out between the bar stools, nodding a glance to the bartender. It was a quiet Tuesday afternoon; the electric buzz of the smoke eater battling for attention with the sporadic mumblings of the small crowd. Swann shuffled across the sawdust floor until he came to one of the two side doors. He flipped it open and walked out, squinting as a sudden burst of bland-gray light—bright only in contrast to the cave-like darkness of the saloon's murky insides—attacked his eyes. He looked across the street to the boardwalk and sea. A palette of grays: the light bleached wooden-gray of the boardwalk, overhanging the silver-gray of the sea, reflecting the bland white-gray sky, interrupted by wisps of frothy-gray whitecaps.

Spring Lake, New Jersey on a gray November afternoon: a ghost-town of sorts. The Victorian summer homes locked up, devoid of their seasonal young professional occupants and their chattering and barbecues and beers. The town's summer rainbow of colors—the bright yellows and reds of its bountiful flowers, the pristine white clapboards and hunter green trims of its freshly-painted homes, the sparkling greens of its manicured lawns—all covered by a monochromatic blanket for winter's hibernation.

Swann walked along the contour of the lake and made a right onto Main Street where he walked up to a door next to a red-striped barber's pole. He opened it, and climbed the musty staircase. At the landing, he stopped in front of a another door, topped with a pane of frosted glass. It read in black block letters: *Edwin Swann, Private Investigator*. He shoved his key into the hole and pushed in.

The office was its usual disheveled mess. On the edge of his desk, his coffee cup, still half-full from the morning, sat in a light-brown halo on a sheet of yellow-lined paper scribbled on in pencil and two colors of ink. At least seven green pressboard folders were strewn around, most of them overstuffed, some bound by rubber bands, others not. A stack of newspapers, that day's *Coast Star* sitting on top, sat on the ledge near the window. The answering machine was wedged in between the telephone and his wooden In and Out boxes. In the right corner, a small cardboard placard read: *A cluttered desk is the sign of a genius.*

Swann raised his eyebrow as he noticed the blinking red light on his answering machine. Two messages. He hoped at least one would be from someone inquiring about his services. Business had been slow for the better part of the last year, he could use a little excitement. But, no, not today, he soon discovered: the first message from a young woman asking if he'd be interested in a free trial subscription to *The Asbury Park Press*, the second an invitation to a surprise seventieth birthday party for Joey Walsh, one of the regulars at the Spinnaker Pub.

As he walked back down Main and around the lake for his regular afternoon boardwalk stroll, he wondered if it was about time he should close his little office. It was hardly more than a glorified two-by-four and his current level of activity certainly didn't justify it, but whenever he considered giving it up, his better judgment became clouded by a queasiness of the stomach. Sure, he could conduct whatever small amount of business he needed to conduct out of the condo. But that wasn't the point, he figured. The little disheveled office over the barber shop gave him a place to hang his hat, somewhere to go every morning at eight-thirty, a place to stretch his legs out on the desk and read the morning paper. But, most of all, as long as it remained open—as long as the local Yellow Pages listed Edwin Swann, Private Investigator, at 4 Main St. in Spring Lake, NJ—he served a useful purpose: there was the chance that he could be of real help to some confused, unfortunate souls most likely on the verge of desperation and, most definitely, scared out of their wits.

He sat on his usual bench that afternoon, on the boardwalk across the street from the old Essex and Sussex Hotel, staring out into the sea. Whether the Atlantic be the sparkling crystal blues of a vibrant summer day or today's drab shades of gray, he always thought first of Marie. It had been five years since he went out in Bill Congdon's cabin cruiser and sprinkled her ashes somewhere out there along the horizon, but every day since had begun and ended with thoughts of his wife of thirty-eight years. The cancer had robbed her of life at sixty-three, long before her rightful time. Although she had lasted six months, it was still a shock to him when it actually happened. But, somehow he had ploughed on.

He smiled, feeling the cold ocean air streaming by his ruddy red cheeks, and remembering Marie telling him how on a good day those cheeks of his could shine like a pair of apples. The thought of her saying that to him always lifted his spirits. He thought also of how supportive she had been after his retirement, allowing him to set up his little office and pursue his avocation, even if half of Spring Lake thought him a crackpot. She had stood by him, allowed him to pursue his holy grail. *Would he be letting her down if he ever gave in to his better judgment and closed his little office?*

Perhaps business had been slow lately—extremely slow—but regardless of what anyone thought, his "hobby" had kept him more than occupied since he retired over twelve years ago: the term Private Investigator was merely a euphemism; in fact, Ed Swann was a psychic investigator, a *ghost hunter*, on the cutting edge of inquiry into psychic phenomena and the paranormal. He stretched back in the bench wondering, as he often did, what his old fraternity brothers at Yale would think if they knew. Al Kelly. Bruce Wilson. Skippy Lindquist. Alpha Phi Mu, Class of '48. They probably all thought he was retired—living the life of Riley—after a long career as a successful contractor down the Jersey shore. They probably thought he spent most of his time on the golf course, eighteen holes a day. If they only knew he spent whatever free time he could chasing down apparitions, poltergeists and other psychic phenomena, they'd be flabbergasted. In fact, if twenty years ago, someone had looked into a crystal ball and told <u>him</u> about all this, he'd have been flabbergasted himself. He took a breath and gazed out upon the fuzzy gray horizon. Something happened to your mind, he figured, when your hair turns gray and your body slows down. Either it closes shut, <u>airtight</u>, clinging desperately to a lifetime's worth of convictions, or something happens to open it up, forcing it to re-examine one's basic beliefs and values. He smiled. How many men his age—after having dealt with the realities of the world for over half a century—would even allow for the existence of something they couldn't see or touch? Perhaps he was lucky, he thought: he could count his mind still among the open.

Ed Swann's flirtation with the paranormal began years earlier, even before he, himself, ever realized it. As far as he could remember, his first encounter occurred on a bright spring day when he was a freckled-face nine year old living with his family in rural Pennsylvania. The circus was due in town and, for weeks, his parents had been promising to take him and his little sister, June, to see the Sunday matinee. Each day leading up to that Sunday, the young child's mind was filled with thoughts of clowns and elephants and acrobats and lions. On Saturday evening, though, the young Swann's heart sank to his stomach when his mother discovered the tell-tale marks on his arms and legs: chicken pox. Instead of enjoying the circus, he spent Sunday afternoon tucked away in his bed, covered with Calamyne lotion. Just about the time they would have left for the show, he ran a fever and fell into a deep sleep. Quite understandably, he dreamt of actually visiting the canvas big top rising above the fields on the outskirts of town. But, oddly, it was like no dream he had ever dreamt before: everything seemed so vivid as he roamed around the circus grounds—feeding peanuts to the elephants, gaping at the three-legged man and bearded lady, and then sneaking in under the tent and watching the show standing by himself beside the packed bleachers. When he awakened later that afternoon, he felt as if he had actually been to the show that day.

The next Thursday when he returned to school, Swann was surprised when his friend, Johnny Williams, asked him how he had enjoyed the circus. He answered that he had been unable to go because of the chicken pox. Nonetheless, Johnny insisted he had seen him there. *My parents and I saw you feeding the elephants and then standing all by yourself next to the bleachers during the show. We're sure it was you!* Johnny told him. The young Swann was shocked as Johnny went on to describe everything about his dream in vivid detail. Confused, Swann sweat profusely: *Had he done something wrong? Had he somehow left his bedroom, traveled to the circus, and then forgot about it because of the fever?* He was scared; so scared, he made his young friend swear to him that he would never mention anything of it again—to anyone.

Eleven years later, during his junior year at Yale, Swann experienced what he believed to be his second brush with the paranormal. Again, it began with a dream. After an evening of carousing with his frat brothers, during which they consumed a healthy amount of beer, he passed out on his dorm room bed. Several hours later he remembered awakening, but something was wrong. He tried to turn over, but couldn't. Then he tried to wiggle his fingers and toes, but nothing happened. *He quickly realized that he could not move a bone in his body. He was completely paralyzed!* After several minutes of desperately trying again to move anything he possibly could, he decided not to panic, figuring it part of his dream. However, he did panic, *definitely panicked,* several moments later when he saw the head of his Uncle Arthur hovering over the bed. Swann could swear this disembodied head was trying to say something to him, but could never quite make it out. When he awakened the next morning, he still felt a bit queasy, but wrote it off to a bad nightmare.

Several minutes later, he was summoned to the phone by one of his frat brothers. It was his mother calling from Pennsylvania. In a somber voice, she told him that his Uncle Arthur had passed away in his sleep during the previous night. When Swann put down the phone, he began shivering uncontrollably, realizing the significance of his dream. It was Uncle Arthur who had taken a special interest in his nephew Ed since the early days of his childhood, it was Arthur who had encouraged Ed to attend Yale, who had even helped with his tuition. And, that night, before he left the world for good, Uncle Arthur wanted to say good-bye to his favorite nephew, wish him a good life.

Years later, when Swann began his formal study of parapsychology, he learned what had actually happened to him during these two incidents from his youth. The first, his experience with the circus, was what parapsychologists would call a classic *Out of Body Experience* or *OBE*, accompanied by the phenomena of *bilocation*. During his vivid dream, some undefinable part of the young Swann's mind *actually traveled* to the site of the circus, this particular OBE being so powerful that it caused an apparition of the young Swann to be seen at the site, at the same time as he slept peacefully in his bed several miles away. The second experience, the apparition of his Uncle Arthur, was what would be called a *crisis apparition*, a form of *synchronicity*. During particularly emotionally-relevant events during one's life—death being the foremost example—an individual's latent psychic powers become so heightened, that person sometimes becomes capable of sending a psychic message to someone of special significance, a special psychic-bond forming between the two for a short period of time. What fascinated Swann most, though, was that psychic experiences like these happened to millions of people every day, but most preferred to ignore them instead of recognizing them for what they were: a very special gift bonding people together over long distances and across decades, even centuries.

The aroma of a sizzling pot roast added a pleasant scent to Swann's condo overlooking the seventh fairway on Spring Lake

Heights Golf Course. Swann sniffed in the aroma and stretched back in the burgundy leather chair in his library. He sipped on a small glass of Pinot Grigot as the third act from *Rigoletto* resonated from his stereo. He reached for a journal in his magazine rack: The *American Journal of Parapsychology*. Flipping through the table of contents, he selected an article entitled *The Near Death Experience: Alternative Theories.* He adjusted his glasses, sat back, and buried himself in its pages.

Swann's approach to his post-retirement "avocation," as he liked to call it, reflected a combination of several influences in his life: the seat-of-the-pants demeanor of a battle-scarred owner/manager of a construction company for over thirty years combined with the academic rigor of a Yale Summa Cum Laude and the heart of a frustrated poet who had majored in English Literature, much to his father's chagrin. But, most of all, it reflected his undying devotion to question things that others would rather ignore or wish away: a passion for discovery that he pursued with the exuberance of a young child.

As *Rigoletto* came to an end, he put down his journal and stood up. What now? *Puccini? Verdi? Vivaldi?* He walked over to the bookcase filled with dozens of LPs—a comprehensive library of the classics and opera—and pursed his lips as he tried to decide. Ah, yes, *Vivaldi, The Four Seasons.* He lifted the plastic cover to his turntable, moved the arm, and replaced *Rigoletto* with his new selection. As he sat back down and continued reading his article, he thought back to the beginnings of his formal study of the paranormal, twelve years earlier.

He was fifty-eight years old and newly retired from the family construction business he had inherited from his father. Business had been good to him, and he and Marie had decided to retire early so they could enjoy life a bit. But, after only seven months and an extended stay at an "adult" community in Florida for the winter, both he and Marie became bored. Homesick, they moved back up to the Jersey Shore and rented a condo near the golf course. Several months after they had moved back, Swann, still very bored, became involved in what began as a pestery little incident, but soon turned into a new way of life for him.

One morning, Swann opened his front door only to be confronted by a messenger who announced he was serving him with papers. Swann learned he was being sued by a Philip Waring, a man whom he had built a house for outside of Trenton several years earlier. Waring claimed the house was haunted and, therefore, uninhabitable, suing Swann to return the original purchase price because, according to Waring, Swann built the house in full knowledge that it stood on the site of "a particularly bloody confrontation during the Revolutionary War." The papers went on to explain that a poor Hessian soldier who had died in the skirmish was intent upon extracting justice from the Americans, even if two centuries too late. Although Swann had to go to the trouble of hiring a lawyer and then sitting in the county court house for what seemed like ages one afternoon, the suit was quickly thrown out. But, even after he had been released from any monetary obligation, something about Waring's charges piqued Swann's interest.

Perhaps it was the distant memories of those two psychic experiences from his past, or maybe the boredom of retirement, but Swann wanted to know more. After the hearing, he stopped Waring in the courthouse hallway and asked if he might take a look around. With nothing to lose, Waring obliged. Swann drove out to Trenton the following week armed with his tool box and spent almost eight hours at Waring's house. He tried to find a reasonable explanation for the phenomena Waring had reported—strange groaning sounds, vivid sightings of the soldier walking across the breezeway between the kitchen and garage—but could not. He tested the entire plumbing and electrical systems, examined all the beams and cross-beams, assayed the foundation, but discovered nothing that might have caused Waring to *think* he had seen and heard the Hessian ghost.

By the end of the day, though, Swann did discover something: no longer was he bored. In fact, he could not remember a time when he had been so enthusiastic about what he was doing. Driven by this enthusiasm, he spent the next day in the Princeton University

Library, studying Revolutionary War battles of Central New Jersey. He discovered that, indeed, there were several important skirmishes involving Hessian troops on the very plot of land where Waring's house had been built; and, interestingly, Waring had described the Hessian's uniform quite accurately. By late that evening, as he drove back to the shore, Swann reached a very significant conclusion: if Waring was basically an honest, sane man as he suspected, and there were, in fact, several Revolutionary War battles involving Hessians on that plot of land, and if nothing else—no physical flaws in the house's structure—could explain what Waring had reported seeing and hearing, *what else could it be but a ghost?*

The next morning he rushed back to Princeton, waiting eagerly for the library doors to open. This time, he flew past the stacks where historical records of the American Revolution were stored, and parked himself at a desk in the Psychology area. He sat there for thirteen straight hours—not even taking a break for a snack— reading every possible book, journal or magazine article he could find on parapsychology. He was fascinated as he read about ESP and the Rhine's experiments at Duke, about apparitions, poltergeists, OBEs, NDEs, and hauntings. Then, he was absolutely shocked as he read about a phenomena called *hypnogogic trances*—a paralyzed state during which one experiences the sensation of being half-asleep and half-awake and becomes prone to seeing certain types of apparitions. He quickly became light-headed: *wasn't that exactly the sensation he had experienced when he saw the head of his Uncle Arthur hovering over his dorm room bed all those years ago?*

Swann soon became a practitioner of his new avocation. He started by reading the supermarket tabloids—a good source for stories of the supernatural—and contacting "victims" who lived in the mid-Atlantic area. Fascinated, he would ask them question after question, and if they allowed him, he would visit the site of their haunting and give it as complete a once-over as he did the Waring house.

Into his second year of investigations, Swann became serious about what he was doing: he and Marie moved down to North

Carolina for six months so he could study at the famed Rhine Center at Duke University. There he underwent a battery of tests which concluded that he was blessed with a modest psychic gift, but no moreso blessed than many others, some who may go entire lifetimes without ever realizing it. More importantly, though, he learned about the latest cutting-edge experiments regarding all types of psychic phenomena, and perfected his investigative techniques. By the time he returned to New Jersey, he was truly qualified as an honest-to-goodness ghost hunter.

Ed Swann's reputation soon spread throughout the Northeast with scores of subjects of paranormal activity contacting him for help. He discovered the ghost of a turn-of-the-century Irish immigrant in a Jersey City tenement. He uncovered a case of RSPK—Random Spontaneous Psychokenesis—or what is more commonly referred to as poltergeist activity, in a Philadelphia suburb, and the apparition of an old retired—but still very much alive—farmer protecting his crops from poachers in rural Delaware. In the next five years, he investigated over seventy cases. Eventually, he became a local celebrity of sorts, <u>The</u> <u>Newark</u> <u>Star</u> <u>Ledger</u> running a feature article on him one Halloween:

> TO ONE SPRING LAKE MAN, GHOSTS AND GOBLINS ARE A YEAR ROUND OCCUPATION—An unexplainable creek in your steps? Strange noises emanating from your attic? A transparent figure of your dead Aunt Elvira roaming around the bedroom? Great fodder for serious Halloween stories? Definitely. But, for Ed Swann, 67, of Spring Lake Heights, it's a way of life. Since 1982, Swann has been pre-occupied with the investigation of para-psychological phenomena. In layman's terms, Ed Swann is a ghost hunter.
>
> "It's really no different than any other type of investigation," Swann explained. "The first thing I always try to do is prove that whatever phenomena I've been asked to investigate is really not due to paranormal intervention. In seven out of ten cases, what people think is paranormal activity can be explained by a flaw in construction or an irregularity in the physical environment. In many ways, my role is to play Devil's Advocate."

Swann's most recent investigation concerned a Hoboken family who claimed they heard a strange voice uttering obscenities in the bedroom of their third floor apartment every morning at about 6 AM. After spending a day and a half examining their seven unit brownstone building, Swann concluded that the "strange voice" was actually that of an early morning drive-time shock jock playing on the clock radio in the basement apartment. Swann had discovered the walls in the pre-war building were constructed of sandstone, an excellent conductor of sound. And the radio in the basement apartment? "It was programmed to turn on at five fifty-seven each morning," Swann said, chuckling…

Swann's popularity crested after the article, his local reputation growing to national proportions. He spent almost two months in the Seattle area uncovering the mystery of a famous haunted house overlooking Puget Sound, he was called up to Toronto to help explain what forces prompted a seventy year old elevator to have an apparent mind of its own, and he was even asked to investigate an old haunted castle in Scotland. Things were going well for him, quite well. But, then he received The Call. It was from Charlie Wainwright, a retired steelworker from Scranton, PA. And everything turned sour.

The article about the investigation was unfair, could prove no connection between cause and effect, but it made Swann look like a charlatan, no more a legitimate scientific investigator than an astrologer or faith healer. Whereas before Scranton, Swann had the luxury of picking his cases—zeroing in on those where sane, honest people needed real help—now almost all the calls, sporadic at best, came from kooks and eccentrics, the outer fringe.

Lying propped up in his bed, Swann snapped off the television as the eleven o'clock news came to an end. He fixed his sheets, clicked off the light on the end table, and buried his head in the pillows. His lips formed a smile as he thought of his Marie. Wavy white hair, a smile across her lips, a love of life, just the way she was before the cancer got the best of her. Thinking of her like that always soothed him, put everything else into perspective.

As much as he missed Marie, he had never used his mastery of the paranormal to try to bring him closer to his deceased wife. It would be too feeble, too trivial. Swann knew the limitations of his craft all too well: he would never be able to talk to her, smile at her, touch her. Ghost hunters couldn't actually *communicate* with the dead, all they could ever hope to do was pick up the imprints the deceased left behind. Ghosts were merely the product of psychic energy projecting images from the past, images locked into the precise set of actions from years ago, *psychic videotapes* so to speak. So why bother? he often thought. He had over thirty-four years worth of fond memories already locked securely in his mind. That would more than suffice. Thinking of her, he smiled, and then turned over.

Happily, he saw her face again as he nuzzled his head into his pillow. She smiled at him and whispered something. He wished he could understand what she was saying, what memory his subconscious had invoked, but couldn't. Then, as he dozed off into a deeper sleep, her face became fuzzy, blurring into some collage in dozens of shades of gray. Quickly, it came together again, its shades coalescing into a distinct image. It wasn't the face of Marie, though. It was the face of another woman. Young, in her late twenties, maybe early thirties. She had a delicate white face and dark jet-black hair tied back into a tight bun. Her dark eyes were penetrating, boring into his cerebellum. Her full red lips moved with a forced deliberateness. She was saying something to him, he was sure of it, *desperately trying to say something*. But only silence came from her lips.

As usual, the next morning Swann left his condo at eight-fifteen, stopped at the Seven-Eleven on route 71, picked up a coffee and the morning papers, and drove to his office on Main Street. He tapped on the window of the barbershop downstairs, signaling a big "hello" to Ernie and the crew, then walked up the musty stairs to his office. First, he checked the answering machine. Nothing. He shrugged his shoulders: *so what else is new?* But, it was too early to expect anything. Maybe later in the day something will come up, he thought. He propped his feet up on his desk and buried his head in the paper. Then, just as he began to scan the local obituaries, the phone rang. Surprised, he almost fell out of his seat as he swiveled around and grabbed for the receiver.

"Hello."

"Mr. Swann?"

"Yes. This is he."

"My name is Jon Pennfield. My brother and I have been having a little problem and I've heard you're the person to help us…"

PART

II

A Murder in Newport, 1928

8

Christopher Pennfield yawned, lifted his fingers from the keyboard of his Smith-Corona, and looked out upon the dark December night from his sun porch. It was Wednesday, the night he reserved for his "quiet work"—grading papers, planning lectures, and, of course, writing the first draft of his address for the one-hundredth anniversary ceremony of Pennfield College. He loved these quiet evenings, sitting at his work desk on the porch, shuffling through his papers and toying with new ideas. It was almost as if he was insulated from everything else that was going on in the world.

It was funny, he thought. Funny how something so extraordinary—so shocking—could interrupt your life, wreak havoc with your emotions, and then, only two and a half weeks later, back to normalcy, as if it never happened. At first it had disturbed him immensely. The thought that some lasting impressions of his brother Robin—and God knows who else!—were lurking within the cottage tingled his nerves. He wondered how many other incidents were etched within the walls of the cottage—or his sun porch, or his own bedroom? He soon realized, though, that if he allowed these questions to chip away at his mind unfettered, they would create a vicious paranoia. He reacted to it all in a typically Christopher Pennfield fashion. Over the last week and a half, he muffled all these distractive thoughts, tucked all the questions away in the back of his mind. Life must go on, he convinced himself. He was proud of the way he had handled it. He looked back down at his Smith-Corona and typed another paragraph for his address:

> *Perhaps the shining era for the Pennfield family came eleven genera-tions after Charles Pennfield landed at Plymouth Rock with his Pil-grim brethren. If anyone in our family's long lineage epitomized the capitalist spirit begun by the Pilgrims, it was my grandfather Ben-jamin Pennfield. The last of a rare breed, Benjamin Pennfield was an industrialist supreme, his name worthy of mention in the same breath as Rockefeller, Astor and Morgan. He had it all: guile, cunning, vision, charisma. His sharp, calculating mind, his cool level-headedness and his cast-iron stomach called the bluff of Wall Street more than once in his time. Indeed, his capitalist spirit spawned nineteen companies, employing over a quarter of a million Americans...*

He smiled: thoughts of his grandfather always lifted his spirits and swelled his chest. When the telephone interrupted his reverie, he regarded it as nothing less than an assault upon his privacy.

"Hello." He answered gruffly.

"Chris, I think I've got a lead for us."

"Jonathan?"

"Susan helped me find this man in New Jersey, a private investi-gator who specializes in the type of problem we had at the cottage. And you don't have to worry, from what I've heard, he's very dis-creet."

"Well..." Christopher whined.

"Chris, don't tell me you're..."

"What happened has happened, Jonathan," Christopher answered. "Lord knows we can't go back and change the past. I just don't know what the whole exercise would prove."

"But, Chris, think of everything you told me that night."

"I know, I know. But I'd just rather not deal with it. Perhaps it'll go away."

"Jesus, we can't stick our heads in the sand."

"I'm not doing that at all, Jonathan. I'm just making every attempt to get on with my life. Now—

"Then perhaps I should let you in on something."

"And what would that be?"

"I'm afraid I haven't been completely straight with you."

"Oh?"

"It isn't only the cottage," Jonathan almost whispered. "You're not the only Pennfield having problems."

"What do you mean by that?"

"Last September, I was out on the Speedwell in Nantucket Sound one day and I was knocked silly by a phantom storm. No one else saw it. Not the Harbor Master, not the Coast Guard, not any of the dozens of boats out on the water. No one, except me."

"Excuse me, what has that to do with this?"

"Nothing, by itself. But, a few days later, I'm home having cocktails with Suz, and in the middle of our conversation, an ashtray floats off a table, as if it's being carried around by an invisible man. The strangest thing I've ever seen. And Suz saw it, too."

"Hmmmm. Interesting, to say the very least."

"We've go to do something about it, Chris, I'm sure of it."

"But. But—

"I made an appointment to see the man, a Mr. Ed Swann. He's going to meet us at the cottage on Saturday."

"But it's Christmastime. How could I possibly?"

"Easy. There's a commuter flight that leaves Rutland at ten o'clock on Saturday morning. There'll be a ticket at the airport for you. I'll pick you up at Providence at ten forty-five. You'll be back in Percer by five, five-thirty at the latest."

"Jonathan, I'm just not sure."

When Christopher finally placed the phone down, he grimaced. *Jesus, he wished Jonathan would get off his case!* He silently wondered if his brother had fabricated the stories of the storm and the ashtray merely to convince him to seek help. He could kick himself for agreeing to meet them at the cottage on Saturday. This whole incident only served to remind him why he had been deliberately avoiding his younger brother for the last several years. Frustrated, he focused back on the paragraph he had just written—if only to take his mind off Jonathan, always the family rebel. He stared at the piece of white bond paper sticking out of his typewriter's carriage. He thought more pleasant thoughts and continued to type:

> *One wonders what it must have been like to be in the company of Benjamin Pennfield during his golden years. The man's reputation and charisma were legendary. Although his ties to Wall Street kept his official residence in New York, he spent what were perhaps his most shining moments at our family's summer cottage in Newport, Rhode Island. During Benjamin Pennfield's heyday, it was considered quite an honor, indeed, to be among the guests invited to dine at that legendary cottage on a summer Sunday in Newport...*

*   *   *

Newport, Rhode Island
July, 1927

"Kindly lead us in Grace, Reverend." Benjamin Pennfield ordered.

"Certainly, Benjamin." Reverend Walter Jenkinson, sitting opposite Pennfield at the far end of the long mahogany table, bowed his head and clasped his hands, waiting for complete silence. His eyes scanned the twenty guests sitting around the table. He cleared his throat and began:

"We thank you, Dear Father, for this bountiful meal you have blessed us with on this day. We thank you with the profound understanding that this blessing comes to us only from your goodness and the grace and sacrifice of your son, our Lord Jesus Christ. Amen."

"Well said, Walter. Well said." Pennfield opened his napkin and placed it on his lap. "And I must say, your sermon this morning was particularly profound. Your comparison to the current times brought a new level of meaning to the parable of the loaves and fishes. Yes, profound indeed."

"Why, thank you, Benjamin. That comes as quite a compliment." Jenkinson nodded his head and smiled. He and his wife Betty had been at Newport's Trinity Church for only eighteen months and it was critical that they win over the congregation's leading member.

Halfway down the long table—seated between his wife, Sarah, and his father-in-law, Charles Pennfield—Thomas Morton took a sip from his water goblet and taunted his host. "I have to admit, Reverend, you were as eloquent as ever this morning, but with all due respect, I find it a bit of a stretch to compare the miracle of the loaves and fishes to the bounty of the Republican party. Many of us believe the President's programs are selling us down the river."

The table fell silent. Inside, Reverend Jenkinson's stomach churned. He had given that sermon for one reason only: Benjamin Pennfield had *demanded* he give it.

Benjamin Pennfield's eyes bored into Morton. "Yes, Thomas, people may say such things, but most of them are neither intelligent nor fortunate enough to benefit from the bounty of the man's programs." A dense puff of smoke from Pennfield's cigar dusted the bristles of his brushy dark-brown moustache and spread throughout the room.

Morton pointed his finger at Pennfield and started to answer, but, next to him, the tightly-wound spring inside his wife Sarah recoiled. *"Thomas! Benjamin!"* She spoke sharply. "A debate over the President's programs is not proper discussion for Sunday dinner."

"Yes, but," Morton insisted, jabbing with his finger, "the man is allowing them to build a house of cards on a foundation of debt. It's just a matter of time before it all comes crashing—

Underneath the table, Sarah slapped her husband's leg, the sound clearly audible. Morton's face reddened. He grit his teeth, embarrassed over being shackled by his wife in public.

Benjamin Pennfield grinned mischievously and dabbed his mouth with his napkin. "Jealousy. Pure jealousy. Anyone with any bit of wisdom will tell you the 1920s are the most prosperous decade in the history of this nation." Through his short stature and stout frame, Benjamin Pennfield radiated confidence; he tolerated Morton only because the man had done his family a service by taking his cousin Sarah off their hands ten years earlier.

"Yes and from this prosperity we must always remember our Christian obligation to those less fortunate than ourselves." Reverend Jenkinson added, glancing quickly at Sarah Morton. Her eyes were riveted on him.

"Yes. Yes. Well said, Walter. The most intelligent words I've heard today." Benjamin Pennfield took another sip of soup, staring defiantly at Morton.

As Pennfield spoke, Jenkinson couldn't help but glance over at Sarah once again. Her eyes were still riveted on him. Indeed, over the years, many female members of his congregations had been seduced by his mellifluous speaking voice and handsome stature. But, what troubled him about Sarah was something that happened last month as he was going through the envelopes containing the monthly tithes. He was alone in his office at the church late on a Sunday night when he came to an envelope with his name inscribed in a beautiful, delicate calligraphy. He did not remember ever seeing an envelope inscribed with such beautiful pen strokes. When he opened it, he found Thomas Morton's monthly check. But also inside was a small note, written in the same delicate calligraphy:

> My Dearest Reverend Jenkinson,
>
> How wonderful has it been to watch you grow in the Grace of God before our very eyes over the last year. You are a learned man, a handsome man, a sensuous man. You fill me with inspiration each time you light up the church with your sermons.
>
> With all the Love of God
>
> Sarah Pennfield Morton

He was, of course, flattered by the note. It had been a long and uphill battle to garner the respect of this congregation and such a glowing approbation from a member of the congregation's leading family was certainly something he could be proud of. Still, several things bothered him. Why the use of the words *handsome* and *sensu-*

ous? And to be proper, shouldn't the note have been signed by *Mr. and Mrs. Thomas Morton?* Why just *Sarah Pennfield Morton?* It was a well known fact that Sarah was a bit different, a bit strange, some would even say unstable.

Admittedly, Jenkinson had thought about Sarah Morton more than once. Behind her restrained manner, hidden beneath her dark dresses and high necklines, *Sarah was an attractive woman.* And in Jenkinson's judgment, a *seductive* woman. Her dark jet-black hair tied back in a tight bun contrasted her soft white skin. Her button nose and deep blue eyes sat delicately above her dainty cheekbones. But, it was her lips, the vibrant shading of her full red lips, against her porcelain white skin that mesmerized Jenkinson so, and many other men he was sure.

"Mr. Pennfield." The maid stood at the doorway, interrupting desert.

Benjamin Penfield put down his silverware and looked up. "Yes, Olga."

"The two gentlemen from New Bedford would like to see you for a moment, sir."

"Tell them I will talk to them when I'm through with my Sunday dinner."

"They say, it's very important, Mr. Pennfield."

Pennfield scowled. "I will see them when I'm through with dinner. And Olga...," his face turned red, "...*never allow those two men to interrupt me during Sunday dinner again! Do you understand me, Olga? Do I make myself clear?"*

The young woman stood trembling in the doorway. "Yes. Yessir, Mr. Pennfield. I'll never do it again, Sir."

After Sunday dinner, members of the Pennfield family and their guests were expected to spend several hours on the cottage's front porch and lawns. Most did not have to be coerced into staying; on a clear, sunny afternoon, the front lawn of the Pennfield's cottage was, arguably, the most tranquil spot in Newport. The fresh aromatic scents from the grass and chrysanthemums perfuming the air. An afternoon sea breeze tickling the guests faces and swirling around the porch. Captains on the Sound trimming their sails to the whims of the elements. The women and children, dressed in their white Sunday finest, playing croquet on the grass and strolling along the cliffs. And the men, after a hearty Sunday dinner, sharing a smoke and discussing the ways of the world on the front porch.

"I have to say the man is clearly out of his mind. Mr. Levine may be a successful impresario, but if he thinks that monoplanes will ever replace steamships as a form of transportation, he's in for a rude awakening," Thomas Morton said, puffing on his cigar.

"I dare say," Uncle Charles addressed Morton, "I've never heard of a Jew frittering away money the way Levine proposes to."

"Perhaps that's why he's intent on using *other people's* money." Morton answered.

They all laughed. Then—

"Do any of you gentlemen realize what Caroll Porter did three Saturdays ago?" Benjamin Pennfield said after a deep puff on his cigar.

Blank stares. "No, what did he do, Ben?" Uncle Charles asked.

"Took a private plane up from New York. Landed on the first fairway at Newport Country Club. Anyone venture to guess how long it took?"

No one had the gumption to answer.

Pennfield pulled his cigar out of his mouth. "Seventy minutes. The way I count, that's one-eighth the time of the steamship, gentlemen. I think Mr. Levine may be onto something. You can't tell me there's not the foundation for a profitable business in that. A drink to Mr. Levine." Pennfield raised his hand.

His butler, Albert, returned quickly with seven shot glasses full of whiskey from Pennfield's private reserve.

"None for me," Reverend Jenkinson held up his hands. He certainly didn't want to cast himself a prude, but drinking in public was beyond the bounds of acceptable behavior for a clergyman in 1927. But, if ever he needed a drink, it was now. Soon, he would be handed the monthly tithing envelopes. He wondered if Sarah Morton's would contain another note.

"Walter! Walter!" Betty Jenkinson called over from the cliffs. "I think it's time we should leave. We did promise to pay a visit to Mrs. Stoner this afternoon."

"Yes. Yes. Of course, Betty." Jenkinson called back across the lawn.

Betty waved at him and momentarily turned back towards Cliff Walk, exchanging goodbyes with the other women.

On the porch, Benjamin Pennfield took a shot of whiskey and puffed on his cigar. As the smoke blew from his lips, his eyes were drawn to the Reverend's wife walking over from the cliffs. Pennfield puffed again. There was a freshness to Betty Jenkinson, an innocence. Her bright blue eyes wide open, captivated by whatever the Good Lord placed before them. Her soft white skin, her golden blonde hair, her youth. Beautiful was not the word to describe her, Pennfield thought. She was still so young, her angelic appearance had not yet *matured* into beauty. Why, she must have been a baby when the Reverend found her somewhere out in Western Massachusetts. Underneath her modest dress, Pennfield could just imagine the soft, smooth contours of a perfectly developed female form. The thought of it, alone, sent a tingle up his spine. He drew deep on his cigar and blew out a generous puff of smoke. He could only hope that the good Reverend Jenkinson had the capacity to fully appreciate the wonderments of that uncut gem with whom he shared his bed.

"It's been a wonderful afternoon, Ben…but I'm afraid its time for Betty and myself to leave." Jenkinson offered his hand to Pennfield.

"Of course. Of course." Pennfield reached into his lapel pocket and pulled out a plain white envelope. "Your monthly tithe. I think you'll find a little extra in it."

"Thank you, Ben, whatever you choose to give is appreciated."

Pennfield looked around at the other men on the porch. "I'm sure that *everyone* has something for you." He looked over at Morton. "Thomas?"

"Yes, Benjamin, I certainly intend to bestow an envelope upon the good Reverend Jenkinson this afternoon. Sarah has it in her purse. Sarah, dearest…" He called over towards the lawn.

No response. He called out again. "Sarah!" The women gathered on the lawn around the croquet hoops looked at each other, shaking their heads. Nadine Pennfield, wife to Benjamin's oldest son Oliver, stopped short just as she was about to swing her mallet, looked up, and called back to Morton across the lawn. "I think she went inside for a moment, Thomas. I'll send Xenobia in to get her."

Xenobia Pennfield, the thirteen year old pig-tailed daughter of Nadine and Oliver Pennfield rushed into cottage at her mother's request. When she bounded into the dining room, she stopped short, surprised to find Sarah Morton in some sort of trance at the large, cherry table.

"Cousin Sarah?" Xenobia whispered, barely audible.

No movement. Sarah stood at the middle of the table, facing out towards the parlor. Her eyes were shut tight, so tight it cast a strange grimace across her dainty face. She placed her hands on the table and bowed her head, the tip of her small nose hovering above the table's shiny top.

"Cousin Sarah?" Xenobia tried again, this time a bit louder.

After several moments, Sarah raised her head. Xenobia began to speak to her, but then noticed her eyes were still shut. As if oblivious to Xenobia's presence, Sarah opened her eyes, looked straight ahead, and then mumbled a strange set of words. She mumbled so softly, Xenobia could not understand what it was she had said.

"Cousin Sarah!" Xenobia called out, even louder.

Sarah shook her head, as if shaking off a deep trance. Then, she looked at the young girl and almost shivered, unaware that she was not alone. "Xenobia?"

"Pardon my interruption, but Mr. Morton would like to see you."

"Yes, thank you, Xenobia." She lifted her purse from the floor beside her and walked off towards the porch, offering no explanation for her strange episode. Once out on the porch, she handed the envelope to her husband.

Thomas Morton accepted the envelope and handed it directly to the Reverend Jenkinson. Jenkinson quickly glanced at it, noticing that his name had been spelled out on the envelope in the same delicate calligraphy. He went flush and then looked at Sarah.

Her face was affixed to him, a warm glow in her eyes. As much as he struggled to resist it, he could not deny that he was attracted to her.

That evening, after dinner with Betty, the Reverend rushed over to his office at Trinity Church and quickly opened the Mortons' envelope. Inside, he discovered another note, written in the same exquisite calligraphy.

My Dearest Walter,

For months, I have stood silently by, enraptured by your bountiful talents, fancied by your handsome stature. Every night I ask the Lord, why must I suffer? Why can I not know him the way I yearn to know him?

With All My Love,

Sarah Pennfield Morton

For what seemed like hours, Jenkinson thought and meditated. Were these the words of a woman smitten? Or were these notes nothing but the product of Sarah's instability? To take them seriously, surely would be an exploitation of Sarah's affliction. Or would it? Jenkinson went back and forth asking himself what he should do. Should he confide in Benjamin Pennfield? He thought about it, then concluded the risk would be far too great. Pennfield could very well consider it an assault upon his family, an attempt to strip naked the Pennfield's unattractive underside. Should he confront Sarah? No, it would be wrong. In her instability, she may interpret even the most innocuous conversation as some sort of advance. Should he do nothing? But, what if someone else—God forbid—should accidentally see one of her notes.

He sat deep in thought for almost an hour. His better instincts told him to immediately burn the note. But, for some strange reason, he desired to keep it. He slowly worked the lock to the congregation's small safe, took one long last look at Sarah's exquisite calligraphy, folded the note, and placed it far in back, underneath a stack of bills. Slowly, he locked the door.

9

From the moment Ed Swann stepped through the cottage's front door, Christopher and Jonathan knew they would have their hands full.

"So you think you got ghosts, do you?"

Swann dumped his old square leather carrying bag on the floor and quickly scanned the parlor.

"Well, let's slow down for a moment, get comfortable." Christopher motioned Swann towards one of the large upholstered chairs in the parlor. "I wouldn't leap to that conclusion quite yet."

"Well then I have to say it's a bit odd you asked me to come up all the way from Jersey if you think you don't."

"I think at this point I'd prefer to say there's been a confluence of events that leads us to *believe* that something out of the ordinary may be affecting our family. Wouldn't you, Jonathan?"

Jonathan nodded.

"In other words, you're scared out of your socks." Swann grinned at the two of them from across the coffee table.

"Scared is perhaps too strong a word," Christopher answered. "I think *intrigued* might be a more appropriate way of putting it."

"Yes, that's it. We're intrigued." Jonathan grinned, enjoying every moment of this exchange between Swann and his brother.

"Well, the only way I know to get started is to dive right into the thing." Swann pulled a notepad and pen out of his bag and placed them on the coffee table. "Why don't the two of you sit back, relax, and let me ask a few questions."

Before Swann could begin, Christopher interrupted. "I think *we'd* prefer to ask a few questions first."

"Sure. Shoot." He answered, without looking up from his notepad.

"Well, first of all, I think Jonathan and I would like to know what is it you do when you actually find a ghost?"

"Good question," Swann answered. "But chances are I probably won't."

"Won't what?"

"Find a ghost. I see my job as trying to prove that you *don't* have ghosts."

"Yes, but I think in our case, we may be beyond that point."

"Oh?"

"Yes, I believe Jonathan already told you that just about three weeks ago, the two of us simultaneously saw an apparition of our dead brother Robin right at the top of those stairs." He pointed up towards the landing.

"Yep," Swann's eyes quickly ran up and down his notepad, "and he also told me about a phantom storm at sea in Nantucket Sound on September 24 at approximately three fifteen PM, several other apparitions at this site at various dates over the last fourteen months, and an apparent poltergeist haunting in Greenwich, Connecticut on September 27 at ten forty-seven PM. But that proves nothing as far as I'm concerned."

Christopher sat straight up in his seat. "Well, certainly you must admit it's a bit odd?"

"Maybe it is, maybe it isn't." Swann answered. "Could be lots of alternative explanations."

"But, *Jesus*, Mr. Swann, we both saw him at the same time. Certainly—

"Auto suggestion. Always a possibility."

"What?"

"The mind's a fascinating instrument when you think about it. So fascinating, that many learned scholars believe if one person is in deep contemplation over a particular matter, and another person's nearby, sometimes the two of them can share the same thought. Particularly when their minds are relaxed, if you know what I mean. The two of you *had* been drinking, hadn't you?"

"How did you know that?" Christopher snapped.

"Lucky guess." Swann grinned. "So it's not too hard to believe that when the two surviving brothers are together, at least one of them is thinking of the deceased, and if you allow for the existence of mental telepathy, particularly considering the mental skids may have been greased by a little liquor..."

"But there was more than that!" Christopher jabbed his finger at him. "A gust of wind blew down the stairway, the temperature dropped to almost freezing. You can't *imagine* that. Right, Jonathan?"

"He's right, Mr. Swann. That's certainly how it happened."

"Good points, both of them. I happened to have checked the local weather report for the night in question. November 29th, wasn't it? Well on that night, this area was influenced by a weather system that generated fifteen to twenty knot winds out of the north and northeast." He stood up from his chair, walked over to the bottom of the stairway, and pointed up towards the second floor landing. "Seems to me that those windows up top face north. So, if they were opened a little, a good puff of wind could blow right down the stairway and cause exactly what you just described."

"Yes, but then how do you account for the drastic drop in temperature?" Christopher asked.

"According to the National Weather Service, the local temperature at twelve midnight on the twenty-ninth was nineteen degrees Fahrenheit. Could've been caused by the same open window and the same puff of wind."

"Mr. Swann, I was under the impression you were here to help us, not confuse us." Christopher said.

"Who said I wasn't?"

"Then let's get to the point. What happens if you *do* find a ghost, how can you assure us it would cause no harm?"

Swann chuckled. "Don't be silly. Ghosts can't hurt anyone."

"You're sure about that?"

"Damn sure." He looked down at his notes. "Now let's go take a look at the master bedroom."

The instant Swann entered the bedroom, he walked right over to the large windows at the foot of the bed. "Gosh, could see what you mean," he looked down upon the grounds. "Could imagine what it might be like on a lonely night. This old house. The sea beating against the rocks down below. A strong breeze off the water. Would scare the BeJesus out of me, that's for sure."

"Well, Mr. Swann," Christopher cringed. "I really can't say they were the most pleasant experiences of my life."

"And when was this old place built?" He tapped the window frame.

"By our great-grandfather in the 1880s," Jonathan answered.

"And your family's lived here continuously since?"

"Our great-grandfather lived here year-round. Then, after he died, it became a summer residence for our grandfather, Benjamin Pennfield." Jonathan said.

"Yep, heard of him. Sounds like he was quite a character. And who lived here next?"

"Ever since, it's been sort've a vacation residence for our families. No one's lived here year-round for years."

"So the old place has been closed up a lot?"

They both nodded.

"Ever have squatters?"

"Not to the best of our knowledge," Christopher answered. "But I suppose there's always the possibility…"

"Unwanted guests have always been known to cause problems. Little changes in the way the place is used can cause an old structure to play all sorts of mind games with you." Swann spun around and scanned the entire room. "Now the way I recall it, you claim to have had five separate experiences in this location. Is that right?"

"At least." Christopher answered.

"And what you actually saw were two large figures approaching the bed, one with a knife."

"Yes, yes. That was it."

Swann looked down at his notes. "During all those occurrences, the apparition was supposedly near the windows. Why don't you show me exactly where you remember seeing it."

"It was there, right over there, near the foot of the bed." Christopher pointed, his finger trembling.

"You okay, Chris?" Jonathan asked.

"Fine. I'm fine, Jonathan." He loosened his collar.

"Now each time you saw the apparition, you were laying in approximately the same position on the bed and the apparition always began at the same spot in front of the windows. Correct?"

Christopher nodded.

Swann walked to the bed's headboard and examined the two windows from another perspective. He paused, then: "Now it would seem to me, it wouldn't be too unusual that late at night there are all sorts of vessels entering Newport harbor, sailing right outside this old house as a matter of fact. I would suppose a lot of them have pretty powerful beacons lighting their way, shining right through those windows at times. Combine that with a little bit of mist off the water and a gifted imagination and it could create a pretty eerie sight right here at the foot of your bed."

"But how come it only happened when I was in that trance?"

"Could be coincidence. Or maybe you just *convinced* yourself you were in a trance to cover up your fear."

"Look, Mr. Swann," Christopher seethed. "If I wanted an analysis of my fears and insecurities, I'd seek out the appropriate professional help. We're here to talk about ghosts. How come these phenomena have only occurred in the last fourteen months? Why haven't they been happening for years?"

"Could be as minor a thing as a change in the shipping lanes. Coast Guard'll be able to help answer that one."

"Excuse me, Mr. Swann, but I find it hard to believe the Coast Guard will be able to help me with anything concerning this. *We're talking about ghosts, Mr. Swann!*"

"Calm down, Chris." Jonathan said. "The man's making a point."

Without responding, Swann walked back over to the windows and tapped on one of the panes. "You know, not too many people realize this, but, over time, gravity causes glass to seep a bit. It's not uncommon if you measure the top and bottom of one of these old panes, that the top would be a few millimeters thinner than the bottom. No big deal, not at all. But, it *can* cause slight variations in the way glass refracts light, perhaps creating certain phenomena that weren't previously there."

"So you're saying what I saw was completely bogus?"

"Not saying that at all. I'm saying it's quite possible you experienced a paranormal event in this room. But, then again, it's also quite possible everything's explainable by the natural laws of physics."

"So what do you suggest we do?"

"Can't suggest anything yet."

"But my brother *does* make a point, Mr. Swann," Jonathan cut in. "What do we do next?"

"Well, if we're going to prove anything, I need to spend some more time at this old place. Listen to it breathe for a few days, if you know what I mean. I'd like to spend the night here, by myself. See if I can come up with any ideas."

"And when would you like to do that?"

"Why tonight, of course."

Swann slept in one of the guest bedrooms on the second floor of the cottage that night. As he lay there, so many ideas were racing through his mind he found it difficult to get comfortable. He would stir around, fall asleep for a short spell, and then wake up again. The same cycle pestered him over and over. One of the times he awakened, he distinctly remembered hearing something downstairs. Perhaps the wind flapping a shutter or rustling against an awning. Then he was sure, *absolutely sure*, he wrapped himself in his robe and walked down the steps. He distinctly remembered hearing the stairs creak.

He looked around the dark parlor. All the windows closed, the doors shut. But it was chilly, cold. He folded his arms, warming himself. He looked around. No outward signs of what had been causing the noises. In fact, the room was silent, so devoid of sound Swann questioned why he had ventured downstairs in the first place. As he reached to turn on the light, he stopped short. A hazy glimmer of light from the dining room caught the corner of his eye. He looked over.

God! Swann stiffened.

Shadowy people, about fifteen of them, maybe more, all seated around the table, eating dinner. At the head, a bald man. A short, heavy bald man with a moustache, puffing on a cigar. At the opposite end, a younger man, with dark hair, gray at the edges. Butlers and maids waiting on them. Everyone dressed in turn-of-the-century garb. He watched as this shadowy banquet continued. People getting up and down, passing plates, munching their food, talking amongst themselves. But there was silence, complete silence. No sound to go along with the pictures. Just shimmery, semi-transparent images going through the pantomime of a banquet.

Concentrate, concentrate, he told himself. Swann strained to etch a picture in his brain, capturing all the details. There was a menacing look on the face of the mustachioed bald man at the head of the table. He said something and blew out a defiant puff of smoke. Then the thin bald man with long sideburns halfway down the far end of the table said something back to him, jabbing his finger at him. Then the woman next to the thin bald man, a stern grin on her face, said something to the heavier bald man at the head of the table and appeared to slap the thin, bald man on his lap. The man's face reddened, embarrassed. The bald man at the head of the table dabbed his mouth with his napkin and spoke. Swann watched in awe, memorizing the details, repeating them over and over to himself. *Fat bald man blows smoke. Thin bald man jabs finger. Woman says something to fat bald man, slaps thin bald man.* Although their deliberate movements flickered like those of an old vintage film, the images were solid, whole, in three dimensions.

Suddenly, all the figures, save one, faded away. The dining room turned pitch black. Only the woman—the woman with the dark hair and white face—remained. Her face was luminous as if a bright spotlight shone on it, the entire sequence staged. His mind raced, straining to record every possible detail. *White face, dark hair pulled tightly back into a bun, button nose, high cheekbones, full red lips.* Suddenly, she stood up and looked right at Swann. She stood there silently with her eyes closed, as if allowing him time to complete his task. Then, she spoke, the movement in her lips slow and deliberate, a distant, hollow resonance to her words:

"Dig deeper, Mr. Swann, dig deeper."

A ray of morning sunlight beamed through the bedroom window. The chilly air seeped through the crevices in the wooden windows, refreshing Swann's reclining bones. An early morning blast from a tugboat out on the sound caused him to stir. Slowly, he pushed himself up from the bed, rubbing his eyes.

Damn! He was so sure it was an apparition. So lifelike, so vivid, fitting all known criteria of a genuine haunting. But then the woman spoke to him and destroyed it all. Only a dream, that's all it was, the only thing it *could be.* Real ghosts don't talk to their observers, don't interact with their present-day surroundings. It didn't fit the model, completely contrary to it. He had no choice: as an investigator, one dedicated to a strict application of methodology, he was forced to conclude it was only a dream.

But what was its source? Why a silent banquet? Why last night? Certainly, nothing in his experience would have caused his subconscious to *deliberately* suggest a silent turn-of-the-century banquet in the dining room of the Pennfield's cottage. But then dreams were so unpredictable. On one hand, he could explain it to himself, explain it easily. Embroiled in an investigation, he was anxious to unravel the mystery, uncover a solution to the Pennfield hauntings. And it was that very anxiety that created the dream, suggesting a plausible scenario, almost tricking him into accepting a false clue. Yes, a dream indeed. But then, those words—*Dig deeper, Mr. Swann, dig deeper*—

So intrigued was Swann, he decided to call a colleague of his that afternoon: Dr. Justin Farber, a scholar in the study of parapsychology from the Rhine Center in North Carolina.

"So you're sure, absolutely certain, you've never seen a picture of this woman before?" Farber asked him.

"Perhaps I inadvertently may have. But I don't think so."

"Still it's the most logical explanation. Somewhere along the line you saw a picture of this woman, forgot about it, and then, for some odd reason, your subconscious mind created a dream episode around her last night."

Swann shook his head. "But I find that hard to accept, Justin. Even if I had seen a picture, why would my subconscious put her in this old house?"

"Then there's no other explanation but coincidence. Think about it. There's nothing really unique about seeing, or dreaming about, a banquet in the dining room of an old, stately Newport cottage."

"Yes, but—-

"Okay, here's one for you. Suppose it really was an apparition. You really <u>did</u> see someone in the dining room in the middle of the night. It's not unreasonable to assume that the Pennfield family, or at least some members of it, have a latent psychic ability. Now suppose the psychic trait is genetic. And whomever this woman is, is a blood relative, had the same trait, but much more powerfully, in some super-concentrated form. Suppose her psychic ability was so powerful, she *anticipated* all this happening years ago."

"Yes, but why."

"Something traumatic must've happened to her. Something she wanted us to know about."

"I follow some of your logic, Justin. But, still, she talked to me. That just doesn't happen. We all know damn well that ghosts can't talk to their observers. That's a fairy tale."

"Understood," Farber answered. "But here's where it gets quirky. Suppose she *staged* the whole thing years ago, whenever this banquet you saw happened. Suppose she stood in that room, put herself in a powerful psychic trance, and talked to you, knowing that you would receive her message years later."

"If she tried to communicate with the future in a general sense, fine. But it all falls apart when she mentions my name. How could she have ever known that someone named Mr. Swann would be investigating this old house so many years later?"

"Can't really answer that. All I can say is perhaps her psychic abilities were so powerful she was able to *prognosticate* everything that's happening today."

"Justin, I'll be first to admit there's a helluva lot we don't understand about psychic powers. But, no matter how strong her's were, I know of no case where anyone, no matter how gifted, has been able to foresee the future..."

10

Naked, Jennifer Winston looked every bit the goddess Christopher imagined as he had undressed her in his mind countless times during sessions of Plato 341. Better, actually. The youthful vibrance of her smooth, firm breasts. Her taut athletic figure: milk white skin, unblemished, stretched delicately over a perfectly sculpted frame. Her firm, tight buttocks. Her lean, muscular thighs. As she sat undressed behind his desk in the faculty building—leaning forward, an inviting smile, her long blonde hair glistening in the afternoon sunlight—Pennfield wondered what he had done in life to deserve such good fortune.

"I enjoy these sessions marvelously, Jennifer, and this is certainly a pleasant surprise, but you do realize we must find a more conventional way of meeting." He sat on the edge of the desk and ran his hand through her hair.

"But isn't it exciting, Chris? I mean you and me and…"

"Exciting, perhaps. Risky, definitely."

"What's the risk? I'm your research assistant."

"And a fine one at that. But, some day in the heat of passion I can just imagine one of us forgetting to lock the door and some misguided freshmen stumbling in without knocking, and—"

"You look depressed."

"Yes, just slightly so. Only because it would be the end of Christopher Pennfield as we know him."

"Chris, you're being paranoid."

"Jennifer, remember, it's *Professor Pennfield* when we're on campus."

"Geez, chill out, will you? Get rid of the negative energy, think pleasant thoughts." She stroked his forehead.

Indeed, Pennfield's mind had abounded with pleasant thoughts ever since the day Jennifer Winston walked up to him after class to ask for private counseling. Soon thereafter, everything fell quickly into place, just as Pennfield had fantasized.

"Now why don't you unbutton your shirt? Slowly, one at a time." She whispered, and placed her hand against his chest, tingling his insides.

Underneath his wool glen-plaid trousers, Pennfield's penis sprouted. She pulled off his shirt and pressed her soft lips against one of his nipples. He looked down her back—the perfect symmetry of her spine, as if a master had sculpted her out of marble. He placed his hands under her smooth bottom and lifted her towards him. By instinct, she undid his zipper and guided him inside. He squeezed her against his hard wooden chair, the spring creaking as the seat rocked back and forth. He took a series of quick short breaths and wrapped his arms around her, enveloping both her and the chair. She wrapped her legs around him, locking at the ankles. They rocked back and forth, faster and faster, the spring creaking louder and louder—

Then, the phone.

"*Shit!*" Pennfield exclaimed, puffing. "There's no one at the front desk to pick up. I'm supposed to have office hours till five." He pulled his boxer shorts over his still-erect penis, pushed himself off her, and waddled over to his desk. "Yes, hello." He snapped.   •

"Chris?"

"Jonathan!"

"Gotta minute?"

"Yes, but you'll have to make it quick. I have a student waiting."

"Ed called me this morning. He thinks he might have a lead."

"Really?"

"He woke up in the middle of the night and saw a woman in the dining room."

"What'd she look like?"

"He said she had dark hair, tied back in a bun, white skin, and full red lips."

"Jesus Christ, yet another one. When will it stop, Jonathan?"

"He asked me if she resembled anyone in the family, anyone we might remember. I couldn't think of anyone, could you?"

"Let me jog my memory a bit, but I don't think so. No one comes immediately to mind."

"That's what I figured. I told him if all else fails, Xenobia might be able to help."

"Jesus Christ, Jonathan, why get her involved! Have you no better discretion?"

"Calm down, will you. I told him she most likely wouldn't cooperate. So he's not going to talk to her, not now at least. But she's an option down the road…"

Coitus interruptus was never a pleasant experience for Christopher Pennfield, especially with a partner as provocative and stimulating as Jennifer Winston. So, it was no surprise that Pennfield found it difficult to bring the afternoon's session to fruition after brother Jonathan had struck such a disconcerting chord.

"Jennifer?"

"Yes." She answered, primed to take up where they had left off.

"I want you to do me a favor." He stuffed his sagging organ back into his shorts. "As part of your research for my address, I'd like you to pursue a slightly different track. I want you to find out everything you can about a Mr. Edwin Swann. He's from New Jersey. I'll give you the specifics."

"Why?"

"He claims he's a ghost hunter."

"A ghost hunter?"

"Yes," he chuckled, "and I fear he's set on using his pseudo-science to rewrite Pennfield family history, tarnish our image. So I

want to know everything you can find on him, no matter what the
expense. Understood?"

"Sure. But aren't we gonna..."

That evening, Swann's apparent intent to meddle in Pennfield
family affairs still gnawed at Christopher. So much so, he found it
difficult to make real progress on his address. He sat on his sun
porch for over an hour staring at his Smith-Corona, no cogent
thoughts surfacing. It was difficult, but finally he typed out several
sentences:

> There are many stories told about our grandfather, Benjamin Pennfield.
> One of my personal favorites is how he always kept his private steam
> yacht docked within blocks of his Wall Street office so that, whenever
> the mood struck, he could escape to Newport at a moment's notice.
> Newport was more than a summer residence for him. It was a tonic, a
> counter-balance to the rigors of high finance. Over the years he
> rewarded the City quite handsomely for this service. Today, many
> Newport institutions continue to benefit from his generosity: the New-
> port Hospital, the Newport Public Library, and, of course, Trinity
> Church...

*   *   *

Newport, Rhode Island
Fall, 1927

A beam of rich orange-yellow light shined from the tower of Trinity
Church, slicing through the soft blue hues of a clear evening sky. It
was quiet on Thames Street and along the harbor, the city resting in
anticipation of another busy week. While most Newporters were
preparing to retire on this Sunday evening, Reverend Walter Jenkinson sat alone in his small office behind the altar, going through
his ritual of opening the monthly tithing envelopes. He worked
methodically, opening each envelope and recording its contents in
the ledger—until he came across one particular envelope. His heart

skipped a beat. On it, his name was spelled out in a beautiful, delicate calligraphy. He ripped it open and looked inside. Another note:

My Dearest Walter,

I can no longer bear my feelings existing as mere words on paper. I can no longer stand you glancing away whenever I set my eyes on you. I need to visit with you, speak with you, touch you. I will be at your office this evening at nine thirty.

With All My Love,

Sarah Pennfield Morton

Jenkinson shivered as he read the words. As much as he feared Sarah would become more aggressive in her next note, he had never dreamed she would be bold enough to confront him in person. He glanced at his pocket watch. Nine twenty-three. One thing he knew for certain: he must get out of here *now*.

He thrust himself up from his seat and rushed, then ran, to the front of the church. He reached for the door and prepared himself to gallop across the street before the last few minutes elapsed. He opened the door.

"Good evening, Reverend Jenkinson."

There, standing before him on the front steps of his church, was Sarah Morton. She stood there so serious, her back so straight, her shoulders so square, the image she projected belied the messages of her notes. Perhaps she was here to explain herself, to beg forgiveness for her indiscretions? But then her eyes, her blue eyes glared at him as if he was hers for the taking. He swallowed hard.

"And how are you, Mrs. Morton?"

The moment seemed like hours. They stood there, their eyes locked on each other, Jenkinson quivering.

"Do come in, please." He opened the door and led her into the church.

His better judgment told him to assume the role of spiritual advisor, to treat this meeting exactly as he would one with any other member of his congregation who had a problem to discuss.

"Sarah, I'd be lying if I didn't admit your notes flatter me, but, of course, you realize—

"I realize I'm in love with you, Walter." She said it so matter-of-factly, the words seemed trivial.

He smiled. "Of course, we all go through periods in our lives when we *think* we feel certain emotions. But, if you ask the Lord for His aid, I'm sure it will pass."

"If I was ever sure of anything, I'm sure that I'm in love with you, Walter." Slowly, she lifted her hand and placed it on his shoulder.

He flushed. The touch sent tingles up his back. But, *no—this is wrong, very wrong*—he had to stop it, put an end to it.

"Believe me, it's all transient, Sarah, the work of the devil! These emotions you feel aren't real!"

"But how can that be, Walter?" Her voice was low and sensuous, her fingers warm. With her free hand, she slowly reached for him. "Is *this* not real?"

He stood there completely still. He looked down at her. Her soft blue eyes glanced upward. Then she kissed him.

Part of him told him to pull away, pull away with all the strength he could summon. *Strike the devil down! Crush the head of the serpent!* Yet that small part of him was defenseless to the greater strength of an inner voice encouraging him to enjoy this moment, to revel in it. He clutched her, running his hand through her fine hair, down her soft neck, and around her shoulder until he fondled her firm breasts.

Every moment of every day thereafter, guilt plagued him. Their short kiss lasted no more than several seconds, but as he slowly pulled away, Jenkinson's brief moment of pleasure instantly shackled him with shame. He looked at her, *ashamed*. He looked at his reflection in the window, *ashamed*. He looked at his pulpit, *ashamed*. He told her they must never do that again. He told her how for several brief seconds, he had lost control. He told her they could never meet again, never even *suggest* that anything happened between them. She stood and listened somberly.

Yet, despite his shame, his libido had been titillated, stroked in a way it had never been stroked before. Now that he had tasted the forbidden fruit, he yearned for more. As the days passed, his entangled emotions tore at his insides. When his mind sojourned towards Sarah, images of Betty would draw him back, clouding his soul with guilt. When his mind dwelled upon Betty, a sudden thought of Sarah would lance his heart, leaving it hollow and empty.

Walking up Memorial Boulevard one day several weeks later, he saw her again. Far across the street, but he saw her. There was something strange, yet marvelously arousing, to the way she stared at him. It was as if she had choreographed the entire event, knowing without one shade of doubt he would be there at that precise instant. As he looked back at her, he felt the exact feelings from those precious few seconds when they kissed. To think she was so intent, *so determined,* to force his affections aroused him in a way he had never been aroused before. Then he came to a realization: *his life would not be complete until he fully pursued his attraction to Sarah Morton.*

But what would be the moral outcome if he did pursue her—*a minister, a servant of the Lord, pursuing an extramarital affair? Why, he was sinning, sinning already, by the mere thought of it!* But, then, wasn't this all pre-determined? Weren't all men sinners? Wasn't it only through forgiveness that the Lord would lead man to salvation? Was he no better than any other man? Needn't he sin to be forgiven and, therefore, saved?

Still, as easy as it may have been to walk across the street and talk with her as he would with any other member of his congregation, he simply *could not* bring himself to do it. But, perhaps, there was another way. Perhaps, if he just were to let her know—in some subtle way—that he shared her feelings, that alone would satisfy his arousals. Perhaps if he wrote her a note?

That evening he sat at his desk, wrestling with his thoughts, twiddling his pen between his fingers, staring at the blank piece of notepaper. How should he begin? Slowly, he started writing, printing block letters so no one would recognize his handwriting.

My dearest S.

I think of our moment together and my mind fills me with...

With what? How can he say it without making it too forward? He stared at the wall. Then, he continued.

...the same feelings I know you feel.

Good. It could be any one of a range of feelings. Sorrow. Happiness. Fear. Even holiness.

Although these feelings can never manifest themselves in a concrete way,...

Okay. Now finish it so that it arouses her in a way that surpasses a *physical* arousal. Yes, that's it, *a spiritual* arousal.

...rest assured that your feelings have been shared and cherished.

Now, how would he sign it, finish it off? Put a final end to it all, satisfying his need to share his feelings with her, and signal to her that her pursuit of him was not in vain?

With all my love,

No, not right. He crossed it out, ripped it up, took another piece of notepaper, and slowly rewrote the rest of the note up to that point. Then, after much thought, he wrote:

With all the love of God,

W.

Jenkinson's heart fluttered as he walked briskly down Thames Street, beginning his long trek to Morton's house on Gordon Street. He would leave the note on Sarah's doorstep before noon, go back to the church, and return by two. If the note was still there, he would retrieve it and try again another day. If it was not, he would know that Sarah had received his message.

As he turned off Bellevue onto Gordon, no one was in sight. He walked slowly up the steps. Halfway up, he suddenly stopped, almost deciding to abandon the whole endeavor. But, no, this is what he must do, what he *had* to do. He walked to the door. Slowly, he leaned over, his hands trembling, and placed the note down. As he began to stand, the door creaked.

"Do come in, Walter."

He looked up. Sarah. Looking down on him so casually, as if this was all to be expected, predestined, he having no choice in the matter.

"Something for me?" She asked, eyeing the note in his hand as she closed the door.

He handed her the note.

As she read it, she smiled, her eyes glowed radiant. A transformation overtook her entire being—usually so straight and stiff, prim and proper—now warm and relaxed. She dropped the note and reached for him.

The moment her lips touched his, he had exhausted his defenses. He embraced her with all the vigor with which she embraced him. And they kissed, kissed with all the energy of their first kiss. Then, without warning, Sarah pulled away.

"But why?" He whispered.

"Come, follow me." She took him by the hand and led him up the stairway.

By the time they reached the bedroom, he was defenseless. He clutched her, running his hands across her back, fingering the buttons to her blouse. She offered no resistance, laying back across the bed, supple and unrestrained. He quickly undid the buttons. She offered him her arms, allowing him to gently remove her blouse and brassiere. He planted a soft, gentle kiss on her firm, white breast.

Through the winter and into the spring, their meetings continued. Each Thursday at noon, Jenkinson would make the long walk along Thames, up Memorial, make a right on Bellevue, stride quickly by its stately mansions—Stone Villa, The Ochre House, Rosecliff, Beechwood and the others—then turn down Gordon. When he passed the Morton house, if the upstairs curtain was drawn, that would mean Sarah was home alone: he would walk up the front steps and knock on the door. If the curtain was not drawn, it was not a good day for them to meet: he would walk by.

"It seems as if our little meetings are stirring up quite a bit of interest." Sarah swept her hand through Jenkinson's hair one Thursday afternoon as they lay together on her bed.

"*Oh?*" Jenkinson propped himself up on his elbows, his bare chest slipping out from under the covers, his face a pale shade of gray.

"Yes," she answered, her jet black hair flowing half-way down to her shoulders. "They're saying things about us, I can sense it. Last Wednesday, Martha Clarke stopped me on Thames and said to me `Isn't the Reverend Jenkinson taking quite a bit of interest in your spiritual welfare these days?'"

"How did you respond to her?"

"I smiled right back at her and answered `Doesn't Reverend Jenkinson regularly visit many members of his congregation? Aren't I entitled to the same spiritual guidance as the others?'"

"Surely. Surely, my dear. Very good answer." Jenkinson slipped back under the covers. Silently, he wondered if rumors of their affair had reached the ears of Benjamin Pennfield.

11

The home of Xenobia Pennfield Harthgate looked like it had once been a desirable place to live. It stood on a large lot of untended land—overgrown brown grass battling unruly weeds and bald patches of frozen earth—on the corner of Roe Street and Allen Drive in Middletown, only several blocks from the Newport border. Set against the day's crisp blue sky, it was difficult to accept the old house as anything other than what it was: an unwelcomed eyesore in what was otherwise a working-class Middletown neighborhood.

As a brisk wind swept in from the south, raking the branches of its naked trees, Ed Swann stood on the corner of the old house's lot, scribbling notes on his pad, studying all the prominent features: the large wraparound porch, the rickety front steps, the buckled front walk, the flaked gray paint on its shingles. A structure so self-absorbed, it had grown oblivious to the present day.

Swann paced around the corner several times, the bristles of the house's overgrown hedges brushing against his golf hat. He observed how the old imposing structure dwarfed the other houses in the neighborhood—mostly post-war capes and summer bunga-lows upgraded to year-round residences. The neighborhood was so quiet in mid-morning, for awhile it was difficult for him to find a neighbor who might help bring his picture of Xenobia into sharper focus. Finally, half way down the block, he spotted a woman getting out of her car.

"You wanna know about Harthgate, I'll tell you about that old witch," Marilyn Cartwright, a husky woman in her early forties, her dirty blonde hair in curlers, told him as she stood in her driveway.

"Yes, what can you tell me specifically about Mrs. Harthgate's—

"When my two year old was a baby, I was walking her in the carriage one day and, from out of nowhere, the old witch turns the corner and leans over like she wants to talk to her. Fine, everybody loves a cute little baby, right? Well, first she touches Courtney's chin with her finger, then says to her, `The mean spirits of the wrongful dead damn their living perpetrators.' Believe me I'll never forget those words. Later I find out she said the exact same words to the Lawrence girl, sent her home crying. Well, I look at her so shocked, I mean you just don't expect someone to say something like that, and then her cat—she's holding this cat up against her chest—her cat actually hissed at me. Hissed at me, can you believe it? There's something strange about that woman if you ask me."

Swann jotted notes feverishly.

"And then, of course, there's the ghost, everyone knows about the ghost.

"The ghost?" Swann asked.

"Yes, I've seen it. Everyone's seen it at one time or another. A woman, dressed in black, walking back and forth across her porch. Eeerie, enough to make you freak. Why are you looking funny at me like that? You don't believe in ghosts?"

"Not quite sure," Swann answered. "Though I do know that many people accept the existence of ghosts without question."

"Well, I certainly do. Especially after living near that ole witch for seven years. At first we just thought that lady was a friend of hers. But, then we got suspicious. I mean, how many people dress in the same old black dress and walk back and forth on the porch all the time like that? And she's not old, not old at all. Can't be any older than me, probably younger. Well, we were suspicious until the mailman, Mr. Greevey, actually saw the woman vanish one day, vanish right before his eyes. Then we knew we had a ghost in our neighborhood, no doubt about it. Ask Mr. Greevey if you don't believe me."

"Yep, I seen it." Lowell Greevey answered Swann's question later that morning as he walked briskly down the street, his sack of mail strapped over his shoulder. "Vanished into thin air. Swear on a stack of bibles. But that's just the beginning of it. Strange lady." He shook his head. "Strange, strange lady…"

"Oh?" Swann strained to keep up with Greevey's brisk pace.

"She writes letters to non-existent people. Dead relatives, I think. Amanda Pennfield. Evangeline Pennfield. Sarah Morton. They all come back, return address. Once she even wrote one to a Peter Pennfield. Get this, the letter was addressed to <u>The</u> *Compass Rose, At Sea*. Just that, nothing else. What a nut."

*   *   *

"Let me make myself clear, Mr. Swann," Christopher Pennfield barked into the phone the next morning. *"Under no circumstances whatsoever are you to speak to my cousin Xenobia about ghosts!"*

"You do realize you'd really be tying my hands behind my back."

"And I really don't care. The woman's unstable, been that way for years. She'd only lead you astray."

"But she's the only living Pennfield who can help me with the history of the cottage."

"Mr. Swann, how dare you tell me anything about a person you've never met!"

"Feel like I know her, though. Must've talked to five or six of her neighbors yesterday…"

"Jesus Christ! You're letting all of Middletown in on our little secret!"

"Haven't let anyone in on a thing. But I did learn something."

"What's that, that all of Aquidneck Island thinks she's deranged?"

"Nope. Not really. Seems as if Xenobia has a ghost of her own."

"What?"

"Her neighbors all swear she's got a ghost as well, right on her front porch. Sort've interesting how so many members of your family have had so many run ins with the paranormal, don't you think?"

"I don't know what to think, Mr. Swann. But I do believe that unless we end this investigation soon, it could cause undue harm to the Pennfield family name."

"You're really jumping the gun on that one. Fact is, we don't know anything at all about that yet. And what difference would it make anyway?"

"All the difference in the world as far as I'm concerned, Mr. Swann. So when will this investigation of yours be over? What else needs to be done to coddle my brother's insecurities?"

"Well in absence of talking to your cousin, there's only a couple of things left that I can really do. I suppose it wouldn't be too early to bring in the heavy equipment."

"The heavy equipment?"

"Just a few little tests I usually run when I come to the conclusion we might have a real haunting on our hands. Set up a few on-site devices. Start with the simple stuff. Of course, thermometers to measure changes in temperature. Detectors to measure the slightest emissions of light, sound or electromagnetic activity. Strain gauges to detect movement. Heat sensors. A Geiger counter. Then, I have a string of infra-red cameras set up to snap a round of pictures once any pattern of variation is detected. It's all controlled by a PC. Pretty interesting set-up, actually. Developed it with a few academic colleagues of mine."

"Geiger counters? Heat sensors? Infra-red film? Academic indeed! Exactly what kind of pseudo-science are you practicing, Mr. Swann?"

"It's not a pseudo-science at all. I think most men of science would tell you it's a pretty sound methodology. Thought I'd set everything up in the master bedroom and watch it for a few days. Hope is, we could maybe catch something on film."

"And then what? Will that be it?"

"Only other thing I plan to do is bring in a few psychics. Sometimes gifted individuals can pick up sensations the equipment can't."

"What are you trying to do, turn our family cottage into a side-show? Why don't we just open up a theme park on the premises and be done with it…

*   *   *

For four days, the printer droned, every several seconds releasing a new line of numbers in a slow deliberate rhythm. Swann sat in the guest bedroom with his knees up on the edge of the desk, his eyes shifting from the readouts on his computer screen to the small printer set next to it. He shifted back in his seat and focused again on the screen. Like watching grass grow.

Ninety-six hours worth of data, practically a week in Newport, and no hard evidence other than the Pennfields' words, his own dream, and a few comments from Xenobia's neighbors. The computer grunted out another row of numbers, filling its eighty column green paper. Swann read across the headings. *Temperature, windows. Temperature, bed. Movement, window. Movement, bed. Radioactivity, windows. Radioactivity, bed.* And eleven measures more. Everything within their normal ranges. The computer kept on churning them out: every ten seconds of every minute of every hour of every day. Already, over six hundred thousand data points. Should more than any four of the measurements deviate significantly within a ten second period, the computer would instruct the five infra-red cameras set up around the master bedroom to snap thirty continuous pictures. But so far, nothing.

He pushed the chair back out from under the desk, disturbing the tangled web of cables running into his equipment from the master bedroom across the hall. He stood up, yawned, and walked down the stairs for a quick break, skipping over several more cables. When he walked into the kitchen, he found his files strewn across the big table, just as he had left them the night before. He unrolled a giant floor plan of the cottage and the surrounding grounds, studying his red pencil marks from the two days prior, indicating where the psychics he had escorted around the cottage had sensed paranormal activity. Two red "x's" in the dining room, two more at the upstairs landing, one in the yard near Cliff Walk, two up in the master bedroom, four in the back near the tool shed. He opened up one of his files and reviewed his notes:

> MARIA PORTUGUESE. Thur, Dec 8. 2PM. Showed up at 1:53. Felt strong vibrations on the landing. Said it felt like an "Impulsive, impetuous" presence. Went into semi-trance and body shook in the master bedroom. Said she felt *strong, strong* presence. Something "untoward, violent." Also felt something in basement, but could not be more specific about it. Said they were "muffled" sensations. Also felt non-specific vibrations out back near the tool shed.

> HILDEGARDE BLOOMFELD. Thur, Dec 8. 5:30PM. Out front, immediately felt something. Led me around to the backyard. Sensed strong vibrations near tool shed, within ten feet of where Maria had felt something. Whatever it was she was feeling, she said it was very, very strong and that this where "we'll eventually solve it." I asked her what that meant and she could tell me nothing more. Also thought she felt weaker sensations near dining room.

> HANK ZEBRINSKI. Fri, Dec 9. 9:30AM. Was late, as usual. Minute he walked in, he walked right up stairs. Stopped at landing, said he felt something. But then was attracted onward toward the master bedroom. Stayed there for awhile, but couldn't latch onto anything specific. When he walked around the outside, felt minor sensations in back and out front near Cliff Walk.

> GEORGE MCPHINNIE. Fri, Dec 9. 2PM. Went downstairs to basement. Felt nothing. But was absolutely convinced there was something in the attic. We climbed up, he was sure there was something strange about the attic fan. But that was all he could say, nothing more specific. Also felt something out back and in dining room, but that was it. Told me it wasn't a great day for him.

It wasn't perfectly clean, but Swann found it interesting how they had all generally focused in on the same areas—the same areas where the Pennfields had reported paranormal activity—although he had been very careful, *extremely careful*, not to give them any clues. But he wanted more *tangible* evidence, some small kernel that might lead him to the *reason why* the Pennfields were being haunted so frequently. Perhaps the gentleman due later this afternoon would help, a very powerful psychic from Boston whom Swann knew only by reputation.

"And how *marvelous* it is to meet you, Mr. Swann, even though you're understandably distraught over being away from your fine home in Spring Lake for a week now."

"Huh?" Swann answered standing in the doorway.

"Dalipe Salaam." The tall, well-manicured man with rich brown skin nodded his head. "And the pleasure is all mine, indeed. I can understand quite easily why your dear Uncle Arthur was so intent upon contacting you at the time of his untimely and premature passing." He smiled, his white teeth sparkling.

"How in the name of God did you—

Salaam smiled, pointed to his temple, and answered. "Correct. A gift from God indeed."

Swann studied Salaam carefully. A very well built man, with broad shoulders and a tapered waist, at least six foot three. His jet-black oily hair was perfectly combed, capping his broad forehead. He sported a proud smile, his bright white teeth shining against his dark skin tones. The man's impeccable grooming—his perfectly-tailored suit, his bowtie, his suspenders, his two-tone wing-tips—and his rich, genteel voice belied his large frame. It made Swann wonder what Salaam's day job was.

"I happen to be a very prominent attorney in Cambridge, Massachusetts, specializing in the intricacies of the rather cryptic tax code of this country."

"Jesus Christ, you *are* good!" Swann answered, stunned by Salaam's extrasensory powers. "So tell me about the house. What do you feel?

Salaam smiled, spread his arms, and squinted. "I must say that the psychic content of this marvelous house rivals that of some of the most famous hauntings of England and Scotland. This house is *immanent* with psychic vibrations, I assure you."

"Had a pretty good idea about that," Swann answered. "Problem is, who the dickens is it?"

Salaam closed his eyes all the way, touched his temples, walked over towards the dining room and stopped at its large antique table. He placed his hands on its shiny surface and paused for a moment. "She talked to you from right around here, did she not?"

"Yeah, but it could've been—

"No, a dream it was not. I feel quite confident about that." Salaam answered, his eyes still closed.

"But then, who was she? What did she want to tell me?"

Salaam squinted hard, carving deep lines in his brow. "There's something she wants you to find. A mystery she wants you to unearth. But I don't feel much more." He opened his eyes. "Let's move on."

Over the next forty-five minutes, Salaam toured the house and its grounds, starting in the back yard. Once there, he stopped, squinted, touched his temples and told Swann he felt something strong, but he could not hone in on it. He then walked Swann back inside the house and up the stairs. Salaam stopped short at the door to the master bedroom and grit his teeth, a sharp pain knifing through his skull. He told Swann that whatever he was sensing was so strong, it interfered with his ability to perceive it. He quickly turned away, the pain far too great to continue there. Salaam then asked to see the attic. As he followed Swann up the stairs, he suddenly tugged on his jacket.

"She wants you to know she's around, Mr. Swann. She's standing right behind you now as we speak. I can see her silhouette."

"Who?"

"Whomever the woman is who's trying to contact you."

Swann's face whitened. "But that's impossible. Ghosts can't do that."

"Let me give you one word of advice," Salaam answered, smiling. "Never allow your imagination to be limited by the bounds of your own rules."

Once at the top of the attic stairs, Salaam again shut his eyes, and touched his temple. He covered his face with his hands and took a deep breath. "There's something here, I can feel it. Something which I think can be quite significant."

"What is it?"

"I'm not sure yet. Please allow me to concentrate."

Salaam paced around the attic, his hands still covering his face, his eyes closed. He walked towards some old wooden storage racks, at one point tripping on some yellow fiberglass insulation and almost stepping through the ceiling. He grimaced, turned an abrupt about-face, and walked slowly towards the opposite corner, a cobweb grazing his cheek. When he reached there, he shook his head, then turned towards the attic fan. He stood next to it for almost ten minutes, then pointed to an old trunk several feet away on the floor.

"It's in there."

"What?"

"A clue. A very relevant one, I'm sure. Somewhere in that old trunk. I'm not certain exactly what it is, but it's in there. The sensations are very strong, crystal clear. I assure you."

"Then let's open it."

Salaam opened his eyes, glanced at his watch, and smiled at Swann. "I'm afraid that would be quite impossible, Mr. Swann. If I leave now I should be home just in time. Cocktails are served promptly at seven o'clock in my household. I'm sure you possess the perspicacity to uncover it yourself." He started for the stairs and then turned back. "And, Mr. Swann, rest assured that your dear Marie is quite comfortable where she resides today. She wants you to know that. And she wants you to know what happened at Scranton was not your fault." He smiled at Swann and then walked down the stairs.

"But. But—"

Swann spent nearly six hours rummaging through the material in the trunk. There were old pictures, stacks of papers, books, journals, diaries. All Pennfield family relics. He examined each piece carefully. What made his task so difficult was that each and every piece in that trunk could reasonably have been *the clue* Salaam had referred to, but it was impossible for him to know. Swann formed three piles. To his left, he placed items which he definitely had ruled out. In the middle, he placed items that he thought may or may not be the clue. And on the right, he collected those items which he considered to be the very strongest candidates. Then, for hours, he shuffled and reshuffled pieces between piles. Could that family portrait circa 1935 which he had ruled out, possibly be a picture of the culprits who were haunting the cottage? Could Elizabeth Pennfield's journal from 1917 which he had thought so promising be, in fact, mere family trivia, irrelevant to the matter at hand? As he sat there, shuffling items between piles, he noticed an old unopened envelope sitting by itself between piles.

He picked it up and examined it more closely. Old, yellowed paper. On it, there was scribbling in a rushed, anxious handwriting. Swann squinted, attempting to read it. He could only make it out partially:

Betty Jenk
11/18/27

He opened the envelope carefully, its paper crackling. When he blew into it, separating the sides, several jagged pieces fell out. He placed them on the attic's creaky wooden floor and examined them under the light. They appeared to be ripped, all part of the same whole. As he arranged them, his hands shook. It was coming together, some sort of puzzle, a short note. As he fit the last piece into place, he reached for his bifocals and observed the note's hand-stroked block lettering:

My dearest S,

I think of our moment together and my mind fills me with the same feelings I know you feel. Although these feelings can never manifest themselves in a concrete way, rest assured that your feelings have been shared and cherished.

With all my love,

W.

12

A surge of cold December air breezed in off the river, swooshing down East Sixty-Fourth Street, rushing over the bumpy concrete unimpeded by the street's usual clamor of cycles, buses, taxis, and bustling humanity. So quiet was the East Side of Manhattan at six thirty in the morning that only the steady *clip-clop, clip-clop* of Winnie Pennfield's black patent leather pumps hurrying down the front steps of her stone-gray townhouse rivaled the whistling wind. She quickly strode the half block to Third Avenue, wrapping her scarf over her chin and evading the swirling debris. She stopped and looked down the Avenue. No taxis to be seen. Funny how on a bright, clear, fragrant spring morning taxis abounded at this early hour; but on a cold winter morning, *nothing*. No use to fight the inevitable, she decided; she would *walk* the six and a half blocks to Coyne Publishing.

And to think people said she lived a charmed life! They should see her now rushing down a dark, desolate Sixty-Fourth Street, lugging an overstuffed soft-leather briefcase, the cold air frosting her cheeks and numbing her legs. *Charm this!* she countered to those who had this image of her. If you listened to *them*—she gritted her teeth—you would think Winnie Pennfield spent every available evening at restaurant-after-expensive-restaurant escorted by heir-after-eligible-heir to every substantial fortune in North America, dancing the night away at *Aria, The Palladium* or *The China Club*. Why, if *they* were correct, she'd be just *returning* now, not braving the morning elements to get a jump on what would be another sixteen hour day at work.

The problem, she figured, was that the people who stirred up the gossip about her—the *"Charmed Life Theorists,"* she called them—dwelled only upon her accomplishments, neglecting to consider the hard work and struggle she had gone through to get there. In four short years she had cut a wide and rapid swath through the corporate maze at *Avanti* magazine. At twenty-three, a mere editorial assistant, a glorified goffer. At twenty-four, Senior Editor. At twenty-five, Executive Feature Editor. At twenty-six, Managing Editor reporting to the renowned Clarissa Mantusso, Editor 'n Chief and one of the founders of <u>Avanti</u>. And, yes, now Winnie Pennfield had achieved it all, Editor 'N Chief, after Clarissa's early retirement. But did they realize what she had to go through to get here? Could they have handled the brutal eighteen-hour days, jumped all the political hurdles, put up with all the over-inflated egos?

She shivered, her teeth rattled as she waited for the light to change at Park. *And what about the tragedy in her life?* How many of the Charmed Life Theorists had lost both their parents in a car crash at age nine and were left to the care of boarding schools and legal guardians during their formative years? That alone would put most people in an institution. How many of the Charmed Life Theorists could have handled *that?*

Winnie crushed her cigarette in the ashtray on her desk, swiveled around in her leather-upholstered chair, kicked off her black pumps, and rested her legs on an open drawer. She pulled a copy of the clean manuscript from a file. She stretched back and read:

> Thomas Westerfeld, always in motion, surveys his world from a perch far above Battery Point. The financiers of Wall Street below. The refineries of New Jersey and Staten Island to his right. The factories of Brooklyn to his left. Cargo-laden ocean liners passing through the Verrazano Narrows on the horizon.

Finance, petroleum, manufacturing, trade. Each plays a role in the world Westerfeld has so carefully engineered, so artfully designed.

But for Westerfeld—known to many as the Whiz Kid of Wall Street—it is impossible to lay back, stretch out, and savor the fruits of his labor. The engine has to be kept running, its wheels greased, its turbines oiled. "If you don't grow, you shrink. And if you shrink, you get devoured," he often tells his corps of hand-somely-rewarded hangers-on.

Despite his boyish good looks and well-manicured exterior, Westerfeld, 31, has the appetite of a pit bull, eager to chomp on any unprotected morsel of opportunity. He flies over the economic landscape with the eye of an eagle, scouting out the marketplace's hidden imperfections: the small manufacturer with a stock price selling at deep discount to net asset value, a three basis point arbitrage opportunity, the multinational corporation in dire need of fat-trimming. The minute he spots his prey, he draws a beeline, nosedives for it, and snaps it up, leaving whomever and whatever in the dust. There is only one survivor in Westerfeld's game.

Instinctively, Winnie lit a cigarette and drew deep on it, holding her breath just long enough to allow the nicotine to tingle her system with a dizzying jolt. She took several more quick puffs, scanned the first three paragraphs once again, and without looking, buzzed her secretary on the intercom.

"Claire, can you get me Julia Bradford on the line?"

"Sure Winnie."

"It works," Winnie told the young associate editor the minute she picked up the line.

"Really?" Bradford answered.

"Ten drafts and half a nervous breakdown, but you did it, Julia. Everyone loves it. It's marvelous. I've already told Winthrop I want to move it up to March. Give it the cover. Bravo."

"It's not a given that he'll agree to a shoot, though. It was hard enough to get the interview." Bradford answered.

"Don't you worry one itsy bit about that. I'll take it from here. I think I can convince Mr. Westerfeld's publicist that posing for the March cover of <u>Avanti</u> is certainly in his best interest. He doesn't seem the type to turn down free publicity."

"You sure?"

"No doubt about it. Just leave it to me. And do me one other little favor..."

"Yes?"

"Check your mailbox tomorrow morning. Don't be surprised if you find tickets to Paris for you and that Social Register boyfriend of yours..."

*   *   *

The photographer's strobe flashed rapid pulses of light, the camera clicking continuously as Thomas Westerfeld fidgeted across the large plushly-carpeted floor of his office. The workers distracted him, made him fidget even more than usual. Winnie stood out of the line of fire, safely behind the photographer. She dragged on her cigarette and observed carefully. There was something unusual about Tom Westerfeld, she thought, eccentric perhaps. Part boy, part man. His smooth cheeky face, the long wavy hair draping over his ears and down the back of his neck: almost sophomoric. But then his patented suspenders and bowtie, perfectly affixed: almost professorial. And his thin, lanky frame: suggestive of world class absent-mindedness—someone too preoccupied with the ways of the world to stop for something so trivial as nourishment.

"Can you stand closer to the window, Mr. Westerfeld?" the photographer asked.

Before Westerfeld had a chance to respond, one of his associates, considerably older, sprang out from behind the lights. "We agreed to forty-five minutes, not a second more. You've already been shooting for forty-three and a half." He looked down at his watch and then up at Westerfeld. "You don't have to continue, Tom. We've already satisfied our part of the agreement."

"Excuse me!" Winnie barged in. "Francesco is the best cover photographer in the world. If you allow him to do his job correctly, we'll all benefit, believe me."

"Tom, you don't have to—"

"How?" Westerfeld looked towards Winnie, ignoring his associate.

"What?" She answered.

"How will I benefit?"

"Simple." Winnie stood right up to him and looked him in the eyes. "People read about you in the papers, hear about you on the news, they think you're some kind of eighties LBO power freak. Post peak, to say the very least. But with Franceso's pictures, they'll see the true you. His magic will bring it out, believe me. They won't even have to read the article to know that you were a philosophy and theology major at Princeton. That there's an essence to you, something deeper."

Westerfeld gazed out his large window, almost absent-mindedly, tweaked his lips, then looked back at Winnie. "And who are you?"

"Winnie Pennfield, Editor in Chief."

"Tom Westerfeld." He offered her his hand.

"No introduction is necessary, Mr. Westerfeld." Her sapphire blue eyes sparkled at him.

*   *   *

Christopher Pennfield sat placidly at his Smith-Corona on an icy-blue Sunday afternoon. He looked out onto the street from his sun porch. Each strand of grass, each leaf on the bushes, glazed with a clear ice coating, as if Mother Nature had taken all of Vermont and dipped it in a vat of liquid crystals. On a moment like this, he never regretted foregoing the opportunities of a career in big business for the academic life on a rural New England campus. There was much more to life than financial reward, he realized. He drew a deep breath and leaned forward on his typewriter. Before he could fully savor the richness of the moment, the phone rang.

"Unk, you'll never believe it!"

"Winnie?" He smiled. "What won't I believe?"

"Who I'm dating."

"Hmmm. Let me see. The President of the United States is married. The Prince of Wales has both a wife *and* a mistress. Who else in the world would be worthy of Edwina D'Ouvrier Pennfield?"

"Let me give you a hint. He's very rich."

"Jesus. That's not a hint. That's a cost of entry."

"And he's very young."

"Well, that narrows it a bit now, doesn't it. So who is it? You have me completely baffled."

"Tom Westerfeld."

"The Whiz Kid? He's practically a boy, isn't he?"

"So what. He's completely infatuated with me. Hook, line, and sinker. We were out till five-thirty this morning."

"Sounds like quite a date."

"Yep, dinner at Le Cirque, a show at the Rainbow Room, dancing at Tattoo, then up and down Manhattan in a stretch limo for two hours and then—"

"Please. Spare me the gory details."

"I assure you, there *were* no gory details, Unk. It was our first date for goodness sake."

For several moments after he hung up, Pennfield wondered if he should be jealous. After all, Tom Westerfeld was the Latest Thing, This Year's Model, the most recent in a long line of hot shot financiers. But, Pennfield soon concluded that the Whiz Kid of Wall Street was a transitory little twerp, at best. A novelty whom Winnie would tire of quickly. There was something magic between Winnie and her favorite Uncle that would withstand the occasional allures of people like Westerfeld. Here today, gone tomorrow: Pennfield smirked. He looked back down on the clean white paper in the carriage of his Smith-Corona and concentrated again on his task at hand. *Grandfather.* Now there was a financier for you. The Original Merchandise. Wonder how Westerfeld would stand up to the likes of Benjamin Pennfield? No contest. Pennfield smiled, and then, inspired, tapped at his keyboard:

Benjamin Pennfield's contributions to Newport were much more than of a financial nature. So strong were his ties to the fair city that in 1928 the Newport Daily News named him the city's "unofficial mayor." Indeed, any person of note who visited Newport could not leave without paying a visit to Benjamin Pennfield's cottage. Herbert Hoover, Charles Lindbergh, and Babe Ruth were among the many luminaries my grandfather hosted there. Indeed, it is probably fair to say that life in Newport during the 1920s revolved around Benjamin Pennfield as he was frequently called upon to offer his counsel and advice to the city's civic, business and religious leaders...

*   *   *

Newport, Rhode Island
May, 1928

Reverend Walter Jenkinson paced back and forth on the porch. Ever since he had received the telegram on Thursday instructing him to meet Benjamin Pennfield here today, Jenkinson worried over what might transpire. He was sure Pennfield summoned him to the cottage so he could censure him over his affair with Sarah. He was absolutely certain. From the moment Sarah told him about the gossip making its way around town last winter, Jenkinson knew this day would come.

Jenkinson shivered, chilled by the blanket of gray clouds hovering over Newport on this unusually dark, cold spring Saturday. Pennfield had arrived late the night before from New York via steam yacht; a rough voyage, Jenkinson had heard. As he paced, he watched Pennfield conversing with two men—those two men from New Bedford, he presumed—far out on the front lawn.

Pennfield waved over to Jenkinson. "Be with you in ten minutes, Walter."

Jenkinson looked out towards the lawn, trying to discern Pennfield's mood from his actions with the two men, both of questionable repute. He often wondered why a man of Pennfield's stature would deal with the likes of those two hoodlums from New Bedford. He watched as Pennfield led them around the perimeter of the grounds. Out towards the rocks at the tip of the point. Along Cliff Walk to the sea wall on the point's eastern edge. Then back onto the lawn.

Pennfield was animated, flapping his arms as he spoke with them. The two of them, both much taller than Pennfield, stood there quietly, apparently taking their orders.

In his mind, Jenkinson had rehearsed this meeting countless times over the last two days. Now he only wondered what the consequences would be. Would he be banished to some small congregation in Maine, never again given the opportunity to be a spiritual leader in a city like Newport? Or would he be banned from spiritual service altogether? In a strange way, Jenkinson was outraged over his predicament. After all, who was Benjamin Pennfield to judge *him*? Fifteen years of dedication and service to the Lord and, now, one small slip and Pennfield was about to pounce upon him. He wondered how many mistresses Pennfield had stashed away, how many times <u>he</u> had lied and stolen and cheated in the course of conducting business?

"I have something *very serious* to discuss with you, Walter." Pennfield's jaw jut out as he bounded up the porch, interrupting Jenkinson's thoughts.

"Yes, yes, indeed." Jenkinson stiffened.

"Something I feel so strongly about it could possibly affect our friendship." Pennfield lit a cigar and drew deep on it, looking out over the lawn.

Jenkinson trembled.

"What I want to discuss shouldn't really be of surprise to you, Walter." Pennfield turned towards Jenkinson, staring at him through a puff of smoke.

Jenkinson tensed. "Of course, Ben, we all—

"You *do* realize this is an election year?" Pennfield cut him off and then paced across the porch, puffing on his cigar. "Especially with Mr. Coolidge not in the fray, I think it particularly important that we remind our congregation of the bounteous programs of the Republican Party. Remember that eloquent sermon you delivered last summer, the one about the loaves and fishes?"

"Yes. Of course." Jenkinson's eyes glowed. Was this it? Was this was all Pennfield wanted?

"I think it wouldn't be a bad idea if you reprised it. Perhaps make it a theme for all your sermons throughout the summer..."

"Why certainly, Ben," Jenkinson answered, his face aglow. "That wouldn't be a problem. Wouldn't be one at all. Is that all you wished to see me about, Ben?"

"Yes, yes, that's all." Pennfield puffed on his cigar.

"Well, then I won't keep you. I'm sure you have many other things to attend to." Jenkinson quickly turned to leave.

"And Walter..."

Jenkinson stopped and turned back. "Yes, Ben?"

Pennfield pulled his cigar out of his mouth and looked Jenkinson in the eyes. "I'm sure I need not remind you that in a year when providing guidance to the congregation is so critical how necessary it is that our *own* houses remain in order..."

Jenkinson's legs wobbled as he walked down the front steps. Pennfield was toying with him. *Toying with him!* Cagey old wolf, Pennfield was too shrewd to confront him directly. Yet, with those few words, Pennfield held his life in a stranglehold.

Whatever it was Pennfield had referred to—even if he knew nothing of the affair—it was merely a stay of execution, Jenkinson concluded. If he and Sarah continued their dalliances, Pennfield would inevitably uncover it. He could not bear to again put himself through the mental torture he had suffered the last two days. He could not bear the thought of Betty finding out. There was only one thing he could do: he had to put an end to the affair now and hope as time separated them from their sin it would all be forgotten. The next Thursday, with much remorse, Jenkinson left a note on Sarah's doorstep.

My dearest S,

Upon reflection, I am forced to the conclusion that we can no longer meet as we have in the past. As much as this hurts me, with all the certitude of the Lord I am sure this is the only way it can be. I will miss you, miss you immensely. Only through cowardice do I deliver this message to you in writing, as I could not bear to look in your eyes as I speak these words.

With all my love.

W.

   The next several days were difficult for Jenkinson. If he forced himself to concentrate upon his work, or his reading, his mind would eventually drift away from thoughts of Sarah. But, then, something would remind him of her: the sweet morning scent of a blossoming flower, a fine piece of china on display in a neighbor's hutch, the exquisitely scripted lettering on a Thames Street placard. After several weeks, though, he thought he had it under control— he thought it was finally over—until he walked into his office one Sunday evening late in the month.
   The lone envelope stood out on his desk, drawing his eyes towards it like a powerful magnet. He rubbed his fingers back and forth over the delicate calligraphy. *Reverend Walter Jenkinson.* For what seemed like a hours, he toyed with the envelope, holding it between his fingers. Should he open it? Should he risk beginning anew something that all his good senses told him he should end? *But how could he not?* As he opened it, a delicate scent escaped, her perfume!

My dearest Walter,

I cannot bear the thought of never seeing you again. I must be with you, alone, at least one more time. Meet me tomorrow evening on the front lawn of Stone Villa at nine o' clock. If not, I may be forced to a rash conclusion of my own.

With all my love,

Sarah

For hours he sat at his desk, struggling over his options. If he did not comply with the instructions in her note, he could not predict what she might do. If he *did* comply, he had no idea where it would eventually lead—he may be again unable to fight her advances. He fretted, staring at the wall. At least she had picked a good location, he thought. Samuel and Martha Parker, the owners of Stone Villa, were spending the summer in Europe, leaving the sprawling grounds of their cottage under the supervision of one lone caretaker. If their meeting were to lead to anything, at least it would be discreet. He drew a breath and looked up toward the ceiling. It was clear. He had no options. He *had* to meet Sarah tomorrow evening on the front lawn of Stone Villa. She had boxed him into a corner.

"It's such a fair evening, I think I might take a short stroll, Betty." He told his wife on Monday evening at half past eight.

Betty looked up from her reading. "That's quite unusual for you, isn't it?"

"What? What's unusual?"

"For you to take a stroll so late in the evening."

"Yes, but, perhaps that's what will make this one so enjoyable." He took a deep breath. "They say there's nothing like clear air to clear the mind." He stood halfway out the door.

"What a pleasant thought." Betty smiled. "Perhaps I will join you." She put down her book.

"Don't feel *obliged*, Betty, I'm only going around the block."

Betty stood up. "No, not at all." She took a knit wrap out of the closet and draped it over her shoulders. "I can use some air myself. Let's go." She pushed him out the door.

Never did Reverend Jenkinson *dream* that his wife would insist upon joining him. It changed everything, threw a wrench into his plans. He was sure if he were able to escape to Stone Villa he could calm Sarah, prevent her from taking any rash actions. But, now, he was here walking along Thames with Betty, trapped.

"What a wonderful idea of yours, Walter!" Betty Jenkinson looked back at her husband. "How peaceful to stroll along the bay at twilight!"

"Yes, I suppose so," Jenkinson clipped back, his mind preoccupied. "Yes, it is a peaceful evening, isn't it Betty?"

A quick thought ran through his mind. If Betty were so enraptured with the bay at twilight, why not just walk along Thames for several minutes and then return home? After all, they were under no special obligation to journey up to Stone Villa. Of course, if that was what he chose to do, there would still be the small matter of Sarah. She would definitely interpret his failure to appear as an effront. But, perhaps, if he walked over to her house early in the morning, first thing—just after Thomas Morton left for the bank—and explained everything to her, he could assuage her. Yes, of course, that's what he would do; play the hand the fates had dealt him. He was safe here strolling along Thames, a good five blocks away from Sarah and Stone Villa. The last thing he wanted to do was to panic.

But, then, Betty took an abrupt turn to the left, up Memorial Boulevard, pulling him with her hand. "Where are you going, Betty?" he asked.

"It's such a fair evening, it might be nice to walk farther…perhaps we should stroll up to the lawns of Stone Villa. Before Martha Parker left for Europe, she encouraged me to stroll the grounds whenever we desired."

He shuddered. *Jesus Christ! Was he hearing correctly?* "Yes, but—

"But what, Walter?" She looked back at him.

"But, by the time we walk there and back," his voice quivered, "it will be at least an hour. The night'll be pitch black by the time we return, Betty."

"Oh, come now, Walter," she chided. "How often do we get to spend time alone together like this?"

"Yes, but…but I thought you were so invigorated by the bay at twilight?"

"Invigorated, yes. But, we see the bay everyday. How often do we come across a chance to be alone together on the sprawling grounds of a Newport mansion on a moonlit summer night?" She tugged on his hand and led him up Memorial toward Stone Villa and Sarah Pennfield Morton.

13

The pictures told the story. Swann placed them in succession across the kitchen table. The first one: a dark night, the two large bedroom windows, sterile and undisturbed. Then the next: two slight wisps dancing in front, perhaps reflections or an imperfection in the film. Then they grew into two dense amorphous clouds, two "cold spots" at the foot of the bed. With each new picture, they took shape. Definitely heads, definitely shoulders, definitely arms. Precisely as Christopher had described them. Murky, but discernible. They grew closer, larger, one of the dense, fuzzy arms drawing back. Still closer, the arm reaching higher. Then, as they hovered close to the bed, the arm about to thrust forward—*Pfft, they disappeared.* The last photograph in the sequence was a carbon copy of the first: two large windows alone in the dark of night.

The computer print-outs corroborated it. Temperature down. Radioactivity off the chart. The strain gauges and motion detectors indicating movement around the bed. Even the random number generator he had placed there deviated from its normal randomness. Everything pointed to the same conclusion: at two thirty-seven AM the previous night, while Swann slept peacefully in the guest bedroom next door, a paranormal "event" had occurred in the master bedroom.

Swann scratched his head and examined the thirty infra-red photographs once again. He found it hard to believe how in each picture the image had grown larger and more distinct and, then, just as the two figures approached the bed, they vanished in a snap. It wasn't the way he was used to seeing it, usually there would be some sort of gradual diminishing, a dissipation of the cloudy images. It made him wonder what had happened at that instant in the master bedroom so many years ago—massive doses of brain activity building to a crescendo then, flat, nothing—what caused the apparitions to shatter so abruptly?

The day before, his eighth in Newport, he had planned on packing his equipment and leaving today, satisfied that he had done everything possible under the circumstances. But, now, he wavered; the event of last night caused him to reconsider. Ever since his second day in Newport, Swann never doubted there was paranormal activity in the cottage, that the Pennfields had some sort of psychic bond with myriad incidents from the past. Now he had concrete evidence, the photographs. And he had no doubt—with just a little more luck—he would be able to get to the bottom of it, crack the mystery of the Pennfield ghosts. Yet, he felt shackled, stopped. The Pennfields weren't about to allow him to take that one step necessary to move the investigation forward. Then—as he stood thinking, looking out the back window at the tool shed—an idea: *what if he just went ahead and did it without asking?*

*   *   *

He stood on the sidewalk and let his eyes run up the front walk's buckled slabs of concrete. He followed them up to the old decrepit steps, rotting wood exposed where the ashen gray paint had flaked away. At the top step, two black wrought-iron numbers—a four and a five—nailed into the wood, slightly off kilter. He scribbled on his notepad, swallowed hard, and walked up. The porch's floorboards creaked as he stepped towards the door. He looked to his left—the old wraparound porch took an ominous turn. He placed his hand on the cold brass knocker and tapped it. Nothing. He pushed the door open slightly, and then called out. "Mrs. Harthgate! Mrs. Harthgate!"

A gust of wind rattled the old house's shingles.

Slowly, he pushed the door again. It creaked from neglect. In front of him, an old staircase. A weathered rug, some sort of oriental design, ran up its steps. The house smelled musty, like mothballs. To his right: the dining room. An old chandelier, its crystals yellowed, hanging like an overgrown exotic plant. Underneath it, a wine-red table: cherry antiquity, he could write his name in the dust. Around it, ten brittle ladderback chairs. Everything still and quiet, as if undisturbed for years. His eyes settled on a large cherry hutch—

"Those who invite themselves over can see themselves in!" an old voice snapped.

His head swiveled. Through an archway, he saw her, sitting in the corner of the parlor amidst odd-shaped lamps, plunging maroon curtains, rickety cherry furniture, oriental vases, and a series of large bay windows looking out onto the porch. Behind her, an ornate marble fireplace, esoteric knick-knacks on its dusty top ledge. He looked her in the eyes, dark and small, set back in their sockets. Thin, dark lines ran across her hardened face. Dry strands of white hair swirled unkempt from her head.

"So, Mr. Swann, we finally meet," Xenobia pet the black cat sitting on her lap.

"The pleasure's all mine, Mrs. Harthgate." He tipped his hat.

"Let me guess," Xenobia closed her eyes and touched her temple with her right hand. "Leo, some kind of leader. A leader of men, aren't you?"

"Very good. Very good," Swann nodded his head. "August nineteenth. And I did run a construction company until I retired, not that that qualifies me as a head of state or anything."

"Well you're here," she harumphed and turned away. "No fault of mine. Might as well make yourself at home."

"Why thank you. Thank you." He sat down and pointed at one of the lamps. "Gee, that's beautiful. The Mrs., she loved cranberry glass."

Xenobia did not look back at him. "You don't care about that. That's not what you're here for."

"You know something?"

"I know more than you would ever want me to know, Mr. Swann. My cousins had the dickens scared out of them, didn't they? How naive, they never knew that Robin still lives. They all still live." She reached into the drawer of the old round cherry table beside her and pulled out a deck of cards. Never turning to face him, she rapped it on the table's ledge. "You read tarot? The cards talk, you know."

"No, can't say I do. But who are you talking about? Who is it that still lives?"

"Everyone. No one ever leaves us really." She arranged the cards on the table in a criss-crossed pattern: the Keltic Cross. "But you know that already, know it very well, don't you Mr. Swann?" She leaned over, her palms rocking the old table, her eyes affixed to the cards.

"I may know a little, but—

"Don't be modest. The cards don't lie."

"Well, then, perhaps we should get right to business?"

"Don't expect me to make it easy. I have no debt to you." She smiled, divining the message in her cards.

"Of course. Of course. I just have a few questions I hope you'll answer."

"Maybe I will. Maybe I won't. That's all for you to decipher."

"Why don't you tell me about the cottage."

"What's there to tell? A vestige, a mausoleum. There's nothing new there, only old." She rubbed her fingertip on the shiny surface of one of her cards.

He scratched his head. "Maybe today, but once it was quite a place, wasn't it?"

"Quite a place? Perhaps millions of years ago. Dinosaurs, the mesozoic, I believe." She picked up a card and held it up to her eye.

He smiled. "You're playing games with me."

"Life's a game, is it not?" She held the card closer and squinted.

"Perhaps. But I wasn't thinking quite back that far. I was thinking more in terms of the nineteen twenties."

She grunted a laugh through her teeth. "Grandfather."

"Pretty interesting fellow, wasn't he?"

"Master of the apparent, aren't you?" She rearranged her cards.

"I beg your pardon?"

"You like to scratch the surface." Her eyes ran up and down the cards, then suddenly she lifted her head and leered at him. "Perhaps if you *dug deeper, Mr. Swann.*" She raised an eyebrow and grinned through her yellowed teeth.

He squeezed the arms of his chair and sat up. "So you know about that?"

"Not I, the cards." She held up one of her decks. "How else can I misinform you?"

"You're doing just fine. But, if you know that she talked to me, then maybe you know who she was?"

"I most certainly do." She shuffled the deck and began placing the cards down again.

"So?"

"No. No. No. No. No." She shook her head, facing the window. "You're presuming I want you to succeed."

"Why wouldn't you?"

"Perhaps they need to learn something, a lesson needs to be taught."

"Your cousins?"

"Sixty-six years she's been gone. Outsmarted by the master. She'll be back." Xenobia turned toward him and winked.

"Who?"

"Shhhhh…" She nodded her head and placed a crooked ashen-gray finger over her lips.

"You won't tell me?"

"How smart." She whispered.

"Then what *will* you tell me?"

"Enough."

"Enough for what?"

"Enough to peel the skin, but not to penetrate the core."

"Can I ask you some more questions then?"

"Why not, perhaps I can confuse you."

"Okay." He flipped through his notes. "Let's talk about your grandfather. What do you remember about him?"

"The master's master. He got her good. Never saw it coming."

"Who?"

"You'll find out soon enough." She giggled.

"What else then? What else can you tell me about your grandfather?"

She sat there and smiled. "Deceptive man. Much below the surface. Yes, yes, indeed."

"Oh?"

"Bootlegger. Kept him going through the depression. No one ever knew."

"How interesting."

"He didn't love Newport. He loved the money. That wasn't a cottage, it was a warehouse."

"Why are you telling me this?"

"Because my imbecilic cousin, the mad fornicator, doesn't understand. Rests on false laurels. But he'll pay. Just wait." She shook her finger at him.

"So tell me more. How did it work?"

A quick toothy grin. "Why, the tunnel, of course."

"A tunnel to where?"

"From the seawall to the basement. Can't you keep up? Must I spell it out for you?"

"So he used the tunnel to sneak contraband into the basement?"

"Irish whiskey. Twice a month. Would send a skiff out in the black of night."

"It would meet a ship?"

She jabbed her finger in his direction. "Jesus, you're catching on, Mr. Swann. Would meet the ships five miles at sea."

"But how was the tunnel built?"

"Lobstermen."

"Who?"

"From New Bedford. Two scoundrels, always around. Did his dirty work for him."

"But I find it hard to believe no one knew."

She shook her head and clicked her tongue. "Deathly afraid, the cottage staff. Deathly afraid."

"I see. I see. Anything else I should know?"

"Worlds you should know. Chapters. Volumes. But if you fancy the waltz, don't expect me to lead."

Quickly, he shuffled through his notes. "Then perhaps I can ask you about someone else, an Amanda Pennfield?"

"Poor, poor, poor, poor Amanda." She shook her head, once more arranging the cards on the table. "Eleven times poor, maybe more. Sixteen Ninety-three. They didn't burn the witches back then. They pressed them to death, crushed their bones."

"She was a witch?"

"That's what *they* said."

"Why?"

"Can't say. She made me promise." She smiled.

"Okay, then, how about Peter Pennfield?"

A long droning squeak from outside interrupted him. He looked out onto the porch through one of the large windows over Xenobia's shoulder.

"Her nephew. Went down in a blaze of glory."

He looked back at her. "What do you mean?"

"You can still see the flames if you're blessed. Where the breakers meet the sandy elbow."

"You *are* trying to confuse me, aren't you?"

A gust of wind whistled in from a creak in the window, ruffling the old dusty drapes. The cat jumped off Xenobia's lap and scampered into the next room.

"Of course. That's what makes it fun, keeps me young." She smiled widely, exposing her yellowed, rotted teeth. "But they both knew her, knew her well."

"Knew who well?"

Again, he heard the same long, droning creak from outside on the porch.

"Her. We're covering old ground."

He shuffled through his notes. "How about Sarah Morton. What do you know about her?"   •

"Nineteen twenty-six or was it twenty-eight? Lived here for awhile, until she took ill." Xenobia giggled.

"Go on."

An amazing sight: through the window, against the golden twilight, he saw a woman. She was dressed all in black and walked slowly along the porch, as if in a trance.   ·

"Captivated by her, aren't you?" She nodded towards the porch.

"Perhaps, but go on. Tell me more."

His eyes followed the strange woman. She floated from window to window. At first, he thought there was something quite placid about her. But as he watched her slow, deliberate gait, he thought differently: something disturbed her, he was sure.

"The young girls, they sang a song afterwards."

"Oh, really?"

Xenobia turned away from him, ignoring the woman. She shuffled the cards. As she arranged them on the table, she began tapping her foot. Then, she sang, softly, never looking at Swann:

> *Sarah, Sarah, a sweet young lass,*
> *A sweet young lass was she.*
> *She fell in love with a clergy-mun,*
> *And then his fate was done.*

Her soft giggle grew into a loud, cackling laugh. Swann scribbled quickly, capturing her words, all the time following the slow, hypnotic walk of the woman in black. She passed to the next window, rounding the porch.

"So what does it mean? What are you trying to tell me, Mrs. Harthgate?" Swann asked, one eye on the porch.

"Told you enough already, maybe *she* can tell you more."

He followed the woman until she came to the last window. She stopped, looked inside, and smiled right at Swann: her face, soft and delicate; her skin, milky white, and her lips, full and red. He gasped. *The woman! The woman in his dream!* Before he could catch his breath, she vanished, shimmering away. Xenobia cackled.

The instant Swann returned to the cottage, he rushed up to the attic. He ripped open the trunk where he had found the note. He rummaged quickly again through its contents, searching for a picture of that woman. After this afternoon, her face was so engraved in his mind—her pure white skin, jet black hair, and full red lips—he would never forget it; he would be sure to recognize a picture of her. If he could find one, then he could possibly identify her, possibly understand why she was trying to contact him. And perhaps he could answer his most pressing question: *was it Sarah Morton, was she the mysterious woman he had seen in his dream and now on Xenobia's porch?* He spent over an hour scouring the contents of the trunk. Nothing. Then he looked up at the old wooden racks lining the attic wall. There were at least twenty boxes stacked one over another. Could the picture he was searching for be stowed away in one of them? He leapt up from the floor and pulled the nearest box off the rack. For the next six hours, he raced through the contents of each. He fell asleep on the attic floor at 2AM, still without his clue.

When the doors opened at the Newport Public Library the next morning, Swann stood waiting on the front steps. He rushed to the archives and pulled out several old weathered volumes of bound copies of the Newport Daily News. He figured even if the Pennfields had not included a picture of this woman among their keepsakes, perhaps somehow one had slipped into the public record. He sat down at a hard wooden desk and flipped forward anxiously. Nineteen twenty-six. Twenty-seven. Twenty-eight. A chronicle of the times. Tales of young, brave aviators daring to best each others' records. Lindbergh, Byrd, Chamberlain. Dempsey readying himself for Sharkey. Coolidge opting not to run. Bobby Jones and the British Open. Ruth and Gehrig. Sacco and Vanzetti. And scores of dignitaries visiting Newport during the summer social season. He studied every picture. Not one of his mysterious woman. Then, a bold headline stopped him. June 29, 1928.

REVEREND AND MRS. JENKINSON FOUND DEAD!—The
Reverend Walter Jenkinson and his wife, Elizabeth Cole Jenkinson, were found dead on the back grounds of Stone Villa early
Tuesday morning. Maynard Paige, a mulatto gardener, was the
first to find the bodies near a row of hedges on the southwest
corner of the grounds at about 7AM. According to Police Chief
Aloysius Ryan, the Reverend Jenkinson appeared to have been
stabbed several times in the chest while Mrs. Jenkinson had been
slit once across the wrist...

Swann's eyes ran up and down the column. Reverend Walter
Jenkinson. Young, stately, eloquent. Only three years in Newport
when he was suddenly found dead next to the body of his wife on
the grounds of Stone Villa. Interested, Swann flipped ahead—the
entire week, Newport's only paper overrun with stories of the Jenkinson tragedy. Wednesday. Thursday. Friday. And then Saturday.

JENKINSONS FUNERAL DRAWS THOUSANDS TO NEW-
PORT—The Reverend Walter Jenkinson and his wife, Elizabeth
Cole Jenkinson, were laid to their final resting places today in St.
Georges Cemetery after a two hour long service in Trinity
Church presided over by Bishop Charles Wilson of Boston. Benjamin Pennfield, the renowned financier and a close personal
friend of Jenkinson's, eulogized the minister as "...a God-faring
man taken from us in the prime of his life with so much more left
to offer the people of his congregation and this fair city." After
the service, Newport District Attorney James Dougherty assured
mourners that a thorough investigation was under way.

Swann's eyes wandered across the black and white photograph
beneath the headline. He studied the grainy picture over and over
again, holding it under the library's fluorescent lights. A team of
four black horses pulling the wagon. Two wooden coffins draped in
purple and black. Throngs of people pouring out of the church,
crowded around the funeral bier. Was his mysterious woman
among the mourners? Then, suddenly, an idea. He pulled an envelope out of his leather bag and emptied its contents on the table.
The note.

My dearest S,

I think of our moment together and my mind fills me with the same feelings I know you feel. Although these feelings can never manifest themselves in a concrete way, rest assured that your feelings have been shared and cherished.

With all my love,

W.

Slowly, Swann began to realize the significance of it. He repeated it to himself several times. *She fell in love with a clergy-man, and then his fate was done.* He sat up straight in his chair. Of course, of course, it had to be. Xenobia had given him a clue. That old lady—that strange old lady with the yellowed teeth, hardened face and cryptic comments, the black sheep of the Pennfield clan—had given him a clue: an honest-to-goodness clue! Of course, now it all fell into place: *Sarah Morton was the "S" and Walter Jenkinson was the "W," they had to be!*

14

"Yes, Sarah Morton lived in that house in Middletown, but only for a very short time. One or two years as far as I can remember." Ethel Martino lifted a white bone china teacup to her lips. "Another cup?"

"No, no. I'm fine, Mrs. Martino. Appreciate your time." Ed Swann answered, silently thanking the Good Lord—and one of Xenobia's neighbors—for helping him find such a cooperative witness.

"People were always saying things about her. She was a *very strange woman*, you know."

"Yes, I gather that from the little I've heard about her. How long did you live in that neighborhood?"

"Until I was fourteen. Then my family moved from Middletown up here to Wickford. Sarah moved into the big house on the corner in…well, it must've been 1929, give or take. That would've made me eight or nine at the time."

If he hadn't known the facts, Swann would have never guessed that Martino was in her early seventies. Her rich, abundant hair—dark streaked with gray—flowed from her crown, each strand falling into its natural place. Her smooth, well-conditioned skin had a slight suggestion of a healthy Mediterranean tinge. Her surroundings reflected her sense of care as well. On her hutch, the teacups and knick-knacks stood proudly in perfect arrangement. The glass face of the old clock glistened so that Swann could see his reflection in it. Everything, even the slightest details, seemed important to her, as if she was too preoccupied to allow time to wither away at her. So it came as no surprise to Swann that when he asked her about 1929, she spoke with the precision and authority of a well-seasoned schoolteacher, which is exactly what she had been for forty of her seventy-three years.

"Sarah Morton and her husband were very private people. Didn't mix at all with any of the neighbors. Actually, their moving in was a bit of a local scandal. Changed the complexion of the neighborhood. We were all working class people, living in our small two-bedroom houses. No plumbing then of course. Then…and I distinctly remember my parents talking about this…a Pennfield, Benjamin Pennfield's uncle we were told, is seen looking at a plot of land that used to be the McPherson's farm. Newporters, Pennfields even, moving into Middletown! Well, you can imagine the stir it caused. Turned out he was looking for a place for his daughter and her husband. Before we knew it, a whole army of construction workers were on the grounds. People were saying that they were rushing to put it up, money was no object. Never remember a place being put up that quickly. I think Sarah and her husband even moved in before it was completely finished. There were people still working on the house a good six months after they moved in."

"Can you tell me anything more about what she was like?" Swann asked.

"As I said," Martino sipped from her cup, "they pretty much kept to themselves. But everyone said there was something wrong with her. Something the Pennfields were trying to hide. The only times I really saw her was when she was walking around the grounds. She did that quite often, actually. She always appeared disturbed, depressed. I remember we used to hide behind the hedges and watch her. It would be fair to say she scared us, scared us pretty good. She always dressed in black. She walked around the grounds, and back and forth on that long porch, as if she was preoccupied, like she wasn't all there. Just back and forth. Back and forth all day sometimes. Rumor had it, of course, that she had been involved with the Reverend Jenkinson. You've heard about the Jenkinson murders, haven't you? Probably the biggest scandal on Aquidnick Island for the first half of this century."

Swann nodded. "Yes, I've read up on it a bit."

She sipped again. "Well, of course, some even speculated that she may have been the murderer."

"Did you believe that?"

She smiled. "At that age, you don't know what to believe. Even if she was, the Pennfields would have covered it up. They were very powerful back then, you know. Benjamin Pennfield practically <u>ran</u> the City of Newport. All I can remember was that after a year or so of living in that house, Sarah Morton wasn't there anymore. Left just as quickly as she came. Some people said she had been sent to an institution, but nobody really knew for sure. Her husband stayed there by himself for awhile. But, eventually, he moved out too, and the house was turned over to someone else in the Pennfield family, a cousin I think…"

*   *   *

The cold wind whistled between the iron spokes. The moon's orange light glowed through the dark flapping branches. Two bright beams peaked over the hill on the lonely country road—a gasping engine choking on cold, heavy air. The old van ca-chunged to a halt, interrupting the night's lonely stillness. Swann stepped slowly out, puffing frosty breaths, a flashlight in his hand. A sign. St. George's Cemetery.

He walked along the perimeter of the fence, searching for an entrance to this plot of odd-shaped monuments. He wondered why he was here. What compelled him to drive across the island to an out-of-the-way country graveyard at eleven o'clock at night? Surely, it was Sarah. Somehow, she had chosen him. From wherever she was, she had made him her mouthpiece, her connection to the world of the living, he was sure of it. After all, *he had seen her, hadn't he?* That woman in black conjured up during the session with Xenobia fit Mrs. Martino's description, fit it to a tee. *And she had talked to him, hadn't she?* The more Swann learned about Sarah, the more he was sure it was not a dream episode that first night. Nor a coincidence. It was her, Sarah, making a psychic connection to him, Ed Swann, asking him to dig deeper, to solve the puzzle for her. To bring out some deeply hidden truths about her and the Jenkinson murders. And somehow her psychic bond with him, her telepathic link from beyond the grave, had told him to come here at this very moment in time.

His flashlight led him to a small gate. He reached for the latch and lifted. A muffled symphony of chirping crickets drew a breath as the gate creaked open. Swann panned the cemetery with his flashlight. An acre's worth of monuments. Slowly, he weaved himself through the uneven rows, flashing his light on the names. Jacob Rathwood, 1888–1936. Matthew Goode, 1848–1917. Harold Bathley, 1835–1892.

Swann stopped, curled his lips, and looked around again. At least a hundred more, possibly two hundred. Brown stone-like bumpy ones sprouting from the earth. Smooth marble ones, decorative figures chiseled into their grainy faces. Flat gray ones, almost afterthoughts, grass growing over their edges. He slowly twirled around, looking at them all again. *Why did you send me here, Sarah? Tell me. Tell me now.* He stepped back towards the gate.

As he turned, he felt a strange twinge on the back of his neck. *Sarah, is that you? Is that your finger resting on my neck?* Now, a buzzing. He turned around cautiously, readying himself to see an ashen white figure of Sarah Morton standing behind him. He gasped. But nothing. Then, a tingling ran down his spine. He attempted to take another step, but his foot wouldn't move. Again, he tried. No movement. He pushed forward with his arms. *Whomp!* A sheet of cold, dense air. Like punching hard rubber. He tried again, making a fist. *Stopped!* By the same invisible force. He turned back, faced the monuments. *It was her, had to be! Invisible, but she was there, boxing him in, not allowing him to leave.* A pause, a moment's relaxation. And then a burst, some glow, pulling him ahead. A vacuum sucking him forward, his legs, like jelly, stumbling over the ground, weaving between monuments. He surged forward, unsure of where he was going, but following some deep, magnetic force pulling him onward.

He stopped under an old crooked tree, an odd-shaped, discolored knot in its side, its twisted branches, devoid of leaves, grasping out over the old, weathered stones. He took a breath and relaxed. The surging force gone, his backbone free of its electric tingle. Yet, directionless. No buzzing force pulling him onward. No clues of where to go from here. He bounced his light from marker to marker. Archer McDonald. Eudora Blake. Rupert Summers. Abigail Stone.

He looked up through the maze of black twisted branches, the orange face of a crusty moon casting a misty glow. A gust of wind breezed by his face, pushing scattered pieces of refuse across the cold, damp turf. A crumpled piece of paper skipped along towards him and grazed his shoes. He shined his light at his feet. *Stone! He was standing on stone!* A large flat stone resting comfortably beneath the tree. He fumbled with his light, looked down and gasped. A cemetery plot. *Rev. Walter Jenkinson, 1890–1928.*

His body shook, the tingling so strong it rattled his bones. He stood just six feet above the remains of the man whose murder must have—*had to have*—played a major role in the Pennfield's problems. *And she, Sarah, had sent him here. Sent him here by some unexplainable psychic connection, by encouraging him to follow his instincts, by actually guiding those instincts!*

He struggled to fall asleep that night. He tossed and turned and fluffed his pillow countless times, yet his mind refused to allow him rest, refused to surrender control of his tingling flesh. Instead, thoughts of Sarah, thoughts of that desolate graveyard, of him being compelled by some outside force to find the marker of Walter Jenkinson, rustled his nerves. As he fluffed his pillow for the umpteenth time and readied himself to turn over yet once again, he suddenly realized it. His heart sank. Of course, the message. The message Sarah was trying to convey to him. Of course, how could he have missed it: *Where was Mrs. Jenkinson?*

It was documented in black and white. He had practically committed the exact words to memory. July 3, 1928. *The Reverend Walter Jenkinson and his wife, Elizabeth, were laid to their final resting places today in St. George's Cemetery after a two-hour long service in Trinity Church.* So why wasn't she there?

The next morning, he drove slowly by the spiked iron fence of St. George's cemetery once again. So different by the light of day. The trees, their twisted branches so threatening against the night's dark sky and the moon's somber tones, reached engagingly up towards the refreshing light of the sun. The stone markers, forbidding in the darkness, now bathed by the sun's tranquil beams. He drove by twice and then parked alongside the fence, gazing across the markers for what seemed like hours. He laughed at himself. To think the night's darkness could trick him into—*scare him into*—believing his own intuition was really the hand of Sarah reaching out from beyond the grave. The blatant egotism—to think she would have chosen <u>him</u>! With the sun's bright rays came a powerful sobriety. But, still, the question perplexed him: *Where was Mrs. Jenkinson?*

That afternoon he again found himself at the library, flipping through The Newport Daily News, looking for answers. 1928. September. October. November. Nothing, until…

DOUGHTERY CLAIMS MRS. JENKINSON MURDERER. CASE CLOSED.—Newport District Attorney James Dougherty announced today that after an extensive investigation his office has concluded that Mrs. Elizabeth Jenkinson murdered her husband and then committed suicide on the grounds of Stone Villa last June 28. Dougherty claimed that over sixty witnesses and suspects were interrogated, including leading suspect gardener Maynard Paige, and no alternate explanation proved plausible enough to warrant further investigation. Despite his office's conclusion, Doughtery stated that no logical motive for Mrs. Jenkinson's act had been uncovered.

Fine, but no explanation of why Mrs. Jenkinson's name did not appear on the marker. Swann continued to flip forward, hoping that while the official investigation had ceased, public interest in the case would still warrant coverage. Less than ten issues later, he found the Jenkinson scandal again in the paper's headline.

MEMBERS OF TRINITY CONGREGATION DEMAND MRS. JENKINSON'S REMAINS BE REMOVED FROM TOMB—A group of congregation members from Trinity Church led by Mrs. Rudolph Swain met with Reverend John Martin today to discuss the removal of Mrs. Elizabeth Jenkinson's remains from the same tomb containing the remains of her husband, Reverend Walter Jenkinson. The group claimed it would be a travesty for the remains of his murderer to be entombed next to the body of so devoted a spiritual leader as Reverend Jenkinson. Reverend Martin, Jenkinson's replacement, promised the group that their request would be seriously considered...

The issue divided Newport down the middle, appearing sporadically in the headlines for the next several months. Indeed, Swann found it a rare occurrence for more than a week to go by without at least a small piece on the Jenkinson controversy occupying space in the columns of the paper. He read everything. For every Newporter supporting the views of Mrs. Swain and her group, there was another not accepting the conclusion of DA Dougherty's investigation or feeling it was best to leave well enough alone. Swann became so entwined with the controversy, he found his own position wavering as the ebb and flow of public opinion changed. It all ended in February of 1929 with one final lead article in the Daily News.

MRS. JENKINSON REMOVED FROM TOMB—The remains of Mrs. Elizabeth Jenkinson were removed from the tomb they had shared with the remains of Reverend Walter Jenkinson today after almost five months of controversy that touched nearly every Newporter. Reverend John Martin told the Newport Daily News the decision was made only after it became apparent that "threats that some might take the matter into their own hands" should be taken seriously. According to Martin, the remains were removed quietly during the night and turned over to Jenkinson family friend Benjamin Pennfield. When asked where the remains would be interred, Pennfield would not comment only to say that Mrs. Jenkinson's remains would be given a "proper Christian resting place."

That was it, the last public word on the Jenkinson tragedy. Swann carefully flipped through another year's worth of newspapers but could find nothing else; like many other tragedies that grabbed the public's attention and seemed to occupy the forefront of their daily lives for a short period of days, weeks and months, over time the Jenkinson tragedy slipped into the background and attenuated into a mere footnote to the city's history.

*   *   *

A dark, cold night. Swann's blue van rambled slowly down Bellevue Avenue, proceeding north towards Memorial. On both sides, mansions, relics of Newport's gilded age—Belcourt Castle, The Marble House, Beechwood, Rosecliff. They stood stately in the night, their ornate facades yawning, never suspecting that time had passed them by. Branches flapped to a southerly breeze. A crescent moon and an occasional street lamp lighted the way. Then, as he moved closer to Memorial Boulevard, the mansions ended. Commercial phosphorescence. A video store. A ski shop. Vicker's Liquors. The shingled, turreted Newport Casino, The Tennis Hall of Fame. He stepped on the brake a half block short of Memorial, the rear lights casting red streaks on the street behind him. He looked over to his left.

A large black parking lot. Empty. Paving its way towards a long, flat strip mall. Glass and cement. An Almac's supermarket. A CVS drug store. A laundromat, the Newport Creamery, a gift shop, an appliance store. At the far left, a women's clothing store. The muffled rumblings from the engine echoed across the large, vacant space. The light from the street dimmed into darkness as the van moved closer in. Nautical odors from the wharf three blocks below scented the midnight air.

He parked the van at the far edge of the lot, across from the clothing store and next to a narrow lane separating the mall from the grounds of the large residence next door. The parking brake creaked as Swann pulled it towards him. Then he jumped from the van, galloped to its rear, and pulled out three folding tripods and a crate full of cables.

After unspooling some cable, he jumped back into the van and connected one end to his computer set up in the rear compartment. Then he connected the cable's other end to a tripod he had placed on the walkway abutting the store's large window. A female mannequin attired in a black velvet evening gown watched over him, the dim security lamp below casting a macabre glow on its molded face. He methodically placed the rest of the equipment around the perimeter just as he had done in the cottage's master bedroom. When his task was complete, he rested and slowly studied his surroundings. So this is it? he thought. The scene of the crime. The site where Stone Villa once stood.

He sat in the driver's seat all night and waited. He was looking for anything, even the smallest sign. A slight change in temperature. An aberrant reading from the Geiger counter. An unexplained exposure on his infra-red film. Even a stream of statistically unexplainable numbers spouting from his random number generator. All it would take was patience and a little luck.

He repeated the procedure for each of the next four nights, occupying the time by counting the number of cars turning from Memorial onto Bellvue, listening to an all-talk radio station from Chicago, and doing the New York Times crossword puzzle. He would leave each morning at 5AM when the large dairy truck pulled up to the supermarket at the far end of the lot. He wondered what the driver thought—being greeted each morning by the sight of a seventy year old man sitting in a van surrounded by tripods, cables, and odd-shaped boxes.

Statistically, he knew he was asking for a miracle. Although, he was sure the psychic imprints of that evening from June 28, 1928 were somehow permanently etched into the very fabric of this plot of land, he was equally certain that the odds of finding a physical sign of them on one of those five evenings was akin to searching for the proverbial needle in a haystack. Too many unknowns entered into the equation. Perhaps, though, he could do something to tip the odds in his favor.

"Mr. Swann, now you *have* gone off your rocker!" Christopher glared at him from across the parlor. "To ask us to do what you're suggesting is utterly absurd!"

Swann sat calmly, gulped from a mug of coffee, and answered: "You brought me here to do a job, Chris. And I'm telling you I have every reason to believe that the Jenkinson murders are somehow related to the hauntings in this house. If you want me to solve this thing, I'll need your cooperation."

"But the whole idea is an effront to every Pennfield who ever lived. To think you have the gall to accuse some obscure cousin of my grandfather's of an act of murder on nothing but circumstantial evidence over sixty years after the fact is a perversion of justice, indeed!"

"I'm not saying she did it. I'm saying she *may* have done it. And if she did, it may give us a very logical explanation for many of the things that have been happening here."

"Jonathan?" Christopher looked across the parlor at his brother.

Jonathan paused, considered the consequences, and then answered: "He builds a logical case, Chris. What he's saying is certainly not implausible. I can't see how it would hurt to pursue his idea. Maybe it would help us, add some insight to this thing. After all, we're here. Why not?"

"Jesus Christ, Jonathan, I can't believe you're agreeing with him!"

"Listen," Swann said. "It may be a long shot, but it's worth a try. I have very reason to believe that you have some sort of psychic gift, Chris. That your entire family has a psychic gift. And there's a theory—more like speculation actually—that says a gifted person like yourself in what we students of the paranormal call a sensitized state—like you were in the bedroom those nights when you felt paralyzed—can actually *induce* an apparition, help conjure up whatever psychic activity is already in the area. If we can somehow see an apparition of the events of that evening, it will confirm to us whether or not Sarah was the murderer."

15

Newport, Rhode Island
June 28, 1928

Reverend Walter Jenkinson grazed his hand against the low stone wall, walking slowly in the night. His mind churned over what he might do to free himself from his dilemma. If he were to do as Betty suggested and walk with her onto the grounds of Stone Villa, he would be walking into his own downfall. Sarah Morton would be there waiting and, for all intents and purposes, his marriage—and his career—would be over. He slowed his pace, hoping that Betty would follow. But, no, her pace quickened, her shoes tapping briskly on the sidewalk.

Jenkinson cleared his throat. "A bit chilly. Wouldn't you say, Betty?"

Betty stopped, looked upward, and sniffed the air. "No, I have to say I don't feel a chill at all, Walter."

Jenkinson winced. "Well, perhaps, it's me. Perhaps a fever's coming on. Maybe we should turn around and walk back. Wouldn't want to make it worse…"

She looked back. "Oh, don't be silly, Walter. If anything, this evening's clear, balmy air will soothe it. That is, if you have a fever at all, Walter." She smiled at him.

Jenkinson looked ahead. The wall ended no more than fifty or sixty paces ahead of them, marking the entrance to Stone Villa. He had only a minute—two minutes at most—to figure something out. But why was Betty acting so strangely, so out of character?

"A beautiful night for a stroll on the grounds of Stone Villa, wouldn't you say, Walter." Betty's voice was affected, different than usual. Jenkinson was sure something was going on beneath the surface of her calm tones, sure that she was taunting him. "I've always loved the way the moonlight glows through the hedges. Almost magic, wouldn't you say, Walter? I just love it."

No, she didn't! She had hardly been on the grounds of Stone Villa. And only a casual acquaintance, at best, of the Parkers. He looked ahead. No more than ten paces to the entrance. He gulped. Once they made that right turn onto the grounds, his fate would be out of his hands.

"Yes, you are *so* right, Betty." He stopped, hoping that she would as well.

She obliged, turning to face him. But, she was different. The hard, straight lines in her cheeks and the venom in her eyes suggested a woman intent on vindication.

"Perhaps we should postpone the moment and return at a time when we can fully appreciate the wonderments of the evening. Perhaps on Friday evening we can return and spend several hours here." He strained to mask the quiver in his voice. "I do understand they expect the pleasant weather to hold through the week."

"Don't be silly." She laughed. "You talk as if you are trying to avoid something, Walter." She stopped again, her eyes boring into him, and grabbed his arm. "Come on, we're here. Why turn back now?" She pulled him forward, dragging him the last several steps.

He clenched his teeth. *Why was she so determined, damnit!* For years, she had been an obedient consort, bound by his every word. But now, what had empowered her to be so insistent upon venturing out to Stone Villa? Within seconds, they would make the turn. And within seconds, Sarah Morton would be standing there, primed for their secret rendezvous.

Swann's blue van sat quietly in the night, surrounded by a configuration of tripods, boxes and cables. A light breeze swirled around, brushing the treetops and kicking up debris across the large black parking lot where once stood the great Newport mansion, Stone Villa. A wispy fog rolled through the mall, misting the long glass windows. The moon—a diffuse silver disturbance in the dark misty sky—cast an anxious glow.

"What now? What now?" Christopher grumbled from the back of the van.

Swann pointed to a large rubber air mattress stretched out across the van's rear compartment. "I want you to lay down right there. All you have to do is fall asleep for us."

Christopher looked at the mattress and scowled. "What in the name of…"

"Chris, just go along with it, will you?" Jonathan chided him.

"We're going to make it easy for you," Swann said as he pulled a small Walkman out of his bag and placed the headset over Christopher's ears. "Recorded sounds of the ocean, just like a seashell. Should put you right out."

"What's next?" Christopher asked, still sitting up on the mattress. "Are you going to put a mask over my eyes?"

"No, just these." Swann pulled two half ping pong balls out of the bag. "When we place them over your eyes, they'll create a bland sensory environment. It'll help us induce what we call a Ganzfeld state."

"Jesus Christ!"

"Now let me just hook up a few sensors and we'll be ready to begin." Swann dabbed jelly on Christopher's temples and wrists.

"And what is this for, Mr. Swann!"

"Just some harmless measures. Pulse, skin resistance, brainwaves. Simple stuff."

"But, but—

"Now just lay down and relax."

They were there, Stone Villa. Reverend Jenkinson followed his wife onto the mansion's entranceway, a winding cobblestone path. He cringed and squeezed his eyes shut. As they made the turn, he was sure Sarah Morton would be there waiting. But nothing. With trepidation, he followed. The path curved to the left, leading them around a cul de sac before the house's large doorway. Stillness. Silence. No lights in the windows. No sound from the rooms. Betty passed right by without looking, following the path towards the mansion's back lawns. The dense foliage created a canopy over them, the tree's leafy branches reaching across towards the building's stone walls.

The long dark, canopied pathway confounded Jenkinson's instincts. Darkness was now his refuge, his safe haven. As long as the pathway's dense foliage shielded him and Betty from the moon's silver light, he sensed there would be no Sarah Morton, no confrontation with his fate. Only God knew what lay ahead once they ventured outside this veil of darkness, once they stepped foot onto the mansion's long sweeping back lawns and gardens unshielded from the moon's illuminating rays. He moved slowly, Betty's brisk pace lengthening the distance between them. At the end of the pathway, Betty stood waiting, impatient. Beyond her silhouetted figure, the moon's evening light shimmered off the lawn's swaying grass just as the sun's morning light glistened off a tranquil sea.

Swann pored over the computer screen in the cramped van. Christopher lay flat behind him, motionless on the rubber mattress, his prone torso almost touching the legs of Swann's small stool. Jonathan sat up front, wedged between the dashboard and seats, pushed all the way forward. With his computer, printer, cables and other paraphernalia crunched in around him, Swann was so cramped his face was practically flush against the screen. The sterile green glow from the precise figures on the display wreaked havoc with his eyeballs.

"What's happening?" Jonathan turned back towards Swann.

"He's out. Deep sleep." Swann whispered without turning his head.

"So what's next?"

"Keep your fingers crossed." Swann forced his eyes to focus on the readouts. "As he comes out of it, he may reach a sensitized state."

Within minutes, Swann began to feel it, a subtle shaking of the van's metal floor. Quickly, the shaking intensified, the entire van rattling as if it were bouncing on a bumpy road. Yet, there was no forward movement—the van's wheels locked stationary in the same spot on the mall's long, empty lot. Then, more pronounced shaking; the entire vehicle bounced up and down on its rubbery shocks.

"What's happening?" Jonathan stood up over his seat, facing back.

"Something." Swann hunched over his screen, his eyes locked on the read-outs. "Temperature's down. Geiger counter's ticking."

"What? Where?"

"Something. Something out near the back."

Jonathan grabbed for the handle and rolled down the window. He shot his head out and looked back.

A slow, dense rolling fog. His eyes froze on the wisps of fog dancing to the whims of the nighttime breeze. Criss-crossing themselves, wrapping into figure eights, overlapping and melding, combining and separating. A maze of cloudy wisps, so thick Bellvue Avenue was lost in their random minglings. Only a feint glow from the street lamp in the distance. The van shook, rocking up and down. Jonathan's hands clutched the window's frame, steadying himself as he looked into the mist.

In the distance, under the street lamp's diffuse glow, a deep, dense cloud. Thin wisps collecting together, drawn to its center. *Vrrrrooooooom!* The ground shook. Jonathan clenched his teeth. Within the dense cloud, a shimmer. He blinked and looked again. The shimmer vibrated into a shape. Or was it? Perhaps. Or maybe just his mind playing tricks. He stared, refusing to blink. Yes. Yes, a shape. No, two shapes. Moving forward. Out of the cloud towards the van. And then mumblings. He heard mumblings. And footsteps. Growing louder, closer. He looked hard, focusing so intently a sharp pain pierced his temples. His eyes widened. The shapes—

the two figures—became sharp, distinct. A woman, a shawl wrapped around her shoulders, extending her arms outward and turning around. Followed by a man, walking slowly, hardly moving.

"Ed, Ed. C'mere, look…"

"A beautiful night, isn't it, Walter?" Betty reached out with her hands, drinking in the night's fresh air, her knit shawl extending out like a set of wings. She turned, making a half-pirouette, dancing on the bristling grass of the wide, expansive lawn.

Jenkinson stood motionless at the end of the pathway, still shielded by the shadow of the foliage's dense canopy. He trembled. "Yes. Yes, indeed, Betty."

"Come on. Come out, Walter. Enjoy the night." She ran over to her husband and grabbed his arm, pulling him out onto the lawn.

He stiffened, resisting her pull. "But, but, it's practically bedtime. We should be going."

"Oh, phooey." She tugged again.

The force of her tug lurched him ahead. He tripped forward, regaining his balance. He shuddered. "Jesus, Betty!" He quickly looked around, jerking his head in all possible directions. Still, no Sarah. But was she hiding somewhere? Behind the trunk of the large tree ahead of them, within the clumps of bushes to their side, in the garden's hedges far in back?

Swann wedged himself into the van's front compartment, leaning over behind Jonathan. He blinked. Once. Twice. Two figures. Two figures, he was sure, shimmering out of the fog near the rear of the van. A woman pulled a man forward. But the man was reluctant, as if he was determined to stay behind some imaginary line, as if something was shielding him. But, nothing. No physical objects in the area other than the wispy fog, his ghost-hunting paraphernalia, and the large black lot.

Finally, the man cooperated. He walked forward, the woman tugging on his arm. His feet moved slowly in small, considered steps. The woman, lively and animated, pulled him onward. But, in front of them, an impediment. A tripod, one of Swann's infra-red cameras mounted on top. The woman yanked on the man's arm and marched forward, walking right through the tripod's wooden legs, unaffected, as if nothing were there, dragging the man behind her.

For Jenkinson, each step brought with it the fear that Sarah Morton would lurch forward from her hiding place and attack him by her mere presence. But from where would she come? From the right? The left? In front of him? Behind him? The fear—real or imagined—tortured him so, stiffening his muscles. He looked forward. A large tree, its trunk surrounded by several small clumps of bushes. *That was it, he was sure!* Sarah was there. He knew it, he *felt* it. Was that her, rustling the bushes? Or was it just the wind?

"Oh, Walter, what bothers you now?" Betty stopped and turned around.

He wringed his hands together as he searched for an answer. Then, as he ran his fingers up his wrist, he felt it. A cufflink, an idea. "I seem to be missing a cufflink, Betty. Perhaps I lost it in the grass behind us." He turned back and crouched over, his hand raking through the grass.

"What makes you think you lost it here, Walter? Perhaps if you came back in the morning, in the sunlight—"

"Just allow me a moment, Betty. One moment, please." Squatting down on the balls of his feet, he ran his fingers through the grass. When he was sure Betty couldn't see, he removed his cufflink and threw it down.

"But, Walter, we didn't even walk where you're looking!"

He ignored her, moving ahead in his awkward squat. He batted the cufflink forward, hoping he could think of a reason to convince Betty they should leave before Sarah jumped out from behind the tree.

The actions of the shadowy figures confused Swann and Jonathan. The man pulled back from the woman, faced the back of the van, and crouched over, rubbing his fingers across the lot's black tar. It looked as if the figures were speaking to each other, but in the van all they could hear were distorted mumbles. The man moved closer to the van, right up to its edge, and leaned forward reaching with his hand into its side—

A glimmer, a spot of white light. Jonathan caught it in the corner of his eye. *"Shit!"* A shimmering spot of white light on the van's inside wall. Then three more shimmering spots next to it, a row. Extruding inward, like three wiggly worms, piercing through the metal wall. Now, a thumb, a palm. A disembodied white hand, squirming around, dusting the van's cold floor with its fingertips. Grayish, cold. Wiggling fingers, reaching around, grasping at invisible straws, its lower sleeve, cuff undone, dipping beneath the van's floor, right near where Christopher slept on the rubber mattress. Jonathan tapped Swann's shoulder and pointed. Swann turned and gasped. *"God!"* A large white tarantula, its tentacles attached to a human wrist, wiggling nervously around its strange environs.

Jonathan looked up. On the van's wall, another larger spot of light, egg-shaped. From out of nowhere, shimmering just like the others. But, different, textured, in bushy flocks. As the wiggling fingers grasped blindly around the floor and then submerged beneath it, the dim light of the larger spot summoned their eyes. Growing, it moved inward. Hair, a flock of bushy hair! A weathered brow, a nose, ears, a mouth, a chin—*an entire head, corpse-white!*—sliced through the wall, unimpeded. It's slow, deliberate motions, pre-planned, etched into eternity years ago. Yet, somehow, it knew, *it knew!* It knew they were there, watching. The head turned, rotating slowly on its neck, towards the front, towards Jonathan and Swann. The white, translucent face of a desperate, nervous man—a grayish tone of death to its skin—looked right at them, staring them down, its eyes glistening at them. And then its thin, quivering lips opened into a fearsome smile.

"Come back, Walter! Come back right now!" Betty summoned her husband, waiting for him near the large tree.

He jerked out of his crouch. "But, Betty. My cufflink, I'm sure it's here."

"How can you be so sure you lost it here? You could've lost it anywhere."

"But, but—

She ran over and grabbed his hand, pulling him onward, back towards the tree. He tried with all his mental faculties to come up with an excuse. But, she was too quick, grabbing him away before he could think of anything else.

In a quick jolt, the shadowy head yanked itself out of the van. Swann and Jonathan shuddered in their seats, shaking their heads as the gray, shimmery light passed back through the van's wall. Then, suddenly, Jonathan jerked his head back to the rear, almost having forgotten about his brother. Christopher lay still on the rubber air mattress. His body, limp and helpless; his covered eyes filled with an uneventful pattern of gray sameness. The van quiet except for the rumbled shakings and an occasional clipped comment from Jonathan or Swann. Caught in a fuzzy state between sleep and wake, Christopher strained to listen. All he could tell was that *something* was happening.

"Oh, Walter, would you please relax." She pulled him onward. Docile, Jenkinson offered no resistance. He had resigned himself to his fate. "Mother warned me that a man of the Lord would be plagued by needless worry tending to the needs of his flock." She stopped and looked him right in the eyes, a wicked smile. "Or is it something else that plagues you, Walter?"

Jenkinson took a long, slow gulp. She knew. From the tone in her voice, the gleam in her eye, that *damned wicked smile,* he could tell. She knew. She knew everything! *But how?* How in God's name? He—no, they—had been so careful, so discreet. He stopped short. Of course: *Sarah had told her!* Yes, that was it. That was the only way she could know. In her instability, Sarah had told her. It was all planned. Sarah and Betty were conspiring against him. They would teach him a lesson. He took a breath and relaxed. He had been beaten, outwitted, lulled into this trap by two women! His mistress and his wife. He sighed. There was nothing he could do. He would follow her, be a man, take his dose of medicine, and live with the consequences. He looked forward. The tree grew in size with each step. Somewhere by it—behind its large trunk, within the surrounding foliage, hidden by its dark shadow—stood Sarah Pennfield Morton. He was walking directly into his fate. He winced, shutting his eyes.

"Evening, Reverend Jenkinson. Mrs. Jenkinson."

He heard it just as he expected, from behind the tree. But it wasn't the voice of Sarah. *It was the deep, raspy voice of a man!* He opened his eyes. Nothing. But, he was sure he heard it, sure of it! He turned his head towards Betty. A gasp, her face white. Scared, truly scared. But something was wrong. If she was part of this, a conspirator, why was she shivering so?

"I wouldn't worry if I were the two of you." A large gloved hand grasped at them. Then, a rumpled burlap sack—eyeholes cut into it—poked out from behind the tree. Underneath, the broad shoulders of a tall burly man, dressed in tattered coveralls. Behind him, another man, an equally rumpled burlap sack covering his head, shoulders, and upper torso. Betty and Walter shuddered; an eerie shock, a jolt to their senses. Two big muscular men, burlap sacks over their heads, jagged holes for eyes, beneath the lonely tree.

"Yep, nothing to worry about, nothing at all." The second one said calmly. "We just have a little message for you."

From behind his back, the man raised his gloved hand over his head. A sharp knife glistened in the moon's soft light. In a swift jerk, his arm whipped down towards Jenkinson's chest. For Jenkinson, time stood still; his eyes followed the knife millisecond by millisecond. By the time its finely-honed blade ripped through his rib cage and slivered his heart, he was well prepared to absorb it, his chest a soft pillow.

Swann watched it all through the windshield, his chin resting on his palm. Everything as he would expect, the phantom man and woman walking together in the lot, approaching the exact spot, right in front of the clothing store. *But, wait a minute, something was wrong!* Two large, broad-shouldered figures, sacks over their heads—like klansman of old—emerged from out of nowhere. Swann's eyes bulged from his face. One of the figures raised its arm and thrust a knife into the first man's chest. The man staggered in awkward, spastic movements, and then fell to the ground. *No, no!* Swann shook his head and leaned forward on the dash. *That's not the way it's supposed to be! What's going on here?* The woman shrieked, but the other hooded man quickly grabbed her, covering her mouth with his large, gloved hand and enwrapping his wide arms around her chest. She kicked desperately with her feet, watching as the other hooded man stood over his victim, waiting for his last gasp of life. He leaned over and sloppily pulled the knife out of his victim's chest. He carried it over to the woman and, as his partner held her, he gently slit her wrist.

16

Christopher Pennfield wondered how Renoir would have captured the moment. The country peasant girl sitting naked on the edge of the plain bed in the spartan room. A ray of light from the window in the background bathing her in silhouette. Her long blonde hair tossed carelessly around her shoulders and down her back. The three-quarter view of her firm rounded breast, its nipple protruding towards the window. And what was going on inside—*God!*—only a true master could bring it out.

Jennifer sat there, nonplussed, her arms wrapped around her knee; her smooth, taut skin glimmered in the hazy light. Pennfield sat across from her at her dorm room desk, his boxers tangled half-way up his thighs. He wiped a fine mist of sweat from his brow, his hand continuing upward raking through his hair. He yearned for a cigarette.

As he sat there gazing at her, he could kick himself for foregoing last weekend. If he hadn't been in Newport at the insistence of his brother and Mr. Swann, he could have spent almost two full days with his young mistress. As he knew all too well, timing was every-thing. His relationship with Jennifer was reaching its apex. He might never be able to recapture what they might have had the past weekend. *Damn!*

There were two minor consolations, though. Firstly, a serendipitous moment like this in a dorm room on a Monday afternoon aroused his erotic instincts in a way that the planned spontaneity of a weekend could never surpass. And, secondly, the time in Newport was certainly not a waste: although he considered Swann's methods pseudo-science at best, they had at least concluded that Sarah Morton was not the murderer of the Reverend and Mrs. Jenkinson. The Pennfield name remained unblemished.

He turned to face Jennifer, concentrating again on the here and now. "I hope you'll think hard about it before you make a final decision."

"But I've already thought a lot about it," she said.

"Granted, it's easy for someone at your stage in life to be seduced by the allures of the big city. But, believe me—and I speak from experience on this, I've seen many students pass through this campus—you only go to college once. And the opportunity to spend the summer on campus as my research assistant is one other students would envy, I assure you."

"But the chance to spend the summer as an intern at an ad agency—

"A great opportunity, indeed. But, there's always next summer. And you'll probably spend the rest of your life in a big city working for an ad agency. Believe me, ten years from now you'll regret it."

"I'm just not sure." She looked in his eyes.

"Well, consider time your ally. I'm sure sound judgment will prevail."

She smirked. "My brother-in-law will kill me if I turn down the offer. I mean, after all he's done for me…"

"If you explain it to him carefully, I'm sure he'll understand."

She stepped over towards Pennfield and sat in his lap, wrapping her arm around his bare back. She tickled his ear with her tongue and then whispered into it. "I have a surprise for you."

He grinned. "And what might that be?"

"Remember when you asked me to find something about that man in New Jersey, the ghost hunter?"

"Yes?"

"I've done a lot of looking around. Made umpteen phone calls, spent hours at the computer…"

"The anticipation is killing me, Jennifer."

"Well, yesterday, I finally found something." She swiveled around on his lap, stood up, and walked over to her dresser. Blood rushed through Pennfield's veins as his eyes followed her lithe naked figure across the room. She leaned over, pulled out a yellow manila folder, and handed it to him. "Here. Pretty interesting stuff."

*   *   *

This time, Swann pushed open the old door with authority, not even bothering to knock. A quick high-pitched creak echoed up the stairway. He looked to his left. Bright afternoon light swept through the bay windows into the parlor. Blinded, Swann covered his eyes and then peeked through his fingers looking for her. Her dark, black silhouette eclipsed the bright light from the porch. He squinted and stepped forward.

"So you've returned." Xenobia said, petting her cat.

"Couldn't have finished my job without seeing you again." He answered.

"You flatter yourself."

"Me?" He pointed to his chest.

"Your job will never be finished, Mr. Swann. You're dealing with an unsolvable riddle. You're not the one. You'll be undermined before you know it." She grinned and pet her cat.

"So that was Sarah Morton I saw on your porch last time."

"How perceptive. I practically handed you the answer."

"She moved here after the Reverend and Mrs. Jenkinson were killed, until her depression required that she be institutionalized."

"Here. Here. You do your homework well." She giggled.

"Why do you laugh?"

"You think you have the answer."

"What, that it was the two lobstermen who killed Reverend Jenkinson and his wife?"

She sat straight up in her chair. Her old brittle fingers tightened their grip on her cat. She grit her old yellowed teeth. "And what would make you think that?"

"Your grandfather, Benjamin Pennfield, paid the two lobstermen to kill the Reverend and Mrs. Jenkinson, didn't he?"

Silently, she looked at him. Her face turned sour. "Perhaps some people were spreading that rumor." She mumbled.

"But there's more, isn't there?"

"I'm not here to do your job, Mr. Swann. Find it yourself, if you dare."

"I wouldn't suggest otherwise. Only need your help confirming a few basic facts. But they wanted more, didn't they?"

"Who?"

"The lobstermen. After the murders, they tried to shake down your grandfather for a bigger payoff, right?"

She sat there silent, pursing her lips. The distinct, dark lines in her face hardened. Her small black eyes bore into him.

Swann continued: "But he refused, didn't he? It went on for awhile until finally, they tried to kill him. But he killed them first, in cold blood. No one ever knew, right?"

Reluctantly, she nodded her head.

"I wondered, though, what did he do with the bodies?"

Her hardened face broke into a slight smile and then she giggled. "Got caught up in their own tomfoolery."

"How's that?"

"The tunnel. Their own tunnel. He snuck 'em out in the middle of the night and dropped 'em at the bottom of the sea. Right with the lobsters they used to hunt." She giggled.

"Interesting. I thank you, Mrs. Harthgate."

She scowled. "I *haven't* helped you. Just gave you some incidentals. There's much more to it, more than you could ever know."

"And what would that be, Mrs. Harthgate?"

She smiled, folding her arms. "She's returned, Mr. Swan."

"Who? Who's returned?"

Xenobia giggled again, petting her cat. "She's returned, Mr. Swann. She's returned."

*   *   *

"My grandfather did what!" Christopher Pennfield snapped at Swann.

"He had the Reverend and Mrs. Jenkinson killed on the grounds of Stone Villa," Swann answered.

"Preposterous! Blasphemous!" Christopher shouted, his face turning bright red. "Stop him, Jonathan. Stop him right now. Talk some sense into this man." He motioned to his brother across the parlor.

"Calm down. Calm down, Chris." Jonathan paced the room. "Let's listen to what the man has to say." He looked over at Swann. "Ed?"

"I know it sounds a bit far-fetched. But if you let me take you through the facts, I think I can build an almost airtight case."

"Go on."

"From the letter I found in your attic, we've already established that the Reverend Walter Jenkinson was somehow involved with your grandfather's cousin, Sarah Morton." Swann placed the note, its ripped pieces held together by scotch tape, on the coffee table.

Christopher studied the letter for several moments and pursed his lips. "I am no longer certain if I am willing to concede even that. That `S' and `W' could be a myriad of combinations of names. Susan and William. Samuel and Wilhemenia. Hundreds of possibilities."

"Fine," Swann answered. "But look at the envelope I found the note in." He placed the envelope, face up, on the coffee table. Christopher and Jonathan focused on the scribbled writing:

Betty Jenk
11/28/27

"So?" Christopher bellowed.

"The handwriting is hard to read at the end, but I think it's not a major stretch to say the name is Betty Jenkinson. From what I could gather, the Reverend wrote the note to Sarah, for some reason decided not to send it, ripped it up, and discarded it. Only, Betty found it and gave it to your grandfather."

"How do you know that!" Christopher barked.

"The handwriting on the envelope. I had it checked against some of your grandfather's documents. Two experts have told me it's his."

"But why would she go to grandfather?" Christopher asked.

"Why not? He was the leading citizen in Newport at the time. I don't find it hard to believe that the wife of the minister of Newport's largest church would confide in your grandfather. After all, Sarah was his cousin. And Mrs. Jenkinson was confused. She needed help."

"And what did grandfather do?" Christopher asked.

"At first, nothing. He probably had someone watch Sarah and Reverend Jenkinson, watch them closely. Then, sometime in spring of the next year, he came to the conclusion they *really were* having an affair. So he proceeded to do something about it. With Mrs. Jenkinson's help, he devised a scheme to somehow lure the two of them to Stone Villa, seemingly so that Sarah and the Reverend could be confronted."

"But, the murders, what happened?" Jonathan asked.

"Here's where it gets interesting. For some reason, Sarah never showed up that evening. For some reason, your grandfather thought he had to have the Reverend and his wife murdered."

"But how do you have the gall to say that it was my grandfather! You have absolutely no evidence!" Steaming, Christopher stuck his jaw in Swann's face.

"Calm down. Calm down, Chris. Let Ed finish." Jonathan walked across the room and stood between Swann and his brother.

"True, I don't have any direct evidence." Swann paced across the parlor. "But I have a very strong clue. Your grandfather used to sleep in the master bedroom, did he not?"

"Of course, I would imagine so. But what has that got to do with the Jenkinson murders, Mr. Swann!" Christopher answered, upset.

"Let me show you these. One night last week my equipment was able to pick up activity in the master bedroom."

Swann spread them down. The infra-red photographs. Those two menacing cloudy figures near the window. Growing larger and more defined in each successive picture. Then nothing.

Christopher winced and tugged at his collar. That was it. Exactly what he had seen those fearful nights in the bedroom.

"Just as you described it, right?" said Swann. "They get closer and closer and closer until they suddenly disappear. Now look at them closely. Look familiar?"

"But they're fuzzy. Not distinct."

"Think about those two figures in the parking lot."

"Are you trying to tell me these are the same two men?"

"Be surprised if they weren't. Look at the way they suddenly disappear. See? Now let's suppose one night sometime after the murder, these two men pay a little unannounced visit to your grandfather in his bedroom, they ambush him because they're trying to extort a bigger payoff. But, your grandfather was too shrewd for them, he was prepared for them. Let's suppose that just as they were about to stab him, your grandfather pulled a pistol out from the bed and shot the two of them. That would explain why the apparitions you saw always ended so abruptly, and why they disappeared so suddenly in my pictures. Their brainwave activity came to a halt when he shot them."

Silent, Christopher paced the room for several moments, then turned to Swann. "So is that it? Your grand conclusion. The investigation now officially over."

"No. Not at all."

"*What?*"

Swann stood up and spoke. "It all fits neatly together, but there's something about this whole logic I just don't buy. While all my evidence points to your grandfather being behind the Jenkinson murders, I just don't buy his motive, it's not strong enough. There's something more to it, I'm convinced. Surely, Sarah's affair with the Reverend would have been a source of embarrassment to the Pennfield family name, but why did Benjamin Pennfield have to go so far as to kill *not only* the Reverend *but also his wife?* There were so many other things a man with his power could have done to put the affair to an end, cover it up. Why did he resort to murder?"

"Mr. Swann, are you trying to tell us you want to continue this scurrilous investigation!" Christopher barked.

"Mr. Pennfield, I don't believe in leaving a job half done. There are leads I haven't even begun to check out." Swann smiled, his red cheeks rising up on his face.

"No! No! Not at all! It's over, done with! We've had enough of your specious logic!" Christopher stood up and barked at Swann.

"But, but, there's so much more—

"No, it's over!" Christopher barked again.

"But you don't understand." Swann said.

"Understand what?"

"There's nothing specious to my logic. It's all been confirmed.

"By whom?"

Silence. Swann stood in front of the large fireplace, folded his arms, and then said quietly. "Your cousin."

"Xenobia!" Christopher shot up off the couch.

Swann nodded, his face blushed.

"Mr. Swann, I specifically told you that under no circumstances whatsoever were you to speak with our cousin!" Christopher shouted.

"Yes, I understand. But I was coming up empty. At a dead end. I wouldn't have been able to proceed without her help."

"Yes, and my mentally deranged cousin was successful in convincing you my grandfather was a mass murderer! Exactly why I *didn't* want you talking to her. She's probably howling over it right now."

"But you don't understand—

"No, I understand everything *very well* Mr. Swann."

"Your cousin may be strange. But she's psychically gifted, just like yourself…"

"Don't *ever* compare me to her!"

"In her own strange way, she's trying to *warn* us. There's something around, some sort've spirit haunting the Pennfield family. The apparitions you saw were only just the beginning. The Jenkinson murders are just a small part of it. There's more, believe me.

You *have* to let me continue. For your own sake, for your family's sake."

"I don't *have* to let you do anything." Christopher answered.

"Maybe he makes a point, Chris." Jonathan interrupted.

"What?" Christopher swiveled his head towards his brother.

"I think Ed makes a lot of sense. Maybe we should let him continue."

"Are you going mad, Jonathan! Doesn't it bother you that in his own personal kangaroo court Mr. Swann just convicted our grandfather of murder, that he spoke to Xenobia in strict defiance of our orders?"

"But think of how confused we were when all these strange things began happening to us. Granted, he hasn't explained everything, but he's helped us at least to scratch the surface. I don't know who else we could possibly turn to."

"Don't you understand? We don't *need* to turn to anyone. The investigation is over, done, finished! If you're looking for something to palliate your mid-life crisis, I suggest you sign up for Outward Bound, not this cockamamie ghost hunting of Mr. Swann's."

"But, I just don't see it that way, Chris. We'd be taking a big risk if we ended it now."

"What?" Christopher blurted.

"As far as you're concerned it may be over. But not for me."

"How dare you, Jonathan!" Christopher's face reddened.

Jonathan paused, looked his brother in the eyes, and said softly, "I'm continuing with Ed, with or without you."

Christopher scowled at his brother. "Well, then, perhaps I should tell you about a little investigation of my own. Maybe there's something you ought to know about this *ghost hunter* of yours, Jonathan. Here. Read this."

He pulled a piece of paper out of his jacket pocket and slammed it down on the coffee table. It was a newspaper article, dated August 14, 1989, from the *National Bugle*:

ALLEGED GHOST HUNTER CAUSES CLIENT'S DEATH—
Charles Wainwright, a retired steelworker from Scranton, Penn-

sylvania, suffered a massive stroke and died during what a self-proclaimed ghost hunter described as a "parapsychological experiment." Wainwright had hired Edwin Swann, whom he believed to be a professional ghost hunter, to help explain strange phenomena which began occurring in and around his home of twenty-seven years shortly after his wife's death. Wainwright, seventy-eight years old, reported waking up in the middle of the night in what he described as a "paralyzed" state and seeing visions of his wife calling out to him from the edge of the bed. The ex-steelworker also reported odd noises and objects "moving strangely" around the house. Upon a friend's suggestion, Wainwright called upon Swann of Spring Lake, NJ. After two months of arduous investigation, Swann was unable to replicate any of the phenomena which Wainright had reported. In a last ditch effort, the ghost hunter brought in a configuration of electronic equipment, including neurological sensors to be attached to Wainwright's brain. As part of the process, Swann had a parapsychologist put Wainwright into a trance-like state which was supposed to help Wainwright establish "psychic contact" with his deceased wife. During the third attempt, Wainwright suffered a massive stroke and was pronounced dead upon arrival at a local hospital. Although there is no known precedent for an incident of this nature, Wainwright's survivors are considering legal action.

Swann simmered as he watched them read the article, then sprang from his seat. *"There's more to it than what's in there! Much more!"*

"And what would that be, Mr. Swann?" Christopher's eyes bore into him.

"I had him checked out. He had a complete physical. There was nothing wrong with him. It was a freak accident. He would've had the stroke wherever he was, no matter what he was doing. The doctor told me just that."

"So, you afforded him a luxury which you denied to me?"

"What? What's that?"

"If I remember correctly, you didn't require that I undergo a complete physical prior to your hooking me up to your Rube Goldbergesque array of equipment."

"But Mr. Wainwright was almost eighty years old. You're fifty-two and in good health. And last time I checked, there's nothing harmful about putting someone to sleep and attaching a few sensors to them."

Christopher walked slowly across the room and looked over at his brother. "Jonathan, you've been awfully quiet."

Jonathan looked up at the two of them, drew a breath, and then said, "I'm thinking."

"What's there to think about?" Christopher asked. "I had every intent to spare him the embarrassment, but the man's a charlatan. He practically risked my life. If I had read the article before, I would never have allowed him to conduct his chicanery in the van."

Jonathan stood silent in the middle of the parlor.

"Jonathan!" Christopher chided him. "You're a respected business executive. The decisions you make affect the lives of thousands of people every day. After reading that article, would you risk doing business with a man like Ed Swann?"

Jonathan folded his arms, turned to face Swann, and looked him straight in the eyes. "I'm sorry, Ed. I'm afraid this casts everything in a different light."

"But, but—

"I'm afraid the investigation is over."

17

Her reflection shimmered in the mirror, the warm light tingeing her image with a subtle orange hue. Slowly, she touched her soft white cheek, ran her hand through the silken strands of her golden blonde hair. She paused, staring into the image. Surely it was her: outwardly, she had not changed. But what was going on inside perplexed her. *What tricks was her mind playing with her, why did her memory surpass her years?*

She strained to recall her first living thought, the oldest imprint etched in her mind. She would go back, all the mileposts: first day of school, blowing out candles at a birthday party, playing with her parents as a toddler, but then fuzzy, hazy, and finally a void. Years of black nothingness. But then more: sitting at a stately banquet in a large mansion, everyone dressed differently from today; a beautiful cove in a tropical village, large tall-masted ships anchored on the horizon; a small New England village, everyone dressed in colonial garb, like in history books.

It always ended the same way, with the same fearful image. Water, she was in water, up to her nose, over her cheeks. She bounced up and down on the soft sandy bottom, waving her arms, straining to catch their attention. *She had made a mistake, done herself a terrible wrong, she wanted them to take her back!*

A lone tear slid down her cheek. *Why? What did it all mean? Why was her mind confusing her so?* She felt queasy, scared. There was a message to it, she was sure. These memories, these confusing memories, were telling her to do something. *But what was it?*

PART

III

Pollock Rip

18

The Vermont snow began to soften in March. Hard and crusty throughout the winter months, its pores opened slowly, sweating out drops of perspiration, oozing gently down the hills until finally settling in puddles over hardened earth. A transition month, Christopher Pennfield thought as he gazed up at the mountains from his sun porch. White, snow-capped peaks rolling downward to moulded mud, preserving meaningless tire tracks and bootprints from the dead of winter. Soon it would all be blanketed by a fresh, glowing green, a new beginning. The coming of Spring especially excited Pennfield this year, signaling that June—and the College's anniversary ceremony—would soon be upon him.

He slid a piece of white bond into the carriage of his Smith-Corona, its gears grinding as he twisted it in. Well into draft number three of his address, he had embellished the story of his grandfather countless times, perhaps *too many times* he thought. But he had a reason, a motivation for dwelling so much upon the life and contributions of Benjamin Pennfield: as that pest Swann repeatedly uncovered details of the Jenkinson tragedy, he felt a strong need to build up the accomplishments of his grandfather, a natural psychological defense. But now Swann was gone, had been gone for almost three months, his discoveries as forgotten as those meaningless tire tracks would be come another month or so.

Now he would go further, extend the Pennfield legacy back several centuries: prove to the world that it wasn't only the family's accomplishments at turn of the century that had made the Pennfields great, that through each generation the family had achieved greatness. Now he would draft a section on the family's accomplishments in the eighteenth century, how Thomas Pennfield and his sons Nathaniel and Peter had built a great trading enterprise during Newport's colonial heyday. As he placed his fingers on the keys, contemplating how he might begin, the phone rang.

"Unk, I'm married!"

"*What!*"

"I married Tom Westerfeld yesterday."

"Winnie, where are you?"

"In the south of France. He surprised me, took me here on a whim Friday night, then proposed yesterday morning. We were married last evening."

"Jesus!"

"You're shocked?"

"Overwhelmed is more like it. I mean, you've only been dating the man several months and I always assumed I would be there to formally give your hand in marriage when that joyous day came upon us. I always thought it would be the social event of the season."

"But it was so spontaneous, spur of the moment. And neither of us wanted a spectacle, no paparazzi."

"But then what about—

"Us?"

"Not an insignificant matter as far as I'm concerned, yes." He mumbled.

"Get real, Unk. Nothing'll change."

When he placed the receiver down, he sat quietly looking out upon the street and the mountains in the distance. He was in shock, his jaw agape. It would take time for him to adjust to this new development. He always assumed that at the proper time Winnie would take a mate, but why so soon, and what was this Westerfeld really all about anyway? It would take some adjustment, indeed, to realize he was no longer the number one man in Winnie's life. He tried to continue writing, but could not. Instead he lit a cigarette—then a second, and a third—silently looking out from his sun porch.

It was not until evening that he continued on his address. He figured if he forced himself to work it would take his mind off Winnie, if only for the moment. Despondently, he tapped at the keyboard:

> *Although my grandfather, Benjamin Pennfield, was only a seasonal resident of Newport, the Pennfield's roots were buried deep in the soil of that fair city, it being the venue of some of our family's greatest successes and accomplishments. Indeed, the Pennfield family first set foot on Aquidnick Island in 1714, when Thomas Pennfield and his family migrated down Narragansett Bay from Rehoboth Colony. Together with his sons, Nathaniel and Peter, he built a business which grew into one of Newport's most profitable mercantile enterprises of that century…*

*   *   *

Newport, Rhode Island
September, 1768

A ray of sunlight teased the frail figure of the old man laying still and weak in the dark third floor bedroom. He coughed, struggling to cover his mouth with his white, bony hand. His chest throbbed as a thick sputum rushed up from his lungs. Flecks of dust tickled his nose and his dry morning throat, causing a barrage of short, painful coughs. He hacked away, gagging. Slowly, he forced his hand to his mouth, his elbow creaking.

So this is how it ends? Nathaniel Pennfield thought as he lay there helpless and limp, pressing his clammy hand over his mouth. *This is what the Good Lord has in store for all men of pride and ambition?* He shifted himself, the bedsores on his buttocks scraping against the overnight crevices carved into his mattress. Now he despised the morning, despised it with all the passion with which he had once welcomed it. What was once such a daily celebration of opportunity yet unexploited was now merely a cruel reminder of his own mortality.

After all, he was one of the privileged few who had helped elevate Newport to its rightful place as a center of commercial trade. Along with the rest of them, Newport's great merchants—the Ayraults, the Malbornes the Bannisters, the Wantons, the Redwoods, the Vernons—he had been there, helping Newport carve out its niche in the wake of the great colonial ports of Boston, New York and Philadelphia. He had risked his capital and his own flesh and blood: *didn't he deserve a fate better than this?*

Drowsy and weak, he was a captive to his bed. Yet, as he lay there, he remembered it all. As if distant memories could compensate for the pain, assuage his fate. He remembered being there as a young man with his father, Thomas, and his brother, Peter, when Newport merchants first discovered the allure of the rum trade with the African coast, when the basic patterns of the triangular trade were first established. Rum from Newport to Africa for negro slaves, to the West Indies for molasses, then back to Newport where it would be distilled into rum, the cycle thus repeating. He was there to see Newport's commerce abound as a result of this magic golden triangle. He had seen the number of tall ships in Newport harbor multiply, the numerous warehouses sprout up across Thames, the shops and inns and taverns proliferate. Because of it all, the Pennfields had become one of Newport's prominent families, leading members of Trinity Church; part of the "genteel" upper class residing in splendid townhouses on Thames Street overlooking Newport Harbor.

He wheezed, struggling to force the cool, heavy air through his clogged throat and swollen nostrils. *Damn this consumption! Good Lord, God Almighty, damn this consumption, damn it with all your power and might!* Viciously, it had attacked him from within, sneaking up upon him. When would the Good Lord release him from his pain? He shut his eyes, hoping also to shut out his grief. But he could not close them for that final time. Not yet. There was one last task to complete.

"Master Pennfield? Master Pennfield, Sir?" A sharp tap rattled the door at the foot of the bed.

Pennfield turned his head slightly, and braced his elbows on the mattress, buttressing himself. He breathed deeply, readying himself to answer, but then gagged and fell back, his arms collapsing beneath him.

"Master Pennfield, Sir?" The door creaked open. A tall, elegant servant with fine light brown skin and thick curly hair held a silver tray at his waist. "I've brought your morning tea, Sir."

Pennfield set his jaw and forced out a whisper. "On my writing table, please." With his chin, Pennfield motioned towards the wooden table underneath the window looking out over Newport harbor.

"*But, Master Pennfield!*" The servant looked over at him, his eyes wide in puzzlement.

"*On the writing table please, William!*" Pennfield answered, struggling to summon sufficient strength to speak.

"Yes, yessir. Certainly, sir." William rushed over to the small table and placed the cup of tea down.

"Now help me up." Pennfield gasped.

"But Master Pennfield, you haven't been up in weeks!"

"Do as I say! Help me up, William."

William stepped towards the bed, hovering over his master. "But Master Pennfield, it wouldn't be prudent. You've hardly the strength to…"

"Help me up. I've something to do. Now, please!"

William carefully placed his arm beneath his master's brittle back, forcing himself not to gag from the stench rising off the bed. His eyes locked in on Pennfield's ashen-gray face, slumped to one side, his skin clammy and wrinkled. Carefully, William lifted, bracing himself. Yet, as he raised Pennfield's frail bones from the bed, he was surprised by the ease of his burden, as if lifting a small child. Just six, seven months ago the man was broad and stout, a satisfied belly slipping over his belt. Today, his master was merely a skeleton of weakened bones covered by a thin layer of wrinkled gray skin.

William took four broad steps across the room and carefully slipped Pennfield into the wooden chair. As William positioned him in place, he hesitated to relax his grip, fearing that this weakened mass of bones and flesh would collapse without his support. Slowly, he loosened his hold, Pennfield slumping back into the chair. The old withered man slowly raised his hand from his hip, as if drawing a pistol, and pointed a shaking finger at the window over the table. "The drapes. Open them, William. I must see."

William responded quickly, drawing the drapes back and fastening them into place. Pennfield raised his head and peered out, his visage reflective of both joy and sorrow. *Yes, the scene of his triumphs!* The rolling wake of a fresh, morning sea. Tall masts moored throughout the harbor. Laborers and sailors and craftsman rushing about the wharf below, practicing their daily trade. *To only be part of it once again!*

"Get out a quill and parchment. Quickly, please."

William fumbled with the wooden desk drawer, obliging his master. "Here, Sir."

Pennfield looked up at the tall, strong figure of William hovering above him. "Good, now leave!"

"But…but…Master Pennfield, I shan't allow you to sit up alone. Why you've hardly the strength…"

"Out!" Pennfield snapped at him again, his quivering finger pointing towards the door.

William stood silent for one brief moment, quickly concluded that whatever his argument, Pennfield would prevail, and walked slowly toward the door. As he left the room, he trained his eyes on his master, wondering if this might be the last time he would ever see him.

Alone, Pennfield reached slowly for the pen. He had waited a lifetime for this moment. Now he would finally do what he had contemplated for over half a century. Now he would commit it all to writing: the story which, until now, had passed only from mouth to mouth in whispered conversations. Now, he would tell it all—every word, sparing no detail—preserve it to insure the chain of words would never be broken, tell it all before his memory failed him. He dipped the pen in the bottle, pinching its shaft with his weary fingers. Perhaps, if generations from now, his act of the next several hours could spare one of his descendents from the mistakes of his ancestors, it would be a fruitful investment of his last living moments. Slowly, he touched the tip of his pen to the parchment and winced as he began to form the letters:

A HISTORY OF THE MEAN AND MALICIOUS SPIRITE
WHICH HAS BEEN THE PLAGUE OF THE PENNFIELD
FAMILY FOR FIVE GENERATIONS.

As I, Nathaniel Pennfield of Newport, son of Thomas Pennfield of Newport, grandson of Richard Pennfield of Rehoboth Colony, and great-grandson of Edward Pennfield of Plimouth Colony, son of Charles Pennfield, the Pilgrim, suffer from the ravages of an affliction from which I am certain that I will never recover, it has become my last taske in life to record the narrative of sundry events which have served to cause blasphemy, shame and disrepute to descend upon my family undeserved...

For three hours, Pennfield toiled as he related his story on twelve pages of parchment. When finished, he squeezed his quill and signed his name, forming a regal tail to the last letter. He had nothing left; each stroke of his pen had extracted its toll. Suddenly, he was attacked with a barrage of coughs, as if signaling a final punctuation to his story. He dropped the quill, jerking his hand up to his mouth.

"William! William!" He gasped out between coughs.

"Yes, Master Pennfield." William rushed through the door, having waited patiently outside throughout the duration.

Sagging back in the hard, wooden chair, Pennfield slowly pointed towards the bed. "Put me back."

William rushed to his master's aid, carefully cradling him in his arms and gently laying him on the bed.

The instant Pennfield's frail body touched the mattress, he coiled himself into a tight ball, bringing his bony knees to his chest and shielding his face with his hands. Helpless, William looked on; he could swear if it were possible for this skeleton of a man to wither away even more dramatically in the time he was alone in the room, Pennfield certainly had.

Slowly, Pennfield slid one of his hands down his face and pointed a quivering finger at the table. He gasped. "The parchments."

"Yes. What would you like me to do with them, Sir."

"Take them."

William rushed over and reached for the parchments. "Yes, but what shall I do with them, Sir?"

"Take them. Just take them!" Pennfield opened a drowsy yellowed eye and barked. "Now leave!" He pointed slowly towards the door.

William rushed out the door, still hesitant to defy a direct order from his master, even if he was convinced the consumption had weakened Pennfield's mind as it had his flesh and bones.

Peacefully, Pennfield closed his eyes and allowed his ashen-gray lips to form a tranquil smile. Yes, now it was time, he was certain. His voyage had ended, his cargo delivered. He could close his eyes peacefully now, knowing that he would never again be victim to the wicked taunts of another Newport morning. It was time to meet his Maker.

Yet, as he faded into a drowsy stupor, he again heard William rustling at the door. *Damn!* he thought. *Can't that simple knave ever get anything right? Can't he allow me to go in peace?* Wearily, Pennfield opened his eyes, laying on his bed in a helpless ball, struggling to lift his head. "William, please!" He stopped short and gasped.

It wasn't William at the door.

A woman dressed in a soggy white gown, dripping wet, stood silent at the foot of the bed and peered at him with her glistening eyes.

No. No. It can't be! It mustn't be! He curled into a tighter ball.

She moved closer, as if floating. Dripping strands of seaweed hung from her shoulders. In knotted tangles, her wet discolored hair enwrapped itself around her neck and shoulders. The soggy bluish skin on her face, a death mask, drew her cheeks into a menacing smile.

As he shivered on the bed, the thought raced through his mind: *Was this spectre real or was it just the product of the last dim thoughts of a dying mind?*

He tried desperately to flush the vision from his mind. He grunted, struggling to close his eyes, but they remained open, frozen in place, forced to watch this ugly spectre as it floated closer and closer to the bed, until it finally stopped, hovering beside him, within an arms length, her deathly blue face leaning into him, filling his eyes with her ugliness.

"No! No! Leave! Go away!" Pennfield pleaded.

She stood over him, looking down on him. She laughed, exposing her rotted teeth, vomit coating her lips. Summoning all the strength he had left, Pennfield tossed back and forth on the mattress, struggling to make her disappear. Yet, the more he struggled, the more power she consumed, unwilling to vanish until he had breathed his last breath.

She left him at last with no final moment of peace.

19

Captain Adrian Stewart, sitting in the cockpit high atop the nose of his 747-300 series jet, looked down upon the dark Atlantic. With hardly a cloud to block his view, he could easily make out the dimly twinkling set of lights below, most likely from an oil tanker heading for Staten Island or Jersey, or perhaps a luxury liner bound for the docks of midtown Manhattan. How insignificant it looked from up here. There was a magic to the moment, though, a sort of cosmic bonding between humans that gave Stewart a small rush, not unlike flying throughout the night across a wide, sleepy expanse of sea or desert and then, pop, like magic, a set of twinkles rises from the sterile horizon. It was that way when he first flew into Hawaii and Hong Kong and Tokyo and Taipei and Sydney and countless other pockets of civilization spanning the continents. It was the sheer magic of flying into a dark, empty space of air and water and discovering that someone else was there, a comrade.

Stewart sat back and eyed his read-outs. Compass. Altimeter. Fuel Gauge. Air Speed. He yawned, covering his mouth. Autopilot took all the fun out of it. Why, these damn 747s practically flew themselves! They didn't need a pilot. What they needed was a microchip connected to a set of arms and legs! In fact, flights like this one—GlobalAir 1428 from Heathrow to Kennedy each evening—had become so commonplace, so standardized, they were almost dull to an experienced Captain like Stewart. He kept himself alert by sipping coffee and peering out his window, scanning the ocean for twinkling sets of lights and wondering what thoughts streamed through the minds of his comrades below.

A sighting like this one could occupy Stewart's mind for almost half an hour. At first, it would be just a faint flicker sitting on the horizon two hundred miles due west. He would catch up to it quickly, the spinning turbines of his 747's giant Rolls Royce engines eating up the ocean between them. Within twenty minutes, he would be right above it, getting his closest view. Then he would watch it drift slowly to the rear as his jet rushed across the North Atlantic. *Peace, Shalom, Au Revoir, my transient friend!*

It was almost unfair, he thought, how he could begin his voyage across the Great Pond three or four days after that vessel below, and then beat it to the coast of North America by another three or four. He wondered what it was like years ago, when it would take much more than a week for a ship to cross the Atlantic, when deep-bellied merchant vessels, their hulls of wood and pitch, relied upon nothing more than the forces of nature to propel them across the mighty Atlantic. What had become such a perfunctory six or seven hour job to him, had been a massive struggle with the forces of nature to them. He looked down upon the dark, lonely Atlantic with reverence. He wondered, if so motivated, how many stories those waters below could tell him.

This night had been a particularly exasperating one for Stewart. GlobalAir Flight 1428—scheduled to leave London's Heathrow Airport promptly at 6:40PM London time and arrive at New York's Kennedy Airport at 9:15PM New York time—had taken off three hours late. First his 747, due in from Bombay, arrived an hour and a half behind schedule. Then, once all two-hundred and twenty-three passengers had been boarded, a malfunction was discovered in the plane's Internal Navigation System. Three technicians had been rushed aboard in an effort to repair it, but when it appeared that it would take several hours, Flight Operations had made the decision to switch equipment. Stewart winced when he heard the news. That meant shuffling two hundred warm bodies back through the jet way and into the lounge area as a new 747 was rolled up to the gate. Then, back through the jet way, and onto the new plane.

By the time they took off at 10:33, Heathrow's usually busy runways were empty. Stewart taxied his jet down the runway, executed a flawless takeoff and waited for clearance to ascend to his cruising altitude. Perfect, by the book, flawless. Stewart was a deft pilot, a pro.

Now, almost six hours into the flight, Stewart's unsuspecting eyes scanned the dark Atlantic, searching for yet another twinkling set of lights, another temporary diversion from his monotony. Unfortunately, though, a thin line of wispy clouds grew into a thick ceiling, blocking the ocean from his view. He had been warned about it in his pre-flight briefing back at Heathrow. The leading edge of a front working its way up the coast from Bermuda. He looked at his watch. Eleven fifteen, New York time. With any luck, they'd touch down about twelve, twelve ten at the outside. That would mean he'd pull into his driveway in Connecticut by quarter of three. If the weather held up. Frustrating, but by tomorrow afternoon he'd be playing with his grandchildren on his front porch, the inconvenience all but forgotten.

He nodded over to his right. "Why don't we get a quick update on the weather in New York, Larry."

Larry Nelson, his young flight engineer right out of eight years active service in the Air Force, quickly obliged. "New York Control, this is GlobalAir 1428 Heavy. What's the latest on the weather?"

"GlobalAir 1428 Heavy, New York Control. Yeah, we got heavy thunderstorms stretching up to fifty miles off of Eastern Long Island. Ceiling up to twenty-five thousand feet. Visibility at Kennedy's two miles. Wind's eighteen knots from the northeast. Might wanna consider diverting slightly to the North. You've got clear skies five miles north right up to the Cape."

"Whaddaya think, Tony?" Stewart looked over to his co-pilot.

"Can't hurt."

When the jet's massive fuselage suddenly bounced on a sheet of heavy air, its wings flapping, Stewart sat up in his seat, a slight smile across his lips. He could sense the collective gasp in the passenger cabin behind them. Some of them are probably shitting bricks back there, he thought. They should've been with him back in Korea if they thought *this* was anything.

He flipped on his microphone."This is Captain Stewart. We're gonna experience a little turbulence for the next few minutes, so I'm gonna ask you to return to your seats and put on your seatbelts. I'll keep you posted." He flipped off his microphone and looked over to his flight engineer. "Request permission to change course, Larr."

"Yeah, New York Control, this is GlobalAir 1428 Heavy, again. Looks like we're gonna take you up on that offer. What've you got for us?"

"Yeah, GlobalAir 1428 Heavy. You can proceed to a course of 310. That's three-one-oh. Maintain altitude at 30,000 feet."

Stewart rubbed his hands together, cracked his knuckles, clicked off the autopilot, and clutched the wheel. *So, we're actually gonna get some real flying time in tonight!* With all the enthusiasm of a young fighter pilot, he banked the giant bird to the northwest as Nelson quickly performed some calculations on his flight computer.

"Looks like we can maintain course until we're just northeast of Nantucket, then proceed to a course of 244 for approach into New York airspace, Captain."

"Let's do it." Stewart answered.

"New York Control, GlobalAir 1428 Heavy. Yeah, we'd like to maintain course until we reach coordinates 41.9, 62.3. Then proceed to a course of 244 for approach."

"You've got it, 1428. Switch to a frequency of 124.8 and notify Boston for us, will ya."

"No prob, New York." Nelson quickly switched his frequency and complied.

Stewart clicked on his microphone. "Yes, this is Captain Stewart again. We're gonna try to smooth out the ride for you a bit. Seems as if there's a thunderstorm off of eastern Long Island that's causing this turbulence. So we're gonna proceed to the Northwest, till we're just a little north of Nantucket Island, and then bank to the southwest to begin our approach into New York air space. Right now, we're looking at an arrival time of about twelve fifteen New York time. Again, we apologize for any inconvenience the delays may have caused you tonight and we hope the next time your plans call for air travel that you'll fly GlobalAir."

Stewart piloted his craft with a renewed vigor, taking the controls himself and feeling the fuselage's vibrations through the wheel as the giant jet cruised to the point just northeast of Nantucket Island where it would make its planned turn to the southwest for reentry into New York airspace. His eyes sparkled as they scanned the instrument panel. If it were always like this—if he could permanently trash that damned autopilot—he wouldn't even *think* of retiring at the end of the year. "Request permission to make the turn, Larr."

"Boston Control. Boston Control. GlobalAir 1428 Heavy."

"GlobalAir 1428 Heavy. Boston Control."

"Yeah. We'd like to request permission to change course to 244. That's two-four-four."

"Affirmative, 1428."

As Stewart began his turn, he felt a rattle in the wheel. And then—*SWOOSH!*—from the southwest, a massive surge of wind knifed across his fuselage. The jet tipped to the right, contrary to the direction of their attempted turn and bounced across the rushing wind, like a stone skipping across a pond.

"Shit! Did we know about this!" Stewart snapped at Nelson.

"According to Control, the skies are as clear as a bell."

"Well, looks like someone in control screwed up again!" Stewart lurched back in his seat, another strong gust pummeling his fuselage. *Shit—" PA-BOOM! PA-BOOM! PA-BOOM!* The plane bounced again and again. He shouted at Nelson. "Put Boston on my radio. I'll have somebody's job for this!"

"Yessir." Nelson flicked some of his switches. "They're on sir."

"Boston. This is Captain Stewart, GlobalAir 1428—" *PA-BOOM! PA-BOOM! PA-BOOM!* "—I just told two hundred passengers that we're gonna arrive ten minutes late because your pals in New York told me we could avoid a storm by diverting north—" *PA-BOOM! PA-BOOM! PA-BOOM!* "—Now we're north and my plane's jumping up and down like a god-damned banshee! What's going on, Boston?"

"GlobalAir 1428, Boston Control. I'm sorry, but we see nothing in the area at all."

"WELL, YOU COME *THE FUCK* UP HERE IF YOU SEE NOTH-ING IN THE AREA, BOSTON!" He clicked off his microphone, bouncing in his seat, his eyes glued to the wind meter. *Four-eighty. Five-fifty. Six hundred miles an hour! Now, a shift! To the northeast! Wait, southeast! No, now, southwest! The winds were attacking the jet from all directions!*

He clutched his controls. Rudder. Flaps. Engines. *The plane bounced, jerking back and forth, up and down.*

"GlobalAir 1428, Boston Control. Begin descent to twenty-thou-sand feet right after you make your turn. That's two-oh thousand."

His mind raced. What could he do? Engine 1. Engine 2. Engine 3. Engine 4. Nothing. *KA-BOOM! Another burst of wind! A swirling whirlpool, drilling the craft from behind! Underneath the left wing, jolting it up! Over the right wing, pouncing it down! Whistling, rushing winds! A violent bank to the right!*

"GlobalAir 1428?"

He struggled with the wheel, begging the plane to respond. *A nosedive! Uncontrollable, racing downward, a bullet accelerating, its wings spinning!*

"GlobalAir 1428? GlobalAir 1428? Boston Control. Please Respond."

"GlobalAir 1428? GlobalAir 1428?"

*   *   *

Earlier in the day, Jonathan Pennfield, COO of GlobalAir, had sold fifteen of his 737s to one of his competitors and laid off another three hundred employees in an effort to keep the financially strug-gling airline afloat. So he slept restlessly, dozing off into a light sleep and then abruptly waking several times during the night. When he had finally settled into a deep sleep, he was interrupted by a piercing ring from his bedside phone.

He decided to wait. Maybe it was the wrong number or a crank call.

It rang again.

Susan stirred. Perhaps he should pick it up, he thought. Drowsily, he rolled out of bed and reached for the phone.

"Hello?"

"Mr. Pennfield?"

"Yes."

"Bruce O'Leary, Kennedy Operations."

"Yeah, what's up, Bruce?"

"I'm afraid I have some pretty bad news…"

Pennfield froze.

"A 747 just went down in the Atlantic."

"Oh my God…," Pennfield bit his lip. "Wha…What flight was it?"

"1428 from Heathrow, the late one, left England three hours late due to equipment problems."

"What do we know? What happened?"

"There were no evident mechanical difficulties. And no distress signals except for the Captain complaining about unanticipated turbulence. The radar blip just disappeared from the screen. Everything we know so far points to…," he paused, "…terrorism."

"God…when did it happen?"

"About an hour ago. It was diverted slightly north on its approach pattern because of turbulent air. As best as we can tell it went down just east of Cape Cod. Control's telling me it's about six miles due east of a place called Monomoy Point…"

The reporters besieged him as Pennfield double parked in front of the GlobalAir Terminal at Kennedy at 4:30AM. Brusquely, he mumbled, "No comment. No comment," as he barged through the crowd, pushed open the terminal's doors, and marched down the corridor. His heels clicked on the hard linoleum floor as he drew a beeline straight for the Flight Operations Center, allowing no one to get in his way. He threw off his raincoat as he opened the door. "What's the latest news?" he asked.

Over thirty technicians, engineers and pilots looked up at him and froze. Silence. Each of them standing by their computer terminals, radar screens, and weather instruments as if in a morgue. Finally, it was O'Leary who answered him. "Nothing really. Nothing new since I talked to you. Coast Guard's pulling bodies out of the water and a rep from the NTSB is on his way up from DC by helicopter."

"Any survivors?"

"None, at least not yet."

"Who was the pilot?"

"Stewart. Adrian Stewart."

Jesus! He knew Stewart, had played golf with Stewart. One of GlobalAir's very best pilots, if not *the* best, Stewart had been with the airline since 1962. There was *no way p*ilot error could have played any role at all with Stewart in command. But that wasn't important, not important at all. It was hard enough to accept the deaths of two-hundred *anonymous* passengers and crewmembers, but he *knew* one of them, considered him a friend. "Get a copter ready," he said, "I'm going up there."

The propeller's constant puttering throbbed away at Jonathan's brain during the seventy-five minute flight up to Cape Cod. He sat there: silently, stoically, waiting to see the tragedy for himself. As twilight began to set in, a thin sliver of sandy beach lined the horizon—the southern shore of Nantucket Island. Then, the lighthouse, 'Sciasconset, and Sankaty Head. All well known to him. And then, off in the distance, to the north, the sandy shore of Monomoy Point. And the helicopters: not too far to the east hovering over the open sea. Frogmen descending from ropes. Bodies and fragments of fuselage being pulled out of the water. And, somewhere among them, somewhere out there, Captain Adrian Stewart, Jonathan's friend.

Though he tried to convince himself not, beneath this strange scene of choppers and bobbing pieces of fuselage, everything looked remarkably familiar. The four red buoys beginning at Butler Hole and stretching out to the northeast, marking the only safe passage through the area's treacherous shoals. The frothy white breakers of Bearse's Shoal and Pollock Rip. Chatham Harbor several miles to the north. As he silently watched, it became painfully clear to him: *this is exactly where the phantom storm had attacked him last September!*

20

Ed Swann gazed out upon the Atlantic from his usual bench on the Spring Lake boardwalk. The waters were still and calm, a peaceful March afternoon. He set his eyes on the long hazy line in the distance where the water's far edge met the blurred fringe of the afternoon sky: he thought how special it was that each day nature provided him with such a stunning snapshot of the Infinite.

At peace with himself, he drew in a deep breath of cool air and glanced at his watch. Two thirty-five. After several more moments on his bench, he would pick up an afternoon paper and then drive over to his office on Main Street. Hopefully, there would be a message on his machine: a new project, something to keep his mind occupied. In the absence of a stroke of luck, though, he would spend the afternoon at the Spinnaker Pub, sipping a beer or two and slinging numerous metal pucks down its smooth lacquered shuffleboard table with a few of his cronies. He pushed himself off the bench and walked towards his van.

His eyes were drawn to it the instant he walked into the 7-11. The headline on *The NY Post:* "DEATH ON THE SHOALS" draped across an arresting photo of several frogmen descending upon a floating piece of airplane fuselage. Swann remembered having heard something about an airplane crash earlier in the day, but had not really dwelled upon it. He rushed to his van and read on:

> A GlobalAir 747 crashed early this morning on the shoals about six miles due east of the sandy shores of Monomoy Point, near Cape Cod's elbow. The flight, GlobalAir 1428 from London's Heathrow airport, took off almost three hours late due to equipment problems. The entire flight crew and all 223 of the flight's passengers are feared dead. GlobalAir President and COO, Jonathan Pennfield, grandson of the airline's founder, financier Benjamin Pennfield, told reporters this morning that, "GlobalAir will have no comments regarding the cause of the tragedy until a full investigation has been conducted."

Abruptly, he stopped reading. Something bothered him. Words, a set of words he remembered. Something Xenobia had muttered in her cryptic mumblings the first time they met. Wasn't it something to do with *flames that rise where the breakers meet the sandy elbow?* He revved the engine and drove off.

Twenty minutes later, he pulled up to *The Sailor's Compass,* a small disheveled storefront near the docks at Point Pleasant Beach. He took a whiff of the salt air as he entered the door. Behind the lonely counter, a youngish man with a buzz cut sat back watching a small portable television, foil wrapped around its antenna.

"Yeah, what can I do for yah?" The young man snapped out of his stupor.

"I'd like to purchase a nautical chart. Need it to cover Nantucket Island north through the eastern shore of Cape Cod."

Anxiously, Swann pulled the large chart out of its cardboard tube and unrolled it on his desk. He searched for the area where the plane had gone down. He found Monomoy Point, the tip of a small sandy island located at Cape Cod's elbow. He pulled out a ruler and measured six miles due east: a series of shoals called Pollock Rip. Then, he pulled out one of his folders from his days in Newport and ruffled through his notes until he found the information he needed, from one of his initial discussions with Jon Pennfield. He examined the chart again, this time measuring up from Nantucket Harbor with his ruler. Sixteen miles northeast. He smiled. *Amazing...*

Within minutes, he grabbed for his rolodex. He flipped quickly through the cards searching for a name he had filed away. But where had he put it? He searched through all the logical headings.—*Newport. Nautical. History. Captain. Pennfields.*—until finally it popped up under *Miscellaneous.* Immediately, he dialed the number. It took several attempts, but Swann finally managed to reach Captain Conrad Scott of Falmouth, Massachusetts.

"They tell me no one knows the waters around Cape Cod better than you, Captain Scott."

"Lemme give yah a piece of advice to tuck away in yer back pocket," the old crusty voice answered back.

"What's that?"

"Never trust someone who gives yah an easy compliment, get it?"

"Yeah, I understand, but—

"My time's valuable, what's yer point?"

"I'd like to talk to you, learn a little bit about the waters around Cape Cod."

"Don't do that. I'm a charter Captain, not a history teacher."

It took considerable arm-twisting, but Swann finally coerced Scott to meet with him in Falmouth Harbor the next Saturday afternoon. Scott was so reluctant, though, Swann wondered if the seven hour drive from Spring Lake to Falmouth would be worth it. *But what else had he to do?*

On Saturday afternoon at 3PM sharp—after a long, bumpy ride on I-95—Swann meandered over to Scott's place of business, about halfway up on the east side of Falmouth's Inner Harbor. Swann took a sniff of air pungent with the odors of seaweed and fish as he spotted the sign for *East Wind Charters.* The weathered slats of an old rickety dock rolled to the weight of his footsteps as he walked gingerly to its end. Three medium-sized vessels, their bows pointing in, were tethered to pilings: a fiberglass sloop, about thirty-five feet long, named *Phoenix,* a beautiful, perfectly-maintained wooden yawl, over forty feet, named *Capt. Jones* and an old black tar-papered, pilot-house twin-engined diesel—a real stink pot— without any name on it at all.

Swann held onto a piling and stepped onto the bow of the Phoenix. "Captain Scott! Captain Scott!" He called out. No response. When he stepped into the cockpit, he noticed a metal padlock securing the slats over the hatch. Undaunted, he lifted himself back onto the dock and walked over towards the Capt. Jones, admiring its finely-lacquered wooden deck as he worked his way toward the stern, again only to find the hatch slatted up and padlocked. He looked over to the third vessel. Of course, the twin-engined black boat with the pilothouse probably served as a combination office and working-craft. He carefully worked his way on board and again called out: "Captain Scott! Captain Scott!"

Swann walked through the open doorway to the pilot house. No signs of life with the exception of an unmade cot, a hotplate on a table next to some navigation charts, and a mug half full of chalky-cold morning coffee. Baffled, he walked onto the dock and surveyed the area. No one in sight. He walked back to his van at the foot of the dock and sat behind the wheel, patiently waiting.

After forty-five minutes and no sign of Scott, Swann decided that a short stroll would be a better way to pass his time. He took a look at the old, historic houses on the Village Green and walked down along Surf Drive, watching the rolling breakers wash up on an empty Menauhant Beach. But, most of all, he spent some time around the docks. Captivated, he watched four or five boats pull up to a fishing pier, unloading their daily take. Lobsters, scallops, bluefish, cod. Tomorrow's entrees at area inns and restaurants. So interested in observing this workingman's ritual, Swann was startled when he looked down at his watch and noticed it was ten before five. He rushed back.

Another sloop had pulled in, docked next to the Phoenix. A paunchy, bearded figure held a rubber hose in his hand, dousing the deck. Swann stopped and studied him for a moment, then grinned. If King Neptune, himself, could have fashioned an old sailing salt, Swann doubted the result would be much different from this crusty old man. A bristly-white beard running from sideburn-to-sideburn. A round bulb of a nose, its deep shade of red tinted by many a swig of good whiskey. An old captain's hat covering his bald patch. A navy blue blazer—worn at the elbows, a set of anchors engraved on its tarnished gold buttons—running over his beltless khakis. Weathered brown topsiders, both leather shoelaces tangled and undone. And a set of stern, deep-blue eyes that required only a ray of sunlight or a puff of wind, Swann was sure, to cure their melancholia.

Swann stepped closer and called out. "Captain Scott?"

"That's me." The man answered, not turning his head.

"I'm Ed Swann. We were supposed to meet at three."

"Twas a test fer yah." Scott did not look up, his eyes fixed on the stream of water spouting from his hose.

"A test?"

"Any busybody who considers himself man enough to deal with me, 'sgotta know with a twelve knot breeze and a slack tide, I ain't gonna be sittin' in no shithouse waitin' round to talk business."

"Never claimed to be a nautical man, myself." Swann worked himself onto the deck. "Although have to admit I did do a little deep sea fishing off of Key West a couple of times."

Pcchww. The side of Scott's mouth propelled a saliva-bullet into the water below. "Tourist crap. Payem an extra fifty bucks and they'll take yah 'n any wench uh your choice on a moonlight cruise."

"Well, as I said on the phone, I'm sort've interested in the nautical lore of the area."

"And what interest would a landlubbin' bellyfulla mush have in the *nautical lore uh the area*, Mr. Swann?" He turned towards Swann and raised an eyebrow. "This wouldn't have nuthin' to do with that plane crash, would it?"

"No, not at all. It's just that I'm a bit of a history buff. Much like yourself, or so I hear."

"Ain't no history buff. Moreuv'n occupational necessity."

"Oh?"

"If you don't understand, ain't worth explainin'" Scott spit again.

"Listen, Captain Scott," Swann said, "I only came here to pick your brain a bit. I'm willing to compensate you for your troubles. But, if you have a chip on your shoulder about that—"

"No, *you* listen to me, Mr. Swann," Scott looked him directly in the eyes. "These weekend sailors with their high phalutin' jobs and their hundred thousand dollar fiberglass toys, think you can negotiate these waters with a few charts, an expensive compass, and some 'lectronic crap." *Pchwww.* He spit again, forcefully. "That's how hundreds of 'em come tuh park their keels on a sandy floor. Nope," he looked out over the harbor, "you don't get 'round these parts with charts or compasses or radio signals. Yah get round these parts by listenin' to what the sea has to tell yah, the collective wisdom of every seaworthy skipper who ever piloted a ship through its shoals and its currents and its winds. When it comes tuh these waters, one man's misfortune is another man's salvation." He looked back at Swann. "That's history fer yah, Mr. Swann."

"Couldn't agree with you more." Swann smiled at him. "So help me a bit. Educate me. Let's start with Monomoy Island, what can you tell me about it?"

"Bird sanctuary," he answered, dousing the deck.

"Anything else?"

"Nope."

Puzzled, Swann tried again. "How about Pollock Rip?"

"Hmmmph," Scott chuckled. "Better to talk to an undertaker if you wanna learn somethin' 'bout a graveyard."

"A graveyard?"

"Yep. Biggest graveyard on the east coast of North America. Confoundin' currents is what does it."

"Interesting. I heard a story once, about some sort of flames where the breakers meet the sandy elbow. A bit cryptic, but I thought—

"So you're trying to add a little myth to legend, are yah? Yep, happened at Pollock Rip."

"But what was it?"

"A conflagration." Scott smiled as he doused the deck. "Legend has it some poor pirate ship, the *Compass Rose*, most people say, went up in flames near Pollock Rip in the 1720s, crashed on the shoals. Some even claim if you look hard enough you can still see the flames today." He glanced up. "How 'bout that for a little *nautical lore*, Mr. Swann?"

"Quite a story."

"Quite a place. Changed the whole history of North America, the shoals at Pollock Rip."

"What do you mean?"

"It's where the pilgrims turned around." He turned his back to Swann and continued dousing the deck.

"Turned around?"

"If yah studied your history, Mr. Swann, you'd know that the Mayflower weren't headed fer nowhere near Plymouth Harbor. Were set for the mouth of the Hudson. Hugged the forty-second parallel all the way 'cross, but reached land two weeks late. Ole Captain Jones never knew his bow was drivin' straight intuh the currents of the Gulf Stream. Didn't know a thing about it back then." He shook his head, smiling. "Musta confounded the hell outta 'em."

"But what happened at Pollock Rip?"

"The morning he sighted Cape Cod, ole Jonesie headed south like he was s'pose tuh. But, at sunset he got caught up in the shoals of Pollock Rip. Woulda grounded the poor ship if it wasn't fer a fortunate puff uh wind from the south." *Pchwww*, he spit. "Yep, if it weren't fer Pollock Rip, pilgrims mighta celebrated the first Thanksgiving in Jersey City."

21

They sat silently around the large conference table. Eight of them, Jonathan Pennfield at the head. The room was hazy with smoke, ashes being flicked into half-full coffee cups. Their fingers twiddled with paper clips and ball point pens. Quietly, they all read copies of the same transcript, the report from the National Transportation Safety Board:

> *Based upon our preliminary investigation, we find no evidence of ballistics of any kind. Security procedures at Heathrow were all strictly adhered to. The only hard evidence we have is the flight recorder which indicated that the pilot and crew reacted in accordance with accepted procedures to apparent heavy winds. However, no other weather monitoring devices in the area detected those same wind conditions. Unfortunately, the cause of the crash of GlobalAir Flight 1428 remains a mystery.*

Pennfield bit on the edge of his cup, munching styrofoam bits. After a long period of silence, Rod Quinn, GlobalAir's Public Relations officer, mumbled:

"We almost had to *hope* it was terrorism. That way the public would have considered it an act against the United States, not a major blunder by us. This is exactly what we *didn't* want."

Silent, Pennfield tweaked his chin and said, "So what have we to look forward to?"

"Bookings are gonna be in the toilet," Bruce McSwain, head of operations, answered as he reached across the table for another cup of coffee.

"Of course, Bruce." Quinn dragged on a cigarette. "We're just talking damage control here."

"It'll be at least six months until things get back on track," Earle Stanton, one of the senior financial analysts said. "I checked back data. After TWA 748 and Pan Am 103 it took about six months for bookings to return to prior levels."

"But it's gonna be worse than that," Quinn said. "The public has no one to blame this one on but GlobalAir. Not the weather, not terrorists, not an act of God. The press'll do a hatchet job on us. They'll dig up every negative story from the past five years and hang us out to dry. If you think GlobalAir's stock price is low now, just wait til the effects of all this set in."

Before Pennfield had a chance to ask another question, the door flung open. His secretary. "There's a phone call for you, Jon."

He looked over at her. "I can't talk now, Linda."

"But he's quite insistent."

"Tell him to call back."

"But he's *been* calling back, all afternoon."

"Who is it, some reporter?"

"No, it's a Mr. Swann, a Mr. Ed Swann. He said you would know him."

Surprised, Pennfield ruminated for a moment, then excused himself from the conference room. He marched briskly down the corridor, carefully closed his office door, and picked up the phone. "Ed. It's been awhile. How are—

"There's something strange going on, Jon. I'm sure you figured it out the moment it happened." Swann spewed out, interrupting him.

He whispered. "Yeah, but what can I do. If I told anyone—

"But it's not only your phantom storm. It goes deeper than you would ever think."

"What do you mean?"

"Your family claims ancestry back to the Mayflower, right?"

"Of course, a direct line. Charles Pennfield."

"Well, I never knew this, but exactly at the spot where the plane went down—at the shoals of Pollock Rip—the Mayflower turned around. It was never supposed to land at Plymouth."

"Yeah, but—

"But there's even more. When I talked to Xenobia that day, she muttered something to me. Something about flames that rise where the breakers meet the Sandy elbow, something to do with one of your ancestors, I'm sure. I looked at a nautical chart and the description fits Pollock Rip. Exactly."

"But what's all that got to do with this?"

"Think of it. Your phantom storm. The plane crash. Xenobia's babblings. The Mayflower, Charles Pennfield. It's too strange to be coincidence. There's something spooky about that spot and it has to do with your family."

"But my hands are tied. There's nothing I can do. It'd be suicide if I divulged the information. The whole world would think Global-Air's being run by a kook."

"But you're wrong," said Swann. "There *is* something you can do."

"Yeah?"

"You can let me continue. Let me pick up where I left off last December, Jon…"

"Don't even mention that man's name to me, Jonathan!" Christopher barked into the phone that evening. "He's a charlatan and you know it. I'm surprised you even had the gall to talk to him knowing how I feel."

"But, Chris, don't you find it very strange that it's the exact spot where I experienced the phantom storm?"

"No, not at all. Wasn't the debris from the plane crash spread over a twenty-two mile radius? There's nothing magic about this Pollock Rip, it just happened to get in the way."

"But—

"But, nothing. Don't let Ed Swann put spurious thoughts in your head. It's all a coincidence. Your storm last September has *nothing* to do with this. And then this malarkey about the Mayflower? And Xenobia? Consider the source. Let's move away from fantasy, and focus on reality."

Jonathan paused, then spoke: "Well reality happens to suck. The whole world thinks the tragedy of Flight 1428 is the result of a terrible blunder by GlobalAir. Right now, no one wants to fly us. Last night, one of our 747s took off from Kennedy to Heathrow with twelve passengers on board."

"But this *has* to be temporary, correct?"

"Problem is, we were already in trouble before the tragedy. A stronger carrier would be able to weather this storm. We hardly have enough cash on hand to get us through another month."

"But surely there's something you can do. Surely there's some friendly bankers you can call on."

"No one, no matter how much they like me personally or how they feel about GlobalAir, is going to loan a dime to an airline they believe is going down the tubes."

"So what's your prognosis, doctor?"

"I think GlobalAir's stock will continue its downward spiral and when it gets low enough, some corporate raider'll try to scoop us up at a rock bottom price. I've already heard rumors. Supposedly someone's quietly buying up our stock."

"Who is it?"

"Don't know. Whoever it is seems to be covering their tracks pretty well."

"But the Pennfield Foundation is still a major shareholder."

"Not major enough, only about eleven percent of the stock. Not enough to fend off a hostile takeover."

"But, I don't understand. How can some inexperienced corporate raider ever hope to be more successful than current management in running a tainted carrier?"

"They wouldn't. They'd load up the balance sheet with debt and then sell off assets to the highest bidder. Planes, routes, gates, and slots. When they're all done, there'd be no more GlobalAir. Unfortunately, we're in a position where the sum of the parts is greater than the value of the whole. I think we can all kiss GlobalAir good-bye."

"*Jesus*, are you serious? Do you really think that'll happen. *We can't let it, we mustn't!*"

Christopher took out his frustration on the typewriter that evening, striking the keys of his Smith-Corona with a renewed fervor. The thought that, for personal profit, some Wall Street opportunist would have the gall to destroy a great company built by his grandfather flamed his insides. *It just wasn't proper, wasn't right, they weren't playing by the rules of gentlemanly business practice.* The only salve to his emotional bruises proved to be the content of the paragraph he was tapping out on his typewriter. Another section of his address: more about the early colonial Pennfields—Thomas, Nathaniel, and Peter—as they built a great trading empire in eighteenth century Newport. A different breed, he thought. They *built* businesses, they didn't *destroy* them like today's profiteers. He typed faster:

> *By the early 1720s, Thomas Pennfield and his two sons, Nathaniel and Peter, had accumulated a modest fortune trading Newport lumber, candles and rum for foodstuffs from New York and Philadelphia, whale oil from Nantucket, and fine European goods trans-shipped from London through Boston. But perhaps their most ambitious voyage occurred in 1721, when they first sailed to Barbados and the West Indies, enjoying a profitable venture trading for molasses and salt. The voyage turned out to be a milestone in the history of the Pennfield family in many ways...*

*   *   *

The Carolina Coast
September, 1721

"Father! Father!" Young Nathaniel Pennfield rushed across the deck. "Look. Over there!" He pointed his shaking finger to port.

Thomas Pennfield squinted. Just tipping over the horizon, he could make out the image of a bobbing mast. At first, his eyesight proved not to be as keen as his son's. But, as the mast slowly extended above the horizon, his own two eyes soon confirmed what at first he believed to be merely the product of Nathaniel's imagination. Flying from the mast, he saw a small black flag. On it, he was sure he could make out that frightful symbol. The Skull and Crossbones.

He shuddered. He had heard many stories of these highwaymen of the sea. How they preyed upon small vessels like his, looting them of their valuable cargoes, wreaking havoc with legitimate enterprise. And—he shuddered again—how oftentimes these wicked marooners would not only loot cargo, but also take the opportunity to replenish their crews, kidnapping seamen from merchant vessels and forcing them to sign articles, turning legitimate sailors into pirates in their own right. Not only did Pennfield fear for their valuable cargo, he feared for their very lives.

A strong northeasterly breeze beat against his right cheek as he considered his options. Surely, if the Captain of that menacing brigantine so desired he could overtake their small sloop with little effort. Pennfield's only hope was the slim possibility that perhaps the Captain's eye was on another more rewarding plunder. Indeed, as the vessel surfaced over the horizon, it appeared to be pursuing more of a northwesterly course.

With less than two hours of daylight left, Thomas Pennfield chose his fate: he would maintain his northerly course until sunset, then tack his sloop about and set his course due east, hoping that the pirate vessel either had not seen him or was not interested in him. If the brigantine continued to pursue its northwesterly course throughout the night, by daybreak the two vessels would be out of each other's sight. It was his best hope.

Pennfield paced the deck of his sloop all night long. Only with the light of day would he know whether or not the brigantine had chosen to pursue him. For hours, his mind haunted him with the vision of a large menacing bow hovering over his small sloop by the light of the morning sun, marauding hooligans bursting onto his deck.

Yet, as the sun edged over the horizon, he was surprised to see no other vessels, friend or foe, within the arc of his eyesight. Only his small sloop and a tranquil morning sea. Silently, he bowed his head, certain that it was only through the aid of the Lord that he had escaped his treacherous circumstances. As he meditated, he realized he had learned a valuable lesson over the last half day: never again would he question the virtue of his mounting riches as the profits of his trade did not come without considerable risk. And, as he took a moment to relax on deck later that evening, he learned something more about the constitution of his two sons.

"No man has the right to plunder a legal trading vessel!" young Nathaniel exclaimed. "All those marooners ought to be hung and left to rot! Wouldn't mind watching a few of 'em wiggle under a gallows myself."

"You talk as if all merchants are full of virtue, Nat," his older brother Peter countered, his long mane of bright red hair flowing down his neck.

"And what was meant by that, Peter?" Their father asked.

"It takes very little thought to realize that most merchants are not of the virtuous sort, father." Peter looked him in the eyes. "How many rules do they bend? How many taxes do they evade? How many seaman do they exploit with their niggardly wages? And to think, some of them have the outright temerity to trade human beings for molasses. Perhaps they're the ones who should be brought to the gallows!"

"Slaves aren't human beings," Nathaniel stood up, "they're savages. Legitimate commodity for trade, no different than tobacco or rum. Right, father?"

"You ask a very difficult question, Nat." He paused, then looked over towards his older son. "But, Peter, to defend the very sort who would have pillaged and plundered away at our very means of livelihood is an act of outright foolishness."

Long before their discussion that evening, Thomas Pennfield had realized it would be his younger son, Nathaniel, who would someday carry the torch of the family business. Even in his youth, Nat displayed a capacity for commerce, always asking questions of his father about finances, expenses, emerging markets, new trading partners. His older son, Peter, was different. At times, he would withdraw and be so quiet for such long stretches—days, sometimes weeks—it was difficult to really know what thoughts flirted with his mind.

Little changed about the two young men over the next several years. With each day, Nathaniel grew more into the adult who would one day lead the family business to a level of prosperity that even he, himself, would have found hard to imagine. As comfortable as Nathaniel was in his role as a merchant-sailor, it was clear that Peter was equally uncomfortable. Indeed, he was looking for something else.

In the summer of 1724, Peter Pennfield discovered what his fate would be. By then, the Pennfield fleet had grown to three vessels, the largest of which was a new ninety-foot brigantine built for them in Newport Harbor. In one of its early voyages through The Vineyard Sound, Peter and several crew members went off to fish in one of the vessel's small shallops towards Tarpaulin Cove, a small protected inlet off Naushon Island. As they sailed peacefully into the tranquil cove, they noticed several other small shallops—carrying other fishermen presumably—approaching from starboard. As Peter beckoned to them, they sailed closer and closer. What was it they wanted? he thought. Perhaps they were not familiar with these waters and desired guidance? But, no! As they ventured closer, it became clear what their intentions were. Just as the lead fishing boat approached the shallop's stern, six of its supposed-fishermen jumped aboard brandishing daggers and pistols. Pirates!

Peter and his small crew were ill-prepared to mount a challenge to the wanton marooners. With little struggle, they were taken prisoner and forced to sail the shallop to the pirates' main vessel, a man-of-war named *The Compass Rose* anchored in a hidden cove in one of the nearby islands.

That evening they were taken before the infamous Captain Thomas Rogers—known for plundering hundreds of trading vessels both in New England and the West Indies—and given two choices: either sign articles or be shackled in the vessel's hold until they could be thrown overboard on the high seas. Having little choice, Peter and the others signed. As the wicked Captain Rogers presented them with articles, Peter's eyes were drawn to the final two:

ARTICLE IX

Other than those taken as proper prize, and under the strict watch of an appointed sentinel, no women shall be allowed on board punishable by marooning or death whichever should be most fitting to the deed.

ARTICLE X

Anyone caught below deck holding an open candle, whether sober or drunk, shall receive forty lashes by the light of the next noonday sun.

At first Peter was a quiet, obedient crewmember of The Compass Rose, playing only a small role in its various plunderings as it worked its way down the coast. Indeed, his intention was only to wait for the proper moment to escape and somehow work his way back to Newport. But, that Winter, as they rounded the Cape of Good Hope and headed for Madagascar—safe haven for all pirates and buccaneers—a change came over him. He began enjoying the adventures of piracy as they pillaged and plundered unsuspecting Moorish vessels in the Red Sea and then drank rum by the light of the moon, divvying up their loot. The following summer, off the coast of West Africa, he became a complete convert when they over-took a merchant slaver, liberated fifty African savages, and then along with them reveled through the night emptying the twenty casks of rum they had confiscated from the slaver's hold.

Word of Peter's exploits brought much remorse to his father and brother back in Newport. The more they heard about this unknown young marooner—with long bright red hair and deep blue eyes—brandishing his cutlass as The Compass Rose wreaked havoc with vessels on the West Indian shipping lanes, the more they were certain that it was Peter. It had to be him, they figured. After all, despite a rigorous search, they could never find the shallop. Peter was much too good a sailor to lose his boat in the local waters he knew so well. And wasn't The Compass Rose sighted in that very area within days of his disappearance? Didn't survivors from some of the Newport trading vessels plundered by The Compass Rose over the past year *swear* that one of its leading crewmembers bore a striking resemblance to Peter Pennfield? With each day, the whispers grew within the merchant community of Newport building to a quiet resentment of Thomas and Nathaniel Pennfield. The rumors became so widespread that even a common seaman alluded to them right on the deck of the Pennfield's brigantine one day.

"Ain't it a shame about poor Peter, Sir?"

Thomas Pennfield, striding across the deck flanked by Nathaniel, stopped short and turned towards the seamen. "*What* about Peter?"

"About how the pirates caught 'em and turned 'em in tuh one uh their own, Sir."

Fuming, Nathaniel stepped up to the seaman and grabbed him by the collar. "Bite your tongue, rogue! No pirates caught any kin of ours. Peter died a noble death fighting to save his crew in a storm off Tarpaulin Cove!"

Despite his family's denials, sightings of Peter Pennfield became more frequent as The Compass Rose ravaged the coast between Newfoundland and the West Indies during the ensuing months. Indeed, Peter turned into such a ferocious marauder, petty jealousies soon surfaced among certain members of the crew. As Peter's infamy grew, mumblings could be heard on the deck of The Compass Rose. *Who was this man—flesh and blood of a niggardly merchant—to think he could ever be a real buccaneer? Why, he has no more right to a share of our plunderings than his father would himself!* Each time such thoughts circled the decks of The Compass Rose, it was Captain Rogers who stopped them dead in their tracks. "Any one of you scoundrels who could match the exploits of this son of a merchant man, be the one to take Peter Pennfield's rightful share!" he would tell them. Yet, in winter of that year, Peter found himself entangled in a situation from which even the all-powerful Captain Rogers could not save him.

He first set eyes on her in a tavern in Martinique. A beautiful young girl with flowing blonde hair, crystal blue eyes, and supple tan skin, Marie Dela Croix had been kidnapped from a merchantman in the Mediterranean and taken to the French West Indies. Perhaps she was a common whore working the harbor taverns, Peter thought, but why was it each time after he was with her he wanted her again and again? Why was it each time they left port to maraude and plunder more merchant vessels, he could not wait to return to her bed? What was this magic spell she had cast over him? During the three months The Compass Rose ravaged the Caribbean, Marie had become much more than a mere belly-warmer to Peter. And, as The Compass Rose was preparing to depart on a six-month voyage up the coast to Newfoundland, Peter learned that he had become much more than one-of-many patrons to her.

"Take me with you, Peter." Her deep, blue eyes soothed him as she ran her hand through his hair.

"But I don't know how I could ever do that, Marie." He sat up on the side of the small bed in the dark room upstairs from a portside tavern.

"Why? Don't you love me as I love you?" Her eyes glistened, overwhelming him with a powerful opiate.

He leaned towards her, his eyes locked onto hers. She was captivating. Beautiful, exotic and captivating. So spine-tingling were her eyes, so overwhelming was her fresh, youthful face, so convincing were her simple words, he was incapable of fully answering her. "Yes, but..."

"But what, Peter?"

"But, it would be in defiance of articles to stow a woman aboard ship. I don't know how we could ever..."

Before Peter could finish, she sat up from the bed and raveled her long blonde hair over her head, covering it with his hat. Then, she picked up his shirt from the floor and buttoned it over her soft, exotic skin, tinged a soothing shade of tan from months in the bright Caribbean sun. Peter fixed his eyes on her, scanning up and down this strange sight. Yes, *he* knew that standing beneath his hat and behind his shirt was a beautiful young woman, but would *they?* If she could cut her hair before they departed, no one would ever have to know.

With the frequent comings and goings from the ship's crew, hardly anyone paid attention to the fair young boy who, along with ten others, signed articles before Captain Rogers on the deck of The Compass Rose its first night from port. Perhaps this new recruit— this Michael Dela Croix—was young and a bit slight of frame, but a life of piracy was known to attract all sorts of outcasts and malcontents. Some of the more jealous crewmen may have thought it a bit strange how this young boy stuck so closely to Peter Pennfield, but it wasn't uncommon for a new recruit to become the protégé of a more accomplished buccaneer. As The Compass Rose sailed northward, young Michael more than proved his mettle, brandishing his cutlass with the rest of them as they raided unsuspecting vessels and then consuming more than his fair share of rum as they reveled over their spoils. But, as the ship approached New England, some of the crewmembers began to question why Peter and this young Michael would go off alone in the shallop for hours at a time whenever The Compass Rose took a brief respite from its mission.

By the time The Compass Rose rounded Nantucket and sailed towards The Vineyard Sound, several crewmembers suspected that there was more to Michael Dela Croix than met the eye. Their suspicions grew so, that seven of them made a pact: whoever was the first to uncover the real story of this slight, young boy would win three extra shares from their next plundering.

The discovery occurred in, of all places, Tarpaulin Cove. Knowing that the cove would be the perfect, secluded spot to sail the shallop, two of them hid in the thick bushes close to shore and, much to their glee, watched excitedly as they spotted the shallop approaching with Peter Pennfield and Michael Dela Croix aboard. Their eyes widened when, once ashore, Michael removed his clothes and revealed a perfect female form. *Why, it was Marie, the wench from Martinique, they should have known all along!*

"And let's empty a cask to the one among us profligate enough to stow his own private wench on The Compass Rose!" One of the two shouted as the crew rattled the deck's floorboards in a drunken fervor that evening.

Captain Rogers, himself having consumed a fair amount of rum, stood up at the bow and addressed his crewman. "And what was meant by that?"

"Peter Pennfield, Cap'n. He's got his own wench aboard, Sir."

Pennfield dropped his cup of rum as the Captain's eyes bored into him. "Is this true, Peter?"

"No. No. Not at all, Sir." He stood up, shielding Marie. "I have no idea of what they say."

"Michael Dela Croix's nothing but a common wench, Sir." The crewman shouted. "I seen 'er naked with my own two eyes!"

Raucous shouts of *Wench! Wench! Wench!* instantly overwhelmed the deck. Within moments, a drunken barrage of crewmen descended upon Marie, several of them holding Peter back, and paraded her around the deck, their shouts building to a crescendo. With Marie's arms flapping like a hummingbird's wings, they furiously ripped off her clothes—frothing dogs fighting for a bone—the others swigging rum as they watched in glee. The drunken pirates pawed at her, running their dirty fingers across her breasts, pawing at her crotch, slapping her buttocks. By the time Marie had been passed up through the throng of drunken marooners to the bow, she was completely naked. Captain Rogers raised his arms to quiet them down.

"And what have you to say for yourself, *Michael* Dela Croix?" Rogers snickered.

"It was just me. I did it all myself. He had nothing to do with it." She pleaded, wrapping her arms over her breasts, shivering from the cold nighttime breeze.

"Peter, is what she says true?" The Captain looked him in the eyes.

Peter drew a deep breath and swelled out his chest. "No. I helped her do it. I snuck her on, Sir."

Death! Death! Death! Immediately, the drunken crewmen cried out the word, all pointing their fingers directly at Peter. He looked Marie in the eyes, and then up to Captain Rogers.

"You leave me with little choice, Peter Pennfield, son of the merchant man."

Death! Death! Death! the crew shouted out again like bloodthirsty heathen, sensing an imminent execution. Captain Rogers raised his arms. The crew was silent, all ears turned towards the bow.

"For an act in strict defiance of the articles of The Compass Rose," Rogers announced, "you shall be shackled in the hold until such time you can be marooned with your wench on a deserted island, your only provisions a flint for fire and a jug for refreshment!"

A gasp of disappointment from the crew. That old salt Rogers had taken it easy on him. In recompense for his many exploits, no doubt. Hoping for a bloody execution, all they would get was a marooning. And that would most likely not occur until The Compass Rose returned to the West Indies or African coast. Until then, though, they'd have his wench to keep them occupied.

Within moments of Rogers' announcement, Peter was thrown into the hold and shackled in irons. From that day on, the rage inside him boiled. *To think those barbarous scalawags would do this to him after everything he had done for them!* Sitting day after day in a stinking hold, hungry and weak—a mockery—barely thrown a bone for nourishment, his former crewmates stoking the flames of his rage each night as they laughed about it in a drunken fervor on the deck above. *And what they were doing to his love, Marie, rubbed salt in the wound!*

The only times Peter could even see Marie—and learn of her sorry fate—was during a plundering, when the crew was so busy ravaging another vessel they would take their covetous eyes off her for the moment. One night, as The Compass Rose marauded a merchant vessel filled with casks of fresh Newport rum off Nantucket Island—amidst the clanging of cutlasses, the shaking of floorboards, the shouts of buccaneers, and the screams of surprised sailors—Marie ran down to the hold.

"Peter! Peter!" She ran to him, out of breath. *"I've seen where Captain Rogers keeps the keys to your shackles!"*

Silent, he ran his eyes up and down her beaten frame. Her bruised legs, her puffed face, her sorrowful eyes. Then, in rage, he shouted: *"Those heathens! What have they done to you?"* He clutched her, the shackles dangling from his arms.

"Peter, don't worry about that. We have little time." She pushed away and answered quickly. "Did you hear me? *I've found where the Captain hides his keys!*"

"Yes, but…"

"But what?"

"But what good does it do us?"

"They're in a wooden locker next to his bed, and no one's watching it." She answered, shaking.

"Can you get at them?"

"I think so."

His mind quickly churned. "Then go. Go. See if it's still unguarded. And…," his eyes slowly scanned the many casks of rum stowed throughout the hold, "…bring me a flint as well."

Bobbing to the swift currents of Nantucket Sound, The Compass Rose abutted the sorry merchant sloop, their wooden hulls crashing. Wild buccaneers jumped back and forth brandishing their cutlasses and waving their pistols in defiance. The nature of their loot whipped them into a rabid, thunderous fury as they passed the sloop's cargo amongst them, unloading cask after cask of rum onto the deck of The Compass Rose. A fortunate plundering, indeed! Amidst all the furor, it took little effort for Marie to sneak into the Captain's unguarded quarters. Quickly, she rummaged through his locker, looking over her shoulder to see if she had been spotted. Her heart beat rapidly. *Surely, they would kill her if they found her here!* As she ran her hand through the locker, her fingers felt a cold piece of iron under several of the Captain's mementoes. *Thank God, the key!* She stuffed it down her shirt, ran for the door, and then stopped short and looked around. *A flint, he said he needed a flint!* She spotted one near the Captain's bed, quickly picked it up and stuffed it in her shirt as well. She burst for the hold.

"Run upstairs and hide in the shallop!" Peter instructed her as she undid his shackles. Then, he lunged towards a cask of rum, broke it open, and spilled its contents onto the floor.

"Peter, what are you doing?" Marie stood there frozen, confused by Peter's sudden actions.

"If we're going to fall, we're going to take those slovenly heathen with us. Now go! Up into the shallop!" As Marie ran for the hatch, Peter ignited a spark with his flint, setting the spilt rum ablaze, now soaked into the brittle wooden floor. With the flames crackling, Peter burst up the hatch behind her.

Despite the action on the deck above—casks being thrown clumsily, raucous crewmen brandishing their cutlasses—one lone member of the crew spotted Peter as he rose from the hatch. *"Pennfield!"* The crewman summoned his mates. *"Hey, it's Pennfield. He got loose!"*

Peter stopped short, looked towards the crewman who spotted him, and then turned quickly, heading for Marie and the shallop off the portside rail. Five of them ran after him, waving their cutlasses over their heads, bloodthirsty gleams in their eyes.

He lunged for Marie in the shallop. But as she looked at him, her eyes glowed a strange hue. Peter gasped. "Marie? What's—

She did not reach for him, didn't help him onto the shallop. Instead, she scowled at him, pushing him back onto the ship within the clutches of the charging buccaneers.

Stumbling to the deck, he looked up at her with bewildered eyes.

The buccaneers surrounded him. As they thrust their daggers towards his chest, Marie smiled wickedly, then whispered: *"The mean spirits of the wrongful dead damn their living perpetrators!"* Her glowing eyes bore into him.

At that precise instant, an explosion of flame cascaded from the hatch, lighting up the sky. Within seconds: a fiery hell, arching flames sprinting across the decks, feeding off the dry, wooden floorboards, quickly bursting over to the merchant sloop, the two vessels fueling a massive conflagration at sea. Shocked crewmen ran for the safety of the shallops. The flames consumed the wooden ships so quickly, though, even the shallops were ablaze. Then, with a sudden lurch, the fate of the two vessels was sealed. *Aground!* In all the confusion, the crew's judgment tinged by rum, the ships had crashed into the shoals of Pollock Rip!

The flames, an orange blaze reaching for the heavens, were spotted as far away as Boston Harbor to the north and Nantucket to the south. Later that week, *The Newport Mercury* gave it its name: *The Blaze at Pollock Rip.* At best count, there were only three survivors. Two young crewmen from the merchant sloop and one from The Compass Rose who hid out until he could join up with another ship of buccaneers. Several months later, his account of what happened worked its way back to Newport: *It was Peter Pennfield, son of the merchant man, and his lowly wench who caused the blaze!*

As the whispers worked their way around Newport, Thomas and Nathaniel Pennfield began to feel like outcasts, snubbed by Newport's merchant community. The mumblings did not escape their ears: *It was him again, the aberrant Pennfield son, burning a worthy merchant ship to ashes!* Thomas Pennfield soon became so enraged over these rumors, that one day he stood on Newport's wharf, waved his fist at his fellow merchants, and announced: "Peter Pennfield, God rest his soul, died two years ago in a storm off Tarpaulin Cove. He's dead now, been dead for two years, and he'll remain dead for eternity. Enough said!"

*   *   *

Thirty-eight years later, the first sighting occurred. The captain of a merchant ship, proceeding eastward from Newport to Newfoundland, spotted mysterious orange flames flickering over Pollock Rip. The legend grew when, sixteen years later, the entire crew of a British man-of-war claimed to have seen similar flames. From then on, not more than twenty or thirty years would go by without someone having reported a sighting. According to legend, they all shared the same vision: *The flames of the mighty Compass Rose set ablaze by some anonymous malcontent pirate bold enough to sneak his woman aboard ship!*

22

"*It's Westerfeld!*" Jonathan shouted into the phone.

"What?" Christopher answered, startled.

"Tom Westerfeld's the one buying up GlobalAir stock."

"Jonathan, are you sure?"

"Damned sure. Our investment bankers were able to trace the purchases to some of his accounts, the bastard."

"I'm shocked. I don't know what to say."

"I know exactly what to say. GlobalAir'll be gone in a year if he gets control. He'll break it up faster than you can say leveraged buyout. Its his modus operandi."

"I can't believe he would do that. How could he ever…"

"Do you think Winnie knows?" Jonathan asked.

"I have no idea. They're still in France. I haven't talked to her in three weeks, since she told me about the marriage."

"Can you reach her?"

"Perhaps. But would that be right, should I meddle?"

"*Of course you should meddle!,*" he shouted. "I'd call her myself if I thought it would work."

"Yes, but—

"But you've always been able to influence her. She listens to you."

"But do you think *she* could influence *him?*"

"Come on, Chris. When have you remembered Winnie *not* being able to influence a member of the opposite sex?"

"Perhaps, but—

"This is GlobalAir, Chris. *Grandfather's GlobalAir!*"

Christopher mulled it over all afternoon. He sat out on his sun porch, gazing out on the street but focusing on nothing. For some odd reason, he was hesitant to dial, punching the first few numbers several times, then halting. He asked himself why he was so reluctant. *It was only Winnie he'd be calling, wasn't it?* Just before dinner, he began dialing again, but this time forced himself to finish.

"Well, I see Mr. Westerfeld has decided to bestow a small gift upon the Pennfields in celebration of his formal inclusion into the family." He said the moment she picked up the phone.

"Huh?"

"Edwina, this is your uncle."

"Unk? What's going—

"While you and the illustrious Whiz Kid have been basking on the shores of southern France, we find out your new husband has been secretly buying up stock in GlobalAir."

"Yes, but that's the business he's in, isn't it? He mentioned it to me—he told me it was undervalued because of the crash, that it was a good buy—but I really thought nothing of it."

"Well, I suggest you think again. Your uncle Jonathan is convinced his intent is to gain control and then break up the airline. You *must* convince him otherwise."

"But if it wasn't him, wouldn't someone else do the same thing? Come on, get real."

"My dear Winnie, the problem is *someone else* is not married to a member of the Pennfield family."

"Yes, but I have a slight problem with that."

"And what would that be?"

"Before we married, we made a promise that we would keep our professional lives completely separate from our personal lives."

"But this is the *Pennfield family* we're talking about, Winnie."

"But, this is business, Unk."

Winnie's confrontational manner bothered him, causing an evening of anxiety. It was the first time he could ever remember that Winnie had stood up to him. By nighttime, though, he sunk into his mattress, allowing its soft cushion to mould to the contours of his back. He closed his eyes and relaxed, flushing all negative thoughts from his mind for the moment. He would worry about Tom Westerfeld in the morning, he decided. Given time, Winnie would come around, he was sure. This was only his first stab at her; eventually, he would convince her to talk sense into her new husband, he was sure he could. She was only being difficult, a common trait of her's.

He shifted, glanced over at Elizabeth, and yawned, allowing more positive thoughts to fill his mind: after all, in six short weeks he would be standing before a select group of academic and political dignitaries extolling the virtues of the Pennfield family at the anniversary ceremony. He closed his eyes and silently repeated the words to himself:

> *Governor Winters, President Collins, Senator Hessler, Provost Murray, Reverend Clergy, Distinguished Guests. We are here today to celebrate the legacy of a great American family. A family of which I feel both humbled and privileged to be counted as a member...*

Drowsiness gently clouded his thoughts and settled his bones. The pleasantly-scented Vermont spring air sneaked in through the open window and tickled his nostrils. His eyes grew heavy and he drifted into a comfortable, restful sleep.

Sometime later, shuffling in the mattress, he awakened. But not a frenzied awakening. A temporary hiatus: the beginning of another pleasant, re-energizing cycle of sleep. He yawned, stretching his arms over his head, and repositioned himself. For a brief instant, he opened his eyes then quickly closed them. He stirred and opened his eyes again. This time longer. He took a short breath as his eyes widened.

Lazily, his eyes wandered around the dark room. The sheer white curtains luffing to a puff of wind from the open window. A beam of moonlight casting shiny highlights across the hard wood floorboards. The throw rug off-kilter at the foot of the bed. He and Elizabeth stretched out across the mattress. His bathrobe hanging from the hook on the door. *What! What was that?* He blinked.

Jesus! Everything was out of place, backwards, inside-out, not where it was supposed to be. One more time, he allowed his eyes to drift around the cockeyed room. The windows, the walls, the dresser, the bed and—he gasped—him and Elizabeth. *He was upside down! Suspended from the ceiling, he was looking down upon himself and Elizabeth!*

It was vivid, everything below, so shockingly vivid. Elizabeth on the right side, stirring as she slept. He, himself, on the left, the covers drawn up to his neck. The night light and alarm clock sitting on the dresser. His wallet and pocket change. Seventy-four cents. Two quarters. Two dimes. Four pennies. Just as he had left them earlier. Then, he shuddered.

No, no, no. Oh, God, no. Don't tell me this is it! It would be such an irony, such a waste to end it all now before the anniversary ceremony! But, as much as he tried to convince himself otherwise, he could not deny the evidence. He was dead. His inner essence had escaped from his bodily trap. Platonic duality was a fact.

Hovering above the room, his buoyant essence bouncing against the ceiling, he looked down upon his corpse, examining his earthly remains. He looked good, very good, he concluded, for a fifty-two year old man who had just expired. His skin with a healthy touch of color, his chin firm, his cheekbones high, and his flowing mane of silver hair sparkling in the darkness. At least in death he would be as handsome as ever. *Yes, open casket, definitely!* But, hold on, it had hardly been ten minutes. His body was still warm. The bacteria had hardly a chance to eat away at him.

Then he noticed something. Small, yes. But confusing. Couldn't he see his nostrils flaring ever so slightly? Was his body still breathing, his chest expanding and contracting? And—*wait!*—now he moved. He moved his arm and repositioned his head. He wasn't dead, couldn't be, an impossibility! *Thank God, Thank God*—he sighed with relief—*it was only a dream!*

Yet, it was unlike any dream he had ever experienced. There was a realism to it. He was sure, *absolutely sure*, he was suspended from the ceiling, bouncing around as if filled with helium. And he and Elizabeth below looked so real. He would swear he could reach down and touch them.

And then, ever so slightly, a soothing wisp of air pushed him. Gently caressing his pseudo-body, it puffed him across the room. Feeling unanchored, he flapped his imaginary arms and legs, searching for something to grab onto. Yet, the more furiously he flapped, the more the gentle wisps of air pushed him slowly towards the partially open window until he passed right through it, streaming through the solid glass like water through a sieve.

Wow! He was outside floating over the street! Yes, he realized it was a dream, but the feelings were so vivid, so pleasant, so real. Hovering over his roof, his arms being rustled by the leaves of a tall oak. He could see the Brookses next door—Jeanie and Clark—asleep in their bed through the darkened window. And down the street, Jimmy Baylor, pulling up in his driveway after his late night shift at the firehouse. *Jesus, this was fun, he was a child again!*

The same gentle breeze pushed him onward. Down the street, right on Main, up the hill, and towards the college. The clock tower, he floated right by it, could practically touch its hands as it turned quarter past two. He looked down. A few students staggering across campus after some late night bash. The campus security van parked in front of Boynton Residence Hall. The bright lights from the infirmary. *The floating, he loved it, loved the marvelous floating!*

And then he rose. The breezes caressing and lifting him, he rose far above it all. He watched the campus shrink: the brick and ivy buildings becoming smaller and smaller until they were enveloped by the surrounding mountains and then obscured by the puffy clouds. He was above it all: far, far above, drifting with the night-time zephyrs!

A paradise indeed! Stars and mountains and trees! He swooped down over the seasonally abandoned ski-lifts. Killington? Stowe?

Or was it Bromley? Whatever it was, he had been there before. He knew it. His eyes followed the winding mountain roads, the two-lane highways. Everything so real. Not visual broadstrokes, but amazingly vivid details. An isolated Volvo, Buick, BMW. Traffic Lights. Power lines. Railroad stations. Two or three stray deer at the edge of the woods. And, now, the rolling green hills of the Berkshires. Yes, the Berkshires, he was sure. So relaxing, this marvelous dream was a tonic, a therapy!

Now a black tar discontinuity in the midst of the hills. *The Mass Pike! Definitely, the Mass Pike!* Building speed, he followed it as it swerved through the landscape. Mountains and valleys and farmland and countryside: a soporific paradise! He opened his mouth wide and breathed in the cool nighttime air as it streamed by his face. *Jesus, was this exhilarating, a natural high!* He felt so calm, so rested, breezing along on his carpet of air.

Then, in the distance, the rolling hills flattened. Far away, to the south, he could make out a craggly coastline and a tranquil sea shimmering in the moonlight. And, peaking over the horizon, a majestic sight: tall spires and swooping suspension cables. *Yes, the bridge, the Newport Bridge! His dream had taken him to the city of his ancestors' greatest triumphs!* Gently he descended, down over the water and then above the sleeping town: circling the proud steeple of Trinity Church, along Thames, up Memorial, swooping around the parking lot where Stone Villa once stood. And then he breezed along Bellevue, past the mansions: Roseclifff. Beachwood. The Marble House. The Breakers.

Now a quick, sharp turn onto Ocean Drive and then out onto the point. Along the old cinder driveway and out to the Pennfield family cottage. *But why here? Why tonight? Hadn't he been here enough?* Like ash over flame, he rose. Over and around its circular piazza. Up even with the crow's nest. Now over the roof: the sight so vivid, he could count the shingles. He flew over to the tool shed, through the branches of the old weeping willow, and looked below.

When he first saw them, he immediately recoiled, lurching back in shock: *the two men, the two big men he had seen—or thought he had seen—that night last November!* They were working, digging with shovels and a pick ax, paying no attention to him, working away as if he wasn't there. Like ghosts, they shimmered, their images transparent. He hovered over them, observing from different angles. Then as he flew directly above, he noticed it: the box he thought he had seen that night. He studied it carefully and gasped. *No box, it was a coffin. They were burying a coffin outside the cottage's back door!*

When he awakened the next morning, he felt more rested than he had in years. Yet he remembered everything about the dream in vivid detail—bouncing up against the bedroom ceiling, passing through the window, the street, the campus, his marvelously exhilarating flight to Newport and—he winced—the two men burying the casket out back, just as he had seen them that night last November from the cottage's kitchen window. Refreshed, he trotted down the front steps, drinking in the clear, fresh air in celebration of a new spring day and writing off the dream's strange ending to the quirkiness of the human mind.

Then he stopped short on the second step from bottom and gasped.

Abruptly, he turned around and bounded back up the steps, wisked through the front door, and reached for the banister as he rushed up towards his bedroom. Halfway up, Elizabeth called to him from the kitchen, the aroma of morning coffee wafting up the stairs:

"What's the matter, Chris, forget something?"

"Yes, precisely," he answered without hesitation. "My wristwatch, dear."

"That's the man I married. The absent-minded professor…"

Once in the bedroom, he lurched straight for the dresser. But it wasn't his wristwatch he was looking for. He placed his fingers on the dresser's smooth cherry top and tapped nervously. He allowed them to wander, trailing with his eyes. Carefully, he fingered the change sitting next to his alarm clock, running his fingertips slowly across the cool metal surface of each coin. He counted: two quarters, two dimes, four pennies. *Seventy-four cents.*

For the next several days, he obsessed over it. Didn't Weisman—
or was it Nordstrom—describe a phenomenon similar to what he
had experienced late Tuesday night during their discussion in the
Faculty Club last November? Something to do with a person's
mind actually leaving one's body? What was it they called it? By
week's end, his curiosity compelled him to investigate further.

He trotted up the corridor stairway in the Faculty Office Building
on Saturday afternoon and stopped at top to catch his breath. Jerking his head in both directions, he opened his office door and
snapped it shut behind him. Then he sat behind his desk and
unlocked his lower desk drawer, his hand shaking. He pulled out
the green pressboard folder and ruffled through the pages of notes
and Xeroxed articles Jennifer had collected for him over the last
several months. He was sure she had found something, that there
was some sort of article explaining it in the folder.

He wiped a drop of sweat from his brow and looked out his
office window for a moment. He felt funny, like a child, sneaking
around like this. A grown man nervous about flipping through an
innocent file in his own office.

Halfway through the folder, he found it. *The Out of Body Experience: A survey of the literature. By S. Manuel Rao, PHd.* His eyes ran
across the small print, too anxious to absorb each individual word
his first time through. Within two paragraphs, he found a definition
of the phenomena: *An Out of Body Experience (OBE) is a paranormal
event during which an undefined part of the psyche leaves the physical
body and travels to a remote location. The most fascinating research in the
area is that of "veridicial" OBEs where a subject's mind travels to a remote
location and afterwards the subject is able to accurately report what had
occurred there.*

Pennfield read the section carefully, intrigued by the story of a
Stanford University graduate student named Arthur "Red" Elliot.
During a series of twenty-seven separate experiments conducted
over a two-year period from 1969 to 1971, Elliot, in self-induced
OBEs, had been able to successfully retrieve undisclosed messages
hidden in a room on the opposite side of campus with amazing

accuracy. Once he was even able to report that a teaching assistant stationed in the room had taken an unplanned phone call, relating the conversation virtually verbatim.

Interesting, yes, Pennfield thought. But that was much different than what he experienced, wasn't it? There wasn't anything at all vaguely related to the flying sensation he experienced last Tuesday night. Clearly, what he experienced was much different. *But then what about the seventy-four cents?*

He strained to remember everything else from that evening, some other verifiable event to latch onto, something to help him prove whether or not his mind *actually did* leave his body during that unusual dream. He concentrated, squeezing his eyes shut. He recalled everything. Hovering over the room. Flying out the window. Seeing the Brookses next door in bed through the window. Flying down the street towards campus. Hovering over the clock tower on the commons. He paused, biting his lip. Yes, yes, the clock tower, of course. Didn't he remember a time? Wasn't it two-fifteen when he flew by? Was there anything else he can link to that time, something he can verify? *Think. Think hard, concentrate.* Ski slopes, winding mountain roads, the Mass Pike, the Newport Bridge. Nothing, no specific event he could think of that he might be able to verify as occurring at two-fifteen on Wednesday morning. But, certainly there must be something, he thought. Go back, start over. Repeat the sequence, *strain!* The bedroom. The street. The clock tower. Campus. The security van. Yes, yes! He slapped his hand on the desk. Right after he flew by the clock tower, he remembered seeing a campus security van parked in front of Boynton. Immediately, he sprang from his chair.

Cap Howard, a veteran of thirty-eight years on the Campus Security Force, sipped on his can of Coca-Cola, leaned back in his wooden swivel chair, and placed his feet up on a corner of the recently re-varnished surface of his cluttered desk. He lifted a copy of *Field and Stream* from one of the piles, propped it up against his paunchy middle, and skimmed the table of contents. Just as his eyes grew heavy, the buzzer from the front Security Office door jolted him out of his drowsiness. His head snapped up as if in revolt. *Damn,* he thought. A quiet spring Saturday afternoon: this was supposed to be gravy time. He never would have put himself on this shift if he thought there would *actually be something to do.*

Slowly, he swiveled around and lifted himself from his chair. Although the door buzzed three more times in the next several seconds, it had no effect in hastening Howard's slow gait from his office in the rear of the Campus Security area to the counter and large glass door out front. If this were some spoiled student pulling a prank, he'd pay for it, Howard thought. He was surprised when he saw not a student at all, but Professor Christopher Pennfield's nose pressed up against the glass. He quickly unlocked the door and let him in.

"Professor Pennfield, what a surprise seeing you here today." Howard forced a smile. "With weather like this, thought someone like you'd be out playing a little golf."

"Had to catch up on a few odds and ends. While I was here, there was something I wanted to talk to you about, Cap."

"Oh?"

"In my frequent conversations with parents and alumni, the same topic always seems to pop up."

"Not getting' enough grads into Harvard, are we?" Howard raised an eyebrow.

"No, quite the contrary," Pennfield answered with a scowl. "Our academic reputation is stronger than ever. It has to do with carousing."

"Carousing?"

"Yes, you know, Cap. Beer blasts and frat parties and drunken brawls and wanton sex and the like."

"Can't say we're immune to it, Professor, but don't think we have any bigger of a problem here than any other place where you got so many young kids on a free ride from ma and dad."

"Yes, I understand," Pennfield drew a breath and glared at him. "But as of late, I've heard the complaints with more regularity."

"You don't say?" Howard answered with a blank stare.

"Yes, for instance Wednesday morning as I took a short stroll around campus, I happened to overhear that there was an incident of rather major proportions on Tuesday night at Boynton Hall."

"Wouldn't know anything 'bout that."

"You *are* head of Campus Security, aren't you?"

"Of course. Of course, but can't make things up, Professor. Don't know anything about *any major* incident at Boyton on Tuesday night."

"Well, I'd appreciate it if you'd look into it. I heard about it from more than one person."

"Hmmmm," Howard tweaked his chin. "Let me take a look in the log." He walked over behind the counter and pulled out a book, straining without his glasses to read the scribbled handwriting. "Well looks like there was something at Boynton. But nothing big, mind you. Just some drunk sophomore makin' a little noise. Sent a campus security van out at 2:11 AM Wednesday morning."

Within seconds, Christopher rushed down the hall and quickly punched out a number on the payphone. "*Jonathan. Jonathan,*" he blurted. "*You must meet me at the cottage. Tomorrow. No excuses.*"

"What?"

"There's been a new development. Something I could only tell you face to face."

"Yeah, but Suz and I, we got…"

"Believe me, no matter what you have planned can't be more important than this. Just trust me."

They began digging at two o'clock on Sunday afternoon. Christopher's memory was so vivid, he did not hesitate in pointing out the exact spot: halfway between the tool shed and the old weeping willow. The earth moved slowly; thick sprawling roots, earthen red clay, and an assortment of stones and rocks made the digging a formidable task. After two hours, their hole was only three feet deep.

"Are you sure this is exactly where you saw it?" Jonathan wiped his brow as he rested.

"Without doubt, I remember it precisely. It's right here, right beneath us."

The early afternoon's bright, clear skies grew dark and heavy. A clap of thunder snapped at them, rumbling the dark clouds above. They continued, working faster as the rumbles of thunder grew louder and the flashes of lightning brighter, a slight sprinkling of rain tapping their shoulders. The wind whipped up in small swirls, kicking up debris. It built to a rapid whistle, bouncing around the dark gray skies. With one more rolling rumble, the sky burst into sheets of rain.

Jonathan tugged on his brother and pointed towards the door. *"Inside, inside."*

"No, no," Christopher pulled away, rain pouring down his face. *"We have to finish."*

"But, there's nothing here!" Jonathan shouted over the hissing rain.

"Wrong! You're wrong, Jonathan!" Christopher planted his foot on the head of his shovel and kicked it into the ground. Barraged by the rain, he kicked and planted and kicked and planted, losing his breath as he threw more and more dirt out of the hole.

"Chris," Jonathan tugged at his shoulder and shouted, water dripping down his face, *"Take a break for Chrissikes!"*

"No. We're close. I can't." He plunged the shovel into the hole, soaked by the cascading rain.

Over the rapid hissing, the shovel clanged. He had hit something. The tone vibrated throughout his knuckles. With the wind whipping around him, he kicked the shovel into it again.

"Jonathan! Jonathan!" He motioned towards the hole.

"What?" Jonathan crouched over the hole, the wind rushing by his face.

"Look!" Christopher dropped to his knees.

His hands burrowed faster and faster, removing mud from the long hard object. The rain teemed upon him, keeping pace with the quick strokes of his hands. The whistling winds swirled the rain around them in thick sheets.

"Stop! Stop!" Jonathan hovered over his brother, *"We'll come back later!"*

"*No! No!*" Christopher yelled back, his hands and knees soaked in mud. "*Now. We'll find it now!*"

A clap of thunder cracked at the foaming sea. Bursting waves swelled over the cottage's sea wall. The wind pummeled sheets of rain into their faces. Christopher's hands slid back and forth in the mud, running across a smooth, shiny object underneath. He quickly squished the mud to the sides, trying to see what it was. Faster and faster, until he finally recognized it. He quickly shivered, then stood up, spread out his arms, and screamed: "*Yes. It's here. It's here. A coffin! The coffin, Jonathan!*"

*   *   *

Wrapped in thick blankets, they stared at the old wooden box which they had placed ceremoniously on the large dining room table. They sipped hot tea as they looked at it, studying all the fine details. Its fine lacquered finish, its exquisite hand-carved woodwork, its muddied brass handles. They walked slowly around it, carefully observing from all possible angles. The adrenalin which had propelled Christopher to unearth the object with such alacrity now drugged him into a stupor, shackling him with caution.

"Why are you waiting?" Jonathan asked in a soft monotone.

"Pandora's box." Christopher whispered as his eyes traveled across the long box's cherry-red surface.

"But now it's inevitable. Nothing you can do will make it go away."

Slowly, Christopher reached for the cover, rubbing his finger across its smooth surface. He placed both his palms on it, and breathed deeply. Then, he burrowed his fingertips into the crevice underneath and lifted, its hinges creaking as the heavy cherry top rose above its base. Their eyes darted inside.

Empty. Aside from some rotted flowers, several earthworms that had wiggled in between the cracks, a King James version of the Bible, and several other small mementos, the coffin was empty. No rotted corpse laying atop the deep maroon velvet to lead them to an easy clue. No face of some Pennfield ancestor from years gone by staring at them through a chalky white death mask. Just an empty coffin resting atop the dining room table.

Jonathan ran his hand along the edge, feeling the old maroon velvet moistened by the teeming rain. He fingered the Bible and the rotted flowers, a corpse of sorts in their own way. Next to the Bible, he touched a small leather pouch, or perhaps purse, wondering what it held.

"But it doesn't make any sense." Jonathan said as he toyed with the pouch's buckle. "Why bury an empty coffin?"

"Perhaps it was done to deceive someone, to make them *think* someone had died…"

"Or perhaps the body was removed years *after* the burial." Jonathan twiddled with the buckle.

"Yes, but why?"

"Perhaps the better question is *how?*"

Christopher squinted, not sure what his brother meant. As he poised himself to respond, Jonathan managed to work open the pouch. He reached inside and touched the contents.

"Look. I think I've—

"What? What have you got?"

"Papers, some sort of papers."

Carefully, Jonathan removed the old papers from the pouch. There were about twelve of them folded over down the middle. As Christopher peered over his shoulder, Jonathan opened them. The first page was covered with fine penstrokes squeezed closely together, running to the edges. Together, Jonathan and Christopher read.

23

A HISTORY OF THE MEAN AND MALICIOUS SPIRITE
WHICH HAS BEEN THE PLAGUE OF THE PENNFIELD
FAMILY FOR FIVE GENERATIONS.

As I, Nathaniel Pennfield of Newport, son of Thomas Pennfield
of Newport, grandson of Richard Pennfield of Rehoboth Colony,
and great-grandson of Edward Pennfield of Plimouth Colony,
son of Charles Pennfield, the Pilgrim, suffer from the ravages of
an affliction from which I am certain that I will never recover, it
has become my last taske in life to record the narrative of sundry
events which have served to cause blasphemy, shame and disrepute to descend upon my family undeserved. Surely the force of
which I recount was the wicked interloper which swept my dear
brother Peter from our midst. Doubtless, it has been the cause of
numerous and sundry disturbances to our collective existences
since Charles Pennfield first stepped upon said rock at Plimouth.
Indeed, it has been a wicked and vicious source of shame and
embarrassment as the numerous scions of Charles Pennfield, our
revered forefather, have battled with the elements of nature to
extracte our rightful bounty from thereon. As I struggle with this
lingering Consumption to committ this narrative to parchment, I
fear that the Curse which has afflicted us in years begone will
plague our family henceforth in the absence of proper and sufficient warning which is why I ink my quill in this endeavor. How
can one give just account for the strange and odd circumstances
surrounding certain members of our proud and abundant fam-

ily without proper acknowledgement of the cruel and malicious curse thrust upon our lineage by a poor woman of youth, misguided by nothing more than confusion and unable to control her affections with proper sobriety? Oftentime, as I lay in contemplation as my bones slowly wither back to earthly dust, I ask our divine Maker why he had chosen to curse our fine Pedigree with such damnable and despicable misfortune. I wonder why certain members of our prodigious clan have caused certain objects of solid materiel to dance and jump as if possessed of a living spirit. I ask the Divine Maker, our Lord, why certain members of Pennfield lineage have observed in the light of day strange and mysterious apparitions which have caused them to be mocked with vigor abusive by others with no understanding of the circumstances which have caused this affliction to be cast upon us. But, alas, the proper answers to such questions come with little difficulties because as I am sure that I sit here wearily on this very day, consuming the last few breaths of a long and prosperous livelihood, I am certain without question that the proper answer is the one that has been passed to us from the lips of father to son in the strictest of secrecy for five generations. Without question I am certain that the source of our infamy and disrepute has grown with wanton abandon from the very circumstances which Charles Pennfield, the great and courageous Pilgrim, first related to his eldest son Edward in Plimouth Colony, the circumstances of which emanated from that great vessel prodigious and historic, The Mayflower of London. Having been a devoute and vigorous member of the Separatist Congregation in Leyden of Holland, our brave and courageous ancestor, Charles Pennfield, made voyage down the Channel in the ill-fated vessel Speedwell which was to meet the great vessel Mayflower in Southhampton and accompany said vessel in a heroic voyage across the great Atlantic to stake claim to the Congregation's legal plantation in Northern Virginia Colony. But, alas, as the two vessels began their brave and historic voyage, the Speedwell sprung a malicious leake which compelled the two vessells to turn back to Dartmouth port where the poor Speedwell was deemed unworthy of the voyage. As the passenger cargoes of the two ships were then to be forced into the one remaining vessel, our dear beloved Charles feared that he and his wife would be left alone in Mother England where they would be subject again to the wicked and unChristian persecution which had plagued the Congregation for many years prior.

Hence our great ancestor Charles, acting only in the best interest of himself and his family, let it be known to the Congregation's leadership that a small child from one of the other families suffered from an early affliction of the smallpox which, if allowed to grow unfettered in the close quarters of a sailing vessel, could very well place the entire historic journey in a state of grave and serious jeopardy. Hence, the astute and revered Leadership, in all their just wisdom, judged that said family must be left with the others in Mother England, insuring passage for our beloved Charles. The voyage proved to be not without incident as one vile crewmember, a profane and haughty young man who contemned the passengers daily, threatened our revered ancestor by telling him that his divulgences of the young boy's smallpox was a vile and wicked lie and he would soon expose such sinful act to the elders the result of thus with all probability causing the early Pennfield family to be outcast amongst this greater group of outcasts. In his malicious threats, the vile young man left our great ancestor with few courses of action save to take whatever actions necessary to insure that he would never blaspheme our family in such manner. Thusly, Charles, after much painful contemplation and serious deliberation, chose to sacrifice the young man, sullying his wine with a secret poison, which proved effective stripping the young man of his wicked life whilst the Mayflower traversed the sea. How can one reach any conclusion but in support of our beloved Charles' heroic action? Was not this vile young man's threats the work of Satan in all his wickedness? Did not Charles' swift and decisive actions preserve the integrity of all Pennfields henceforth and their bounteous acts of many decades to come in their new and bountiful world? Yet, our forefather's heroic act was not without complications further. The vile young man, before his timely death, chose to share his wicked secret with a young servant girl who bore his child. The shocking and swift death caused such grief to this unstable young girl, that she, in her lack of true sanity, again threatened our beloved ancestor with the same wicked fabrication. In turn, our great ancestor Charles threatened to expose her state of being with child to the leaders, which he had learned of fortuitiously unbeknownst to her. Such threat caused much grief and consternation to come upon this young unstable girl which so overcame her that she chose to take her own life as the Mayflower battled with dangerous shoals and roaring breakers on the coast of their new homeland. As she jumped off the ship as the Captain tacked it aboute to avoid the dangerous shoals, the winds shifted in a sudden and dramatic manner pushing good vessel to the northeast as the young servant girl was left to wallow in the breakers unmerciful, the Good and Seaworthy Captain having made prudent decision not to risk his passengers and crew in a reckless and wanton rescue endeavor. Indeed, many an eyewitness believed that it was the young girl's actions themselves that took grip of the forces controlling the winds pushing them safely off the shoals! Yet, as the good Mayflower sailed up the coastline of Cape Cod that dark night, our heroic Charles found a message from the young sinful girl whereby she threatened to return throughout the generations henceforth to haunt him and his children and cause much infamy and disrepute to come upon him and his descendents. At this juncture I must rightfully ask was not this young girl a sinner, a fornicator? Had she not conspired with that vile and wicked young man whose threats were the work of the dastardly Satan, Prince of Evil? Indeed, the forceful winds which pushed the good Mayflower off the shoals successful with the hindsight of history proved to be winds tyrannical as the Pilgrims suffered unmerciful losing near half their number in that cold New England winter. One can rightful ask would the great assemblage of courageous Pilgrims and Forefathers lost near that number in the more forgiving climate of Northern Virginia Colony, their rightful and legal destination until they were forced by the fate of God and that young woman misguided and unstable to turn back to the north? And, indeed, the unstable woman, the sinner, the co-conspirator with that vile young man I am sure has been at the very root of all the shame and disrepute which our family has suffered since that fateful day off the dangerous shoals of the New England coast. Seventy years after that fateful date our poor Great Aunt Amanda was pressed to death, her bones ground to dust, in Salem province, charges leveled at her by a woman not too neighborly claiming that she caused a broom to dance and the crops to fail. As certain as I am that I sit here today in the City of Newport in the Colony of Rhode Island, I am indeed certain in terms equal that the very woman with whose unjust accusations our dear Amanda was sent to her death, was indeed that very woman who jumped into the shoals of Cape Cod from the deck of the Mayflower. With equal certititude I am convinced indeed that the same vile woman had a hand in the circumstances untoward by which my dear brother Peter came to bring shame and disrepute to us all of like blood as she did in every other shameful circumstance of disrepute which have defiled our good name for five generations. I have sit here at great length as a very sick and miserable dying vestige of my true self to give proper witness and true testimony to the wicked circumstances which are the progenitors of our disrepute. With like certitude, I serve due and proper notice to all Pennfield scions henceforth to become forewarned to the vile and wicked acts of that miserable woman misguided. As I close my eyes upon the world of mankind living, my final prayer to God Almighty, Father of our great Prince Christ Jesus who suffered wounds numerous at Calvary, would be to come to the aid of my true descendents as they battle the deceitful and malicicous power that stems from the death of this one misguided girl of servititude. With every weakened breathe, of life which still I breath, I swear with the Lord God as my witness that every word of this testimony is imbued with the truth of Christ. I give this true and honorable testimony in the fair and pleasant City of Newport on the twenty-first day of September in the year of our Lord Seventeen hundred and Sixty-Eight, so Help me God.

Nathaniel Pennfield

Neither Jonathan nor Christopher said a word as they read the entire twelve pages, straining to decipher the tightly squeezed penstrokes. Everything became clear to them as they consumed the very words their great-great-great-great-great-great-great-great grandfather, Nathaniel Pennfield, a merchant from colonial Newport, penned in his own hand over two centuries earlier. They shivered as they realized the significance of it, almost as if he was speaking directly to them from across the generations—as if he had anticipated this very moment—warning them of the terrible curse that had been cast upon their lineage by the likes of a poor servant girl on the Mayflower.

"Oh my God." Christopher mumbled in a somber tone.

"Everything that Ed told us, everything he warned us about. It's all true." Jonathan whispered.

Before they exchanged another word, they noticed something else at the story's end, underneath Nathaniel Pennfield's signature.

Scribbled diagonally across bottom, A different handwriting, a different colored ink. Added long after Nathaniel Pennfield had written the original saga:

Betty Jenkinson, agent of curse, disposed of 2/17/29
Benjamin Pennfield

24

After what seemed an interminable debate, they placed the call at 11PM.

"Ed?"

"Who's this?" Swann answered, groggy.

"Jon Pennfield. I awakened you?"

"'Fraid I'm not a night owl like I used to be. But I suppose anyone with brass enough to call at this time of night would have good enough reason. What's on your mind?"

"How quickly can you come to Newport?"

"What?" He twisted himself out of his covers and sat up on the side of his bed.

"We need you here. No, that's wrong, we *want* you here. There's been some new developments."

"Are you sure?"

"Absolutely. You're the only one who can help us, we're sure of it. Everything you told us last December has become more clear to us."

A pause.

Swann scratched his head, pushing back the unkempt strands of hair swirling around his shiny pate. "Wait a minute. Slow down. This isn't just *you* wanting me back, is it? I hope you *both* feel the same way about this."

"Of course. Of course. Chris wants me to assure you that he is one hundred percent with me on this." He looked up to his brother.

Reluctantly, Christopher clenched his teeth and nodded his head.

"Hmmm. Well, in that case you make me an offer that's difficult to turn down. Any idea when the first flight out of Newark is?"

"We already checked. There's one that leaves for Providence at 8:45. Can you be on it?"

"Count me in."

By noon, Swann had read the parchments three times. In silence, he scoured over them at the dining room table, straining his eyes as they ran up and down each page, deciphering the penstrokes. The third time through he pulled out a magnifying glass and focused on several passages. Then, abruptly, he placed the parchments down, wrapped himself in a light spring jacket, and walked out on the porch. He stretched out in a rocking chair and drank in the cool spring air, gazing out onto Narragansett Bay. Forty minutes later, he pushed himself off the chair and returned to the parlor, enlightened.

"Amazing. Now it all makes sense. A battle that's been going on for generations. The spirit of that servant girl versus the psychic powers of the Pennfield family."

"Slow down. Tell us exactly what you mean by that," Christopher ordered.

"The only reason she hasn't been able to claim complete victory is your family's psychic gift. It's kept her in check for almost four hundred years."

"Be careful how you say that. There's nothing *peculiar* about the Pennfields." Christopher said.

"Wouldn't call it peculiar," Swann answered, "I'd call it lucky. Think about it. Read the parchments again. Dancing objects. Apparitions. Witchcraft. Your family's had psychic powers for generations. It's genetic, a gift. Each time she returned, someone in your family must've been able to sense it. Must've frustrated the hell out of her. And what your grandfather did must've *really* flamed her innards."

"How?"

"Snookered her. Lock, stock and barrel. Got her so bad, she must be *aching* for revenge. Unfortunately, now she wants to take it out on the two of you."

"But what do you mean by that?" Jonathan asked.

"She's back. She has to be. No doubt in my mind."

"How can you be so sure?" asked Christopher.

"Everything's out of balance. Her presence upset the psychic equilibrium. There's a reason why the two of you began having all these strange experiences last Fall. She returned. Threw everything out of kilter. Your latent psychic powers were able to sense it, were trying to tell you something. Jon gets close to Pollock Rip and this psychic imbalance creates a phantom storm. Whenever Chris spends time around the cottage, his presence conjures up psychic imprints left by the events of the late 1920s—the lobstermen, the burial of Betty Jenkinson's casket out back, whomever else you may have seen. Even your brother Robin tried to warn the two of you that night. Then a GlobalAir jet goes down right over Pollock Rip. And, finally, last Tuesday night, an Out of Body Experience leads Chris directly to the evidence out back. It's amazing, really is. Never seen anything like it."

"But are we in any kind of *danger?* Christopher asked.

"Probably."

"What kind? How much?"

"Don't know."

"What can we do about it?"

"Learn from the past. Do like your grandfather did. Find her, then defeat her."

But *how?"* Christopher asked. "I don't understand."

"Remember when I told you I didn't completely buy your grandfather's motive for killing *both* of the Jenkinsons? If his intent was to put the affair between Sarah Morton and Reverend Jenkinson to an end, why did he have to kill *Mrs.* Jenkinson, why not only the Reverend? Or why did he have to kill anyone at all? But now it all becomes clear. Your grandfather's real intention from the get-go was to kill *Betty Jenkinson*. Killing the Reverend was never his real motive."

"Why?

"Because your grandfather knew Betty Jenkinson was the agent of the curse."

"How?"

"Sarah."

"What?" Christopher exclaimed.

"Sarah's psychic powers were very strong. Perhaps the strongest *ever* in the Pennfield family. She must've been able to sense that Betty Jenkinson was the agent of the curse early on. She warned your grandfather."

"But why do you put so much stock in Sarah?" Christopher asked. "She was mentally disturbed. She died in an institution, did she not?"

"So? With it came an immense gift. She's helped us, has since the beginning. She guided me throughout the weeks I spent investigating your case in Newport. I saw her that first night in the cottage. She actually talked to me, mentioned my name. Then, on another night, she guided me to the graveyard, forcing me to question why Betty Jenkinson was not buried with her husband. When I was at Xenobia's, I saw her again, gliding across the porch. I'm sure she's still with us today."

"But what happened in 1928? How did Sarah and grandfather outsmart Betty Jenkinson?" Jonathan asked.

"There are lots of holes to fill in, but let me mix a little speculation and a few hunches with the facts. Somehow your grandfather got his hands on the parchments. We know that for certain, his signature's at the bottom. He knew that someday the girl from the Mayflower—or her spirit—might visit the Pennfield family again. After all, she had a history of causing no good. It's all over the parchments. Amanda Pennfield in Salem, Peter Pennfield in Newport, all in black and white. So once they realized Betty Jenkinson was the agent of the curse, they contrived a plan to beat her at her own game."

"How?"

"From everything I ever read about your grandfather, he was the master poker player. And I'll tell you, this must've been his most impressive hand. That's all I've thought about since I read the parchments. He got inside her mind, figured out her motive, and then worked from there."

"But what was her motive?" Christopher asked.

"To bring down the Pennfield family, of course. I'm sure Betty Jenkinson somehow *encouraged* the affair between Sarah and the Reverend, hoping it would someday get messy and that, in a lovers' spat, Sarah—known to have emotional problems—would do something rash, maybe even murder him. Maybe even murder the *both* of them. Remember, this spirit is immortal, has lasted for generations, she doesn't really *care* about her own material existence. I'm sure she was trying to set the whole thing up. Then the Pennfields would have had a major scandal on their hands and her task would have been completed. For then, at least.

"But instead, your grandfather and Sarah had her play right into their hands. They *contrived* the affair, Sarah seduced him. Betty confided in your grandfather when she learned of the affair—that would explain the love letter I found in the attic. She probably hoped that, as the leading member of the congregation, your grandfather would put pressure on the Reverend to put the affair to an end. So, when Betty Jenkinson approaches him, your grandfather complies: in no uncertain terms, he tells the Reverend that it's over between him and Sarah, has to be. The Reverend tries to go along with him, but Sarah balks. Intentionally. She threatens him. Tells him to meet her at Stone Villa, or else.

"So then your grandfather tells Betty that through his sources he's learned of the meeting at Stone Villa. They decide *she* should be there to confront them. Betty goes along with it because she thinks her presence would only *increase* the chances of Sarah losing control, killing him—or them—in a fit of rage. Or at very least, uncovering this scandalous affair, going public with it. She thinks everything's falling into place. But, when they get there, there's no Sarah. Just like we saw, your grandfather's two hired hands—the two lobsterman—kill both the Reverend and Mrs. Jenkinson, making it look like a murder and suicide. Your grandfather gets rid of Betty Jenkinson, the agent of the curse, and has a built-in alibi, to boot. And for the past six decades, she's been in a stew over it, just waiting for her chance to get back at his heirs."

"But what can we do?" asked Christopher. "It seems as if we're trapped by this spirit of her's, that somehow she's in our midst and will refuse to leave until she extracts her just dues. How can we ever—"

"Not sure yet. All I know is we've got to find her or you and your families could be in real trouble. She's already killed two hundred innocent people in that jetliner. Who knows what else she has up her sleeve."

"But where do we look for her?" Jonathan asked.

"Only one place I can think of."

"Where?"

"Where it all began. Pollock Rip."

"But are you sure? Wouldn't that—

"Yep, it'll be risky all right. But I'd say the bigger risk is not finding her at all. I'm convinced. We *must* go out to Pollock Rip."

*   *   *

Captain Conrad Scott bellowed out a deep snore, his face contorting into a sleepy grimace, as Swann tapped on the door to the pilothouse of Scott's old stinkpot early the next day. Falmouth Harbor was overcast, the morning wet and damp from a nighttime thunderstorm. Swann stood at the door, watching Scott's lips vibrate from gasps of heavy breath, his stout frame twisted around a blanket on a small cot cramped into the corner, his face covered by his weary arms.

"Captain Scott? Captain Scott?" Swann called over to him, just above a whisper.

Scott shook his head and grazed his hands across his face. He looked over towards the door, his eyes barely focused, somewhat disoriented by the figure of Swann hovering outside. "What in the name uh—" He shook his head.

"Ed Swann." He offered his hand.

"I know who the hell you are, Mr. Swann." Scott pushed himself up off his cot. "I only wanna know who in the name of BeJesus gave yah the right to rustle me up outta a sound sleep."

"More questions. I have more questions for you. Hope you don't mind." Swann winked at him.

"The hell I *do* mind. Whaddaya have another nautical legend you want me to elucidate fer yah? Haven't I done enough?"

"Surely. Surely you have. It's only that—"

"Anyone ever tell you you're a very strange man, Mr. Swann?" Scott tripped across the floor, grasping for a small table to balance himself on, and then poured a cup of coffee with his shaky hand. "Well, what is it that's caught the fancy of your imagination this time?" He gulped the entire cup and then burped.

"I was wondering if you'd be interested in chartering me one of your fine vessels. Captained by you, of course."

Scott stumbled over to the sink and spit. *Pchhhw!* "Can't yah find some poor charter captain in Chatham or Nantucket to take yah on a little cruise. Don't yah believe in spreadin' 'round the wealth?"

"Nope," Swann smiled at him. "I'm afraid my associates and I want you."

"And where would it be that *yer associates* and yerself would like me to take yahs?"

"Pollock Rip."

He stopped short and looked up. "And why would a landlubber like yerself and yer mollycoddle green hand friends want me to risk parking the keel of a fine vessel on the shoals of Pollock Rip. Yah got some sorta death wish or somethin'?"

"No, we simply have an interest in the nautical lore of the area and we'd be glad to compensate you—compensate you handsomely—if you'd help us."

"Ain't money that's the object." Scott looked him in the eye. "The object is *why?*"

"Why?"

"'Sgotta be more'n an academic interest in the *nautical lore of the area*. Not sure if I buy that crap. Level with me, Mr. Swann. Tell me the truth. Is it that you and yer landlubbin' colleagues fancy your-selves as modern day bounty hunters? Think yah have the inside track on some old, uncharted pirate ship, do yahs? Or is it that you and your vulture friends wanna gulp up the debris uh that poor jet-liner for fun and profit?" *Pchww.* He spit into the sink. "Amazin' what the allure of a few greenbacks'll do to the gumption uh crea-tures who have no reason takin' off their neckties and suspenders. 'll makem think they're real sailors. 'll makem fantasize 'bout livin' their lives on the high' seas. *Hmmppph!* Then when they're shittin' in their pants and heavin' their breakfasts over the rail, they figger out the only real worth of their God almighty greenbacks'll be tuh paper the insides uh their caskets."

Swann paused, gazed up at the soupy gray sky, drew a breath, and answered, "You asked me to level with you, Captain Scott, so I will."

"Oh?"

"Our interest has nothing to do with any of what you just said. Has everything to do with the Mayflower. From everything I've heard, you'd know more about that than anyone on the Cape."

Scott smiled. "So you want me tuh track down ole Jonesie, do yahs?"

"Jonesie?"

"Captain Christopher Jones. Most seaworthy skipper ever to sail these parts. Least in the opinion of this old salt."

"But there's more to it. My associates, they claim ancestry back to the Mayflower."

"So? Over twenty-five million pompous blowhards claim ances-try back to the Mayflower. That and a dime'll get yah 'bout ten cents."

"But something happened. Something happened concerning their ancestor on the Mayflower. And we believe we may find something strange in that area, maybe something untoward even."

Captain Scott tweaked his white bristly beard and squinted. "'Zackly what yah mean by that?"

"I have to confess. I usually wouldn't tell someone about this right away. But you asked me to level with you." He paused. "The business I'm in. What I do. I'm a ghost hunter." Another pause. "Does that bother you?"

Scott tweaked his beard several more times. Then his eyes widened and his cheeks lifted. "A man after my own heart. The high seas are full uh spirits, Mr. Swann. All sorts of 'em."

25

The skies cleared in Falmouth Harbor later in the day, the drab grays replaced by white puffy clouds and then clear azure tones until eventually they dimmed into gray again, then a starry-patched curtain of ink-blue. Oblivious to it all, Swann and Scott huddled in the pilothouse. They reviewed nautical charts, chewed over a few of Scott's sailing anecdotes, and, finally—after he became convinced he could trust the Captain—Swann shared a copy of the parchments with him. Scott's eyes glowed as he absorbed them, as if they were unlocking the mystery to some great age-old riddle.

"Jesus Christ, Swannie, yah got me a goldmine here." He mumbled out loud, his face flush and his mouth wide open.

Silent, Scott read them again and again, taking almost two full hours. Then, late at night, after he had walked out on deck to contemplate everything—tweaking the bristles of his white beard as he thought—he rushed back into the pilothouse, pulled an old book out of a locker, and threw it down on the table:

"If yah wanna understand what we're attemptin' tuh do, best yah get it right from the source."

The book was an old weathered copy of *Of Plymouth Plantation* by William Bradford, the account of the Pilgrims journey from Holland to England to the New World as relayed by their most inspirational leader. Swann squinted and read a passage from the yellowed pages:

> But after they had sailed yt course aboute halfe ye day, they fell
> amongst deangerous shoulds and roring breakers, and they were so farr
> intangled there with as they conceived themselves in great danger; &
> ye wind shrinking upon them withall, they resolved to bear up againe
> for the Cape, and though themselves happy to gett out of those dangers
> before night overtooke them, as by Gods providence they did

Silent, Swann shook his head, then said, "That's exactly how Nathaniel Pennfield explains it in the parchments. But what about the servant girl? Why no mention of her?"

"Know what yer thinkin', but don't worry 'bout it. Nope, it happened, that's fer sure."

"How do you know that?"

"Read on." Scott pulled the old book from Swann, licked his fingers, turned back several pages and pointed to a passage:

> There was a proud and very profane young man, one of the seamen; he
> would always be contemning the poor people in their sickness and curs-
> ing them daily with grievous execrations; and did not let to tell them
> that he hoped to help to cast half of them overboard before they came to
> their journey's end, and to make merry with what they had; and if he
> were by any gently reproved, he would curse and swear most bitterly.
> But it pleased God before they came half seas over, to smite this young
> man with a grievous disease, of which he died in a desperate manner,
> and so was himself the first that was thrown overboard.

"For thirty-five years—ever since I started studyin' ole Jonesie and the good ship Mayflower—I wondered what killed that poor ribald chap. Kept me up nights tuh tell yah the God's honest truth. Thought about heart attack, aneurysm, stroke, all sorts uh exotic afflictions. Now I know. Its all in those parchments of yers, was poisoned cuz he knew too much."

"But, still—"

"Yep, if Nat Pennfield was able to explain that riddle, 'sgood enough fer me. I believe his whole story, no reason not to. Guess ole

Willie Bradford didn't think it important enough tuh mention the girl. Either that or he didn't want tuh."

"Why?"

"Shittin' me? Wouldn't be nuthin' to brag about—leavin' a poor young girl to drown in the breakers of Pollock Rip—now would it?"

*   *   *

Villa D'Este fit snugly on the shore of Lake Como, nestled between the lake's clear, reflective waters and Lombardy's ascending alpine mountains. By reputation, the villa—once home to Catherine de Medici—loomed larger than life, a jet-setter's paradise, featured countless times on the thick glossy pages of trendy travel magazines. Yet, in person, the villa's grand marble structure, fastidiously-manicured gardens, and quaint, restful terraces seemed unexpectedly compact, a surprisingly small refuge on the outskirts of the Italian village of Cernobbio, just several miles from the Swiss border. A refuge, however, not outside the reaches of modern technology.

"Sixteen and a half?" Tom Westerfeld mumbled into his cellular phone as he lounged on a deck chair overlooking the lake. "Let's go for another hundred thousand shares right away. Tell Simon to buy it in the name of our Triangle Partners account. Let's find a broker in Des Moines or Peoria or someplace like that to place the order. And tell—

Crash! A rolled up magazine descended upon his head.

"What are you, some kind of moronic nerd? Can't you get your mind off your silly Wall Street numbers for more than five minutes." Playfully, Winnie pulled the phone from his hand. "Here, help me." She handed him a bottle of suntan lotion and flipped over on her chaise lounge, motioning for him to apply it to the back of her thighs.

"Jesus Christ, Winnie, we've bought up four percent of the stock and it's still going down. Target practice." He rubbed the thick, viscous liquid across her smooth golden skin.

"The only practice I want you to get has nothing to do with numbers. I'm beginning to think all this Wall Street mumbo jumbo has fried your brain and left you impotent."

"Impotent? Just because my sexual appetite is slightly south of insatiable, don't count me as abnormal."

She flipped back over and looked him in the eyes. "Westerfeld, face it, you're an egghead. A cute one, but an egghead. We've got to get you a life, pronto." She lifted the fluted champagne glass off the table beside her and sipped on a Bellini.

"But this, what I do, *is* my life. Don't you understand?" He pulled the phone back and began dialing.

"How boring." She settled back into her chaise and hid beneath her Armani sunglasses.

"Sixteen and an eighth?" Westerfeld blurted into the phone. "Jesus! More, buy more. Spread it all around. Accounts, brokers, whatever." He tugged on Winnie's arm. "We're getting it, Winnie. Bit by bit, we're getting it."

"Wow." She almost whispered, patting her mouth underwhelmingly.

"One more percent and we have to file papers with the SEC. Then it really gets hot and heavy."

"One can only wish." She yawned, stretched out on the chaise.

"Don't you understand? We'll have to officially divulge that it's Westerfeld Investments that's been buying up all this GlobalAir stock under different accounts. It'll become more apparent that I'm trying to gain control. Your Uncle Jonathan's slow simmer may cascade into an outright boil."

"Oh really?" She sat up, interested, then sipped on her Bellini once again.

"Has your Uncle Chris tried to call you again?"

"Not since last week."

"I'd suspect you'll be getting another call in the next couple of days."

"Can't happen." She answered, sipping again. "Still thinks we're in France."

"Interesting. It gives us the opportunity to have already filed papers *before* you and I return to the States. Does that bother you?"

"Why should it?"

"By the time we get back, it'd be a done deed. I'd have shown my cards. He'd have had no chance to get to you first."

"And why would a megalomaniacal control freak like yourself want to give them a chance to get to me?"

He shrugged. "Don't know. Family courtesy, I guess."

"Do me a favor."

"Yes?"

"Don't worry about family courtesy." She stood up, and threw off her top. "Come on, let's get wet." She dove head-first into the clear blue waters of Lake Como.

*   *   *

"Convinced meself, Swannie. Thinkin' 'bout them parchments been keeping me up nights." Captain Scott banged his cup on the table in the pilothouse one morning later in the week. "If we're gonna do it, got tuh follow Jonesie's path zackly. Can't crimp no corners. From the forty second parallel right down the backside uh the Cape. Time uh day, tides, winds, phase of the moon, everything's gotta be in sync."

"Sure, but how do we—

"Good question." Scott cut him off. "If yer askin' what I think yer askin', the answer's *no*. Ain't no real record of the Mayflower's path. That's what's gonna make this one tricky. Only two sources I know of. One's Willie Bradford's, the other's *Mourt's Relation*. Problem is, neither of 'em has more than a couple hundred words 'bout the Mayflower's actual voyage. Fortunate thing is, committed 'em all tuh memory years ago." Captain Scott smiled proudly and pointed to his right temple.

"But do we know enough to make a reasonable go at it?" Swann asked, taking a healthy gulp.

"Just a few basic facts," Captain Scott answered. "We know at daybreak on Thursday the ninth uh November in the year sixteen hundred and twenty, the Mayflower sighted land. We know at a certain point the ole ship tacked about and headed south fer the Hudson, then in the afternoon got caught up in the shoals uh Pollock Rip. And, then, after a display uh fine seamanship by ole Jonesie and a fortunate puff uh southerly breeze by God Almighty, the ship freed itself from the shoals sometime just before nightfall and headed back north to deep water."

"Then what course do we follow?"

"Gotta infer it." Scott answered. "Been studyin' this one fer most me life. On November ninth, sixteen-twenty, local sunrise was six fifty-five. Means you coulda sighted land about six thirty-five. Now ole Willie Bradford tells us it wuz a fair day which means wind most likely was blowin' from the northwest quarter. With a fair northwest breeze, most sailing men 'round these parts'll tell you visibility's 'proximately twelve miles that time uh day. So they wuz no more'n twelve miles off the coast uh the Cape when they first sighted land."

"But where?" Swann asked.

"Here's where it gets tricky," Captain Scott grinned. "Gotta work backwards. We know they reached Pollock Rip in the afternoon and freed themselves just before nightfall. Whole thing sorta intrigued me so I spent years calculatin' it all. If the wind were blowin' from the northwest in the mornin', but then puffed from the south to free 'em from the shoals in the afternoon, wuz what we call round here a sea turn day. Cuz as the day unfolds the wind circles out tuh the sea. So that gave me a rough idea uh wind direction and speed. Now on that same day, moon was nine days past full makin' high water slack tide nine AM at Nauset. This all means, Jonesie wuz facin' a favorable current most uh the mornin', slack tide 'bout one, one-thirty in the afternoon, and would have a current streamin' into his bow after two PM. Now figger once they reached Pollock Rip, woulda taken 'em two hours to tack about and free themselves from the shoals. Local sunset wuz four thirty-five that day, makin' nightfall 'bout four fifty-five. All tells me they musta first reached Pollock Rip 'bout three PM."

"God, is there anything you *don't* know about the Mayflower?" Swann sat across from him, his jaw hanging.

"Not much. Been sorta an obsession uh mine." Scott tweaked his beard and smiled at him. "So like I said, gotta work backwards from there. According to ole Willie, took 'em 'bout half a day's sailing to get to the shoals. So I sorta figgered they first tacked about at 'proximately nine AM. It'd givem six hours. Takin' winds, currents and boat speed intuh account, woulda placed 'em 'bout twenty one miles north north east of Pollack Rip and five and a half miles east by south from South Wellfleet beach. Woulda given 'em a straight shot tuh the shoals on a south south west course. So workin' back from there, and allowin' fer the fact that they most likely covered five and uh half miles 'tween six-thirty and eight in the morning before they hove-to, I set the position where ole Jonesie first sighted land nine miles offshore east by south offa Eastham and nine miles offshore east by north off the beach at East Orleans." He paused. "Quite a historic spot if yah ask me."

*   *   *

Jonathan twiddled with the paper clip on his desk. He wondered if he should make the call. Would Winnie listen to him? Now that she was back from Europe would she be more cooperative? He shook his head and then looked down on Park Avenue from his window on the forty-second floor. Thousands of people enjoying noontime on a sunny spring day. He focused on a group of young secretaries eating lunch on the Avenue's grassy median. Somehow he felt it would be easier to influence one of those strangers lounging on the grass below than it would be to persuade his own flesh and blood. What ever made him think he would have even an iota of a chance? Chris was practically a second father to Winnie and *he* hadn't been able to persuade her. But, still, a company was at risk. He couldn't allow himself to go down without a fight. Slowly, he reached for the phone, but was stunned when it rang right before he grasped it. Quickly, he grabbed for it.

"Jonathan, are you sure we're not going just a bit overboard?"

"Chris?"

"Swann just called and told me about May 24th."

"Overboard? How can you say that? The stakes are sky high."

"Yes, but I'm just beginning to wonder..."

"Don't. Just don't. We have to do it. We have to go out to Pollock Rip."

"You do realize it's only nine days before the ceremony. The timing couldn't be worse. Could we at least move it back?"

"Can't."

"Why not?"

"Something to do with the tides and the moon. The old captain Ed found is a purist. Conditions have to be as close to that original day in 1620 as feasibly possible. His rule, not mine."

"But the risk," Christopher whined. "If this spirit is anything at all like we theorize, I mean she's already killed two hundred people. And he's asking us to go to the precise spot where she might be at her most powerful."

"But we have to do it, Chris. We just have to. We have to find out who she is. I can't see any other way out..."

As he hung up, he again asked himself if he should place the call to Winnie. Silent, he stared at the phone. He dialed the first several digits, then suddenly stopped short. For several moments, he went flush. Something bothered him, something he found very discomforting. All afternoon, he found himself unable to concentrate on anything but *it*. When he returned home, he immediately ran up to the attic, pulled several corrugated boxes off a rack, and burrowed through them. He pulled out several old albums of photographs, ruffling through them quickly until his eyes stopped abruptly on one particular photo from 1974. He fixed his eyes on it for several moments, then went flush again. His fingers trembled. Of course, of course, he should have realized it all along...

"I've solved it!" Jonathan blurted into the phone.

"What? What did you solve?" Christopher answered, startled.

"I've figured out the identity of the agent of the curse."

"Who?"

"Winnie!"

"What?"

"Winnie's the agent of the curse. It's so obvious, been staring us right in the face."

"Slow down! What is it you mean by that?"

"Just like Betty Jenkinson was that girl from the Mayflower, was here to embarrass the Pennfield family. Winnie is the same person, I'm sure of it."

"Jonathan, have you gone mad? She's your brother Robin's daughter for goodness sakes."

"We don't know that for a fact."

"Jesus Christ, have you gone *completely* out of your mind?"

"Think about it, when was the last time we saw Winnie with Robin and Gabby?"

"Wasn't it was when they visited in seventy-four? She was about seven or eight, right?"

"Precisely."

"Precisely what? What are you driving at?"

"That's the last time we saw her before Robin and Gabby died. Then she spends the next fourteen years in boarding schools only to show up unannounced one day as a twenty-one year old. We don't know that the Winnie we know today is that same little girl."

"Of course we do."

"How? Tell me how you know that?"

"Well, it's—

"Think about what she can do. Think about how she can embarrass us."

"But I fail to see—

"It's all so apparent. All of a sudden, after years, Clarissa Mantusso unexpectedly retires, leaving Winnie in charge of Avanti. Then she becomes involved with Westerfeld, marries him after only a two month courtship. Then, flight 1428 crashes making it an easy mark for Westerfeld to come in and buy up GlobalAir stock at bargain basement prices. She's using him, I'm sure of it. Just like Betty

Jenkinson used the Reverend. She's using him to gain control of GlobalAir."

"But what has that to do with this?"

"If she *is* the spirit of that girl, think of all the damage she can do. She already runs a major magazine and soon she'll have a God-damned airline. It would make whatever Betty Jenkinson tried to do look like child's play."

"But, Jonathan, what you say is so far fetched, makes no sense."

"Has *anything* that's happened to us since last Fall made any sense?"

"Yes, but, I just find it so hard to believe that Winnie would ever do anything to hurt the Pennfield family."

"But don't you get it, she's *not* Winnie. She's that girl from the Mayflower *masquerading* as Winnie."

26

The young blonde woman with the soft white skin rushed down the bustling avenue, adrift in a sea of flowing humanity. Her eyes darted around the cityscape: skyscrapers, traffic lights, taxis, trucks, cars. And people. Everywhere, people: rushing about, bounding around, caroming off in all directions. Paying little attention to anything but themselves, their own busy worlds. Just like before. Like in 1928, 1865, 1726, and, of course, like in 1620.

She walked under the Forty-Second street overpass and peeked inside the large doors to Grand Central Terminal. A magnificent structure. Surely, this must be the proper place, a fitting venue. She smiled: her thoughts focused only on revenge. They damned her on the Mayflower, let her float off in the breakers, left her to die. All due to one man, one cowardly man. And now that man and his progeny must suffer. In due time, they would suffer. She gazed again at the grand marble structure and giggled.

The mean spirits of the wrongful dead damn their living perpetrators!

27

The sun peeked its crown over the misty horizon, casting a shimmer across the sleepy sea. A crescent-shaped moon hung in mid-sky. Eastward bound gulls squawked their morning songs. Precisely the way the day began: November 9, 1620.

Captain Conrad Scott drank in the salt air and stretched out his arms. "Not a threatening cloud around us, six knots of northwest breeze. Perfect! Betcha ol' Jonesie lowered the dipsy lead right from this very spot." A glow on his face and a fire in his eyes, he hugged the wheel as *The Captain Jones* undulated to the slow, languid rhythms of the sea: a small speck on the North Atlantic crawling toward the Cape Cod coast.

Jonathan tapped Scott on the shoulder. "Where's the readout for your windometer, Conrad?"

Scott spit over the lifeline and turned towards him, a scowl across his face. "No real man uh the sea measures the wind wit 'lectronic crap." He thrust his thumb towards his face and barked, "Yah measure the wind wit ycr cheek."

"How we doin' guys?" Swann popped his head up from below.

"We've just approached Point S, we'll stay precisely on course from here on in…" Jonathan answered.

Swann looked down at the chart. *Point S:* the point where the Mayflower first sighted land at 6:30 AM on November 9, 1620, nine miles southeast from the Nauset Coast Guard Station in Eastham and nine miles northeast from the beach at East Orleans as calculated by Scott. From here they would proceed five and a half miles northwest to *Point T*, the point where the Mayflower tacked about and headed southward. Then they would proceed to *Point P*, Pollock Rip.

A lump formed in Swann's throat as he fixed his eyes on the shimmering water before him. No monument marked this lonely spot off the coast, not even as much as a buoy or lobster pot. Yet, it signified the end of an heroic voyage and the beginning of a new chapter in history. After several failed attempts at getting underway in England, after countless financial squabbles with their sponsors, after losing the most favorable seasonal winds and the breakdown of *The Speedwell*, after sixty-odd days of bucking a steady two-knot current of which they had no knowledge, from this spot in the Atlantic Ocean the pilgrims finally set their eyes upon land.

Funny, Swann thought, how the Pennfields had now come full circle. They had first arrived at this unknown spot as outcasts. Shunned by a world that wanted nothing to do with them, they escaped across a vast sea to a bountiful but unruly continent. From there, they turned their disadvantage into advantage. They had risen with the fortunes of the young continent to the highest heights of prosperity. And their very linkage to that small, ninety foot boat that weathered the historic voyage in 1620 placed them in a position of privilege reserved for the very few.

But underneath all the prosperity, there was always a dark gray tinge. Witches and pirates and murderers, rearing their ugly heads only every so often, but often enough to temporarily detract from the family's mad dash to the highest levels of affluence and privilege. And now, it had appeared again: stirring up ghosts of the family's past, throwing a jetliner into the sea, and, most of all, forcing them to confront whatever it was that had cast this dirty tinge.

And so, after three hundred and seventy years, they returned. To put an end to the past and start anew. Swann could only wonder what they might find out here on this misty morning.

"Hard-a-lee!!" Scott turned the *Capt. Jones* toward starboard and watched the luffing jib pass across the bow. Christopher quickly unwrapped the port sheet, assuring it ran free, and Swann cranked rapidly on the starboard winch.

Scott carefully eyed the jib, watching it fill with morning air. Okay...okay...ease up on 'er, Swannie... Don't wannna stall 'er, do yah..." Scott rested his right hand at the very top of the wheel, looked up beyond the top of his mast, and whispered to his mentor. "Okay. I'm wit yah now, Jonesie..."

For what seemed like an eternity, Scott rested his left foot on the risen portside deck, clutched the wheel with his hands, and looked out onto the sea around him. Then, he eyed the thin strip of land far off the horizon and barked out. "Let out the sheets, Swannie...we're makin' too much speed."

"Exactly how fast are we going?" Christopher scowled, pushed back by a sharp downward slant into one of the leeward corners of the cockpit.

"Too fast. Four and a half knots and were gonna slow us down to three and a third."

"Three and a third! That's like watching grass grow for goodness sakes!"

"The plan is to do it the way Jonesie did. A deep-bellied merchantman close-hauled to a westerly wind with a flood tide pushin' her to windward couldn't have done no better. Three and a third knots, Mr. Pennfield."

Christopher scowled at Scott, resigned to the fact that his fate was in the hands of this bearded martinet for the balance of the day.

"Hey Conrad!" Jonathan called up from the nav center below. "We're close to Point T. About a quarter mile off our bow."

Captain Scott licked his finger and held it up the air. "Wind's clockin' tuh the north. A sea-turn day, just like Jonesie had it..."

For the next six hours, The Captain Jones followed the Mayflower's path down the backside of Cape Cod. Conrad Scott leaned on his wheel and watched the distant shoreline with a gleam in his eye, wondering how similar the view might have been to his mentor three centuries earlier. The highlands of Truro, surely they must have appeared the same to Captain Christopher Jones in 1620. Then, the low shores of Eastham—today marked by civilization's footprints, but how different could they have really been back then? Point Care and the Isle of Nauset were no longer there, years ago covered by the ocean's flow, but white breakers still marked the location of the "bad bars" of Nauset or *Malle-barre* as the early French navigators once called them.

"Captain Scott, how can you be so cocksure we're on the exact path of the Mayflower?" Christopher spoke through clenched teeth as he sat impatiently in the back of the cockpit, his arms folded across his chest.

"Sgotta be. Very few other alternatives." Scott answered without turning his head.

Just as it did for the pilgrims three hundred and seventy years earlier, the fading wind clocked from the northwest to the east as *The Captain Jones* approached the shoals of Pollock Rip. So preoccupied were they with their instruments, their pace, and the unraveling coastline, they didn't notice the fair skies gradually sneaking away from them. The fresh May air of mid-morning grew hot and damp bringing with it gray skies and an afternoon of impending turbulence. It was almost two-thirty when they first heard a muffled rumble of thunder tumbling against the distant horizon.

"From what I've read I don't recall them facing rough weather that day," Christopher tugged on Scott's shoulder. "Shouldn't we turn back?"

"Can't." Swann hugged onto the wheel, his eyes transfixed on a spot in the water far off his bow, "Into it too far."

With the darkening of the skies, the clear blues of the Atlantic's placid morning waters turned dark and green barreling into massive swells and lurching the small boat back and forth. It became a rhythm to them: the bow plunging into the crevice of a swell and then springing back up, dipping the stern into the dark waters abaft. A constant spray washed the decks. The winds whistled and rumbles of thunder echoed against a sky of hollow gray.

"Break out the rain gear," Scott barked, "we're in fer a ride."

"Seriously, shouldn't we turn back, Captain?" Christopher mumbled as his stomach churned.

Without answering, Scott twisted himself into his rain gear. They all huddled into the cockpit as the boat jerked them back and forth. It lunged with the mounting swells, forcing them to brace themselves however they could. The clouds around them thickened, enwrapping the *Captain Jones* in a dense fog. Then, with a flash, a crack of thunder punctured a hole in the threatening sky. Sheets of rain barraged them. Their eardrums rang from the clamor of the cascades.

"Whadda we gonna do, Captain!" Swann shouted over the torrents.

"Don't know. Can't see." Scott hung onto the wheel.

The boat twisted and turned, tossed about by a whirlpool of swells. The fog was so thick they could barely see their bow. Quickly, though, the sound of the barraging rain was overwhelmed by something else. A deep whistling sound from above. As if a missile—or a flaming meteor—was about to dive into the sea. They looked overhead, but the top of their mast was lost in a soupy fog. Still, the sound was there, building; getting deeper, gaining power, becoming closer, now rumbling above them.

Jonathan pointed up to the sky. "Look."

"Holy Shit!" Christopher cried out.

The sky filled with a radiance, burning off the gray fog. The sound grew deeper and closer, a gigantic motor churning. Above them, they could see it. A jetliner: diving, twisting as it fell from the sky. On the tail, they saw the writing. *GlobalAir.*

With a wham, it smashed into the water off their bow. The sea unfolded, surging swells exploding outward, catching the boat in the path of their fury. The bow of the Captain Jones sprang straight up, drenching the four with sheets of water and tumbling them onto the stern. They all grabbed for the lifeline.

Grand Central Station was just awakening from its mid-afternoon nap. The crowds of lunchtime long gone, there was a civility

to the building at this time of day. The marble steps leading up to
Vanderbilt Avenue were sparkling and white, unobscured by hundreds of shuffling rush-hour bodies. Stools at the bar on the west
end balcony—the crowd around them usually three deep and
smoke-infested at five thirty—stood vacant and lonely. The lines at
the ticket windows moved quickly, not anywhere near the length
they would be in an hour or so when they would stretch halfway
across the station's vast floor. As was the natural course of events
each work day since the inception of this grand old structure,
everything stood poised for the five o'clock rush.

From the forty-second street entrance, she stepped inside.
Slowly, she walked forward, stopping right before the information
booth at the station's center. She looked up at the ornate four-sided
clock on top of the booth, capped by its prominent knob grasping
up towards the station's ceiling. She gazed upward, her golden
blonde hair dipping just below her shoulders. Her crystal blue eyes
sparkled, following the signs of the zodiac on the ceiling above
from west to east. A light red blush tinged her soft white cheeks.
The stars talked to her. She smiled. Today, just as she had for some
three hundred and seventy-odd years, she had returned, just as in
1726 and 1795 and 1865 and again in 1928. Today, as she had for
each succeeding generation, she would extract her due and rightful
revenge.

The sea was silent and still. Wisps of mist rose above the water.
Flat and glassy, the Atlantic reflected the silver sky, a white-gray
radiance surrounding them. Slowly, they began to awaken.
Jonathan rolled over in the cockpit, grazing his shoulder against the
hard wooden corner. He raised himself off the deck and looked out
off the bow. He rubbed his eyes to escape the blinding brightness.
Quickly, he shook his brother.

"Chris. Chris. Are you okay?"

"Wha? Where?" He opened his eyes, disoriented by the bright
whites and still sea.

"What in the name uh…?" Captain Scott bellowed out like a fog-
horn.

Something was missing, skipped over. Minutes ago—seconds ago—they remembered bucking back and forth to the swells of a furious sea, their small craft running straight up a wave and throwing them astern. Then, blank: everything changed. A jump. Peaceful. Flat and glassy. Silver beams of light sneaking between white and gray clouds. A strange surrealism.

"Jesus Christ!" Swann whispered as he wiped off his dry work pants.

"Say *dat* again." Scott rubbed his eyes.

"What the hell happened? Where in the name of God are we?" Christopher mumbled.

Scott pulled a pair of binoculars up from the cockpit, stood up on the upper deck, and surveyed the waters. As his head slowly turned, his lips formed a smile. "Well don't know what the hell happened. But pretty damn sure where the hell we are."

"Where?" Jonathan asked, hovering behind him.

"Where we always wuz. At Pollock Rip. Breakers are just off our bow."

She stood mesmerized in the center of the giant terminal, looking up, occasional passers-by grazing her. She read the sign in the painted stars again and again. Euphoria. The feeling overwhelmed her. What she had always waited for, her mission about to be completed, until one day years into the future when she would do it again: some other time, some other place.

"Spare a quarter? Gotta quarter, m'am?" She bumped into him as she drifted across the floor. A black man in a beat-up Army jacket and with a speckly gray beard. He held out an empty paper cup.

"Sure. Sure." She answered, fumbling through her purse and placing a quarter in his cup.

"Much obliged, m'am. Much obliged."

Without responding, she looked up, above the information booths. Her eyes followed the stairway to the secluded office windows running seven stories up the rear side wall. At the very top, the entrance to a catwalk stretching through a bank of four giant windows on the station's eastern wall. Each five stories tall. And at the far end, the ledge. Nine stories above the hard marble floor. She looked at her watch. It was time to begin.

Rays of bright white light glistened off the smooth glassy sea. Captain Scott stood on the upper deck holding his binoculars snuggly against his face. The foamy white crests of the breakers off in the distance cast a blinding glow. The other three stood behind him in the cockpit, confused by the silver panorama stretching around them.

"What happened? Where in the name of God did that plane go? There's nothing here. No debris, nothing." Christopher followed.

"Think I have an inkling," said Swann.

"What? What do you mean?" Christopher quickly turned and looked at him.

Swann paused and then answered. "Simple. If I know anything about what I'm doing, I think what we just experienced was another apparition."

"Yeah, but we practically capsized. That couldn't have been caused by an apparition." Jonathan said.

"Not sure if it could or couldn't have been," Swann answered.

Scott paid no attention to the conversation in the cockpit. His binoculars slowly roamed across the horizon searching for a clue, an anchor, something to place everything in context. A fishing boat. A nautical marker. Anything that might ground their experience of the last several minutes back into reality. But nothing. Just a still sea stretching from horizon to horizon, a silvery glimmer shimmering off its surface, the foamy white breakers of Pollock Rip his only landmark out to the west.

"What you see, Conrad?" Jonathan called up to him.

"Nothing worth getting excited 'bout," he answered.

As if out of exasperation, Scott twisted himself around, pointing his binoculars off the stern. The sea shimmered, silent and still, just as it did in all other directions. He backtracked, re-covering the same stretch of sea again. Right to left. Left to right. With a jerk, he stopped. It sat like a brown dot on the horizon, bobbing up and down.

"What is it, see something Conrad?" Christopher asked.

"Not sure."

As Scott peered out over his stern, the hard lines in his face gradually softened. The corners of his lips turned upward. His knuckles whitened as he grasped on his binoculars.

"C'mon, what is it Conrad?" Jonathan tugged on his shoulder.

"Here, give it a gander." Scott shoved the binoculars at Jonathan.

The image was wavy and diffuse, flickering on the horizon. A ship. Deep bellied and tall masted, its brown timbers a dark contrast to the blinding whites of the sea and sky. He could make out people on board: on the deck, in the crow's nest, climbing on the shrouds around the mast.

No one below noticed her. To any one of the thousands of shuffling rush-hour bodies she was merely a speck, an aberration in the architecture sitting high above the terminal's vast floor. She looked down upon them all. *How dare they? How dare they not notice her?* No one cared moments ago when she discreetly walked through the door and up the seven flights near the terminal offices. She blended in, part of the woodwork. No one batted an eye when she tiptoed across the catwalk in the giant windows. An anonymous tourist to the crowds below. And now no one noticed her standing on the ledge nine stories above. *Didn't they know? Had they no knowledge of her powers? Didn't they realize she was capable of changing the course of history?*

She despised them, despised them all. To them, she had always been different. Different from those puritanical hypocrites on that stinking wooden ship. Different from those hoarding merchants and war-mongering marauders who scavenged colonial ports. Different from the privileged elite lounging on the lawns of Newport mansions. But now it was her turn. Soon they would all know her, know her very well. For one last time, she looked down upon the distant floor.

"Jesus Christ!" Jonathan dropped the binoculars.

"What? What is it?" Christopher hovered over his shoulder.

"Look for yourself."

Christopher squinted into the binoculars, looked for several moments and then quickly put them down. "Of course, it's one of those tall ships they parade around on holidays."

"Then it's one helluva coincidence, wouldn't you say?"

"Ain't no coincidence," Captain Scott jerked the wheel sharply and pulled on one of the sheets, "If I know anything 'bout what I'm doin', I know exactly what it is. And if I got anything in me, we're gonna chase 'er down."

The Captain Jones fell off the wind in response to Scott's maneuverings, cutting through the water like a sharp knife. Scott fixed his sight on the old deep-bellied ship in the distance, his face aglow, the waters before him parting almost magically as his boat plowed through the sea.

"It's as if it was all meant to be," Jonathan mumbled loud enough for Swann to hear.

"The skeptic in me wants to tell you not to jump to any conclusions," Swann answered.

"So?"

"The romantic in me hopes you're right."

The brown dot grew larger and larger as The Captain Jones slowly bore down on it. Indeed, it became clear to them: what they were now seeing with their own naked eyes was a tall ship, manned by a full load of crew and passengers, slowly approaching the breakers of Pollack Rip.

"Isn't its Captain taking a big risk sailing so close to the shoals?" Christopher asked.

"Would be." Scott answered.

"What do you mean?

"Would be, if it was one of those ersatz tall ships you hope it is. Shoals would pop up clear as a bell on their radar down below."

"Exactly my point."

"'cept maybe that ship we think we're seeing don't have no radar." Scott pulled the binoculars up to his face.

It took him very little time to sort through the figures on the ship and pick out the one whom he was sure was Captain. It was the way that one particular figure carried himself. One of the others, but then really not, every few minutes drawing himself away into his own little isolated world, leaning on a rail, surveying the coastline or the clouds, apprising the way the ocean's water streamed around his hull, the way the wind flirted with his telltales. To Scott, it was clear this was the one who carried the fate of them all on his broad, sturdy shoulders.

Something was going on, Scott could tell. At least twenty of the figures were running about the deck, responding to some command or emergency situation. Every several seconds, one of them would run up to the one Scott presumed to be Captain, ask him something, and then quickly run off as if responding to his directions. The rest of the figures on board—by far the vast majority—just stood sullenly near the rails, in an apparent state of confusion over what was happening to them.

As The Captain Jones approached within several hundred yards of the tall ship, Scott turned to port and tightened his sheets hardening up to the wind, giving himself a better view of the stern. He pulled his binoculars up to his face and looked again. He smiled. He could clearly read the large painted letters: "MAYFLOWER OF LONDON."

"Shoal water ahead, Sir! Shoal water ahead!" The Mayflower's lookout shouted out to the Captain from the maintop, sighting breakers and shallow water ahead.

Crewmembers ran about in a fury. The passengers buzzed around the deck, asking each other what it all meant. Captain Jones stood silent on the half-deck, determining his options. The most prudent course of action would be to turn back to deep water. In fact, the more Jones thought about it, it was his only possible course of action. After everything they had been through, he couldn't risk having the voyage end with The Mayflower run aground in shoal water, roaring breakers thrashing at her sides, only miles from the shores of their new continent.

"Three fathoms, sir!"

Jones bit his lip and called out to his chief mate. "Tack her about, Master Clarke. To the Northeast."

Suddenly, the old ship—growing closer every second—began to swing around on its keel. From his binoculars, Scott could see the passengers lining the rails, watching the thin strip of coastline in the distance spin away from them. The breakers of Pollock Rip drenched its timbers and sprayed the starboard deck. Scott swung his head around and fixed his binoculars on the Captain. Quietly, as if in his own world, the Captain looked repeatedly at his telltales, hoping to spot a puff of wind that would push them off the shoals.

"That's it Jonesie, any second now." Scott mumbled.

"What is it? What's happening Conrad? Why is the ship turning around?" Christopher asked.

"He's avoiding the shoals of Pollock Rip. Just like he did in 1620."

"What do you mean by that?"

"Mean exactly what I said."

"Three and a half fathoms, Sir."

The stiff jaw of Captain Christopher Jones masked his concern. He knew that the next few minutes would be critical. The tide was on the ebb, working in his favor. But without the cooperation of the wind, it might all be for naught; The Mayflower still might shiver her timbers on the shoals. He stood calm, his defiant confidence, itself, propelling his ship.

Then, suddenly, from across the deck:

"Man overboard! Man overboard! Man overboard!"

The old deep bellied ship shimmered over them, so close now they had no need for binoculars. Slowly, it swung around on its giant keel.

"Shouldn't we get out of it's way, Conrad? Won't we get caught in its wake?" Christopher asked.

"Ain't gonna be no wake."

"Why not?"

"Cause what we're seeing ain't really there." Captain Scott had such a look of certainty on his face that no one dared challenge him.

As they looked at the shimmery hull hovering over them, they could almost believe his words. Then Jonathan saw it.

"Look." He tugged his brother on the shoulder and then pointed to the old ship's stern: standing there, by herself, a lone figure dressed in white with long blonde hair flowing to her shoulders.

"What?"

"Jesus Christ! I think she's going to jump."

When Christopher saw her, his face turned white." No! No! It can't be. That parchment can't be true." He shivered. "Something bothers me, Jonathan. *Something bothers me very much!*"

The young blonde girl in white looked down upon the crashing breakers. This was it, everything was right, the elements were properly aligned. It was time to make Charles Pennfield pay for his cruelty. It was time to make them all pay. Because of her, they would never reach Virginia Colony. Because of her, they would suffer the ravages of a cruel northern winter. *Damn them! Damn them all!"*

Once again, she looked down upon the water, took one last gulp of air, and then hurled herself into the crashing sea.

Their boat was now so close, they could all see her clearly as she stood on the Mayflower's stern and considered her fate. They could see her when she took that final gulp of air, just before she decided to jump. They could see her as she bellowed out over the water—almost in suspended animation—just before she hit the rocky shoals. So clearly could they see her, they could read the lines in her face.

Christopher's face turned chalk white. He gasped. Without doubt it was her. *"JENNIFER!"* He screamed.

Small flecks of blood spattered around Grand Central Station's white marble floor. A crowd buzzed around the information booth. Several police officers controlled the growing throng. As commuters rushed to their trains, they turned their heads wondering what it was that attracted so much attention. A minor scuffle? A pickpocket being arrested? Maybe a celebrity? But, no, nothing so mundane. Even hardened New Yorkers were shocked by the sight, a bizarre incongruity. Those who could stomach it for more than a brief instant saw it clearly: a young girl dressed in white, her hair golden blonde, impaled upon the information booth clock.

·*   *   *

The next day, the Post's headline said it directly, if not delicately: COED FALLS FOR PROF. Before she had entered Grand Central station, before she had climbed up to the ledge, before she had jumped, she had left a handwritten note at the Post's editorial office. It was printed in its entirety on page three:

> How could he do this to me? How could he expect me to stand for it? Did the mighty Professor Christopher Pennfield think he could get away with it? Did he think he could get me pregnant and then discard me like rubbish? Did he think the mighty Pennfield name would protect him? Didn't he realize that all mean spirits eventually fall?
>
> To be continued…
>
> **Jennifer Winston**

*   *   *

The sun shone brightly on the Pennfield College campus on the morning of June 2nd—the grass of its expansive lawns a radiant emerald green, the skies clear and crystal blue. On the commons, temporary stands had been assembled. A hushed crowd of four hundred waited for the proceedings to begin: government officials, faculty, prominent alumni, the press. Today was the day that had been carefully planned for almost a decade: the one hundredth anniversary of the founding of Pennfield College. Beneath the solemnity of the occasion, though, there were undercurrents of what was already referred to as The Tragedy:

"Christopher had to have realized that one day his libido would come back to haunt him."

"A very disturbed young girl. Yes, very disturbed."

"Tragic, the way the incident marred what should have been such a wonderful tribute to the Pennfield legacy."

"Where is he? Has Elizabeth left him yet?"

"Will Jonathan dare acknowledge it in his speech?"

"Was she really pregnant?"

Professor Christopher Pennfield, the scheduled keynote speaker for the occasion, was nowhere to be found, having tendered his resignation to the College and gone into seclusion nine days earlier, the day after Jennifer Winston's note was printed in the Post. In his place, his brother Jonathan had agreed to address the assemblage.

"It's unfair," Jonathan confided to Swann the day before the ceremony. "She's made Christopher shoulder the blame for something that happened centuries ago. As much as I've had my differences with Chris, it's unfair."

"Never seen anything like it," Swann answered. "What's happened to your family defies everything I know. The fact that she jumped at the *instant* we saw the apparition of that girl. Well, it's just…" He shook his head, never ending his thought.

Jonathan handed Swann a folder. "Chris gave me this before he left for Maine. It's the final draft of his speech for the anniversary ceremony."

"Are you going to deliver it tomorrow?"

"Not sure."

"Why not?"

"You know, I've leafed through it several times and it's quite an impressive story. Charles Pennfield and the Mayflower. Nathaniel Pennfield and the early days of Newport. Benjamin Pennfield and his industrial empire."

"Maybe you *should* use it. After all, you can't let the bad timing of one unfortunate incident destroy generations worth of achievement."

"Yes, but I know too much. If I did deliver it, I'd be perpetuating a fraud." He looked Swann in the eyes. "Wouldn't I?"

When Jonathan walked up to the podium, he still hadn't decided. Almost out of indecision, he placed the speech down before him. He looked out over the crowd and across the college commons. How tranquil it looked: deep green ivy climbing up large stone gray walls, bright green leaves rustling in the wind, and the campus clock chiming out through the cool summer breeze. He thought how the campus was such a wonderful testimony to the Pennfield family's philanthropy. Yet, what good was it if their philanthropy was a product of tainted accomplishments? He took a breath, looked out over the crowd, and paused as he considered his options one final time. He began:

Governor Winters, President Collins, Senator Hessler, Provost Murray, Reverend Clergy, Distinguished Guests. We are here today to celebrate the legacy of a great American family. A family of which I feel both humbled and privileged to be counted as a member...

Epilogue

Manhattan:
October, 2052

From his office on the 125th floor of the Pennfield Technologies Tower, Jimmy Mashimoto-Pennfield gazed over New York harbor: the bubblized cities on the Hudson and Battery Sound, the skyscrapers of New Jersey and Brooklyn, the Seaboard Zephyr Maglev zipping down the coast. He tapped his fingers on the large clear desk floating before him.

He had good reason to be hyper today. He had awakened in London, sat in on a quick meeting of the Global Consortium on Common Standards for Electromagnetic Transubstantiation Technologies, tubed back to New York in the afternoon, and then was briefed by several PT executives on the status of their interplanetary colonization projects. *Whew!* Enough to drive even the most stable personality-type to the point of frazzylysis.

As he sat there and paused, he wondered if it was all worth it. So maybe he was Chairman of Pennfield Technologies Inc, a giant among giants in the world of high technology. So maybe he was only forty-seven years old. So what! Was it worth three broken marriages, four children he hardly knew, and an inability to sustain even the most trivial of relationships? He had tried to deal with it, tried desperately. How many times had he convinced himself that it was such a little price to pay for the chance to achieve greatness? But was it? Did he achieve this all on his own, or was it just a very fortunate case of luck?

His grandfather, Jonathan Pennfield, once Chairman of the now-defunct GlobalAir and then later U.S. Senator from Connecticut. His father, Alex Pennfield, a boy genius—entering MIT at sixteen and graduating with a PHD at twenty-one; now retired to the Thai Coast, he had his name on over a thousand patents. His mother, a world renown psychiatrist, had developed the Mashimoto Theory of Behavioral Analysis. Really, it all boiled down to a good set of genes, he would often convince himself. And then his Aunt Winnie—a billionaire by the first of her five husbands—took an interest in him at an early age, bankrolling him from the day he stepped foot out of Cambridge. How many boy-geniuses had a billionaire aunt who would write them blank checks without even batting an eye?

So, maybe it had nothing to do with him at all. Maybe he was just the one in the-ten-to-the-nth case in the random variable of life. Sullenly, he stared out his window again. Thoughts like these discomforted him.

Then there was also the small matter of *The Dream*.

A recurring image: for some strange reason, he found it disquieting. It had started several months ago and was slipping into his sleep more frequently as of late. It always began the same way: an elderly couple sitting peacefully on a boardwalk bench overlooking the clear blue sea. It had a postery feeling to it: the setting turn-of-the-century, but in many respects timeless. After allowing this image to settle in for several moments, his mind would always be directed to focus on the man. A ruddy, friendly face with apple-red cheeks, a bald top and white sideburns. His lips always formed a set of words, but they were muffled, hard to understand. Through some combination of lip-reading and interpretation, over several weeks Pennfield concluded the man was attempting to say *"Beware mean spirits"* but had no idea what that set of words was intended to mean.

No doubt about it, Pennfield was distraught. He couldn't let his over-pressured life—and that damn dream!—get the better of him. He had to leave and do something impulsive. He had to modulate himself back onto a different wavelength. He barked into his Compusec and ordered it to cancel this evening's appointment with his Brain Stimulation Therapist. Tonight he would do something different. Tonight he would drink. Defile his bloodstream.

Pennfield derived an almost erotic thrill out of doing something virtually taboo like alcohol. He remembered the stories his father had told him about his Great Uncle Christopher. About how after some scandal at Pennfield College, he retreated to the Maine Coast and drank himself to death by the time he was in his early sixties, the prime of life. And wasn't his great-great grandfather, Benjamin Pennfield, an industrialist-bootlegger? In some strange way, his memory of those stories made this little spontaneous escapade that much more exciting. He faxed himself down the elevator and hailed a netcab.

He would have to go to an unrestricted zone to get a drink. From the Pennfield tower on the eastern end of lower Manhattan—an area once referred to as Alphabet City—he would take a netcab through Little Arabia to Greenwich Village, that traditional bastion of licentiousness.

It was a cavernous little hellhole. Dark and dank and mostly crowded with sub-100s, those whose intelligent quotients were less than the threshold considered worthy of educating beyond the basic rudiments, The Greenwich Pub was a virtual zoo. If anyone of note caught him here, he would take flack for it. Take flack for it, for sure. He squeezed through several sweaty neanderthals and held up a handful of cash, summoning a bartender.

Then he saw her.

"Need any help?" She smiled at him.

"Huh?"

"You'll get what you want quicker if you let me order it for you."

Makes sense, he thought. The neanderthals tending bar would respond more quickly to a good-looking female—at least in this part of the Village.

"Sure, thanks."

"What's your pleasure?" She asked right back.

"Scotch," he answered. "Scotch 'n water."

For the first time, he examined her closely. She was cute, very cute. No, *beautiful*, beautiful was more like it. A much more deserving descriptor. Long, golden blonde hair down to her shoulders. Not one touch of make-up on her perfectly sculpted face. A lithe, athletic figure rendered almost transparent by her tight-fitting jeans. And those firm breasts that protruded beneath her loosely-fitting blouse...

About the Author

One eerie night in the mid-1980s, Roger Chiocchi awakened with a strange feeling of paralysis. Out of the corner of his eye, he thought he saw a figure of a person moving across the room. The incident rekindled his fascination with ghost stories and ultimately lead to his writing *Mean Spirits*. During the day, Chiocchi is an advertising executive in New York City where he has spent the last twenty-three years helping to develop award-winning campaigns for some of America's most famous brands.

www.meanspirits.com

0-595-22840-2